Vigilatus Book 2
Rendered Book 3

Vigilatus

Use the loyalty of your heart to drive your passion

Brenda Heller

Brenda Heller
—— and ——
Jimmy Adams

Copyright © 2018 Brenda Heller and Jimmy Adams
All rights reserved
First Edition

PAGE PUBLISHING, INC.
New York, NY

First originally published by Page Publishing, Inc. 2018

ISBN 978-1-64424-037-3 (Paperback)
ISBN 978-1-64424-038-0 (Digital)

Printed in the United States of America

In writing historical fiction, the writer spends a great amount of time in research to check for accuracy. Thus, we have found with the novel *TimeWorm*, the first in this series of three, and with *Vigilatus*, the second in the series, those who aid us in accuracy are valuable players who work behind the printed page.

We dedicate this novel to Nathan Marshall for his patience and persistence in pursuing correctness in science. Any fault within these pages in building an explosive lies wholly on the writer and not on the young scientist who instructed.

We also dedicate this novel to our friend and fellow colleague John Nichols for helping us translate words and conversations into the German language.

We thank Jacob Deffenbaugh for a truthful reminder that technology of the twenty-first century is not a matter that can be easily be replicated in a past century.

We thank Xan Faber for the kilometers traveled and the distances brought together on German soil to aid our desire to be historically correct.

Simon, we humbly thank you for your priceless role.

Brenda and Jimmy

CARRYING FORWARD

Early Spring 1937

THEO MARSHALL SAT beside his robotic dog, looking out across the evening sky of Frankfurt, Germany. It had been only hours earlier when two German strangers, Fritz and Nina, rescued him and his friend Gracie from an evil too horrible to believe was real. Now, sitting on the roof of the Kaiserdom, Theo knew the old church gave him a place to rest and sanctuary from the evil of the Reich.

Murphy glanced up at his master, whose memories squeezed his heart. His memories were immersed in a world of technology halfway through the twenty-first century, surrounded by driftboarding tricks and HoloGame competitions, feeling too lazy to get excited about the commands of his integrated robot information system he called IRIS. Most people of his world had personal robotic systems, but he lived with a chip on his shoulder, having to accept IRIS as a maid in place of his mother, who had died in a tragic air vehicle collision. Life wasn't fair. It wasn't fair to lose his mother to death. It wasn't fair that his dad, Luke Marshall, could drown his sorrow and fill his loneliness with his scientific research at the facility owned by his scientist friend, Viktor Brack.

It seemed a million years since he witnessed his father's scientist friend, Viktor Brack, try to destroy anyone and anything in his path as he used their creation, the time machine, to take himself back over a hundred years to complete his great-grandfather's role in the Nazi regime. He remembered watching the TimeWorm spin Brack into particles, leaving Theo's wounded father in an outer room and leaving Theo and Murphy in a room filling with water that would drown all living creatures and render the TimeWorm inoperable. With his dog in his backpack, Theo's only escape from drowning was falling victim to the coordinates of the time machine.

Theo scarcely remembered the experience in the TimeWorm, but he would always remember the journey that started in the concentration camp of children where he awoke and began his journey.

Theo rubbed his hand over Viktor Brack's journal with the word *Societatas* etched in the leather cover. "He won't stop, Murphy. Brack won't stop his evil vengeance until he has this book in his hands again. I can't let that happen, boy." The beagle's big brown eyes blinked. "I stole his book because it has formulas that Brack would use to change the world. Change it for worse." Theo shook his head.

He tapped the journal. "Brack wrote his plans in this book. How about if I write mine?"

Flipping pages, Theo stopped on a blank page. "Fritz said people like the society of *the Watch* fight against the powers of the Reich when victory seems impossible. I'm going to write his words into this journal. Fritz is more than the leader of *the Watch*. He's my hero. His words are right. They're my plan, Murphy. My plan." Theo took a pencil from his backpack and began to write the words of Fritz Malleczewen in the leather journal.

> *Theo, we can't help them all. But we can help them make decisions for themselves and their families. Not everyone down there is good and honest. Some are not good people at all. We can't—we don't have the right to change who or what they are. All we can do is give them the freedom to make decisions—and be there to stop anyone or anything that wants to take that from them.*

PART I

Pirates

Northern town of Bremen, Germany—Early Spring 1937

While Theo continues his journey with Gracie to escape the evil of the Third Reich, other youth across Germany are taking stands of their own.

Performer

Spring offered its presence to the town of Bremen. Nestled on the ocean's edge, the German town had suffered through winter's northern blast of icy air and snow, but now the south wind began to make its claim on the land.

A large dog stood unattended without a leash, looking up at the roof of a tall building in the middle of the city. People began to notice the brown-and-black German shepherd when it started barking. One old woman stopped and followed the dog's stare then staggered from the shock of what she was witnessing.

"*Polizei!*" the woman screamed and pointed up to where a man balanced precariously on the edge of the hotel's roof.

"Someone summon the police and stop the idiot!"

People stumbled into one another as their gazes followed the quivering arm. Some had just stepped from the doorways of buildings after enjoying their lunch break. Most had left their work to catch a quick breath of refreshing weather. The gathering crowd murmured together, with an occasional scream piercing the air. Everyone was certain the man would soon be splattered on the ground.

From his rooftop perch, the strange little man watched the throng below grow until it billowed across the street and from building to building. He smiled as Ulla, the German shepherd, barked and circled nervously, pulling more and more people around to comfort her.

"Yes!" Joseph whispered to himself. The small-statured man with handsome chiseled features couldn't conceal a wide grin that contrasted the gasps and staccato screams from the faces tilted upward. He hopped up onto the walled edge of the roof and perilously balanced on first one leg then the other. He promised his beating heart that this would be sure to attract even more onlookers. Then he started mimicking a drunken man, weaving and bobbing on the ledge. For Joseph, the act had become so practiced, so perfected it became part of his patented routine that drew newspaper reporters and cameras and the attention he craved. The louder the crowd below screamed, the braver he became.

"Please don't jump, sir!" a voice below bellowed while the crowd screamed in unison, throwing arms up as the man on the roof's edge slipped then regained his footing. A woman collapsed against the chest of a stranger.

Joseph's soul inhaled the cries of concern and worry. *I've got them now. Time to pour it on!* He relished the thought of controlling the hearts and emotions of the people, and the thought invigorated him. By this point, the crowd had worked itself into a frenzy. Mob mentality set in, and people began shouting and urging the man to come down safely. Others ran to prompt the delayed emergency services to hurry rescuers to the scene.

Bystanders hadn't been made privy to information the *Polizei* constable received a few days earlier. The hotel owner, Hans Cleve, had fallen on hard times like most of the German people. The country was still trying to recover from the disaster of World War I. The tyrannical power of the führer increased, and society was economically, politically, and morally stifled. Herr Cleve hired the performer with hopes to pull a few onlookers in for a bite to eat after the show. He had alerted the authorities that he was providing a gentleman with room, board, and a small stipend to perform his acrobatic feats from the rooftop of the Cleve Hotel and Restaurant.

Even Herr Cleve watched from the steps leading into his main foyer. Alert and aware of the man's performance, he kept his eyes mostly on the crowd. Once he thought the crowd was near breaking from the excitement, he clapped his hands together three times as he had been instructed. Hearing a signal she was trained to obey, Ulla's ears perked up with a howl that brought a shivering hush over the crowd. Eyes dropped from the ledge to the dog and quickly looked to the ledge again. High above, the small-framed man promptly sat down on the ledge at the sound of his dog issuing her cue, his feet dangled over the edge.

"Ladies and gentlemen, may I have your attention!" Hans Cleve stood on the top marble step that led into his hotel and announced above the heads of the crowd. "Give a hand to Herr Späh and his wonderful assistant, Ulla." His hand, with his arm extended, swept from pointing toward the rooftop and a grinning Joseph Späh to a tail-wagging brown-and-black German shepherd sitting back on her haunches.

The people reluctantly took their eyes from the rooftop to glance down at the dog with an empty and upside-down hat clamped in her jowls waiting for money to be tossed in. Murmurs pervaded the crowd that were both awed and a great deal relieved. After the realization that they had just witnessed a performance, the mass of onlookers turned questioning faces to the short man standing on the steps of the hotel, running a hand across his forehead and along thin, wispy hair slicked back on his head.

"Ladies and gentleman, the amazing Joseph Späh! Give him a round of applause!" Herr Cleve felt a bead of sweat slide down his forehead almost bouncing through the furrows of wrinkles that had developed from worry of the economic times. The thick silence of the crowd made him worry that his gimmick had backfired. He would be without new money, without funds to pay Joseph Späh, without friends, and without a last financial hope to support the needs of the hotel.

Joseph Späh, who had been performing gymnastic stunts for friends, family, and crowds of strangers since he was a young boy, could sense the restlessness in the crowd. He feared the crowd was turning on Herr Cleve, and it would be up to him to bring them back around. He had learned that one unwritten rule of performing was to capture the crowd in attention and in heart. Today, like others he had known before, would be a day to pull out the stops to capture the hearts. Joseph tipped his head and raised his eyebrows in reflection and decision. *So time to save the hotelkeeper and hopefully add a few more coins in Ulla's hat.* Joseph lifted his head and sat up straight as he uncrossed his arms resting against his chest. An unseen signal commanded Ulla to gingerly set the hat on the ground before she rose up on her hind legs, releasing another loud howl, driving everyone's attention from the dog back up to the ledge.

Späh remained poised and sitting as he extended his arms and pushed himself up with his hands, legs straight out in front of him. His arm muscles strained with the move. He drove his hips back and brought his legs through his arms as he pressed himself into a handstand on the ledge. Again, the crowd breathed a collective gasp in reaction to the impressive feat of strength and daring, then they erupted in a roar of applause.

In an instant, the crowd was pulled back from the edge of anger and swayed into a childlike state of awe. Watching the man perform his death-defying handstand and fearless acrobatics gave the villagers of Bremen a chance to sink to the back of their minds the talk of the looming conflict on the horizon for the nations of Europe.

In a long, inverted inhale, Joseph absorbed the excitement, driven by the crowd's noise, but he fought against the strength depleting in his arms inconspicuously beginning to tremble. He held the handstand a moment longer, causing the crowd below to voice a deafening level of exhilarated fascination. Then just before he calculated his arms would collapse from the strain, he bent his elbows and allowed his body to explode from the taut arm muscles and land lightly on his feet, unwavering on the rooftop.

The crowd, near fever pitch with excitement, fell silent. They stared with mouths wide open and eyes glued to the ledge fifteen stories high. The flowing performance ended with a barely perceptible grin and an enormous bow. Emotions of the crowd shifted gears yet again and combusted with more noise and excitement.

Joseph deliberately emerged from his long, dramatic bow as a butterfly unfolding from a cocoon. His attention lifted from the crowd to shadows across the street between two local shops. Forcing his grin of appreciation to freeze on his face, he stood fully upright and waved to the crowd below. The tilt of his head didn't reveal his eyes riveted on a group of boys dressed like miniature SS officers as they dragged a young girl and two boys back into the alley. His eyes panned back to the crowd, but his thoughts continued to sift through the shadows. He had heard rumblings about a growing conflict within the youth of Germany. He exhaled, letting the corners of his grin sink with his feelings. He had hoped the rumblings were only rumors.

In the streets below, whoops and yells began to compress into murmurs. Hotel proprietor Herr Cleve took advantage of the chance to be heard above the crowd from where he stood on his hotel steps. "Ladies and gentlemen, once again, Herr Späh and his pet, Ulla!" This time, his announcement was exclaimed with true excitement in his voice. "Please come in for a nice lunch! The staff is eagerly waiting to serve you!"

Herr Cleve gestured with a sweeping arm, while the crowd, crawling like a single organism, began to ebb and dissipate. Some returned to their places of business. Some appeared to blend in with the dull color of the street and monotonous masonry of the storefronts. Yet Hans Cleve stepped briskly back through the doorway at the top of the stairs as a large group, either starving from the excitement or having hopes to meet the amazing little man from the rooftop, made their way inside the hotel restaurant for an afternoon meal.

Unflinching in his muscular stance, Joseph waited until the crowd whittled down to a few onlookers before he took one last look, willing his eyes to see any movement of the victims dragged into darkness, unnoticed by the crowd. With nothing to answer his hopes, he opened a hatch in the rooftop and descended from a ladder leading into a musty hallway bordered with doors that opened into rooms long void of any lodgers. Giving a quick tug to his coattail and brushing his hand across the black satin lapels, he walked with an air of importance into the dining room to mingle with those who had come in for lunch and, more importantly, to collect his percentage from the meal tickets and the money from the hat that Ulla probably still had clamped in her jaw.

As Joseph wove his way through the tables of hungry diners, he kept his ears alert for mention of *Hitlerjugend*, youth trained to follow Hitler's ways. As he was trained to be steady in mind and muscles, his grin never faded as he stopped and shook the hands of excited patrons. He knew the trick of looking each person directly in the eye to hear the invigorating repetition—over and over again—of how afraid for his safety they were.

For years, Joseph had adhered to long, grueling hours of practice to keep both mind and body as honed as a knife's edge. He had learned as a child playing on a playground that one misstep could mean weeks of downtime while a broken bone healed. As he grew older and bolder, stunts increased in difficulty and elevation. It was a certain death-defying risk that he craved and that pushed him to stay in peak physical form. For Joseph, it was an elixir of life that stimulated him from the depths of his soul. He knew only one other source of an insatiable drive, and that was the love for his country and family.

A scratchy voice brought his eyes down to a hand that had gripped his forearm. An old woman's eyes searched his face as she told him how she almost fainted when she first laid eyes on him on the hotel roof. He laughed to himself as he patted her weathered hand and nodded in appreciation of her confession. Joseph's mind reached into the past as he visualized how he had performed these same skills on top of New York skyscrapers. The thought of the United States made him yearn to be home—to the hearth fires of his birth and to the home he shared with his loving wife and three children. He had been in Europe for what seemed an eternity. He longed to see his family and to introduce them to his gift for them—Ulla. But for now, he had a mission to complete while the hotelkeeper kept his end of the bargain and saw that Ulla was moved to a friend's home in Frankfurt, where she could receive care until Joseph could arrive.

Joseph smiled politely as the aged woman chattered, beginning to repeat herself. As he listened, partly out of propriety and partly out of covert intent, he scanned the crowd for faces or behaviors expressing concern. Caught in the gravelly sound of the old woman's story and the hum of voices, he heard from behind him the word *Hitlerjugend*. With a tilt of his head to feign attention, he straightened yet kept his hand lightly upon the gnarled hand that held his wrist while he mentally focused on the conversation a table away.

"Those poor *Kinder*," a feminine voice whispered.

"What do you think will happen to them?" The voices at the table seemed to erupt into whispers piled on top of one another.

"I'm not sure, but I heard that the *Albatros* is headed this way. My nephew said it docked last night. That can only mean one thing!"

"The *Albatros*? The torpedo boat? So he's coming here?" A man's voice did not cover his surprise. "Why is he coming here?"

He—the word caught in Joseph's thoughts. *Who is "he"?* The acrobat knew time had come to make a smooth break from the old woman's prattle so he could innocently hover close to the next table before the conversation changed or dropped too quiet to hear. He lifted his eyes and his hand as if to gesture to an invisible person across the room. He did not let his eyes fall upon the next table for fear of quenching conversation. He could not risk their detecting the eavesdropping of an outsider and tightening loose lips.

In a move as smooth as his acrobatic stunts, Joseph withdrew his arm from the lady's clutch. With a step back to allow a waiter a closer stance beside the table, Joseph welcomed the innocuous opportunity and slid with his back to the neighboring table to listen a little longer. If not for Joseph's stealthy intents, the scene would have almost been comical. A stout man was busy devouring his food and almost choked when the star of the show appeared at his side. Two young women at the same table were deep in the middle of the newest gossip and didn't even notice the acrobat.

"Good afternoon, Herr Späh," the man spit out.

Using the uncouth diner as a cover, Joseph smiled and looked over the man's shoulder to read expressions and to hear more conversation concerning the teens. He thought he overheard and made out the name *Wolfram Sievers*. He knew that name, knew he was personally associated with the *Albatros* torpedo boat, and if the teens dragged into the alley were being taken to him, then they were in ruthless trouble.

Oh please, dear God, is that the "he" these people speak of? Surely, Sievers will not disrupt this already-depressed town. Perilous thoughts battered Joseph's soul, threatening to distort the expression of calm worn like a mask on his face.

Rumor had begun to spread that the Third Reich conducted experiments, first in Nuremberg then in obscure places. Under the guise of being for the good of Germany, some experiments were considered humane when depth of the blue eyes and lightness of the blond hair were qualifiers for a "pure" race. Yet other experiments, numb of feeling for life itself, were brutal, such as tanning human skin for use as leather converted into everything from furniture to book covers.

Turning to barbarism, Director Wolfram Sievers served the SS of the Third Reich and earned notoriety in human experimentation with living humans in studies that may or may not have included death before bodies were discarded in the name of research.

Joseph's concentration and concern increased.

Aware of a pause of silence, Joseph glanced down at the man staring up at him waiting for a reply. For now, Joseph knew his attention must remain riveted to the talk of the teens.

"Thank you" was all Joseph could think to say while he dismissed himself from his present company. He willed his ears and mind to absorb conversation as he purposefully moved and stood with his back to the chair of the man who mentioned the name of Wolfram Sievers. Whatever the teens' involvement, the danger reached beyond the world of the *Hitlerjugend*, who were pawns in the hands of the Third Reich.

Joseph's fears escalated with confirmation as he was sure he heard the name Viktor Brack. Joseph clenched his teeth, ignoring the pulse of blood that threatened to explode through his temples. Twice he had come face-to-face with Viktor Brack, whom he hated. The Reich hid the truth of his role as a mastermind of concentration camps. Thriving on power, he became an egotistic parasite to Heinrich Himmler, a man whose ruthless power built the SS into a powerful force. Together they were demons, and their power was explosive when combined with the implementation of a euthanasia program controlled by a deranged medical doctor named Philip Bouhler.

At all costs . . . The salty night air fueled Joseph's thoughts. *I'll find and help those teens at all costs. Dark victory . . . Yes, dark victory.*

Night Rescue

"Demon! I'll kill.—ugh!" Blood spewed through words spit from the mouth of the *Hitlerjugend*, doubled over by the blow from Joseph Späh.

Joseph's tight fists hung loosely at his side as he stood over the teen who had been sucked into Hitler's youth program. "Fool to walk alone on a dark street." Words seeped through his clenched teeth while his heaving chest slowed to a calm. Joseph mentally blocked any guilt for roughing up the boy. This would not be his last punishment.

Hitler's decree employed all of Germany's youths—both male and female—as henchmen of the Reich. Obliterating their age of innocence, together they stood as a brutal force attacking even adults as they played war games of vengeance they didn't understand for a führer they didn't know. But one *Hitlerjugend*, a mere boy who tried to stand his brainwashed ground, was no match against the small-framed man who had more passion in his fists than the youth had in his heart.

With more thought for the youths pulled into an alley than for this mindless minion, Joseph knew only brute force could pry information he needed. He spun on his heel and walked away without looking back. He now knew the location where the abducted teens had been taken. Joseph climbed into a car that had been left unattended along that same dark street and headed for the harbor almost an hour drive away.

In stealth to draw no attention, Joseph stopped for a drink in a bar on the outskirts of the town of Bremerhaven, Germany. His innocent chatter formed questions concerning the docked *Albatros*. The pub patrons offered little truth other than the presence of this ship that signaled a demon in flesh called Director Sievers, who would make an appearance in the town or the town would be missing a citizen when the sun rose the next day. Joseph noted that even in the dregs of society, Wolfram Sievers' reputation had become known and confirmed that he was as diabolical as the stories floating around about him.

Though Joseph did not know the teens dragged into the alley that day, his heart beat a little harder and a little faster with determination to rescue them. Just as 1936 had given birth to Hitler's compulsory membership by all youth into the organization of Hitler's Youth, teens who opposed the führer's forced participation did what adult rebels would have done. Sans force, sans registration, sans military maneuvers, and sans government control, both boys and girls joined efforts in underground associations to oppose the Hitler's Youth. Joseph recognized from the rooftop of his acrobatic stunts in Bremen that the abducted youth had to be *Edelweisspiraten*, the Edelweiss Pirates. Moreover, they were *Kinder*, mere children, with a determination to stand against the Third Reich—a government so powerful that Joseph daily thanked God that he was able to move his own three children and their mother to a safer government in America. Driven by right and by thoughts of his own children, Joseph vowed to fight for teens who held similar beliefs to his own.

The frigid, salty night air stung Joseph's throat as he brought his breathing under control. He hadn't scaled a wall this difficult for some time. Tonight the wall he climbed was a building along the wharf that had been constructed of stacked stones tightly mortared to withstand the northern sea breeze; thus, very few footholds offered leverage. The performance from earlier in the day had been set aside, and he was rested, but this vertical, all-upper-body climb further fatigued his muscles. As he gripped the ledge of the roof, he was grateful to use his palms and relieve the burning ache in his fingers caused by the pull of his weight up the wall. He swung a leg to straddle and pull himself onto the roof. His eyes adjusted to the lack of light. Perched on the rooftop, he had full view of the quay that serviced a few docked ships and a couple of one- or two-story buildings sprinkled along the wharf. His thoughts momentarily wandered back to his canine companion when he saw the car he had used to travel to this coastal town. *Ah, Ulla, that car was too small for both of us to make this trip. I'll soon return to get you. For now, be nice to the landlord. He gets a little cross when you pee on the rug. I'll see you in Frankfurt, soon.* He smiled to himself and continued scanning the area.

In the silence of the night, he crept across the rooftop without so much as a sound of a footstep. Joseph blended into the shadow of darkness as if he had been created from it. He inched to the corner of the building, inconspicuously watching a few people moving in the passages below him, intent on their treks of the night. He noticed a few secret meetings huddled in the lower alleyways. *Come on, old boy, you have work to do. Focus.* This time, the performer hadn't scaled a building for entertainment. He had a job to do, and those kids needed him to complete it as quickly as possible. He returned to scanning between ships and buildings. From this height, he could watch without being noticed. From this view, he would see evil wrapped in a human form as it left the *Albatros* and entered a building that stood above ground but held evil that could only be birthed in the depths of hell. *How can such a beautiful city hold such a seed of evil within?* Joseph allowed his thoughts to fuel his heart for his mission.

Strange how moonlight on water has a calming effect when my soul is in turmoil. At least I can be thankful and take advantage of the scant light proffered. Joseph shivered in the brisk sea breeze as he noticed activity on the only boat with weapons attached. The boy who followed Hitler and who now lay unconscious in an alley had confessed to Joseph that the small war boat named *Albatros* had docked in this northern sea town of Bremerhaven where the teens were locked in a closet of a *Hitlerjugend* meeting hall. Joseph knew the boy would alert other *Hitlerjugend*. In reaction, SS security would be amped up to an absurd level. He feared the captured youths, whom he suspected to be young *pirates*, would be moved to a more secure location. He understood the need for swift rescue from the observations and experiments of Wolfram Sievers, a sick and twisted man.

Through shadows flicked upon the deck of the *Albatros* by the abetting moon, Joseph noticed a giant shadow grow from a lower level of the torpedo ship. He watched as the shadow divided into pieces that took the shape of men scaling a short ladder to step with long stride from boat rail to pier. In unison of step, automatic from years of marching drills, the shadows moved ashore until they blended with the darkness of buildings lining the narrow street. Joseph knelt and leaned his chest against the short wall that rimmed the roof. Without noise or farewell, one form split from the other shadows that continued toward a pub where they could unwind for the night. Joseph squinted to track the lone shadow, intent on finding the location of the *Hitlerjugend* meeting room. The shadow disappeared into a side door of a weathered building, so close to the shore as to receive a battering by waves thrown to shore during storms.

Joseph straightened his back and tilted his head with a nod—a nod of reassurance—and whispered into the salty air, "Thank you for giving me direction. You're so confident in your orders that you shroud yourself in ignorance. But again, I thank you."

From his perch above the streets of the town, Joseph knew that to hurry or move in haste would be futile and even dangerous. His watchful eyes turned back to the ship playing a bouncing tug-of-war with the ropes mooring it to the quay. Minutes passed before the moon, in her game of hide-and-seek, exposed to Joseph a shipmate who emerged from below deck. Methodically, the seaman patrolled the deck before taking his post at the aft of the ship. Minutes passed as the waves against the *Albatros* heaved and sighed almost as silently as the breaths in Joseph's chest. Eventually, the young sailor sank cradled in a squat against the foredeck as the quiet of the night and the gentle lilt of the ship made him feel secure and sleepy. After three or four nods and quick jerks of the seaman's head, a smile spread across Joseph's face. *Good night, young crewman. Your slumber has come more quickly than I anticipated, so good that your commander cannot see and reprimand your sleep.* The lack of any threat must have eased the crew member of the torpedo boat into a relaxed state of mind. His face dropped down to his chest as his breathing slowed and quickened his journey to sleep.

The eyes of the stealthy acrobat scanned the sector around the wharf to ensure there would be no surprises by guards or random passersby. Convinced it was safe to proceed, Joseph shook the gutter pipe affixed to the side of the building from the roof into the alley below. Even with his acrobatic skills, he wasn't excited about the loose pipe being his passage to solid ground, but the rooftop didn't allow any other choice. He double-checked that the people below had completed their business and slipped back into the night.

Hesitating no longer, Joseph rolled his legs over the side of the roof and planted his feet firmly on either side of the rain leader, still holding a firm grip on the rooftop ledge. He released his right hand and grabbed the pipe as the guttering swayed under the stress of his weight. He studied the ground below to judge distance in case the rain leader dislodged from its brackets. He exhaled then took another deep breath, letting his fingers open their grip on the rooftop while falling into motion of a vertical shimmy down the pipe. He descended a few feet before he heard bolts pop from the side of the building and felt himself lurch backward with the pipe. Instinct kicked in, and he gripped tightly with both hands, letting his feet and legs sway away from the building. The force of kicking out with his feet intensified his weight, propelling him toward the ground. As the downward hurtle threatened to smash him into the asphalt, Joseph powerfully pushed off the pipe and twisted midflight with his face toward the ground and his legs semitucked under him. He hit the ground with his legs forcing his momentum to carry him into a forward roll as soon as his tiptoes felt the surface. He came out of the roll like a springing cat and dived into garbage piled along a building on the opposite side of the alleyway.

Joseph didn't move as he held his curled landing, listening for sounds that might have questioned or responded to the snapping rain leader against the quiet night. He could feel something stabbing the middle of his back, and his hands screamed with pain, rubbed raw from the rapid descent on the rusty iron pipe. He bit into his lower lip as the salty air stung the open nerve endings in his palms. Joseph forced the pain out of his mind. He focused on the youths he had come to save—youths strong enough to rebel from the führer's compulsory military service under the Reich.

Again, visions of three youths pulled into the Bremen alley bolstered Joseph's determination. Teens, the *Edelweiss Pirates*, rebelled with hearts threatened by a tyrannical government. Through covert diligence, youths formed their own groups, a diligence that did not come without cost. If caught walking alone, they would be beaten and taken to a *Hitlerjugend* indoctrination headquarter. They saw themselves as outlaws or rebels—*pirates!* Joseph huffed in the refuse of the wharf. *Maybe that's why I am lying here in this filth. I was always seen as a bit of an outsider. While other boys my age were playing stickball and getting into minor brawls, I was at the gym practicing my backflips and juggling. Get up, Joseph! It's time to rescue some pirates before they have to walk the plank.* A simple laugh accompanied his grunt as he stood up in the rank darkness. Joseph allowed himself a few more seconds of safety in the rancid piles of garbage that had softened the impact of his crash landing before he stepped into the night.

As he emerged from the alley to the main walkway, Joseph ripped off the bottom of his shirt and wrapped the strips of cloth over his palms, giving them a little protection from the biting, salty air. With swaddled hands, he rummaged through the satchel strung across his shoulder.

The nimble gymnast felt a smooth wooden surface brush the back of his hand. He grasped it and its brothers then slipped all three objects into his coat pocket. He made his way down the cobblestoned boardwalk toward sentries standing in front of a nondescript door. Nothing about the entry suggested importance except the ambiguous placement of two brawny guards standing firmly on either side. Slipping into character, he began to stumble and mumble to himself.

Two husky teens, each of whom could have passed more for men than adolescents, enjoyed the prestige of their monotonous guard duty and watched as yet another drunken bum stumbled down the street. Typically, they would have ignored the man, but having been on watch for too long, they ached for entertainment. The unsteady man stopped at the corner of the building and retched into the alleyway, making both hulking teens cringe at the sound of the drunkard emptying his stomach. They looked at each other in disgust but smirked at the opportunity to harass the silly fool.

The drunkard pulled his forearm across his mouth and hidden smile then clumsily continued his way toward the door, despite the giant obstacles in his path. He fell against the front of the building, mumbling loud, incoherent noises, getting a laughing response from the two behemoths. He knew they looked like men, but they were still teenagers who would give in to their instincts.

The taller boy was the first to leave his post as the man with the satchel strung across his shoulder leaned heavily against the wall to hold himself upright. "What's wrong with you, drunken fool?" The young sentry shouted and used great force to shove the man away from the building and sprawling into the street. "Can't even walk. You should be ashamed of yourself." He puffed out his chest, proud of his rebuke for the befuddled man.

Joseph rolled to his hands and knees. "Beggin' your pardon, young sir." He looked up just in time to see the second guard step toward him and lift a boot to kick him to his back. He flipped himself over hard, sprawling around and feigning an inability to turn over. Both boys chuckled at the drunkard looking like a turtle stuck on his shell, helpless and needing assistance.

"Beggin' your pardon, I seem . . . seem to be in a bit of trouble. Could . . . could one of you young men help me up?"

The teen who had used his boot on the man lumbered over as a small twinge of guilt prompted him to bend down and flip the drunk onto his stomach.

"Thank you, young man. Thank you." Joseph pushed himself to his hands and knees, baiting the ignorant brutes to push him over again. To his surprise, both youths backed away. Joseph stood up on his knees and swayed back and forth, selling his drunkenness a little more.

"Get on your way, silly man!"

"Yes, you shouldn't be here. Be gone with you and your stink."

"So, so sorry, sorry. I've . . . I've fallen on rough times," Joseph slurred his words.

"We don't care what you've done. Get outta here before we throw you into the sea!" the tallest ordered.

"I can't . . . I can't sw-sw-swim!" Joseph cried. Both boys broke into hearty laughter and started walking toward him. Joseph surreptitiously pulled one foot under him and dropped a wooden juggling ball from his pocket to distract the boys. The two *Hitlerjugend* stopped and watched as the ball the size of a large orange rolled past and came to rest at the door they guarded. The shorter of the two boys bent down to pick up the wooden ball. A sharp cracking sound caused him to turn in time to see his fellow watchman hit the ground beside him.

"What the—" He didn't have the opportunity to finish his question as the third ball made a dull whistle through the crisp night air and found its target. With reflex, one hand jerked toward the back of his head but never touched the bloody skull before he collapsed in an unconscious heap beside the first victim.

Joseph brushed a layer of dirt and debris that had collected on the front of his jacket and pants from his theatrical rolling around on the filthy street. In a flow of motion, he stepped toward the two massive boys and lowered his arm like a pendulum to retrieve all three heavy wooden juggling balls. Next, he checked their pulses just to be sure he hadn't done any more damage than planned. He had gauged a throw forceful enough to bring down each sturdy young man and ensure neither had the opportunity to recover and pursue him.

"Fight smarter, not harder, my boys." Joseph brushed his hands together, clearing them of dirt as he dragged the last youth from where he had fallen. Moving their heavy bodies had been more difficult than scaling the seawall. Not confident that he could have handled either one in a fair contest of strength, he was grateful his aim was true. He shook his head and stepped across the threshold, pulling and quietly latching the door, leaving the salty night air blanketing two giant teens slumped against the side of the building.

Hidden

THE LONG HALLWAY was devoid of anyone—no wandering *Hitlerjugend*, no SS, and no hulking teen security guards. Someone in charge must have been confident that the giants guarding the entrance to the headquarters were impassable and the fear of dabbling with Hitler's Reich would keep people away. Despite the emptiness of the hallway, Joseph remained on high alert. Earlier, from his perch atop a neighboring building, he had watched an SS officer walk through the same door he just entered. He had witnessed no other entering or leaving, a good sign that someone was still on-site. One false move or lapse in judgment and Joseph knew this situation could easily throw him into the defensive.

He glided across the wooden floors without a single tap escaping from his shoe. With his back pressed against the wall, he edged down the hallway that ended abruptly with a single steel door—so out of place with the rest of the architecture, it threw up a warning flag for the nimble intruder. He froze in stride a few feet from the ominous door and searched for hidden alarms or traps. Joseph checked behind him one last time and then closed the distance between himself and the door.

Though a challenge was expected, Joseph did not hide a deep sigh while his hands on his hips demonstrated concern. The huge youth guards had been simple to fool, but the three lock combinations on the door in front of him would not be so easily defeated. Joseph mentally ran through numerous techniques he had used in the past to get into places that had blocked his entry. He focused on the three iron knobs, each shaped like an arrowhead. Each dial was surrounded by a gold-plated number wheel.

"Three locks, each with eight number choices. I'm in trouble." He searched his brain for possible number combinations.

Frustrated, he reached out and aggressively ran his hands over the number dials, giving them random spins. Thoughts halted as his ears and eyes noticed each dial stopped with a barely perceptible tick. When the last cylinder stopped rotating, a solid click thudded from behind the door as the locking latch lifted and freed the handle. Joseph extended his hand, hesitated, then clasped the door handle.

"Dear mother of this troublesome child! Look what I've gone and done now!" The stunned intruder turned the handle. The hinges gave to Joseph's tug, allowing it to swing open with quiet ease. Just inside the door, rough wooden stairs descended and disappeared into a dark corridor. "Well, this is spooky." Joseph chuckled, trying to bolster his confidence. He knew from experience that the farther he got pulled in, the longer and more harrowing any escape would become. It was always the escape that was the trick; no one seemed to notice him arrive, but it seemed he found the limelight when he tried to leave. "Here's to another adventure." He shrugged off his jittery nerves and began his descent into the dark.

Darkness offered no suggestion of location as he mentally ticked off three twisting flights of eight steps each before he reached a landing. He calculated that he was below ground level. A touch with one hand confirmed what his nose suspicioned. Cool earthen walls held dim lights nestled into carved niches to light a tunnel. He reached into his satchel. His hand brushed the cool, smooth wooden juggling balls and locked around a metal cylinder. *Ah, light and weapon. I love when I come prepared.* Joseph pulled the heavy flashlight from the bag that swung around to his back. He spun the long, sturdy flashlight around in his hand, gripping the end, ready to swing and fend off any attacker. The light provided by the wall sconces lit the tunnel floor that was edged on one side with a rivulet coming in from the ocean.

A sound of ocean surf hinted the tunnel opened into the harbor. The river widened and darkened in depth. Joseph quickened his step but stopped when a faint muffled sound echoed from a side direction. A quick glance into the breeze offered no forms or shadows, so he turned toward the noise. Mechanically, he spun the flashlight from hand to hand. Joseph riveted his vision into the tunnel rimmed with both darkness and light that swirled like a confused omen. Sound came through the darkness again as he neared a bend in the tunnel. A few steps closer to the bend brought the sound that stopped Joseph's breath and movement. Pain suspended in the darkness.

"Here we go," Joseph encouraged himself as he repositioned his satchel and tightened his grip on the end of his makeshift billy club. Joseph poked his head around the rock wall where the tunnel curved and quickly pulled back, hoping his movement had not been heard by a guard standing around the bend. Flattened against the tunnel wall, his mind spun through scenarios and plans. Although he hadn't seen anyone except a lone person from the torpedo boat enter, he reasoned that an SS standing in a seaside grotto was there to either keep someone in or keep someone out. He entered the tunnel from the same direction as the one who came from the boat. *Think before you react, Joseph.* He promised himself to be sure of what he was rushing into. A false jump into an innocent meeting would promote harm to the youths and to himself as well. *I followed the man from the boat. Around this bend, I saw the back of an SS soldier. If he's facing away from me, then he's watching something farther in.* His thoughts were interrupted by a thud, followed by a high-pitched wail and moan. Joseph's heart swelled with rage, thinking a trained soldier of the German Reich might be torturing a child. *It's about time for curiosity to kill this cat.*

Joseph spun his body in a full rotation as he rounded the bend, giving power to his extended arm. The flashlight in his hand violently pummeled into the neck and head of unsuspecting guard. Though well-built, the guard was short enough that the muscular acrobat connected with full-body force. The guard's *Schirmmütze* fell sideways from his head, embedding the SS hatpin into his forehead as the blow drove his head into the rock wall. Red blood spurted onto the black swastika stitched onto the red armband as he slumped into unconsciousness. Joseph lunged to the front of the guard, catching under his lifeless arms before he crashed to the earthen floor. He eased the man to his knees then lowered him to the ground with more care and concern than he deserved. Joseph swiftly searched for the luger holstered at the soldier's side. He removed the magazine and ejected the chambered round before he slid the pistol inside his waistband and made his way toward an illuminated antechamber farther into the tunnel.

"Director Sievers asked you a question, scum!" A large man spewed spittle as he screamed at a badly beaten, nearly unconscious boy. The petty officer removed his cover in frustration and tucked it into the pocket of his naval peacoat. The low-ranked officer of the Nazi war navy wanted to move up in the ranks. This young rebel's refusal to answer the director wasn't going to help his chances. Exasperated, the petty officer ripped the boy off the ground and lifted him by his collar to eye level. "I said that the director wants to know from what town you hail. If you don't answer, perhaps your sweet little friend upstairs will be much more cooperative when I'm done with her." He hoped his barbaric threats to harm the kidnapped girl would sway the young *Edelweiss Pirate*.

The pirate boy had been living outside the law of the Reich for a few years and had been beaten on more than one occasion. Hitler Youth would seek out *Edelweiss Pirates* and see how far they could antagonize. Most fighting spawned from hearts not yet hardened and fists, still regulated by conscious, stopped after a light beating. But today, this man holding him up had taken it to another level. The innocence of the boy's age was usurped by a hatred for tyranny that threatened his country, threatened his family, and bolstered his loyalty to stand against wrong, regardless of cost. The boy smiled at the red face screaming at him, spewing saliva on him, and beating him near death. His head was pounding against the deafening ringing in his ears. All he could see was the man's mouth moving, but he was unable to comprehend any words mixed between the blows.

"He will not be able to answer anything if you kill him, Bren." Director Sievers placed a hand on the zealous petty officer's shoulder. "Look at him. He can't even understand you. I can see you have much to learn on the pain thresholds of these swine. You need to take your time and slowly push these animals to their limit." A smile flashed from beneath the thick midnight-black beard and handlebar mustache. "Enjoy the process, Bren."

Bren looked over his shoulder at Wolfram Sievers and could see the man was enjoying himself. He gained confidence that he had not offended the director and turned his attention back to the teen in his grasp. The officer sucked in a breath to fuel his tirade as he caught a glimpse of blackness hurtling toward him. In trained reaction, the petty officer dropped the youth he had been mercilessly beating and crossed his arms to block the path of the pistol.

The luger bounced off the forearm of the cringing war navy officer. "What was . . ."

Sievers pulled his sidearm and held it with awkward unfamiliarity. Quickly, he turned to face their attacker but was further disturbed by the blackness that engulfed the tunnel outside the antechamber. "What happened to the lights?"

"Perhaps the generator is out of petrol." Bren shook his head in embarrassment, knowing the director watched as he picked himself up off the ground and rubbed his forearms.

"Go see. That boy's too beat-up to answer any questions, and we need to cast off soon." The unsettled director used his command to cover an irritated and nervous burning in his voice.

Petty Officer Bren wanted to refuse, but he saw the set jaw behind the groomed long beard and recalled rumors and realities he had seen the man do. The tunnel was an abyss of uncertainty, proffering no sign of movement. "Jens, you okay?" His words bounced off the rock wall of the tunnel and swallowed any hope of a response. Only a few times had the two sailors met when they docked in Bremerhaven for the director's special business. He didn't know the other guard well, but he mentally pleaded to hear his voice.

No voice came from the abyss. The young officer pushed his thumb down on the hammer of his weapon and stepped into the darkness, moving slowly toward the bend in the tunnel. He held the gun in his left hand and ran his right hand along the wall, keeping himself away from the water that trickled down wall and rock floor to his left. "I don't see any—"

Wolfram Sievers heard Bren's words cut short by silence interrupted by a thud and a splash of something falling into water. Only a few seconds lapsed before he lunged into the dark passageway to confront whoever would dare approach. An arrogant man of action, Sievers had been handpicked by the Reich leader of the SS, Heinrich Himmler. Who would be so daft as to try to interfere with the power of the Reich? Often he had walked this tunnel; he knew its winding path well. Though the darkness was disconcerting, the blood of the devil himself seemed to pulse through Sievers' veins. Nothing that lay ahead caused his footsteps to falter. He walked briskly to the bend in the tunnel where both of his men slumped in an unconscious heap on the ground.

"Fools." He grimaced down at the two young guards bested by an intruder. "Show yourself!" he demanded into the empty tunnel with a tone of entitlement. Turning, he searched the way he had come then spun back around, thinking he heard footsteps coming from behind. He lowered his pistol when he realized his imagination was creating noise where there wasn't any.

A scraping noise echoed from the interrogation room, causing Sievers to snap his head back toward the antechamber and snap his pistol back to a ready position. The cold-souled commander was determined not to be beaten at the game of mystery. He ran over the earthen floor toward the room, but his rush ended in the center of an empty room. The boy who had been beaten near death was nowhere to be seen. "*What? How did?*" He was baffled by the disappearance of the unconscious pirate. Then he saw what he was looking for and squeezed off a few rounds into the splashing water. Greasy blood smears divulged where the boy had been dragged into the water inlet rimming the grotto. Sievers blasted three last shots into the water and reloaded as he sprinted back into the tunnel, destined for stairs at the far end.

Halfway through the short tunnel, he rounded the bend and came to an abrupt halt, nearly tripping over a mass on the floor. The unconscious, beaten boy was lying soaked and still dripping water into a puddle in the middle of the passageway. The SS director stood without moving while his heart and mind pulsed to understand what was happening. Cautiously, Sievers pushed the boy with the tip of his boot and waited for a movement or a sound to escape from the prisoner. The body lying on the unrelenting ground gave no reflex, no reaction. He knelt down beside the boy and turned him over, raising his hand, ready to slap the pirate's face.

The unresponsive body ended the roll with a thud just as a hand reached out of nowhere and grabbed Sievers' wrist. He flinched and grunted in reaction and shock.

"You shouldn't treat children this way," Joseph's low voice growled uncharacteristically.

A foul smile crept out of the beard on Sievers' face after he looked up, feeling less threatened by the small-framed man who was squeezing his wrist. "Do you have any idea who I am or whom I work for?"

"I have a pretty good idea on both," Joseph muttered through clenched teeth, showing no fear of the man or the power that backed his secret experiments. "Nothing gives you the right to do that to a child!" Joseph's voice bespoke his anger as he flung a pointed finger toward the teen who paid the price of rebelling against the Reich, now lying motionless on the damp earth floor.

"Throw your judgments elsewhere. The only thing saving his life is the pure German blood running through his veins," Sievers retorted, disgusted by the man's notion that he was doing anything wrong. "Go ahead. Save this one. I've got more."

With reflex of mind and strength, Joseph tightened a twisted squeeze of the monster's wrist and felt a tinge of satisfaction when the director winced and tried to break the small man's grip. "You're not the only one with powerful friends. We won't let you get away with this despicable evil."

Bolstering his own emotions and giving cover to a barely perceptible quaver in his voice, Sievers tipped back his head to laugh. "Good luck. You'll regret this."

"Maybe." Joseph brought the flashlight down across the face of evil, knocking him unconscious. With a glance at the water, his first impulse was to push the man into the salty sea, striking this problem once and for all. He looked down and noticed his knuckles were white where he maintained a grip on Sievers' wrist. He dropped the unresponsive hand. For a moment, Joseph cringed as if an evil odor wafted up to his nostrils. He shook his head in frustration. *No. This isn't the way—not mine or the Watch's. To kill him, I'd be no different from the evil creature who lies at my feet.* Joseph pulled his foot out from under the man who lay crumpled on the ground.

Though a small-framed man, passion of mission and passion of right gave him strength as he bent down and raised the boy, struggling yet able to lift the youth to his shoulders. The darkness of the tunnel that connected seaport and building seemed to lighten with a mysterious glow as the man carried the youth in body and in spirit up the winding stairs and back through the massive door still hanging open.

Joseph wiped cold ocean water from his eyes, not caring that his clothes dripped on the floor, the droplets joining the puddle around the boy. He removed his jacket and rolled it to cushion the battered head. He propped the unconscious pirate against the huge steel door now closed and locked, preventing anyone from sneaking behind him and catching him off guard. He bent down once more and placed his fingers on the boy's neck, feeling for a pulse. He prayed for a heartbeat and convinced his mind that a faint yet steady beat lay under the bruised and torn skin. With interminable hope, he breathed a sigh of relief and sat on the floor beside the victim of the Reich.

"I'm afraid, dear boy, that any further medical attention is beyond my knowledge. Rest yourself." The rescuer ran the back of four fingers down the swollen cheek of the unresponsive teen. "I have a boy. He's younger than you. I pray he too learns to stand up for right and that someone will rescue him when evil fights back." Joseph sniffed into the sleeve of his shirt and propped his chin on his arms resting across his bent knees. "It's a harsh world, dear boy. But I'm proud of you. I'm proud of you." The moment to rest and drink in the silence nurtured Joseph's soul.

Confident that the boy could rest without immediate medical attention, Joseph stood and turned in place, trying to think where the other two *Edelweiss Pirates* may be imprisoned. From where he stood, the building looked innocent of holding any war crimes or prisoners of war. *Just hallways, rooms, and cleaning closets. Like man, the appearance conceals what lies within.* His eyes moved with his thoughts, never resting in one place for long but looking for answers. *I must find the other two pirates. Kids. They're just kids, really. Kids pulled into a war that they can't win, yet they keep fighting. Kids fighting for an age of freedom from oppression that they'll never live long enough to see.* He shook his head to clear his mind of such worries.

As if speaking aloud would put pieces of a puzzle into place, Joseph spoke softly into the silent hall. "The brute mentioned a girl upstairs." He swiveled to look at a wooden staircase worn in the middle by climbers and cracked from the salty air and seawater carried in. "No." He shook his head. "I don't think he meant the top level of the building. If a kid is throwing a kicking, screaming fit of rebellion, dragging him up a staircase would only bring more problems. No. A kid can be thrown down a set of stairs." He swiveled with his hand on his hips and looked at the battered youth. "Ah, so you're the leader, eh? They tossed you down flights of stairs to hurt and threaten so you'd talk. The others saved for later." He turned back to look into the empty hallway. "So from the underground, this is the upstairs. Now, Joseph, think. Where and how could they keep two kids quiet and hidden?"

"Well, standing here thinking is getting me nowhere." The soft sound of his deliberate steps was the drumbeat to encourage him onward. He lifted the flashlight used as a *Knoppel*—though not as long as a billy club used by the guards—prepared to meet interference. Joseph let out a long, slow breath then twisted the handle on the first door he reached. The door swung open and revealed an almost-empty storage closet. He lowered the flashlight and moved to the next door. Over and over again, he opened doors to see unused rooms or vacant spaces sparsely littered with cleaning supplies or bordered with hooks for hanging garments.

Weary in mind and discouraged in heart, Joseph stalked back to the motionless boy. He assumed the other teens had been taken to another location and worried how long to invest in searching for the missing teens. In time, Wolfram Sievers would wake up and arouse the German war machine. Their focus would shift. For now, beating and torturing youths would be set aside. Vengeance would be unleashed. They would hunt until they found their newest prey—him. He squatted to hoist the boy over his shoulder. Alone, he would be fine, but with a boy slumped over a shoulder, escape would prove to be much more difficult.

The hairs on Joseph's neck prickled in alarm. He was sure his ears didn't deceive him. He moved his head away from the silent boy draped across his shoulder. Sound. They were not alone. Swiftly, he lowered his parcel back down to the floor. As if performing a silent tumbling feat, he turned in one smooth movement to face whatever challenge dropped the noise into the silent hallway. Flashlight raised and ready to swing, Joseph saw nothing. He lowered the flashlight, closed his eyes, and reached out with his senses. Long ago, he learned that eyes could betray if an anxious heart misled the mind. He listened, deciphering first the heartbeat pounding in his ears then the sound of wind and sea beating against the building, but nothing more. Nothing.

Precious minutes that he did not have time to waste passed without a sound. A sigh mixed with a deep breath sucked in a new noise. He stepped forward with one foot, softly planting and shifting his balance. *Yes. Yes, I hear you. Are you beast of evil or mice teasing my senses? Speak again, little sound. I'm listening.* Then as if the sound heard Joseph's thoughts, a light scratching answered. With eyes closed, he stepped farther away from the unconscious boy but closer to the noise. His mind kept cadence with each step. *Don't stop. Good or evil, don't stop. Don't . . .* Something overpowered but did not arrest the sound that rasped along inside the wall. Joseph placed the palms of his hands on the wall beside him. He shook his head, trying to understand the hoarse humming. Sound and vibration from the wall were slight but real. Puzzled, Joseph turned in both directions of the hallway. He had opened every door to emptiness. How did a sound come from nothingness? Confused and with too little time to think, he slipped down the hallway.

Had the noises stopped, or had he gone too far to hear them?

With a pirouette, Joseph retraced his steps until the sound came to him again. This time, he stood in front of a door he had opened before. For several minutes, he stood with his eyes closed and his head cocked to be sure the noise came from behind this door. He concentrated, bringing a visual into his thoughts. *Last time, there was a mop and bucket some low-ranking soldier probably used during cleanup detail.* Carefully, he twisted the brass knob then pulled the storage closet door as he opened his eyes. Again, only mops and a bucket. "Is the noise louder, or am I letting my ears play tricks on me?" The dark closet offered no answer to his whispers. Standing on one leg, he used the other to hook the rim of the bucket half filled with muddy water and roll it into the hallway. In the dark closet, he pressed an ear against a wall. *Where are you? Are you mouse or man?* Both hands flattened against the wall, swirling in windmill circles. He didn't touch cracks, bumps, or anything out of the ordinary. He pursed his lips in exasperation and turned with his back to the wall. The sounds behind the wall where he rested his head were more like grunts than talking. He wondered if he was even hearing a heavy sound, maybe like a pound.

"Augh! Where are you?" This time, he turned his cheek to the wall and spoke in more than a whisper. The grunts and thuds seemed to accelerate. His heartbeat gave an excited skip. He wanted to communicate, but he didn't want to be heard. He swiveled and reached for the doorknob and pulled, this time closing himself within the closet. In the darkness, he heard the popping sound of a latch. *A hidden passage?* Joseph's thoughts raced with excitement. Still he could see nothing as he pushed on the back wall of the storage unit.

Again, he opened his palms against the barrier between himself and the noises. Obediently, the plaster wall slid smoothly back under the pressure, revealing a large room lit by red lights peering out of sconces on the walls. A strange glow cast across the room and landed on forms squirming away from him. Their gyrations alerted Joseph that their wrists and ankles were bound by heavy, thick ropes. Joseph quickly held up both hands. His voice cracked in a hoarse and forceful whisper. "I'm not here to hurt you!" Unable to speak through the gags cinched through their mouths and tightly tied, the two bodies continued to roll and kick away from him, fueled by coarse, panting cries.

"You're just kids, aren't you? I'm here to help," Joseph whispered as he extended his open palms away from his body and slowly closed the distance. He slightly smiled as the boy, even with his arms and legs bound, crawled between Joseph and the girl to protect her. The youth's chivalry and bravery reminded him of his own younger days. He knelt down to eye level with the boy but had to dodge the boy's violent attempt to kick and headbutt the approaching man. "Boy, calm down! Shhh!" With one open palm suspended so the boy could see he meant no harm, Joseph placed a finger from the other hand across his lips. "I have your friend out in the hallway. We must get out of here, *now*!" His abrupt stop of movement and words hung in the space between himself and the frightened youths.

Eyes that feared the danger of men in the dark searched the stranger. Distrust and anger swirled in sinking eddies of the boy's mind. He searched the face of the man who sat on his haunches with palms extended, saying nothing more, but waiting with glances that he threw over his shoulder. The small man's voice expressed both calm and panic. Never did he lift a fist or a foot to punch or kick as the soldiers had earlier done.

"Please . . ." Joseph started to move toward the youths but recoiled as they flinched and cried past the wads of cloth that bound their mouths. Lifting his arms with palms out, trying to convey no threat or danger, Joseph moved one hand to the sleeve of the other arm. Slowly, he began at the wrist and unbuttoned and tugged the shirtsleeve, exposing his forearm. With a nod toward his arm, he rolled his wrist to show an arm marked with a tattoo of three elongated circles crossing in a center. The boy's eyes changed from anger to confusion. The triquetra inked into the stranger's arm gave him courage to turn away from the small man and look at the girl behind him. He laid his upper body on the floor where he sat and stretched his bound hands toward his rescuer.

Joseph moved quickly to unbind the youths then turned to the closet that had been the secret passageway, gesturing for them to follow. At the back of the closet, Joseph held out to the teens who had silently followed a hand of friendship and freedom.

A window at the end of the hall prompted a beam of light to lie across the unconscious youth. He did not know or see when his friends emerged from the prison of their kidnappers, but they saw him. Joseph stood in the hall, letting the two fall upon their unconscious friend with tears and emotions they were too weary to hide. Anxious to move to safety, Joseph allowed only a few minutes of reunion before he squatted beside the beaten youth and lifted him across his shoulders. No words were spoken as the rebels against the Reich left the building in daylight in search of shadows of trash-filled alleyways and backstreets. The unconscious burden became heavier as the rooftop performance and ensuing rescue had begun to tax Joseph's muscles. One close call with a patrol of *Hitlerjugend* taunted the two alert pirates who wanted nothing more than to get revenge for their beaten comrade. By the time Joseph led the youths to the car he had driven from Bremen, he was out of breath and ready to put down his burden.

In a swift move, the girl crawled into the small sedan to share the back seat, where Joseph laid the wounded boy across her lap. "Adalric, you sit in front." Her voice was scratchy from the abuse of crying out, but it had been so long since anyone had spoken; the boy turned briefly to look before he nodded and opened the passenger door.

Joseph turned the key, forced the transmission into gear, and tromped the gas pedal. The engine of the borrowed car squealed, shattering the morning's silence. He wanted to get these kids as far from the sea town as possible before Sievers and his dogs suspicioned that a member of *the Watch* had rescued them. He allowed himself time to gather his own thoughts and emotions before he spoke.

"I suppose you're wondering who I am and why I came for you."

Adalric let a pause hang in the air before turning the questioning to the rescuer. "Where are we headed? Will you stay with us?"

"My young friends, eventually, I'm headed to Frankfurt. I can get you to a safe district, but I can't stay with you. I'm meeting with my friends of *the Wa—*" Even though the listening teens had been through a brutal beating by the Reich, these were days for every word to be guarded. "Um, I'm headed to a meeting." He rubbed the sleeve that hid the triquetra. "I purposely rescued you, but I'm afraid the powers that be will be determined to retaliate. It's not safe for you to be with me."

"We live in Wiesbaden. We've been gone from home for too long, and our parents will be looking for us." Minne smoothed Jakob's hair with her fingers as she talked. "Is there a place where you can leave us without taking us to Frankfurt?"

"Wiesbaden?" Joseph rolled the name of the town around in his mind. "Actually, your hometown isn't too far from Frankfurt." He tapped the steering wheel with a finger as if counting. "I'm thinking it's somewhere around thirty-nine kilometers. Yes, I've just changed my plans. I've got a couple of days before I'm expected in Frankfurt, so I believe I'll take you all the way to Wiesbaden. I know a quaint cottage where I can stay until I need to move in and out of Frankfurt. Yes, this may be perfect." The acrobat almost mumbled his last sentence, but both teens noticed a satisfied smile on Joseph's face.

Neither teen interrupted the silence that filled the small car until Joseph left the new thoughts swirling in his mind and returned to the need to answer Adalric's questions. In choppy sentences interspersed with pauses, Joseph explained what he had seen during the rooftop performance. Words had momentary lapses, while the small acrobat watched his car mirrors and avoided open roadways. "I recognized the *Hitlerjugend* were up to no good when I witnessed them drag teens into an alley. That was my cue to find you, hoping you were *Edelweisspiraten* like my heart suspicioned. You could have been Hitler youth, but I had to take the chance." He glanced at the boy beside him. "Always a fine line to balance on." He smirked to himself, amused by his acrobatic play on words.

"What's so funny?" The boy known as Adalric did not hide his leery expression.

"Life." Joseph looked directly at the youth and understood why he had chosen to be part of the anti-Hitler regime. The boy caught his glance and quickly looked away, a move he must have done a thousand times. "Your eyes," Joseph continued though he faced only the road before him. "You sport the German fondness of blue in one eye, but the other eye has brown sharing the blue. In the *eyes* of the

Reich, such heterochromia makes you impure." Joseph swallowed an inappropriate giggle at the emphasis of his wordplay. He shook his head to clear it of distractions and refocused on his task. "Sorry. We all have something the Reich doesn't like." A little ashamed of his lightness of speech, he shifted the focus by encouraging the teens to talk.

"Well, you're right in my eye discoloration, but even if my eyes were the choice of the Reich, my heart is not. I'm Adalric." He nodded to the back seat. "This is my friend Minne." He grinned at the pretty *Fräulein* watching him talk. "We have different backgrounds." He paused. "Her father . . ." He smiled at the girl before he continued. "I think it's okay, Minne. His arm bears the triquetra." Adalric turned back to face the road ahead. "In military, her father serves the Reich, but he understands as Minne shares our passion."

Joseph looked in the mirror to see the reaction of the girl in the seat behind him. It was the first he had taken a good look at her. She was captured and tortured by the Reich, but her sharp blue eyes, long blond hair, and innocent beauty would have gotten her far in this empire. He smiled when his gaze in the mirror caught her eye. "I hail your bravery, Minne." He turned back to Adalric. "And your friend who cannot speak for himself right now?"

"His name is Jakob. He's my brother." The whisper from the back matched the tenderness that stroked the unconscious boy's forehead.

Jakob was beaten very badly, so badly the future for him was unknown, but Joseph was determined to encourage the teens. "Well, he'll sport some scars that won't win any beauty pageants, but he'll live to fight another day. For now, for Jakob's sake, we'll count this one as a victory."

Joseph didn't look in the mirror or even at the passenger beside him, but he was sure a soft cry was lifted on the wings of a prayer in the silence.

PART II
Vigilatus

Tower of the Kaiserdom

THEO GAZED OUT over the beautiful land that was Frankfurt. It seemed days instead of hours since Fritz and Nina had rescued Theo and Gracie from the underground passage between the Alte Oper and the Kaiserdom. Theo felt safe on the roof of the church tower, yet he couldn't help but reach down and touch his ankle where the hideous creature had grabbed him and had pulled him into the tunnel.

That was too close. If Fritz and Nina hadn't shown up to pull me from the tunnel and blow up that stinkin' jaeger, I'd probably be . . . Theo shuddered and squeezed shut his eyes in a long blink to erase the thoughts of the tunnel. He returned to his focus around him. The sun had passed its highest peak and was throwing strange evening shadows over the picturesque city architecture. From his perch high up on the roof of the Kaiserdom's tower, the city seemed at peace. People of Frankfurt were moving through the streets and parks heading for their homes to spend time with families and intimate meals. They looked like tiny ants moving around in a chaotic yet systematic pattern that they had rehearsed many times throughout their lives.

A colder wind whipped stronger across Theo's face. He wondered how high up he actually was; he could see most of the city from this vantage point. The heavy fleece that Fritz had given him was doing an excellent job of keeping out the bite of the cold. He shoved his hands down deep in the pockets where they felt warm and protected.

He again peered over the railing of the rooftop, studying the scurrying people and wondering which one of them was looking for him. "Which person down there will jump at the chance to stop me and Gracie from getting to the airfield? Who will keep me from leaving Germany? Which one of you pretends to be a typical citizen of the city yet secretly wants nothing more than to capture us and send us to Viktor Brack, or whatever my father's former friend is calling himself these days?" Nothing in the cool air spoke back to him.

Theo's mind flipped back to see two twenty-first-century scientists working side by side on a time-travel project that was intended to help the future. How many days did the doors to the laboratory of Dr. Luke Marshall and Dr. Viktor Brack shut on what seemed to be the science of something good? Even in his mind, his father's expression on his face was cheerful and hopeful. Theo shook his head in response to his thoughts. *Dad, how could you know that Viktor was evil? How could you know that his German heritage was a link to the Third Reich? How could you know he was using your intelligence to build a machine to rewrite the past, huh? How could you know Viktor would go back in time to complete the work of his grandfather and to destroy so many people of Germany in concentration camps? Even the nightmare that is about to be unleashed on Europe, yet again, will pass, and people will forget and make the same mistakes in other places.*

The voice of his father surfaced in his memory. *How you use your time is what matters. No matter how famous or powerful you may be, time will not stop for you.*

A shiver ran down his spine, shaking his entire body to its core. He couldn't tell if he reacted to the cold or to the thought of seeing Brack again. He couldn't shake from his memory the sound of Brack's voice in the dark concentration camp where the time jump had landed him. He could still remember his first moments in the concentration camp with Yari and the other children. He could still feel the dead bodies of the children who had been shot and dropped into a pit dug into the ground, pressing on him from every direction. The horrors of so many innocent deaths were seared into his young heart where they would haunt him to his last days. Anger overwhelmed Theo. He ripped his hand from its warm pocket and slammed it down on the bannister as he stared down at the ground below.

"Whoa, tough guy. What's with the hostility?" came a soft voice. "What did that thing do to you?"

Theo straightened up at the sound of Gracie's voice. Thrown together by circumstance unplanned, she was becoming his dear Romani friend—a gift from Germany—raised yet hunted by the country that wanted to annihilate anyone who was not Aryan. He turned his head to give her a faint grin then turned back to staring out over the city. A terrifying thought gripped his mind and stifled the breath in his lungs. He gripped the iron banister.

Gracie's guardian, Jahile Möeller, set a plan in motion to get both Gracie and Theo safely to American soil, away from the danger of a secret society of the Reich. Herr Möeller feared their capture by members of *the Society*. Theo huffed, letting the chilled air come out in a vapor as if he were an angry dragon. *The Society*, the group working for the Reich, was destroying its own German civilization.

He narrowed his eyes as if scrutinizing the thoughts rolling through his mind. *The Society—huh, what an irony. I'm seeing what you tried to tell me, Herr Möeller. You—the Watch—are fighting a force bigger than you can ever bring down. If only I could tell you about the future, if only . . .* Theo bit his lip. *I stand here from the future. It kills me to know this city, this country, even this continent will be devastated by war!*

He wanted to run down all those stairs he had climbed and rush through the streets of the quiet city and warn the good people. He wanted to tell them to leave Frankfurt, to leave Germany, to get as far away as they could from the oncoming nightmare. He wanted to tell them to take their loved ones and just go, leave everything and go! Flashes of the hologram scenes from the war that Mr. Medi had shown in history class started to materialize in his mind. Vivid scenes of the mass devastation and ruin that would become known as World War II flashed in reality. For most of the days since he had landed in the boxcar, he hadn't felt safe. Today a false impression of security had lifted him from reality as the tower of the Kaiserdom had lifted him above the land. Fear had become dislodged, replaced by a smothering feeling of dread and despair for the future—the future he could do nothing to change. What could a young man do to stop the desires of a führer gone mad?

"It's just too much," Theo mumbled. He fell to his knees and began to weep, bowing his head into his outstretched arms with hands still clutching the rail. "Why can't I stop it?"

"Stop what, Theo?" Gracie knelt down beside him, wrapping her arms to hold him, to comfort him. "Theo, what's wrong?"

Theo shook his head in hopelessness. He didn't want to look weak in front of a girl, but he knew somehow that Gracie would understand. For half a year, they had seen and even, at times, shared strengths and weaknesses. They had shared hearts—shattered in different place and time—yet both struggled against loss and both determined to reunite with family. They had grown fond of each other. Theo dropped his hands from the banister to hold the arms of concern and understanding wrapped softly around him.

"I don't know how to tell you the truth, Gracie."

"The truth about what?" she spoke cautiously.

"About what is really going on here." Theo gestured with a nod toward the dusk-soaked city. It was so beautiful; how could anyone want to destroy such a peaceful, serene place? Another wave of nausea hit him as he recalled scenes—scenes from movies that he had dispassionately watched as Hollywood acting but now he knew as reality—heinous scenes from his father's old war movies. He was also hit with a powerful punch of guilt from video games that used the death and destruction of World War II as their backdrop. He shook his head again, this time at the irony of his gaming. How many hours had he spent playing those HoloGames, wishing he could step back in time and save the day? He had been so sure that he could stand up to the Nazis and single-handedly defeat them. That was such a joke; he had never been more scared in his entire life than he had been the last few weeks. He wasn't sure he would ever be able to watch a movie or play a game again without being crushed from the memories, the brush with reality.

"Talk to me," Gracie pleaded. She moved between him and the banister so she could look him in the eyes and maybe shelter him from the cold wind. "Please, you know you can trust me." She wiped tears from his face with her delicate hands.

He smiled then motioned for her to help him back to his feet. He stood silent for a few moments then pointed in the general direction of the Alte Oper. "That wonderful building that you love so much," he paused, reluctant to tell her the truth, "it's going to be destroyed in a few years, Gracie."

Gracie turned, staring out toward the opera house, scanning the landscape so beautifully laid out in front of them. She took a deep breath and exhaled slowly. She turned to look at Theo. Gracie could see a sadness in his eyes that warned her not to further question what he was implying.

Steady now, Theo shifted his eyes from her questioning face to the city as he wrapped an arm around her shoulder and drew her to him. "In about two years, I think, Germany is going to attack Poland. That attack will set off a chain reaction much worse than the Great War. Hitler has a new method of warfare that makes him almost unstoppable. In just a few short months, he will have control of most of Europe. Great Britain will hold out because they are an island, and he can't use his warfare tactics on them."

Theo paused for a moment, trying to choose his words carefully. "The United States will get involved a few years later because of Japan. They, the United States I mean, will focus on Europe and push the German soldiers back into this country. Even the Russians will get involved because Hitler didn't learn anything from the First World War, and he will attack them as well." He could feel his throat tightening as his voice got louder. "Eventually, the Allied Forces will bomb every inch of this country toward the end of the war. Planes will be made to drop huge bombs all over the countryside, annihilating more than military targets. The Allies will try to break the German spirit by bombing the civilians too. The British and Americans will lay waste to Germany. *No one* will be safe from the bombing raids!" Theo fought to control the rage building in his voice.

Gracie remained silent, trying to understand and believe everything Theo was explaining. She couldn't control a tear that dropped from her eye as she looked out over the city, wanting to capture its beauty and serenity into her memory.

Theo cupped her hand in his and lifted it toward his face. "That isn't even the worst part, Gracie."

She jerked her head to face him and spoke almost in a shout. "How can anything be more destructive or crueler than the World War my world suffered? We have not recovered! Things have been so awful here with the depression and all the tension between nations. I just want things to go back to the way of life Papa used tell me." Gracie paused to take a deep breath and squeeze Theo's hand in hers. "Sorry. I didn't mean to interrupt. Please, tell me. Go on."

Theo laid his cheek against her forehead. He gulped in the night air before he continued. "The Nazis have a terrible plan. This oncoming war isn't just about land and resources. It's about purifying the human race."

"Purifying the human race?" Gracie tilted her head as Theo's words caused her to remember her first days and conversations with Herr Möeller.

Theo shook his head, understanding her doubt. "Already, the German government has created awful camps where . . ." He paused, thinking of the children he left in the pit. Everything he had learned in school about the Holocaust became vivid pictures in his mind. "They—the Nazis—will try to annihilate all the Jews, not just Europe, but everywhere on earth!" He looked at his own hands and wrinkled his brow as if what he spoke was falling on his own understanding for the first time. "I guess if the Germans hadn't eventually been stopped by the Allies, they would have become more powerful and even come into the United States." His last words came out barely above a whisper. Theo lifted his eyes to look out across the city, but reality blurred his vision and he only saw a black abyss in his mind.

"Theo." Gracie's voice hung in the thick air. "Theo." She shook his arm. "Theo, listen to me."

A bubble of breath lodged in Theo's throat as he realized she was talking. He pulled back to look at her questioning eyes. "What?"

"What happens in the camps, Theo?"

The dark eyes shone from the soft caramel-colored skin and penetrated the space between them as she moved her face closer to his. "What happens, Theo? Tell me."

He tipped his head back to search the darkening sky for answers. *Why did I keep talking? Why didn't I just keep my mouth shut? This is a heck of a time for me to care about history!* Theo bit his lower lip as he mentally reprimanded himself and wished for a way to avoid the truth. The dark eyes were now riveted into his soul. *If someone tries to hurt her, I will . . . I will . . . protect her. She may be Li'l Grey, but she's my Li'l Grey.* Theo dropped his shoulders and looked at her as he touched her hair.

"The German people will believe they are being shipped to work in factories. In truth, they will be shipped to work camps and extermination camps hidden away from the public eye. The Nazi SS will do awful things to the Jews, but not just Jewish people, Gracie. They will eliminate anyone they deem inferior."

Unseen by either teen, a meteor fell across the sky as if to cry for the fall of humanity.

"Like Romani?" Gracie dropped her head. "The rumors on the streets . . . so . . . they're truth?" she muttered in disbelief. "Herr Möeller tried to tell me. I didn't want to believe such terrible rumors could be real. What kind of person or people do such things?"

Theo's hand brushed across her curls as he wrapped his arms around her to pull her closer as if sheltering her from the future. "It's hard to believe. In school, I learned about the Holocaust, but I never really understood." He spoke slowly and softly to himself and to the sweet girl in his arms. "I don't think I really believed the terror until I came into contact with it here in . . . in your country. I'm still having trouble understanding, but things will get much worse before the war ends."

He held a long, deep breath before he exhaled memories from studies before his time jump had brought him over a hundred years back to Nazi Germany. "Hitler and his Nazi madmen will kill eleven million people by the time the war ends. Six million of those people will be Jews." He rubbed his forehead as numbers written on a history test in a twenty-first-century classroom were now—in 1937—

being etched into his heart. "Two-thirds of all Jews in Europe will be annihilated. I've been in one of these camps already, Gracie. I barely got away. They were just kids—kids, Gracie! Most of them younger than we are!" Theo choked down the bile working its way up his throat and fought back more tears as his memory showed him again the children left lying in the pit.

In the quiet night, a young American stood holding a tender German girl—two worlds pulled together by circumstance, two hearts of determination pulled from the crucible of a madman's Reich. Theo and Gracie stood motionless. They turned to face the skyline and quietly take in the last few minutes of the setting sun. The air temperature dropped rapidly as the sun slid to the other side of the world.

"Gracie, look out at the beautiful country. We must remember what Herr Möeller told us: 'Not all people are evil'. Some, many, like this countryside, are beautiful, and they too are Germany."

"Why don't the governments do something to stop these camps? Why can't my people leave Eastern Europe and get away from it all?" Gracie asked, still stunned from the thought of the camps actually existing.

"*Your* people, Gracie?" Theo asked with confusion lacing his words.

"My mother is Jewish. Papa was not, but he was fine with me being raised in my mother's culture, religion, and lifestyle. I've been out on the streets for so long that I haven't even thought about praying for help anymore," she added solemnly.

"Gracie, I am so sorry. I didn't realize. I didn't know. I knew you are a mix of cultures, but I never questioned, I never guessed what your . . ." Theo apologized, tripping over his words in embarrassment and horror at what she must be going through hearing about his history—her future.

"How *could* you know, Theo?" Sadness filled her whispered response. "My dark skin has kept me safe so far. It has been a blessing in disguise, given to me from my papa." She told with proud emotion how her papa was "Mama's black knight" and how the other children had treated her for looking different. She held her hands out in front of her and gazed at the soft caramel skin that looked much darker as the remainder the sun slipped quietly away.

"Your skin is beautiful, Gracie. Beautiful girls like you wouldn't talk to me at my school," he added, shocked at his own bravery or stupidity. He was sure that his face was red with embarrassment but was glad for the twilight hiding it from her.

"Then they are foolish, silly girls, Theo."

"Uh, yeah, anyway . . ." He fumbled, trying to move on from the awkward conversation.

Silence hung between them. "Actually, there's more that you haven't noticed. True, I'm not a blond-haired, blue-eyed girl, but there's more. It's not just my looks that are different." Gracie stood up a little straighter out of habit of self-defense. "I'm a Romani—a *Mischling* Romani."

"Okay. So what does that mean?"

"That means I'm a target. I'm a half-breed, half German and half Jewish. We are gypsies, the Romani." She raised her head as she raised her voice and looked Theo in the eye. "We had a good life, though." Gracie wanted him to know she loved her life with Papa and Mama.

"I don't care. You don't deserve to be—" Theo stopped short of admitting Gracie and her family would be victims of the annihilation. "I don't care what color your hair is. I mean, I do care. I care about you."

Theo walked away and moved along the rail that bordered the rooftop as he stumbled over his awkwardness. He snapped his head around to face the girl still standing at the rail where they had both stood just moments before. "Uh, is there something we're supposed to be doing?"

"Oh," she said, surprised at his abrupt change. "Yes, um . . . Oh, Nina said to come get you. A friend of theirs, someone named Herr Späh, will be here shortly with an update on our travel arrangements. I better get going. I told Nina I would help with dinner." Gracie spun around without another word and ran to the trap door. "*Garçon stupide*," she mumbled as she started down the ladder.

"What did you say?" Theo asked, not sure why she left in such a hurry. "You know I don't understand German without Murphy around."

"It wasn't German! It was French." Then interpreting in English, she said, "You stupid boy!" With that, she slammed shut the door above her and descended the ladder.

"Okay then," he quipped aloud. "Glad to see girls are just as confusing here as they are back home in the twenty-first century." He took one last moment to take in the shadow-covered view then turned toward the trap door, hoping she hadn't locked him in the cold night air.

Theo walked toward the door in the rooftop. He stopped after just a few steps as something made a strange, static noise. He scanned the rooftop for the source. *Maybe it was just a weather balloon or antenna popping*, he convinced himself and started back toward the door.

"T . . . e . . . er." Theo almost jumped out of his skin at the sounds mixed with heavy static. He stopped as a chill of fear invaded his skin.

"Who's there?" he yelled and waited for a response. "Gracie, is that you messing with me? I'm sorry if I upset you!" he shouted as he bent down and jerked open the trap door, trying to catch Gracie in the act. No one was on the ladder.

"B . . . a . . . t." The static-laced words crackled around him again.

Theo tore the warm, furry hat off his head and could instantly feel the cold evening air on his forehead, ears, and scalp. He pulled out his earbud to examine for damage. It had only worked for Murphy's language translator, which, in its own right, had kept him alive up to this point. He rolled it around in his hands a few more times but could not find anything wrong. He slipped it back into his ear and pulled on his hat. He stood still and waited, straining to hear more static. The only audible sound was the whistling wind. He dropped his head in concentration and waited. Nothing. *Maybe Murphy is translating someone's conversation.* He felt a surge of disappointment;

he wasn't sure what he had hoped to hear, but no further sound disrupted the silence.

Never did Theo suspicion that his father living in the twenty-first century was tirelessly programming his integrated robotic intelligence system to bridge a gap of centuries.

Living Monument

Theo made his way down the old wooden ladder. A heaviness covered his soul as he shut the tower access door behind him—a disappointment of words, of sounds, of silence still lingering in his chest.

Theo slipped out of the warm and cumbersome fleece as he descended the stairs to reach the ground floor of the church. Back home in school, he was never really into architecture or art in general, but he admired the beauty of the church.

The high archways displayed intricate carvings crafted by the hands of a master woodworker. Scenes jumped out of the wood and told stories of German heroes and emperors. He couldn't believe this gigantic church hall and tower started by King Clovis I in the late four hundreds was still standing. Granted, it had been burned down more than once and parts had been added onto the main structure throughout the years, but he was amazed at the determination of the Franks then the German people to rebuild this church over and over again with remarkable beauty. He could see why Fritz was so passionate and eager to share the history and his knowledge of the Kaiserdom—the Emperor's Cathedral.

"Whoa, look at this stuff!" Theo's senses were on high alert.

Theo ran his hand along the walls of corridors that twisted and turned as he returned to the center of the church. He was glad to be alone in the enormous basilica. He didn't care for a girl to see him impressed by the breathtaking surroundings. Theo slowly turned a full 360 to take in all that the church had to offer his senses. He breathed in the scents from the candles placed throughout the sanctuary and around the stunning windows, altars, and paintings. He thought his head might explode from sensory overload.

"Teo! Tere you are," echoed a deep voice. "Ve have been lookink everyvhere for you!"

Theo looked over his shoulder to see Fritz standing with hands on his hips and a look of exasperation on his face. "Sorry, I was kinda looking for Murphy."

Fritz grinned. *"Ach ja, ein Junge und seine Liebe zu seinem Hund."*

Theo stood staring for a moment. Not only did the echoes distort the words, but without the language transmitters on Murphy's collar, Theo couldn't understand the foreign language.

Fritz noticed Theo's confusion. "Sorry, Teo. I don't speak Enklish often. I said it's a special tink, a boy's love for his dog."

"Come, come, Teo. Ve need to go. Nina can be . . . ah, vhat is the vord in Enklish?" He stumbled over his translations, his infectious smile still spread across his face. "*Ach, mürrisch,* you know—grumpish, maybe?"

"You mean *grumpy?*"

"Ja, tat is the vord. She can be very grumpy vhen late for *Abendessen.*" Fritz laughed and shook his head. "*Supper* is vord."

"Excellent, *Ich bin* starving," Theo replied using about the only words he knew in German, patting his stomach to give Fritz a visual for "starving."

"*Goot! Ist goot* you are so starvink," Fritz added cheerfully as once again he motioned for Theo to follow him. "Alvays, goot time vhen ve all can sit at same table and tell stories, some true and some not so true but all entertainink."

Theo followed Fritz through the main hall, past the awe-inspiring *Maria-Schlaf-Altar.* Superior craftsmanship of the statue depicted the apostles at the side of the dying Virgin Mary. *Okay, Gracie. This amazing artistry did not escape the eyes of this clueless boy,* Theo mused in silent conversation to no one, remembering her rebuke at the Alte Oper concerning his lack of appreciation for beauty.

"I vas not raised as a Catolic, you know, but of course not, how could you possibly know tat?" Fritz asked then answered himself.

"But I did meet my second vife because of my belief. I say tat ist a pretty goot sign from God. Vouldn't you say?"

"Uh, I guess so, Herr Malleczewen." Theo wasn't exactly sure what to say. He stared at the statue, unable to take his eyes off the scene before him. Seeing all those men crowding around the dying Virgin Mary reminded him of the emergency room, the doctors and nurses scrambling to try to save his mother's life after the air-car accident. He felt a small twinge in his heart as the memory of his mother replayed in his thoughts.

Fritz was halfway down the hallway before realizing Theo was not with him and he had been talking to the air around him. He stopped and turned to see the boy still staring at the statue before slowly walking back to him. "She's beautiful, Teo, isn't she? Tat altar has been here since early 1400s. I pray tis maknificent piece, tis entire catedral," he said passionately, waving his hands around to encompass the entirety of the church, "can survive tis blasted upcoming var tat our führer seems all too eaker to start." Fritz paused for a moment when he realized the boy hadn't heard a single word. "My boy, are you okay?" His voice was thick with concern for this strong young man.

"Please take good care of her," Theo whispered to the marble statue as he lowered his head and wiped a mist from his eye. He took a long deep breath then looked up to see Herr Malleczewen watching him.

"My dear boy, do not be ashamed of feelings runnink trew your veins." Fritz closed the distance and placed a consoling hand on Theo's shoulder. "You, me, and tis group of extraordinary people you are about to meet—ve're all made human by emotion."

Theo took one final glance at the sculpted altar then nodded that he was ready to go. He followed closely behind Herr Friedrich Malleczewen, his new friend known as Fritz.

"I'll take you to a room vhere you can rest. Gracie vill be in a room in tat same hall. Soon, you'll meet more tat share in our qvest." Fritz never stopped his brisk walking until he bent over and clapped his hands at a beagle that was loping toward them with a tail that threatened to wag off. "Ah, goot pup! Here's your master!"

With a forearm that swung under the belly of the gamboling dog, Fritz picked up Murphy, gave a quick rub between the floppy ears, and offered the dog into Theo's extended arms.

"Hey, boy! Did you find Gracie and get some special attention from her? Yeah, you're not suffering from neglect." Theo and Fritz both laughed and patted the wiggly dog in Theo's arms.

"Here's a room for you. Relax. Come downstairs by six o'clock. Gracie vill come vit you. Nina showed her vhere to meet." With a gesture toward a hall door, Fritz swiveled on a heel and started off down the hall with a hand wave over his head.

"Impressive old church, huh, Murphy?" Theo opened the door and walked into a room where everything from floor to bed seemed covered in softness.

Necessity

Theo plopped into an overstuffed chair and was quickly joined as Murphy jumped to his lap and wiggled to share the soft cushion. "Well, Murph, at least you seem to understand me. Maybe it's because with your robot *artificial intelligence* you don't try to overthink me. The beagle nuzzled against Theo's neck, snuggling onto his chest. Theo rubbed under Murphy's collar, giving a good and long-overdue scratch. "Maybe I should wear your collar for a while and see how I like it, huh, Buddy."

Theo continued to rub Murphy's neck, weaving his fingers under the collar. "Good thing no one knows the technology in this silly old . . . Hey! Murphy! Your collar! Maybe that's a good place for me to start." Theo's vague ranting and sudden sitting up from his slouch in the chair made Murphy give out a good dog huff as he suspected his momentary massage was ending.

"Murphy, I need to look at your collar." Theo unfastened the collar from Murphy's neck before his dog even had the chance to plead with puppy-dog eyes for more petting. "I think if I study the technology in this collar, I may be able to remember some of the experiments and connections I did back in Dad's lab. If I can somehow connect to my good ol' integrated robotic information system, I can see what progress Dad is making on getting me to time warp back to America and back to our century." A half smile puffed out one side of the young man's face. "Living in a world without even as much as a radio satellite is like living with cavemen. Communication is, like, impossible! Zikes, when we get home, don't tell IRIS that I missed her robotic way of talking and taking care of me." He ran his fingers over the collar, feeling the nearly imperceptible computer chips inside. "I just want to know the future hasn't forgotten me. Hey, Murph, I may have an idea. I may not be able to talk directly to IRIS, but there's more than one way to skin a cat!" Theo glanced at Murphy, who cocked his head to show confusion then plopped down on the overstuffed chair.

With more energy than Theo had felt for days, he began looking around the room, gathering odds and ends. A desk drawer offered a pencil, ink pen, and paper clip. A discarded pair of wire-rimmed reading glasses seemed a potential use possibility and were quickly added to the collection. His eyes stopped at a radio on a table.

"Surely, there's some way I can use that old relic. Okay, locked treasure box. If there's any way you can help me, it will be with what you have inside." Picking up the battery-powered radio, Theo turned it over in his hands. "Either I smash this casing or I find a screw driv—oh, of course. What would Gracie do?" He lifted the lanyard from around his neck where the slightly bent driftboard charm dangled. Just as swiftly as Gracie had used the charm to pick a lock what seemed so many months ago, Theo turned the charm into a tool to open the casing. "Well, radio, it's time you give up your life because I need your battery, wire, and diode." Within minutes, the treasures were added to the collection on the table, and the lanyard holding the driftboard charm was secured around his neck.

By early evening, a knock on the door was not enough to capture Theo's attention as he fingered through a table covered with the graphite rod whittled out of the pencil, the spring out of the ink pen, a piece of wire with insulation trimmed from one end to expose two bare and twisted wires, glasses, radio parts, a wire coat hanger from the closet, a small pyrite rock, a rusty safety pin, and the foil from the wrapper of a nutrition bar that had lain crumpled in the bottom of his backpack. His thoughts ran as swiftly as his fingers twisted, rolled, and connected the fragments of refuse into a tiny transmitter.

The soft knock became a pound produced by a fist hitting the door. Theo looked at the door. "Okay, okay. Keep your pants on!" He swung open the door just as Gracie's fist connected with his eye that stood where a solid door had been.

"Ugh! What the heck! Whaddya do that for?"

"Stop screaming at me! Why didn't you answer the door? You've been in here all afternoon. Did you forget we were supposed to meet *the Watch* for dinner to go over the plans?" Gracie whipped her body around and huffed down the hallway without waiting for the boy standing with one hand over an eye to offer an explanation.

Theo lunged to the bed, where he raked odds and ends and his new transmitter into his backpack. He knew that if he didn't want to get lost in the Kaiserdom, he would have to run to even catch Gracie's shadow as she moved down the hall.

Sheepishly, Theo walked into a vestibule where Fritz, Nina, and Gracie were waiting and talking in hushed tones. He hoped to reach the group with Murphy trotting along beside him with no one noticing his late appearance.

"Teo," Fritz spoke, and the buzzing conversation stopped abruptly. "Ve must keep deadlines vhen our friends depend on us." Silence hung like a heavy drape as the young man nodded. "Now, vhat has kept our friend from us, huh? A nap? It can't be a pretty girl as she made it to der table on time." Gracie's dark eyes widened before her face dropped to hide her embarrassment.

"Tsk. Fritz, perhaps you can stop with the teasing. You were once a young man. Maybe we should ask what occupied your secret time, huh?" A sweet grin from Nina gave everyone permission to break into laughter. Murphy lay down on the tile floor and put his muzzle on his paws with a snort as if to take part. Again, laughter erupted, making the embarrassed teens appreciate Murphy's tension breaker.

"Forvard, friends! Ve have a meetink to attend!" Fritz swung his arm in a "come along" gesture and started down a series of halls, doors, and descending staircases.

Vigilatus

YELLING AND ROUGH voices broke Theo from his trance as Fritz pushed open a heavy oak wall panel behind a bench in a chapel basilica allowing them to descend a flight of hidden stairs to a meeting chamber. He was grateful for the personal escort through the maze of the church. It seemed the building had many secrets, and without a guide, Theo would have been lost in them.

"What do you mean, he has other plans, Sophia?" a vaguely familiar voice erupted from the room.

"I am called Keila—*not* Sophia! TAR, you would do well to remember that," a young girl snapped back at the British military officer.

"Keila, that's a beautiful name." Nina's soft voice offered to soothe the tension in the room. "What does it mean? Why did you choose it for your new name?"

"Thank you, Nina. I am glad someone can appreciate it," Keila spoke through clenched teeth as she glared at the British officer. Then as if nothing had been said, she gave Nina a friendly smile. "It is Yiddish for 'vessel.' I see myself as a vessel for God's will," she answered in soft tones.

"Honestly, Sophia, I don't—"

"It's Keila!" she spit, stopping TAR midsentence.

"*Genug!*" Fritz's voice boomed, bringing immediate silence to the room. Theo shivered at the transformation. The kindhearted, almost-silly man changed in an instant. He could see under Fritz's short body and muscular frame sat a strong determination and fierce leadership.

"People, people, ve have guests, and all tis fightink vill not get us any closer to our goals. Ve are supposed to be fighting tose tat vish to bring harm to tis vorld, not goot people" Fritz shifted back to his softer voice in the quieted room. He stepped to his chair and sat down; the rest of the members took their seats after he was seated.

"Tommy, my dear friend, vhat ist all tis fuss?" Fritz asked, soothing the usually calm and charming Secret Intelligence officer.

"Why don't you ask *Keila*?" TAR responded putting special emphasis on the woman's new name. "I'm surprised she hasn't already started calling us all *comrade*."

Fritz put his hand up to stop TAR from continuing his rant. All adults at the table knew that Keila had recently adopted Marx's teachings, which did not sit well with many of the members of this group. A few months earlier, in underground efforts to quell the Reich, another arm of *the Watch* had sent word of Stalin's purges. The group hadn't been heard from since that telegram had been received.

Fritz smiled softly at the handsome Scotsman who served in the British Secret Intelligence then turned his attention to Keila, who was sitting at the far end of an ornate, massive table that served as the group's meeting place. "Keila, vhat has our friend so upset tat he has forgotten ve have some special guests vit us tis eveninek?" Fritz glanced around the table. "Has anyone heard from our friend Johann?"

Keila pushed her freshly dyed red hair behind her ears and gave her best smile to TAR, seated at Fritz's right side, a position at the table to designate him as the leader's right-hand man. "Our dear friend Johann has apparently decided to single-handedly take on the entire Nazi war machine. He has fallen off the face of the earth. None of my contacts in any city has been able to locate him."

Keila paused for a moment, giving a glance and a flick of an index finger toward TAR. "I honestly have no idea what he was going on about, Fritz."

With a wave of his hand, Fritz dismissed the young woman's worries. "Vonce I return home, I vill send someone to check up on our entusiastic friend to ensure he doesn't get hurt or expose us in any vay."

"You know he would never do that, Fritz," remarked a voice that caught the attention of both Theo and Gracie. Sitting beside Keila was a young man who could have passed for a schoolboy, but the deep resounding voice let them both know that he was not a teenager at all. The teens looked at each other. Seeing the reaction in each other's face was all they needed. Both put their heads down and did their best to suppress laughter from the surprise of what looked like a boy with a man's voice. Oblivious to the teens' reaction, the young man continued to support the missing *Watch* member. "He is just unimpressed by the slow nature of how things are done here."

"Ah, Erich, I didn't mean to imply tat our missink broter ist a turncoat. I merely mean tat ve need to make sure he ist not biting off more tan he can chew." Fritz flashed a smile toward the youthful man to imply that the matter was closed from further discussion. With a pleasant inhale and lifting of both hands as if to welcome all at the table, Fritz smiled. "Can ve please dispense of any vork conversation? Ve have all night to argue about such matters."

"Here! Here!" cheered a very handsome man, at whom most of the women in the room, including Gracie, stole quick glances when they felt unnoticed. The man, at least fifteen years older than Gracie, was seated beside his wife. Gracie recalled Nina's calm demeanor and ability with explosives during their rescue from the tunnel. She wondered how Nina met and married someone who appeared so different in mission. Truly, the man's good looks encased in the enemy's uniform stirred questions in Gracie's curious mind. Claus was dressed in the finest clothing the National Socialist German Workers' Party could supply its young SS officers who had come up through the ranks of Hitler's Youth program. Claus was Nina's husband, which brought him into their presence, yet at first, his military uniform of the Third Reich repelled acceptance into Theo's and Gracie's hearts.

For what seemed long, uncomfortable minutes, the two teens stood at the side of the room as the adults settled around the table. Theo could not imagine what would happen if an outsider walked into this room and saw the hodgepodge of people from all walks of life sitting around a large wooden table carved in the center with a symbol he had seen before.

The three ever-flowing elliptical spheres of the triquetra were deeply carved into the wood table and inlaid with what looked to be real gold. A silver circle encompassed the symbol and wove its way through each of the ellipses where it ended at the centermost point—an all-seeing eye. The eye was formed with many valuable and precious jewels. Theo realized the triquetra was the same symbol he had seen the night Herr Möeller bared his forearm, exposing the tattooed triquetra, causing the jaeger and an SS officer to back away into the night.

"Do you see the marking in the center of the table?" Theo leaned over and whispered to Gracie. She stared at him for a moment then just nodded. Theo let his gaze move away from Gracie because he was sure of one thing: she was still not very happy with him.

"Gracie, Teo, please come and join us. Don't let TAR's and Erich's sour faces scare you off," Fritz invited with levity.

Without even glancing at Theo, Gracie moved to the far end of the table where there was only one empty seat. Theo gave Gracie a minute head start then went to sit next to Fritz, directly across from the man they called TAR. Theo recalled that he had briefly seen this man once before at Herr Möeller's home.

"I'm sorry, lad, but that seat already has an owner," TAR said in his thick Scottish accent.

"Theo, sit beside Nina." Theo had not met the man called Claus, who gestured as he pushed the chair back to the table, reinforcing the Scotsman's statement.

"Sorry, I . . . I didn't realize." Theo stammered over his words and felt the blood rushing to his face, making it warm and red with embarrassment. He ducked his head and moved quickly to the other side of Claus and Nina, avoiding nearness to the empty yet spoken-for chair.

"Well, let's get to eating, shall we?" Nina remarked to refocus the group. She stood up and called for the cook to bring out the meal. The angry taunts and foul mood were quickly erased by a feast that had been prepared. Pints of beer were refilled before the members could see the bottoms of their mugs, which removed any ill will that lingered after the dinner was over. Theo watched the group get louder and louder as the food disappeared and the beer flowed non-stop. He smiled as Fritz tried to tell a joke he must have told often because everyone at the table finished the punch line before he did. His laughter was infectious and spread throughout the diners at the table.

Theo was convinced he was in for a special treat when he pointed a finger to count the layers in the cake placed in front of him. Nina explained that *Donauwelle* was a traditional dessert similar to America's sheet cakes, prepared with cherries, chocolate, buttercream, and layered batter. Theo shoveled in the last bit of the sweet pastry before he had eaten his fill.

Food plates were being cleared from the table, and drinking slowed to a controlled pace, while carefree talk about art and theater dwindled. Each member anticipated an upcoming conversation about the group's next move—a small piece in a much-larger machine.

Fritz cleared his throat and tapped his beer mug on the polished oak to bring the group to attention and alert them that the time had come. "Ladies and gentlemen, I tink ist time tat ve get on vit *das Treffen*, ur, meeting." He nodded in apology to Theo. Fritz tried to communicate in English to help the young American, unaware of the translation powers of the robot dog recharging in a position of rest near Theo's feet under the table.

"Today grows late, and I do not vish to put any of you in any more danger tan ve are in, already over our heads." The Table fell silent at his announcement. Everyone's attention turned to the head of the oak table where Fritz's demeanor had changed. The lighthearted man was in leadership mode, and the transformation happened without missing a breath.

"I hope our special guests enjoyed tis vonderful meal and even tastier dessert tat our lovely caretaker has provided for us," Fritz commented with a nod first to Gracie then to Theo.

"Vury much sooo," Theo answered with his mouth still full of his last large bite. His quick reply gave the rest of the Table a reason to chuckle and appreciate the youths who were present this night.

Theo realized the all-too-familiar feeling of blood rushing to his face in another embarrassing moment at his expense.

"Yes, thank you, Herr Malleczewen. I think that's what Theo was trying to say," Gracie answered as politely as possible, making Theo feel even more foolish for having spoken with his mouth full.

"I am glad our American friend vas able to enjoy a *fines Deutsches* meal. It seems our beloved country has not been seen in a most positive light lately." Fritz smiled. "I do believe you kids have had qvite a long journey and shoult turn in for der eveninк."

Theo shot Gracie a quick glance and caught her look of disappointment that vanished before anyone else could see it on her face. "It has been a long couple of days, sir. I think I would like a good night's rest, which should come easy with my stomach not rumbling," Theo spoke before Gracie could protest. "I think Murphy and I are both ready for some overdue rest, but . . . um . . . sorry, but may I ask one question before I go?" he added hesitantly.

"Of course, Teo. Vhat is pressink on your mind?"

"First, I did not mean any disrespect by trying to sit beside you. Second, who usually sits in that chair?"

Fritz and TAR shared a quick glance. Theo could feel Gracie's glaring stare, letting him know that he had overstepped his bounds.

"It belongs to my uncle," the young-looking man named Erich quickly answered trying to help the young American out of yet another awkward moment. Theo then remembered Herr Möeller's words to say hello to his nephew.

"Jahile has gone into hiding for a while. Having to expose his identity to those SS officers during your rescue in Brack's office has put his life in extreme danger. The *Society* will not rest until they get their filthy hands on a champion of *the Watch*," TAR explained with a hint of controlled anger in his voice.

Silence dripped thick over the table. Both teens had visual memory of a night in Viktor Brack's office when they were caught by a jaeger and an SS officer as they looked for Brack's journal. From the time Theo first saw the journal when Viktor Brack destroyed his father's science and research lab, he knew the words and drawings in the book were plans to destroy and rewrite the history of Germany.

Not only would Viktor Brack do all in his power to destroy anyone who was not Aryan, he would destroy Theo's great-grandfather and obliterate his existence before it even began. Theo let his chin drop to his chest as he closed his eyes and slowly shook his head. He didn't intend Herr Möeller any harm. He just knew—and he could not explain to these people—the time jump back to this period of history could not be ended without taking the journal away from Brack. Theo rubbed his temples to end the pounding in his head and to hide the burning behind his eyes that threatened to explode into tears.

"Herr Möeller never mentioned he would be in trouble because of us." Gracie gasped softly. Even stoic Li'l Grey couldn't stop a tear from welling up in her eye. She had fought letting anyone into her heart, but the unconditional love of her guardian had taken root not only because of what he had done for her but also because he loved her papa.

"No, no, tender angel. Rest in knowing Jahile wouldn't have shown the triquetra of *the Watch* without knowing the consequences and without it being the only way out of the situation." Claus tried to ease the young girl's emotions. He walked to Theo and put a large hand on the young man's shoulder. "It's no one's fault. It's a risk we all take just being here, and the risk grows greater every day that the führer's power is left unchecked."

The Table members all nodded in agreement with Claus. Keila put a reassuring hand on Gracie's shoulder and whispered into her ear something that no one else could hear. After a few moments and a quick wipe away of tears, Gracie raised her delicate face to look around the table and smile at everyone.

"Why is he called a champion?" Theo asked, unable to contain his curiosity boiling over.

"Tat, I'm afraid, ist for anoter day, younk man. Now off to bed vit bote of you," Fritz politely ordered along with a shooing motion of his hand.

"Good night, everyone." Gracie offered her warmest farewell to the members of *the Watch*. She wasn't sure how many of them would be there in the morning. "Mr. Robertson, I mean, TAR, will you tell Herr Möeller I appreciate what he has done for me and my parents? Of course, I'll tell him myself someday." She paused at the door with her hand on the brass handle, trying to decide whether to say any more. She sighed and turned to face the table full of unsung and secret heroes. "I never meant to put him in danger. Will I get to see him again?"

"Uh-huh, gmh . . . well." TAR feigned clearing his throat, stammering over an answer.

"Of course, you will, darling," Nina spoke over the struggling TAR, who nodded his thanks to her for saving him. She shot him a quick nod then rose and walked to Gracie. Just in front of the young lady struggling with reality, Nina stopped and cradled both of Gracie's hands in her own. "We all enter this circle knowing full well the danger this secret society brings to our lives. If anyone would survive a manhunt, your Herr Möeller is the most prepared. He has had very special training and has probably been in worse scrapes than this."

"I hope you're right," Gracie's voice lifted in a whisper to Nina's words.

"Let me show you both to your rooms, shall I?"

"That would be awesome." Theo was anxious to get out of the room without making himself look like any more of a troublemaker than he already had. "I'm sure I couldn't find my way back from here anyway. This place is a maze!"

"Quite right." Nina dropped Gracie's hands and opened the door to lead them through the convolution of hallways and rooms under the church. Fritz had arranged for the teens to stay in private chambers under the basilica where they could remain safe and hidden.

Gracie gently closed the door and waited until she could no longer hear Nina's soft footsteps echoing in the ancient hallway. She pressed her ear against the thick wooden door and held her breath, straining to catch the faintest sound coming from the hall. Waiting so no one was within hearing distance, she lifted the latch and winced as the metal clunk resounded through her room and, she was sure, through the hallway too. She froze in place and waited again to make sure no one who might come to check on them had heard the latch. Finally, convinced she hadn't set off any suspicions, she cracked the door just enough to peek one eye out to scan the immediate area. Nothing moved or caught her attention. She inched open the door only slightly to slip into the hall and take three striding steps to the door across the hall.

Twice she rapped on the door just enough for the pounding to be heard from inside. She heard feet shuffle across the floor behind the door, then a pause; the door latch clanked with an audible self-tongue-lashing from someone behind the door. The door opened a crack, allowing Theo to see Gracie standing in the hall. "What are you up to?" she demanded accusingly.

"What on earth are you talking about?" Theo tried to sound insulted and surprised by her accusation.

"Where's Murphy?" Gracie straightened to her full height and stood with hands on hips and a scowl on her face.

Theo looked down at his feet for a minute then up at her and winked. "You noticed that, didn't you?"

"You never go anywhere without him."

Theo took a full step into the hall and looked up and down in both directions. Without another word, he grabbed Gracie by the wrist and pulled her into his room, shutting the wooden door behind them. "Aren't you the slightest bit curious what they're talking about?"

"Of course, but we can't hear them from here, and they'd hear us coming from a mile away in these echo chamber hallways, so don't get some goofy spy idea in your head."

"Relax! We don't need to be down there as long as he already is."

"Who?"

"Murphy! Duh. Why do you think I left him down there?" Theo couldn't help flashing a sly grin.

"I honestly have no idea what you're going on about, Theo," Gracie snipped in confusion. "He's a special dog, I'll give you that, but he can't speak to us." She paused, suspicious of what that dog could and couldn't do. The light show in the fountain outside

Frankfurt's Alte Oper flashed in her mind and made her seriously rethink Murphy's abilities.

"Well, he does have recording chips. Actually, that's a really good thought. I'll have to check his—" Theo stopped rambling when he noticed Gracie's annoyed expression. "Uh, right, sorry. He can be used to eavesdrop."

Gracie's scowl slowly formed into a smirk. "So how do we listen if your incredible Murphy dog is down there and we're up here?"

Theo smiled and held up his finger. "Hold that thought!" He took two large strides to his bed and started rummaging through his backpack. His hand went in, first scouring the side pockets, then he was up to his elbow. "I know it's in here somewhere, dang it. I can't . . ."

"You know, if you were just a bit more organized, you wouldn't have such a—" Gracie stopped as Theo turned the pack upside down, dumping its contents onto his bed. "How did you get all that?" she asked, flabbergasted, waving a hand at his bed then pointing to the backpack. "In there?"

"I have no idea," he admitted as he threw unneeded items on the floor. "Bingo!" he cheered as he grabbed his watch and turned to show Gracie that he had found the treasure.

Gracie gawked at the object dangling from Theo's hand. "So what? It looks like a watch my papa bought once on a trip to Berlin."

"That's exactly what it is!" Theo smiled, glad she was sharing about her family. He hoped her anger was subsiding.

Gracie squinted one eye at Theo. "Oh, let me guess. It does a lot more than just tell time." Her voice suggested a mixture of doubt and hope beyond reason.

"You're learning," Theo answered. "This is connected to Murphy." He waved the black wristwatch with chrome buttons inlaid in the face and sides of the watch. "I can use it to hear and see what he does. We won't be able to use the optical link without bringing attention to the fact that he's in the room. However, if we use his audio relay system, we should be able to hear what they're planning and talking about."

"Okay. Say I understand half of the gibberish you're saying, are you serious? He can do that?"

"And a lot more. I truly have no idea what he's capable of doing," Theo answered with awe in his voice, thinking about everything he had seen his best friend do and the absolute endless potential of his abilities. "Pull that chair over here," he said, pointing across his small but cozy sleeping quarters.

Gracie dragged the chair over and sat down next to Theo's bed. She watched with anticipation and wonder as Theo pulled from his ear the earbud that looked like a rain droplet and set it down next to the fancy watch from his pack. "What are you doing now? The meeting will be starting soon. I'm sure we won't understand what's going on if we don't hear it all."

"One second." Theo held up an index finger without looking up from his position on the bed. He moved the watch and earbud rapidly in his hands and finally looked up and gestured with a thumbs-up. "There we go! We're synced and ready to listen!"

Always Watching

"*HONORARE VOVEMUS AMOR atque deféndat omnes homines,*" Fritz spoke the Latin words in his soft yet commanding voice.

In unison, the group responded, "We shall always be watching." The sound of people sitting down and chairs sliding across the floor exploded through the transmitter on Theo's bed. "Good boy," Theo whispered, although the dog could not hear from where he was innocently sitting on Nina's lap as she petted her new friend. Earlier, when Nina escorted the teens to their rooms, Theo convinced her that the dog had found favor with her and would allow the teens better sleep if he was not in their rooms. The tenderhearted Nina agreed and hurried to the secret meeting room with the loving beagle in her arms.

"First tings first." Fritz inhaled with an audible breath. "I know ve're all vorried about Jahile. Do ve have a location or even a general area of relocation vhere he vas headed?"

TAR scoffed at the question. "You know that the only reason he is still breathing this long into his life is because he knows when to share valuable information and when not to. He never mentioned a fallback point when I've met with him over the last few months." TAR sighed in frustration. "We'll not find him. He will find us when he thinks it's safe to reemerge from the shadows."

Claus jumped into the conversation before anyone else had time to respond. "Maybe this was his plan all along."

"What are you talking about, Claus?" Erich questioned him angrily. "You think he wanted to leave us? Leave the cause, the fight?

I know my uncle, and you do too. This is his passion! It's his whole meaning of existence!"

"You misunderstand me, my friend," Claus explained, trying to placate the young man's anger. "He has been at this longer than any of us. He has seen many of these very chairs empty and be filled again with new soldiers against the evil that plagues our world."

"What my husband is trying to say is that we believe Jahile has softened a bit. That beautiful young girl upstairs has somehow found a way to erode the hard shell that he built around his heart." Nina voiced thoughts she and her husband had earlier shared in the privacy of their home. "He wrote to me, and there was a tenderness in his words that I had not noticed since his wife and daughter were slaughtered in front of his eyes." She glanced to the silent head of the table. "Fritz, you and TAR have known him the longest. What do you think?"

Fritz sat for a minute staring at the empty seat to his right. "I too have noticed a softness in his vords that vas not tere before tese younksters came into his life. However, ve shoult not delude ourselves in tinkink ve vill see our friend anytime soon. I believe *the Society* had a pack of filty hunters lookink for him and tose kids."

"Why would they be looking for those two?" Keila tilted her head as an eyebrow raised.

"I believe they have a few secrets that Viktor Brack and Hitler do not want anyone—especially people like us—to get a hold of," TAR suggested. "We've all heard rumors about the camps that are up and running. More are being built. Every time we send someone to get information, he doesn't come back. The boy, Theo, told Jahile about a camp where Jewish children were destroyed." Uncharacteristically, TAR tapped nervously with his fingers against the solid oak table. "You know that Brack is involved with that wretched SS leader, Heinrich Himmler, in a euthanasia program." His voice took on a huskier, almost shaky tone. "You can bet that Philipp Bouhler has Hadamar involved."

"Hadamar?" Erich's curiosity built as he watched Claus's face tense and redden with each name that TAR mentioned. He had heard the names but was unfamiliar with the word *Hadamar*.

Clearing his throat, TAR hesitated, knowing some of the eyes that had been looking attentively at him had dropped to look at the empty table. "It's a delicate topic with these fine ladies at the table."

"Go ahead, TAR. He needs to know. If we women can't stomach what you say, we are fooling ourselves about the dangers of the Reich that we fight against."

TAR tipped his head to the side in a nod. "How true you speak, dear Nina. Well, then," he looked directly at Erich, "Hadamar, once an institute for innocent mental and psychological research and healing, has been converted into a place where medical experimentation is maliciously practiced—half for pleasure of insane minds and half for ridding our homeland of anyone who is not Aryan."

"Pleasure?" Erich couldn't understand the tie between what TAR termed medical experimentation and pleasure.

"Most of us would call torture such as skin removal to be made into leather for books or gloves or even a man's trophy anything but pleasure, dear boy, but these leaders of the Reich are barbaric madmen who would carve and splay even their own flesh and blood if their depraved minds had such an inkling to do so."

Erich looked quickly at his girlfriend, Keila, in response to her soft gasp and involuntary response that brought her hand to cover her mouth.

After a long pause, Fritz spoke softly and cautiously by first addressing his friend who helped rescue the two youths then turning to other faces around the table. "Nina, I vould like you to have a talk vit our two younk companions and see vhat, if anyting, tey actually know. Jahile seemed qvite convinced tat Brack vas very interested in Teo and his furry friend. I believe Gracie ist a victim due to her parents' love. Black and Jew—a very dangerous combination and marked tarket tese days."

"I would be happy to talk to them for you, Fritz," piped in an anxious Keila before Nina had the opportunity to respond. "I am closer to their age. They may feel more comfortable talking to me."

"*Nein*! I vant Nina to do tis!" He pointed at the woman with short black hair and a beautiful smile sitting quietly next to her husband. "Do not qvestion my orders again, Keila!" Fritz's soft demeanor disappeared for a moment as he scolded the young and ambitious follower of Marx.

Nina merely nodded in understanding and looked across the table at the younger woman, whose face was red with a combination of anger and embarrassment. The Table sat silent for a moment as all members of *the Watch* collected their thoughts and then looked back to the head, who was sitting calmly as if he never raised his voice. Each person sitting there knew that even if he or she was reprimanded by Fritz, the chastisement was over as quickly as it was spoken.

Fritz sniffed air into his lungs and glanced at the door. "Joseph... Vhere is tat silly man now? Vasn't he to be here yesterday?"

Claus pushed back and stood up behind his chair in a fluid movement. No one could miss his body language as he squeezed the top of the chair in his hands. "Ach! That man missed his train again! He's driving here, and who knows what simple thing has caught his attention this time? It doesn't take much to distract him. He's like a child."

"He is an artist, my sweet husband, not a structured man of the military like you. He does not understand things the way you do. He sees life in a very different way," Nina spoke gently, reaching over and placing her calming hand over her husband's white knuckles.

Fritz sat in silence at the head of the table for a moment, deep in thought, forming a peak with his fingertips below his chin. He took a minute to look at each of the present *Watch* members. He exhaled a chuckle to himself. How many different faces had he and Jahile seen in each of those chairs. He thought back to when he was a young maverick. Oh, how he had rebelled against his father's wishes for a son to follow him into the political ring. Would his father be proud of the man he had become, earning his way from sitting in the lowest chair to the highest for longer than most? This seat was cursed, he had been told. No more than two years could someone sit there and still be breathing. Hunted and captured by *the Society*, they always seemed to know who sat in the top chair, leading each Table for *the Watch*. Each top chair was responsible for his members and those who aspired to become a part of the underground society.

Fritz shook his head to bring himself back to the present; the stares of an almost-full table made him realize he had been thinking to himself longer than he had realized. "Sorry. I am growink nostalgic in my old age." His words were laced with a smile. "Ve all know tat Joseph ist a . . . vell . . . a free spirit, I guess ist der best vay to put it. But he ist our link to America's High Table, and tey have put a lot of trust into tat little nimble performer."

TAR seized the moment of pause to pass new information to the group. "My XX committee has been able to discern where *the Society* has decided to strike next."

"Really?" an astonished voice quipped.

TAR jumped in. "Yes, Erich, really. We could stop this upcoming war in its tracks if the prime minister would just grow a backbone and stand up to the führer for a change. Instead, he gives and gives to avoid a war that we all know is going to happen. Look at the mess in North Africa and Spain. It won't be long until all of Europe is once again immersed in bloody combat!" A quiver in his cheeks was enough to show TAR was angry and frustrated about the political state as a whole.

Keila jumped into the conversation, excited to get her new views expressed to the group. "The USSR will not sit idly by and allow this uncontrolled führer to take whatever piece of Europe he wants. Stalin will defend his people and beloved country. It's what he strives toward."

"Sophia, ur, sorry, Keila." TAR caught his mistake. "I am not going to let a Soviet madman like Stalin dictate to the rest of Europe what Hitler does and doesn't do."

"*Madman?* How dare you insult the champion of mankind!" Keila stiffened as she screamed at the British officer.

"Easy, *Fräulein*. He has a point, you know. Josef Stalin did not come to power peacefully. He has murdered tens of thousands of his own people to keep control from slipping through his iron fist." Claus turned and looked at Keila as he spoke in defense of TAR's accusations.

"We will see who is standing at the end of this, won't we?" Keila spit with venom in her voice. She quickly stood as her temper flared like a flame that had been fueled. Her chair tumbled down behind her. Unfazed by the upset, she snapped her leg back and kicked the toppled chair out from behind her. "This Table is no better than the people we are trying to stop!" Her arm flung in a circular gesticulation. "Seems to me that the only good that you want to do is to further your cause!"

"Keila! Tat ist enough!" Fritz exploded from his chair at the unacceptable accusations and insults from the young Communist. "I understand your frustration, but you must see evil in Stalin's heart. Even Lenin did not vant Stalin in charge. He viped out our entire Table in Russia, and you vant us to help him?"

"He does what he feels is best for his people!"

"He does vhat ist best for him. He ist not a Socialist at all. He ist a dictator!" Fritz shouted. "A true Socialist society coult be a vonderful place to live, but everyone must be eqval for tat to happen. Do you see him eating soup and stale bread like millions of starvink people in his beloved Russia?" Reprimanding himself for exposing his emotions, Fritz sat back down and placed his folded hands on the table.

"He has a plan to save his people and make Russia an example for the rest of the world to follow. Come, Erich, I no longer wish to be near these people," she ordered her young boyfriend.

TAR reacted with a stern yet controlled anger in his voice. "Keila, take a moment and think about what you're doing. If you leave this meeting, you will not be welcome at this Table or any other Table and will not be provided any protections to which you have become accustomed." He moved to stand beside Fritz in a defensive posture.

"Whoa, whoa! What's happening right now?" Erich slowly stood up from his seat and placed an arm across the shoulders of his seething girlfriend. He whispered something in her ear that, by the look on his face, did not have its intended calming effect. "TAR, Fritz, forgive Keila. She is very stressed right now."

Keila glared at Erich for a moment with a warning look in her eyes. He looked back at her with concern, bearing an internal struggle between the woman he loved and the need of the great good.

"You should tell them," he finally whispered, lowering his head to stare at his feet, avoiding the piercing eyes of the woman who could hold or crush his heart.

"Keila, what is he talking about?" Nina queried with a low, calm voice. Against the outbursts, she slipped into her role as peacemaker of the group, almost the mother figure of this Table.

Keila looked at the group, terrified of what they all must be thinking. She looked sadly at her much-younger suitor for she knew that this would be the end of her association with this Table of *the Watch*. His youth and naivety of the world, which she loved the most about him, had just caused her greatest upset. She looked down at the dark table then slowly back up to the faces staring and waiting for her to explain Erich's plea. She gave a nervous laugh then looked at the end of the table where Fritz sat seething with rage. "We . . . uh, you know . . . Stalin and . . . and others . . . have a plan to undermine the appearance of the führer's boundless power and technological advancements."

"Vhat have you gotten yourself involved vit, my dear Keila?" Fritz asked with words of concern for the woman and no evidence of his earlier rage. "Tell me tey don't know about your involvement vit us."

"I . . . I'm . . ." Keila's eyes met an explosion of expressions as she scanned the faces around the table. "I'm sorry, everyone, but they will kill me if I mess up their plans." Her voice dropped in volume, but not in strength.

TAR caught her attention with his voice as he subtly motioned Claus to move in the opposite direction around the oak table, slowly closing in on the Communist traitor. Neither ignored a peripheral watch toward her wide-eyed young boyfriend. "Keila, we can and will protect you from whomever you've gotten yourself tangled up with."

"Stop! Don't come any closer to her," Erich ordered once he realized the men were maneuvering into a position to entrap his beloved Keila. "I mean it. Stop or else!" Erich pulled a small revolver from a hidden pocket inside his coat. He aimed his shaking gun first at Claus as he pushed Keila back from the table and stood between her and the two aggressors. His attention swung to TAR, who had pulled his gun and attempted to approach their blind side.

Fritz's chair scraped against the floor as he stood. "Stop, all of you! Keila vill not be harmed in tis room or by members of my Table. Everyone sit down and let Keila—our friend and partner in many past endeavors—explain to me, to us, vhat the Communist society, *Red Peace*, has in store for Adolf Hitler and his Reich."

Keila pushed Erich out of her way as she lunged at the table, grabbing it with both hands in an attempt to contain her rage. "You knew? You knew the *Red Peace* is involved?" She shook her head in disbelief. "Of course, you did. You probably have us all tailed, don't you, Fritz Malleczewen?"

Everyone turned to look at the short man who had sat back down at the head of the table and was adjusting his bow tie. After what seemed an interminable pause and distraction with his tie, Fritz ran his hands over his thick hair and flattened the sides of his scalp. "I did not have you followed, younk lady, yet I don't divulge my vays. How do you tink I have been able to keep tis chair for so long?" He paused, giving her a moment to collect her thoughts, then gestured with his hand for her to be seated.

"Those were my men trailing you." TAR spoke up to defend his beloved leader. "Two of our less experienced agents. I had them follow because I don't trust you. I learned a long time ago that I should always stick with my first impression." He smiled his devilish grin and holstered his gun. "Erich, you would do well to try to keep this little minx from clouding your mind with her honey words."

"She isn't—" Erich started to defend the older woman he loved.

"Boy, she's using you." TAR's charm was gone, and his words were thick with his Scottish accent as he interrupted. "How long ago did she admit to you that she's been with the *Red Peace*?"

"Just . . . just a few weeks. Isn't that right, darling?" Erich tilted his head toward his redheaded love.

"She's been lying to you for a very long time, son."

"Keila?" Erich pleaded for her to answer his denial. He looked at her with longing in his eyes. He was young, but he knew he loved her, and he was sure, at least he had been sure, that she loved him.

Keila sighed loudly. She turned and looked at her overturned chair then back to Erich. Without even a word, he darted to the chair and lifted it behind her and helped her slide up to the table.

"Thank you, darling," she whispered and placed her hand gently on his smooth face and pulled him in for a soft kiss.

TAR scoffed loudly at the display of affection, knowing that the woman had the gullible young man wrapped around her little finger. Erich's mind was so clouded by love she could have told him the world was at peace and he would have searched every government power to prove her right. "We need to have a rule against relationships," TAR grumbled.

"Excuse me, TAR?" Nina responded jokingly, knowing exactly what the British Intelligence officer was referencing. Nina found TAR's remarks even funnier given the officer's reputation as quite a ladies' man himself. She leaned over and kissed her husband's cheek, causing TAR to roll his eyes in mock disgust.

Erich picked up his hat, which had fallen to the floor during the commotion, then he too sat down and fixed his eyes on the owner of his heart. He felt his heart was beating a thousand times per minute in anticipation of her answer. His thoughts tumbled in painful confusion. *Am I deceived? Doesn't she love me?* Erich's head pounded with his heart, and a wave of nausea threatened him.

"Vell?" Fritz held his hands clasped and fingers entwined with his chin resting on them as he waited for Keila's response. The usual twinkle of kindness that always seemed to be present in his eyes had sunk into the depths of his soul, and now a very dangerous and determined man sat at the head of his Table. His demeanor thickened the silent air.

"*Red Peace*, Keila!" TAR ordered.

Keila cleared her throat and placed both hands on the table, trying to stabilize the nervous shake in her hands. "I have been working with members of *Red Peace* for . . ."

Just as the truth was about to pour from Keila's lips, the heavy wooden doors flew open, and a blast of cool air from the outer hall blew in along with the man the Table had been waiting to see. The look on Joseph Späh's face prompted immediate reaction from all in the room. Like a well-oiled machine, everyone pushed away from the table and grabbed any belongings they had brought with them. Members of *the Watch* always traveled light. It was just part of the life they lived. The ability to move quickly and disappear even quicker could be the difference between one more day and taking a last breath.

"The north tunnel has been compromised!" Nina shouted. "Follow me to the sister chapel. Claus, go get the teens and meet us at the chapel."

Without another word, the group hoisted their belongings and followed a very calm and very in-charge Nina to a low overhang and a small oak door that led to an underground kitchen. Most of the men had to lean forward to get under the door header without getting a bruised forehead. They snaked their way through the tiny kitchen space. TAR was the last to enter the room and turned and slammed the secret meeting room door shut behind them then laid a heavy wooden beam across the door. The beam would stop a normal pursuer, but if his fears were correct, it would just annoy the odious evil that was tracking them.

Theo and Gracie both looked up from Theo's watch that had allowed them to listen to the secret meeting. Theo hurriedly stuffed the objects scattered on his bed into his backpack. "Get back to your room before Claus gets here. Act surprised!" he ordered, jumping off his bed and running over to unlatch the heavy lock and open the door for Gracie.

"Don't forget Murphy!" she puffed as she ran past him into the hallway and across to her room.

Without hesitation, Theo pushed on one of the chrome buttons and spoke into the watch's transmitter face. "Murphy, follow Claus and get up here, boy."

Just as Theo was relatching his door, he heard yelling and loud pounding footsteps coming from the far end of the hallway. He ran to his bed and threw his backpack over his shoulders. He took a second look at the bed and searched for any loose objects he might have missed. Satisfied that nothing was left behind, he ran back to open the door. A well-built, blond-haired, blue-eyed member of the

Hitler's *Schutzstaffel* was almost at his door. A silver flash caught his eye. Theo squinted past the charging soldier to see a metallic ball rolling behind the man dressed as an agent of evil but determined as a double agent fighting for good.

"Gracie! Theo!" Claus yelled, sprinting toward their rooms. "We must go! Now!"

Theo shivered hearing Claus's heavy German accent call his name. It had an eerie familiarity to it—just like when Viktor Brack would say his name. The memory brought a flood of anger and emotions surging through his veins, giving him a renewed boost of energy.

"Hurry! We're not safe!"

Gracie's door flew open. She pursed her lips to ask about Murphy just as Theo pointed to the silver ball streaking up the hallway. Gracie watched as the ball shot unnoticed past the sprinting German, bouncing as it got nearer to Theo. With one final bounce, the ball launched itself into the air and morphed into a metallic beagle then a brown, white, and black beagle, which landed in his master's outstretched and waiting arms.

"That was amazing!" Gracie gasped.

"What? Where did he come from?" Claus reacted in surprise to see the dog lying in Theo's arms.

"Special dog." Theo smiled and rubbed Murphy's big ears. "Aren't you, boy?" Murphy pushed a wet snout to Theo's face.

"We must go!" Claus ordered. His military training urged him to focus on the task at hand—to get as far away from the oncoming threat as possible. He was in real jeopardy. If Nazi soldiers saw him in uniform, terrible repercussions would be set in motion against his family and his future as a double agent. He was confident he could handle any threat, but he couldn't handle something happening to his family. If *the Society* had tracked and followed Joseph right into the heart of their Table, he knew it would be more than Nazi soldiers chasing them.

"What's going on?" Gracie's mock surprise caused Theo to lower his head and hide a smile.

She's good, he thought, rubbing the smile from his face and jumping into the action. "Okay, let's get moving."

With that, Claus turned and sprinted down the hallway in the direction he had just come. He never looked back to see if the teens followed, but the pounding feet hitting the stone floor behind him told him they were in tow.

Escape

NIGHT WAS STARTING to lose its grip over the city; the sun was minutes away from pushing over the horizon. At the mouth of the concealed tunnel, a rusted gate, hidden by years of overgrowth and neglect, creaked and cracked under the pressure of three men slamming their bodies into it full force.

"Be strong for us!" Nina encouraged with words that never reached the men who stood farther up the tunnel attempting to breach the gate holding them as prisoners in the tunnel. She stood looking back down the tunnel, which was slightly touched with the last light of the moon as it tried to seep down into their darkness. "Theo, are you okay?" Nina and Theo locked eyes for a moment. Nina recognized panic on his face.

"I really just want to get out of this tunnel." Theo's breathing was labored, and sweat poured down his face despite the bite of the cool air. "I really don't like these things at all!" The force of his emotions punched out from the anxiety constricting his confidence.

"He's claustrophobic," Gracie explained. "You should've seen him in the underground tunnel before you rescued us. Let's just say he wasn't happy." To soften what might have sounded critical, she reached over and gave a pat to Theo's arm, allowing her hand to stay wrapped around the tense muscle within his sleeve.

In the darkness, Nina's soft smile was imperceptible. "I don't like being down in these tunnels either, Theo. But I do appreciate them a little more for their protection in times like this." She spoke to assure that he wasn't alone in his fears.

VIGILATUS

The sound of TAR, Claus, and Erich ramming into the rusted metal gate made the others turn and watch. "One more time, men." TAR encouraged in a low voice. "Let's go. One, two, three." The men drove their shoulders into the wrought-iron gate and felt it finally give way under their weight, spilling them facefirst onto the dewy grass soaking into their clothes.

"Excellent vork, gentlemen." Fritz gave a single clap of his hands in excitement and appreciation for their efforts for him and the rest of the group. "Ve mustn't rest. I do believe that ve're not alone." All three men nodded in agreement, picking themselves up off the grass at the mouth of the tunnel.

Theo crawled upward past Gracie, Nina, and Keila to escape the smothering passageway, leaving Joseph at the back, alone in the tunnel. He sucked in a large breath and closed his eyes, allowing the early dawn air to soothe his nerves. He opened his eyes but struggled to keep focus. His head swam with swirling colors. His nose picked up scents from the garden foliage battling for his attention.

"Where are we?" Theo knew he was disoriented. Even the dim light from the descending moon caused his pupils to contract in reaction to the drastic change from the impenetrable darkness of the tunnel skimmed only by the few flashlights procured from their packs.

"A very sorrowful and special place, Theo," Claus whispered in a softness that contrasted their situation. His voice offered a reverence as clear and penetrating as the fresh air. "This is a Jewish cemetery that dates back to the late 1200s. It met its capacity over a hundred years ago and hasn't been used since the early 1800s. You would think the German government would be sensitive to the suffering already inflicted on the Jews."

It was a strange visual for Theo: Claus—dressed in the official uniform of the German war machine, the destroyer of the Jewish race, yet openly expressing care and respect for a people whom his commander in chief determined to decimate. Theo remembered Mr. Medi saying that the views of Hitler were not the views of all the people. He remembered his teacher trying hard to drive home the point that it only took a few people in powerful positions to lead masses in assault on the Jews. He watched as the handsome German officer ran his hand gently over the tombstones. Theo wished that his technology could work right now. He so badly wanted to take a picture of Claus and show Mr. Medi if he ever got back home.

"If we don't get a move on, ladies and gentlemen, they may bury us here as well." TAR quietly announced the reality though all stood entranced by the overwhelming sight of nearly seven thousand tombstones, most with small piles of stones balanced on top. "Remember this place. It's what we're trying to stop from happening on an even greater scale!" TAR's words snapped their thoughts to the dire situation of the moment. Fritz shook his head as if he were trying to throw the vision of the graveyard out of his mind.

Fritz stepped back into his role of leader. "The teens vill come vit Nina, Joseph, TAR, and me. Ve vill get tem to you later, Erich." Even in the faint light, Erich's look of confusion caught Fritz's eye. "Perhaps tese young people are as confused as you, eh, Erich? No, he's not vit us, but Jahile set a plan in motion to save his kids." The corner of Fritz's mouth tipped upward as he turned to wink at Theo and Gracie before he continued. "Joseph already has a ticket for travel to das States on your airship, Erich. Ve vill get Teo and Gracie to der airfield." Fritz kept looking at Erich but waved his hand between Erich and Joseph. "Ten, vonce you land, it vill be up to the two of you to get tem safely to Amelia and her Table members."

"It's going to be tough to get passage for the kids this close to the flight, Fritz. The SS has been digging into all passengers who have booked so far, making sure they're not a threat to the Reich." Concern was thick in Erich's voice. "We have to report back sooner than normal to have the ship inspected aft to bow by a special unit sent from Berlin."

Fritz leaned against the ivy-covered brick wall, rubbing his forehead as if the touch of his fingers would bring solutions to mind. His head dropped as his eyes looked to Erich with determination. "Be ready for a special delivery, Erich. Joseph vill need to purchase some cargo-hold space for his *recent purchases*." Through the emerging dawn light, a slanted grin was seen on Fritz's face as he punctuated his words.

With a quick nod to Joseph, Erich's face brightened under raised eyebrows before he grabbed Keila's hand. The couple took off through the thousands of graves and vanished in the morning mist rising from the ground.

"Everyvone get vhere you need to be! Claus, be sure not to be seen leavink tis place. It vould get you kilt." Fritz snapped his orders, making eye contact with the courageous double agent.

"He's right, my love. Be safe, and return to me soon," Nina whispered, not caring who overheard or saw her stand on tiptoe to wrap her slender arms around his neck. She brushed his cheek with a kiss before embracing in a long, passionate kiss. She was no stranger to his missions, but she never became calloused to saying goodbye. Leaving each other was the hardest part of this life. Each time could be a last time, but they shared a passion for the people of Germany.

"Wait!" Theo reacted in panic. He had found trust and safety in this small group. "Claus, where are you going? Can't you come with us?"

"Sorry, young man. This uniform I wear is part of my daily life. I wear it now to help avert suspicion from all of you and all my countrymen who are doing their best to survive against the wishes of the Reich. If I'm gone from my post too long, I'll be hunted, and I can't be found in your presence. It would do much harm to you and to the good people of Germany."

Claus wrapped his muscular arms around his wife's tiny waist and lifted her until her face lay against his. He felt the wet tears rolling down her cheek. "My wife, I love you and will be back before you know it. Take good care of this lot. They'll need your love and guidance to get away safely."

One last long kiss ended as Claus set Nina down on the dewy grass. In a fluid move, he shut the gate they had just forced open and did a hurried job to lock it tight. As the metal made a final snap, Claus looked at Nina. Fighting his own desire to stay, he ran along the cemetery wall until he was on a mulched border that left no sign of footprints. Nina's last glance saw Claus athletically jump the wall and disappear.

Nina wiped streaks from her cheeks and swallowed a swollen breath before she turned back to the group. She caught a whiff of something pungent and rank coming from the tunnel entrance. "We must go! Now!"

The fear in Nina's eyes needed no explanation. Without speaking, Fritz started an agile weave through the tombstones on the Jewish graves and out to the street. He never turned back to the others. He knew—they all knew—to live meant to follow.

The streets were still empty of life. A few scattered lights from windows were illuminating the morning for early risers. When their feet hit the brick pavement, the small group of renegades swung north. They welcomed the cover of the first alleyway they found. Theo put his shirt over his mouth and nose as the stench coming from the trash and sewage made him gag. He noticed a pair of shoeless feet protruding from underneath piles of garbage bags and debris.

The sight of the feet stopped him. How long had it been since he had seen his father's motionless feet under the debris from the lab explosion? The TimeWorm jump that sent him back over a hundred years seemed to have happened a thousand years ago. Sadness billowed inside, threatening to overtake and to weaken him; but with the memory came Brack's face, and the sadness was overcome by anger and rage.

"Keep moving, son." Joseph laid a reassuring hand on the youth's shoulder. "That poor soul probably just disagreed with the wrong person or said something to the wrong friend. Dangerous times to have an opinion."

Theo shook his head and picked up the pace to catch up. Nina and Gracie ran close to TAR just behind Fritz, guiding the group. Theo jogged to the muffled cadence. Joseph took his position at the rear of the pack, where he constantly looked over his shoulder for onlookers or aggressors.

The wet, slick cobblestones challenged the run through the trash-filled alleyways. With each slip, a hand of rescue would reach out for support and recovery. Only the nimble and agile gymnast took no notice of the wet conditions or clutter strewn about their path. Joseph leaped and dodged obstacles without a second thought and kept his footing as he ran gingerly on his tiptoes while looking backward most of the time.

Theo heard the tiny acrobat swear in German under his breath. He looked in amazement as Joseph sprang past. With little effort, Joseph jumped a large pile of crates then caught a window ledge with his hand. With his one-handed grip, he pulled himself up and pushed off the side of the building, rolling in a full 360. He tumbled gracefully through the air and landed on tiptoes before he broke into a full sprint past the women of the group.

Theo tripped on an uneven cobblestone and had to tuck and roll to avoid a solid and painful face plant onto the ground. The ball of metallic dog did not feel good as his back slammed down onto his sleeping friend hidden in his pack.

"You okay?" Gracie huffed her concern without turning around to check on Theo.

"How did you—"

"I'm not deaf," she interrupted, knowing he would question how she knew he had fallen.

"Fine, but I landed hard on Murphy." Again, Theo had to catch up with the group. Worried about his pup, Theo slipped one arm out from the strap and swung his pack around to his chest. He opened the top flap and looked into the pack. The silver ball of dog was still intact; he didn't see a single dent or mark on it. *Wish I were made of a metallic alloy!*

"Hey, boy," Theo whispered as he looked up just in time to duck a low-hanging clothesline. He shook his head then stood still long enough to glance down into the pack. "Wake up, Murph. I need you to—"

Before Theo finished his sentence, the motionless ball of metal sprang to life and exploded from the backpack. Murphy landed with four legs touching down on the cobbles and tail in full wag mode. "Keep an ear out for whatever's following us." Theo knew Murphy was as adept as Joseph when it came to being trailed by evil.

Murphy rubbed against Theo's leg almost catlike, waiting patiently for a quick ear rub, which he got, then fell in step behind his winded master. Theo had learned a few tactics of survival from

Gracie and his time on the streets. Turning his head slightly and depending greatly on his peripheral vision, he mentally took note of his surroundings. Every few steps, he purposely set his eyes straight ahead to check that he was still in line with Fritz. *For an older guy, either he's in great shape or he's really scared. Either way, I'm not sure how much longer I can keep this relentless pace!* Theo kept his thoughts to himself though he noticed Fritz and Joseph were intently whispering as they ran. Theo assumed they discussed whatever was behind them and planned the way ahead. He saw Fritz nod then point. Without another word, Joseph ran full speed down an alley until he disappeared around a corner.

Within seconds, Fritz took a hard left and disappeared around the same corner. One by one, members of *the Watch* approached the corner of the brick building and made a sharp left turn. Theo watched as Gracie vanished from his sight. An emptiness tightened his gut once he couldn't see her or the other members of the small group. Exhaustion threatened to overtake him, but the sensation of being alone helped him bolster one last burst of energy. He closed in on the turn and grabbed for the wall to turn and navigate the corner. He caught a scream in his throat as he nearly smashed facefirst into a wooden fence, but an opening appeared with Gracie's outstretched hand waiting for him.

"Murphy, wait for Murphy," he panted as he caught her hand guiding him into yet another dark and damp place. "Seriously."

"Only a few steps more, and we'll be in a larger space," Nina whispered. Theo knew so little of her, yet she had a way of calming his nerves.

"I'll be all right, just bit on edge." Theo's voice came out as a pant, partially due to danger and partially due to his energy being sapped by his tense muscles. Nina's words gave him hope. He appreciated knowing that he wouldn't be forced to endure tight, enclosed spaces much longer. He gained composure by taking long, deep breaths.

"Here, boy." Theo heard Gracie call to Murphy.

"Can we have light in here?" Theo's voice came out louder than he'd planned.

"That should be fine, but we don't have any lanterns or candles—only small flashlights." Fritz's profile showed him scanning the outside of their small group.

The darkness of their hiding place hid them from their attackers. "I think Murphy can help. Hey, boy, could you give us a little light?"

A soft-blue light pushed the darkness back and cast scant shadows on the walls surrounding them. "Will someone tell me where we are now? I almost smashed my face on a wooden fence, then the next thing I know, I'm back in a very tight, very dark space."

"It's just another mode of egress for us, Theo." Joseph could be heard in the dark shadows. Theo wondered if being elusive was another of Joseph's tricks.

"Egress. Isn't that a bird?"

"No, Teo. Tat's an egret." A small chuckle from Fritz echoed in the tight corridors. "*Egress* is just a fancy vord for *leave*."

"Oh, okay. Well, what kind of *egress* spot are we in then?" Theo tried to get away from his blunder. He was shocked that Gracie had not piped in to make fun of him; she so rarely missed an opportunity.

No one answered for a second, making Theo very nervous. Nina broke the silence. "We are in the wall of a building that the company of Fritz's father built many years ago. We have many little hideaways and tricks all over this city as well as in other cities in Europe and the world."

"The trick is to remember where to find a refuge in the heat of the moment—how to get *to* it then *into* it," TAR added to her explanation. Theo was surprised to hear TAR's voice; he had been quiet since they made their way from the graveyard. "Each Table of *the Watch* has its well-known hideouts. When you get the chance to interact with the American Table, they may be nice enough to share a few with you."

"Cool" was all Theo could muster. He had been thrust into the middle of a fascinating world of spies and secret societies, but all that didn't help him deal with his claustrophobia. "So how long do we need to stay in this wall?" He was sure he heard Gracie giggle.

"He does have a point, Fritz. Why are we waiting, dear?"

"I found it!" Joseph's voice answered from around another hidden corner. "Just a little twist and . . ." A popping noise filled the enclosed space, followed by a scraping noise, grunting, and Joseph mumbling improper words, hoping no one could hear. Nina quickly scolded him for his indecency. The reprimand got a small chuckle from everyone inside the wall, including Joseph.

Fresh air flooded into the hidden corridor, easing some of Theo's apprehensions but not enough for him to breathe easily. A few more grunts, and a dim light was welcomed into the corridor, showing the rebels the way out of the hiding place and into a small room. Each gave his or her thanks to Joseph, who was still holding the secret door open with an air as if he were the doorman for an upscale hotel.

"Sorry about the language, Mother," Joseph quipped as Nina walked by. She, in turn, gave him a playful slap on the cheek but then took his hand for assistance, stepping down into the room. The hidden door was a few feet off the ground and opened from behind a large framed painting.

The room was small but cozy and sparsely decorated. Other than a large painting concealing the secret entrance, only one other wall had anything hanging on it. A few couches took up most of the space shared with two small bunk beds at either side of room and a linen closet. Nina went straight into mother mode, opening the closet and pulling out blankets and pillows for everyone. Once she had everyone blanketed, she made another loop, stopping at each person to check on how he or she was holding up and if anything else was needed.

Theo realized pretty quickly that this room wasn't for comfort; it was for safety and survival. He wondered how long they would stay hidden. It wasn't a tunnel. It wasn't dark, but without any windows, it still felt like the walls were closing in on him.

"Find something to occupy your time, Theo. It will take your mind off your worries." Sensing the boy was troubled, TAR offered his words of wisdom before settling down, allowing snores to be heard from under the blanket he pulled over his head.

"Sounds like an excellent idea. Thanks." Theo opened his pack and started rifling through its contents. Soon the bed he had claimed was filled with odds and ends. He lifted the false flap in the bottom of his pack and pulled out two books—one that Herr Möeller had given him, the other still in its protective case.

Curious about a book Herr Möeller had insisted the teens keep in the pack, Theo lifted a novel with a faded silhouette of a woman on the cover. "*Dark Victory*. Never heard of it. Here, Gracie. Maybe Herr Möeller thought you would enjoy reading this book." He tossed the book to the top bunk where Gracie sat cross-legged, petting Murphy.

"Maybe I'll do a little reading. I'm not really sleepy yet." Gracie perched on an elbow and stretched her legs to the end of the soft bed. Before finding the first page, she did a quick flip through the pages. A red line under a sentence caught her attention. *"Nothing can hurt us now. What we have can't be destroyed. That's our victory—our victory over the dark."*

"Find a good book, Gracie?" Nina's tender voice drew Gracie's eyes to the woman's face peering into the top bunk.

"I'm not sure. Maybe. It looks good." Gracie gave a half smile back to the pretty woman. "Herr Möeller sent it with us. Funny enough, there's an underlined passage that makes me curious." She handed the book down to Nina.

Nina's eyes danced silently across the words as the corners of her lips drew upward in reaction. "Even now, our dear Jahile speaks to us. Keep these words in your heart, dear girl, and know all we do for our homeland, for yourself, for your parents is a victory."

Gracie reached for the book handed back to her and was sure the sparkle in Nina's eye was a glistening tear. Her thoughts warmed her as she watched Nina walk away. *She's like my mom, brave and bearing more on her shoulders than she wants me to know.* Gracie rolled to her stomach and let Murphy snuggle beside her as she began reading, looking for an adventure to take her mind away from the feeling of anxiousness their escape had left in her heart.

The etched title *Societatis* was visible through the waterproof case. Theo carefully removed the leatherbound book and carefully started to inspect the pages. It seemed a long time since he had read through the book in Herr Möeller's home. This would be a good time to examine it closely.

Theo leafed through the pages, unable to decipher most of the writing. He assumed it was German and thought about asking Gracie, but he didn't want to feel ridiculed. He flipped a few more pages and came to the diagram of the TimeWorm. He stopped and studied the diagram and notes, some actually written in English. Just seeing the sketch of the TimeWorm made his heart pound a little harder. He didn't know why he was so excited; he had been a very small part of the creation of the machine scratched onto the paper in front of him.

Maybe it reminded him of a time before all this craziness, before the ability to jump through time went from theory to reality—before secret societies, before Brack turned from a friend to an enemy, before his dad was paralyzed by the explosion, before he had such a firsthand, terrifying understanding of the teachings of Mr. Medi. It was hard for him to wrap his head around a number like six million Jews being killed. He had only seen fifty or so in that horrible pit, but it was enough that he knew he would never forget it.

"What's in that book?" a familiar voice asked from above him. He twisted his neck and saw a mass of curly black hair and a hint of caramel skin hidden behind it.

"Nothing." Theo shut the book and pretended to start looking for something else in his empty backpack.

"Nothing? It's obviously *something*. We could have lost our lives stealing it, remember? I know Herr Möeller was interested in it." Gracie had lain above him in quiet observation for longer than Theo had realized. "That's how you got here, isn't it?"

"I told you how I got here." Theo wanted to sound annoyed by her questioning.

"I know how you got here," she pointed around the room, "here—Germany, Europe. But that thing in the book is how you got *here*," she repeated with emphasis while pointing to his watch.

Theo shook his head, trying to throw her off-topic. "You're confusing. What are you talking about?"

Gracie seized Theo's opening to talk. She sprang from the top bunk and landed lightly on her feet and was sitting beside the handsome boy before he knew what happened. "When I first got to Herr Möeller's home, I had a terrible time trying to sleep. He showed me his small library that he had hidden away. I would read some nights to help me sleep, but it never worked. My favorite book was an amazing story of a man who traveled from his home on a machine he built."

"Like a car or something?" Theo asked innocently, refusing to understand what the girl was implying.

"No." Gracie placed her soft hands on the book and looked into Theo's eyes for permission to open it. He nodded, and once again, she moved quickly and gracefully before he could change his mind. She flipped through the pages until she got to the hand-sketched diagrams of the TimeWorm machine. "The man in the story built something like this and went into the future. Except in my mind, I pictured it differently. I always pictured it as a seat with many wheels and wires moving around him."

"What on earth are you talking about, Gracie?" Theo acted shocked by her intuitive accusations. "Are you saying that I built the time-traveling machine that brought me here?" He tried to muster up a fake laugh.

"No, no, no! You don't think I'd give you that much credit, do you?" She smiled slyly. "Your father and Brack built it, and somehow you ended up here. You told Herr Möeller you came from another time, but you didn't say how. This is what brought you, isn't it? That's why you seem to know so much about the stuff going on here."

Theo had a million thoughts and yet no words trapped in his mind. He knew the truth of her discovery was evident on his face because Gracie just sat looking at him and smiling. He did have to give her credit for piecing it all together and taking a leap of faith about the time travel. He just took for granted that a concept so abstract and advanced would be fiction in a madman's mind in the 1930s. No matter how impressed he was, he was afraid of the ramifications if too many people found out. A familiar quote snaked through his thoughts: "*Never underestimate the power of the imagination.*"

"What?" Theo tried his best to sound clueless. "Who talks about time travel?"

"You know, vonce vhen I vas a younker man, I met H. G. Vells." Fritz piped in from the couch next to the bunk beds, where he remained motionless with eyes closed. Theo thought he had fallen asleep long ago. "Clever man, tat Vells fella. He knew, like us, the goot advancements of men vould come at a price."

Gracie looked at Theo for a moment then over to Fritz, who had sat up on his makeshift bed. "What price do you mean? Like money?"

"Not exactly, my dear. However, greed can play an important role in hearts of men and make tem do amazing tings—and terrible tings—just as easily." Fritz's voice had a soft tone. "Robert Goddard, for example."

"Who?" Theo and Gracie asked simultaneously, neither recognizing the name.

"A man who dared to dream." The soft tone turned to excitement in Fritz's voice. A glance at the two teens sitting on the bottom bunk, staring at him made him realize they didn't understand. "He invented der very first rocket propulsion. His first test flight lasted only forty-vone seconds, but tose few short seconds turned into much more tan he ever imagined."

"Oh, I see," Theo muttered. "Missiles."

"What are missiles?" Gracie didn't hide her curiosity.

"Basically, bombs that can be launched from a safe distance." Theo quickly jumped at the chance to tell her something for a change.

"That sounds awful!"

"Ah, missiles are awful. But technology vill only continue to get verse." Fritz looked at Theo for a reaction.

Theo quickly looked down at his feet to avoid eye contact. He didn't know what to do or say. He understood that even as a young man, he could drastically change the future with one or two misplaced sentences. *Knowledge really is power.* He swallowed hard.

"Ist tat das book Jahile told me about, Teo?" Fritz lowered his voice, noticing that they were the only ones not asleep. "Let me see it."

Theo hesitated and pulled the book closer to his body. "Is it really a good idea?"

"My goot friend put himself in danger protectink you two and tat book. He believed you vhen you said it vas important. I'd like to see vhat he sacrificed a lifetime of secrecy to protect." Fritz's reply came with a sadness in his voice as he mentioned Jahile.

Theo looked at Gracie, who gave a slight nod to encourage trust. He reached out and handed the book to Fritz. The leader of *the Watch* slowly thumbed through the pages.

Theo rubbed his eyes and yawned as Gracie climbed back up to the top bunk. "I have an adventure waiting. I'm going back to my book to find a new adventure." Theo closed his eyes as Fritz opened the leatherbound book. Neither acknowledged Gracie's words.

Where There Is Good

*T*HEO'S ARMS CLASPED *around Gracie with fingers on both hands woven together to strengthen a solid grip. Something was pulling Gracie from his arms. His fingers ached. He knew he had to hold the grasp or lose Gracie forever. Something or someone beating against his arms threatened his muscles. The more he squeezed his fingers and hands and pulled his arms toward himself, the more he felt Gracie being pulled from his arms. Huffs and grunts turned to fighting with all his might against the pull—answered only by screams.*

No! You can't have her!

Theo's silent nightmare screams blended with other screams that were fading away. His mind—lost between sleep and precognition—caused his heartbeat and breathing to increase. His eyes bulged open to the nothingness of a silent room's soft light. Surroundings came into focus with the sound of someone scuffling across the floor. A slight throb in his temples begged him to close his eyes.

A half stretch produced a half moan wrapped in a deep breath while Theo's teenage body pleaded for more rest. *How long have I been asleep?* He opened his eyes fully and stared at the underside of the top bunk. *Where am I?* His thoughts were confused. His surroundings weren't familiar. He didn't want to move too much. Paranoia prompted a need to be careful, and every movement—no matter how small—needed to be calculated. He looked to his right as far as he could by turning his head still nestled on the pillow. A man sitting on a couch, flipping through a brown leather notebook placated his anxiety. *Fritz, that's Fritz. Okay, I recognize him, but where am I? We left the church in a hurry. Why?*

The man thumbed through the book, stopping and hovering at times, letting the fingers of one hand move across the paper. For long moments, he stared as if memorizing whatever lay on the pages.

The soft bed beckoned Theo to let his eyelids close again. *We were chased by . . . by . . . Brack? Or . . . I don't know. Who was chasing us? That smell in . . . Where were we? That last tunnel smelled so bad . . . so like . . . jaegers!* Memory of the black-cloaked creatures squeezed Theo's chest with intense fear. He bolted upright, hitting his head on the top bunk.

"Gaah! That really hurt," Theo mumbled loudly, rubbing the goose egg knot swelling on his forehead.

"Ouch! You okay, Teo?" Fritz voiced concern, but his eyes remained riveted to the pages of the book.

Theo shook his head without speaking, turning to put both feet on the floor; his bowed head hung toward his chest, and his hands gripped the mattress on either side of him. The cold floor shot a cooling sensation up through the socks on his feet, sending a slight shiver up his spine. He noticed Fritz's concern had not disturbed his studying the book.

"Teo, I have a few qvestions vonce your drowsiness passes." Fritz kept his voice low.

Theo tilted his head with a slight nod toward Fritz. "I figured you would. Maybe I can answer."

"Take your time. Nina set out some breakfast food for you two before she left."

"Where'd she go?" Theo liked Nina. She had been very patient and sweet to him. It had been a very long time since anyone doted over him in a motherly fashion. He hadn't realized how much he had missed that.

"Vherever she felt she needs to be, Teo." Fritz's answer was vague and matter-of-fact. "It's how ve do vhat we must. Ve develop a plan, and each person does vhat he or she needs to do. Ve are a vell-oiled machine. Ve have vorked together for so long tat little needs to be explained or discussed."

From slumped shoulders, Theo's arm extended to reluctantly grasp the wooden bunk frame. With a hard push off the mattress, he stood quickly. A wave of dizziness threatened to knock him back down. Both hands held the frame until the spinning faded, allowing him to cross the small room and plop down at a table.

He poured water from a large pitcher sitting in the middle of the table. Thoughts began to waken as Theo uncovered bread and cheese. With mechanical movements, he pulled pieces of bread from the loaf. His muscles acted for what needed to be done. In a strange way, he understood what Fritz was saying about members of *the Watch*. Like a body, each plays a part to help the entire system. He raised his eyebrows and grinned a crooked smile at the mental picture.

Fritz sat down beside him and laid the open book on the table facedown while he too poured a glass of water. Theo stuffed the food into his mouth. "Slow down, Teo! You'll choke!" Fritz's chuckle and infectious laugh made Theo smile, despite his full mouth.

"I um starwing," he replied, mouth completely full.

"Vell, you've been asleep for about tvelve hours. Ve all voke and tought our noise might vake you, but you never voke up—even in some times of fitful sleep. Your body probably needs to refuel."

"Twell hour?" Bread crumbs fell out with Theo's mumbles, confessing his shock at the news that he had slept so long. He hadn't slept so long since Herr Möeller saved him from the attack by the Hitler's Youth.

Fritz laughed louder. They continued a snack in silence. When the last crumbs from the severed bread had disappeared, Fritz flipped through the book to the page with the diagram of the TimeWorm machine. "Vas she right?"

"Huh?"

Fritz shook his head. "Gracie. Vas she right?"

"Oh. Uh, you're not gonna believe me." Theo intentionally held skepticism in his voice in hopes of avoiding conversation.

"My boy, I have seen a lot of tings tat most people vouldn't believe even if tey had seen vit der own eyes. How about you tell me and let me decide for myself vhat I choose to believe."

Theo looked down at the sketch for a moment, remembering all the late nights and effort put into the construction of what would become both dream and nightmare. He remembered his dad's passion to take the ideas off paper to make an impossible theory a very real, very stark reality. His memory also brought back how he felt from the force of the explosion throwing him like a rag doll from the laboratory to the outer room. Then his mind went white with the memory of the painful jump. He felt he was dying when the machine tore him to pieces one molecule at a time. He shuddered violently then looked up to the waiting eyes of Fritz.

"You okay, Teo?"

"Funny how a memory can hurt." A shiver came with the whisper.

Fritz clasped his hands together and tilted his head to analyze the young man sitting across from him. Long brown hair and dark eyes made him a perfect specimen of an enemy in the eyes of the Third Reich, but there was something different about him. Theo was part of a much-larger puzzle that Fritz hadn't been able to piece together. "Powerful tings, memories. Tey help us remember and shoult keep us from makink der same mistakes over again, but over der past decades, the world has forgotten a lot."

The man and youth sat in silence—a sad silence of understanding how in each of their own worlds, one man can be a powerful, dangerous force. Theo sighed and interrupted the quiet air between them. "I'm not sure where to start, Fritz."

"How does it vork?" Fritz hoped to spark the young man into a talkative mood.

"It harnesses the light of stars. I'm not sure how much you understand about light, but the light of the stars we see at night are not current. The light travels millions of miles to reach us. That machine—what my dad and Viktor Brack named the TimeWorm," Theo pointed at the sketch, "breaks the traveler down and basically shoots him back along the light of the star calculated and chosen to reach a destination." Theo paused to let his words settle in Fritz's mind.

Fritz said nothing for a very long time. Theo stared from across the table. Eventually, the silence became awkward, so he did what any teenage boy would do and reached for more food. He finished the small piece of bread and washed it down with another glass of water.

"Jahile, vas right. I tought all tose foolish books had filled his head vit nonsense. H. G. Vells and Jules Verne vrote such fantastical stories of jumping trew time and different vorlds. I tought tey had corrupted my oldest friend's mind."

"I've never heard or read anything from anybody named Wells or Verne," Theo admitted reluctantly, embarrassed by his lack of literary knowledge.

"Most people see such stories as fiction, gibberish. I know I did—until now." Fritz exhaled through a crooked smile.

"Teo, how much of tis . . . tis madman's journal have you read?" Fritz asked, holding the leatherbound notebook up and twisting it around in his hand.

"I've only had a quick glance. I can't even understand half of it, maybe less than that," Theo confessed.

"I too have same trouble. Terminology and science are foreign to me. Vhat I do understand feels like I'm reading a fantasy novel."

"I can explain a lot of the science." Theo lowered his head. "I was with Viktor Brack and my dad while they were building and developing the technology that landed me here. It's the German I can't read."

"Vell, unless you're fluent in Italian, French, and Russian as vell, you're completely out of luck. Tis Brack—for all his madness—is a very educated man. He seamlessly svitches betveen languages and makes for a difficult read." Fritz hated this man for helping the Nazis create their death camps, and he hated being impressed by Brack as a scholar.

"How much have you read?"

"I haven't been to sleep, only dozed a short time, if tat tells you anyting. I read more, ten I get disturbed more." Fritz shrugged. "And ten I want more to continue. *Societatis* talks about your American President and a man named Churchill, bote involved in great vays, but vritings in das book suggest tey are responsible for defeatink the German var machine in an upcoming time." Fritz sat back and crossed his arms against his chest. "How familiar are you vit der upcomink var, Teo?"

Theo pushed his plate away and took a long drink of water before he wiped the back of his hand across his face and pulled himself closer to the table. "Well, Mr. Medi would tell you I don't know anything after my last test score, but I do know that FDR and Churchill will end up being a pretty solid team. They will organize a massive land invasion called D-Day, and that will push the Germans back to Berlin. Oh yeah, and before Hitler can be captured, he will kill himself."

"Vait, vhat? Hitler vill commit suicide?" Again, Fritz couldn't hide his emotions as he bolted upright in his seat at the news.

Theo watched the man regain his composure. As Fritz was feeling delighted and optimistic at the news of his enemy's demise, Theo began to worry about the repercussions of all the information he was giving away. He began thinking about the times he and his father had discussed the *grandfather paradox* theory. What if the information he was telling Fritz or anyone else somehow changed the course of history? He and his father had argued at length, neither one able to convince the other that his theory was correct. Theo, the dreamer, wanted to believe that even if he told Fritz something, it still would happen; whereas, his father warned that telling history could alter the course and have devastating repercussions throughout time.

Theo's mind churned with the possibilities. He could feel an internal rage coming up from his gut as he recalled what Brack had said before he jumped. Brack's words swirled and shouted in his memory. The scientist who had gone mad and who had betrayed his father had threatened to kill Theo's great-grandfather. Viktor Brack had sneered that Theo would never exist.

"Vhat's botering you, Teo?" Fritz sensed that the young man was dealing with inner turmoil.

Theo shook his head in frustration. "This is all confusing and complicated. It was fun when it was just possibility and theories, but now it's reality, and I could be responsible for messing up the world!" He could see from Fritz's expression and knitted brow that he didn't understand or perhaps even know what to believe. "What if I tell you something you're not supposed to know and your reaction changes even a small event? That event could change something else then something else and so on. The changes wouldn't be right. They would rewrite the course of history!" Theo had worked himself into a panic, causing him to spring up to stand behind his chair.

"Ahh, I understand, Teo." Fritz leaned back in his chair, lifting the two front legs off the ground and pinning his knees on the underside of the table. He clasped his hands behind his head and stared at the ceiling. "The real problem isn't how much you tell me but how much Brack tells officers of the Reich. This could explain his rise trew the ranks of the *Schutzstaffel*—vhat you call the SS. He must only be giving tidbits of information. Otherwise, they vould have no use for him."

"As much as I hate Brack, I have to admit, he is very driven. He'll do whatever it takes to achieve his goal. He's already proven that by trying to kill me and my dad," Theo spoke angrily. "Did you find anything in there that might tell us what he has planned?" Theo shook a finger at the open book on the table.

At first, Fritz didn't move or respond. Eventually, he leaned forward and brought his chair back down to rest on the floor. He flipped the pages to the back quarter of the book, skimming for something he had read earlier. "As far as I can tell, tis book has been handed down from one leader of *the Society* to the next. Brack being back here puts *the Society* in a place that it has never been—two leaders at der same time. Ve've not been able to figure out de identity of de oter leader. Ve suspicion a relative, maybe a fater or grandfater." Fritz kept his eyes on the book as he slowly turned the pages. "Every time ve tink ve are closing in, ve hit a dead end or vone of our own goes missink. Ve tink maybe someone in America.

Fritz stood and walked a few paces, keeping his frustration in control. "Ve have been tracking Brack's immediate family, but tey keep a low profile and have shown no signs of activity."

"You are fighting with *the Society* in the United States too?" Theo had believed *the Society* was a European problem.

Fritz's nervous pacing ended as he gripped the back of his chair and snapped the last few words of his rant and looked Theo in the eye.

"Since de dawn of mankind, tere have been men tryink to control and disrupt de vorld. Goot people like *de Watch* and tose fightink for common man stand for people tat don't know how to take a stand. Too many innocent people have been caught up and paid extreme price."

Theo collapsed back into his bunk, overwhelmed, curious, and confused.

Gracie awoke and rolled over, giving a gentle shove to the book she had been reading the night before, toppling it to the floor. She grabbed at the falling book, unable to prevent the fall, but noticed something fell out of the pages. Flipping the snoring Murphy to the side of the bed against the wall, Gracie climbed down from the top bunk to pick up the paper.

"Hey, look at this. It's a picture." Gracie turned the paper over in her hands. "Oh, no, it's not. It's a postcard. There's a big fairy-tale-looking castle on one side and writing on the other." She looked at Theo lying with his eyes closed on the bottom bunk then over at Fritz, who turned one ear in her direction.

"It has words on it. One word, *P-salm*, has numbers written beside it." She glanced up, but no one acknowledged her talking. "Here's what it says: '*I will lift up mine eyes unto the hills, from whence cometh my help.*'" She flipped the postcard over to look at the picture then back to the writing. "The other sentence says, '*He that dwelleth in the secret place of the Most High shall abide under the shadow of the Almighty.*'"

Again, she looked up, and this time, it seemed Fritz had his head cocked as if he was both listening and thinking. "That's strange. I thought the back of the card would say something about the castle." She flipped to the picture. "Well, maybe it does. It looks high and kinda secret."

When she raised her eyes, Fritz had moved to stand in front of her. "I suppose you don't mind if I take a look at your pretty card?"

He held out his hand. "Vhere did you find tis?" He turned to look at the card in his hands.

"It fell out of the book Herr Möeller put in Theo's backpack." She glanced over and pointed to the bottom bunk where the backpack lay and Theo had rolled to his side in curiosity of Fritz's question.

The teens could see Fritz's lips move as he reread the two quotes and again turned the postcard to the side with the castle.

"I don't see a connection." Theo's words mumbled with insignificance as he rolled to his back. "By the way, Gracie. It's not *P-salms*. The word is *Psalms*. The *P* sound is silent. It's in the Bible."

Fritz lightly tapped the postcard against the fingers of his other hand. "Yah, I tink you're right, but I vonder if tere's more. I know tis castle. Eltz Castle, not a bad journey from Frankfurt if you travel by river. Tree sides of vater around tat castle. Alvays in the same family for hundreds of years. Gracie, let me see tat book. Anytink else unusual?"

Gracie stepped on Theo's bunk to reach for the book where she had tossed it after picking it up from the floor. She grabbed Murphy, who was waiting to be lifted into her arms, as she jumped back down to the floor. "I didn't see anything. As a matter of fact, it kinda seems like a romance, so I'm not sure why Herr Möeller thought it was important to bring." She handed Fritz the book. "Oh, there is one sentence underlined in red ink."

Theo climbed out of the lower bunk, holding out a hand to see the postcard Fritz held. He wondered if it was just his imagination that Fritz's voice was tightening in intensity. "What are you thinking, Fritz?"

Deep in thought, Fritz shuffled the pages of the book until his eyes found the underlined sentence. Again, Gracie and Theo noticed his lips moving, but no sound came as the leader read to himself. *Nothing can hurt us now. What we have can't be destroyed. That's our victory . . . our victory over the dark.* He closed the book to look at the title. "*Dark Victory*—ah, code vord in *de Vatch*—our rally cry to attack evil." Fritz's voice had dropped to a barely perceptible whisper as he handed Gracie the book.

The older man silently looked at Theo, then Gracie, then back at Theo before he answered. "I tink der sly fox gave Gracie more tan a book to read. Das picture you holt in your hand is Eltz Castle. Teo, read der back." Fritz pointed at the card in Theo's hand.

"Which part? You mean, '*I will lift up mine eyes unto the hills, from whence cometh my help*'?"

"Yah, stop! *De Burg, auch!* Sorry, Teo—I mean castle—is set high on a hill, nutink so high to the heavens in tat part of Germany. A goot man tat vill stand against der führer lives in tat palace. So keep readink." Again, he pointed to the card as if his finger allowed Theo's voice to be heard.

Theo stood with his mouth open and swallowed to moisten his throat, surprised at what he was hearing and amazed by Herr Möeller's secret plan. "Uh, yeah. Okay. The other quote says, '*He that dwelleth in the secret place of the Most High shall abide under the shadow of the Almighty.*' Fritz, does that have a special meaning too?"

"Yah. Peter Paul Freiherr von Eltz-Rübenach ist a goot Chvistian man, a priest, yah, but de verse means more. Eltz is a secret place vhere *de Vatch* can take shelter under de hidden protection of bote Peter and God himself." Fritz reached for the postcard and tucked it back into the book in Gracie's hands. "I need to sleep. Tomorrow vill be busy. Teo, Gracie, put your books back into your pack." A smile briefly crossed Fritz's countenance as he walked to his own couch.

"I tink I know vhere ve can find our dear friend, Jahile Möeller."

PART III

Tiergartenstrasse 4

T4

Adolf Hitler pushed back from his desk and deliberately rose to turn his back to his chief of the chancellery. "Philipp, your position as chancellor is to assist my whims. It is not by accident that I have retained this position separate from the Nazi Party. You are to act as my right arm without incident and without questioning." The führer plunged his hand into his coat pocket to procure a handkerchief to wipe across his brow before he continued. "Your role is to advise—as I believe you can do so well. Philipp, do so. And," the führer motioned, "sit down." Hitler placed his hand on the back of the desk chair and spun the seat so he could again sit behind his desk, too large for the office but large enough to demonstrate his power.

Philipp Bouhler had not unlocked his knees from the time he had been called into the führer's office until this moment. Although his position ranked under the heavy hand of the führer, he knew he could influence the man of position. For most of his life, Bouhler had watched and learned and supported a Germany that could be an Aryan nation. This was his time to act.

"First, Führer, let me state: I did not and will not ever blame Germany's current economic lapse on any of your directives. We are casualties of war, but by your power, we survive." Bouhler crossed his legs and uncrossed them again as his body language showed he wrestled with wanting to be familiar enough to be persuasive but forceful enough to be convincing. "You have in your Reich people of knowledge who can help Germany become the nation you desire."

"How can Germany be what I want when we have masses within who are too boorish and ignorant to recognize my power!"

Hitler interrupted, pressing the buttons of his coat against his desk. The chair springs groaned as he fell back into the soft leather and again wiped his forehead with the handkerchief. "Continue."

"You speak correctly. We are too heavy at the bottom of the population. Scum is best discarded. Thus, those who are true nationalists can control the removal of the sludge, so to speak."

"Go on." Hitler's chin rose in curiosity.

"It's quite simple, really. We annihilate any who are not Aryan. We refine our nation."

"Short of gunning down people on the street and answering to nations who are already monkeys on our backs, how do you propose such *refining*?" A raised eyebrow accompanied the last punctuated and drawn-out word as Hitler folded his hands on his desk.

"Your own personal doctor, Karl Brandt, has medical knowledge that can give—or take—a life." Bouhler tipped his head and raised his shoulders. "And I myself have just under my position a most talented scientist, Viktor Brack, who is eager to experiment in most unorthodox means. Both men have heart for this regime. With their knowledge and aggressive measures, we can dispose of the sludge and purify our fountains of power."

The men sat in long, uncomfortable silence. The expressionless führer pursed his lips until a smack of his hand upon his desk caused Bouhler's face to raise in attention. "Good. Where is this Brack you speak of?"

"His office is at the address of Tiergartenstrasse 4 in Berlin."

"Get him here. And bring Brandt. I can wait no longer."

Philipp Bouhler stood and snapped his heels together as his arm raised in honor to the führer. He turned and stepped out of the office of Germany's leader of the Nazi Party, while outside the office window, a cloud crossed the sky, casting a shadow of darkness across the desk of the führer.

By early afternoon, Philipp Bouhler stood waiting just inside the conference room of the new Reich chancellery specially designated for top Reich meetings and the only conference room with doors that bolted shut. Footsteps in the tiled hall stopped outside the door that stood ajar, and greetings could be heard as the door opened to the entrance of Bouhler's two invited guests.

"*Guten Tag*, Dr. Brandt and Dr. Brack!"

"*Auch!* Because he is young, you welcome Dr. Brandt before me? I see how it is with the society of you younger men!"

The handsome Philipp Bouhler looked surprised, but Karl Brandt's usual face of stoicism broke into a wide smile at the dry-witted jest of Viktor Brack. "Perhaps he fears your maturity, Viktor." Brandt's quick reply evoked handshakes from all three.

Eager to discuss business and return to a late-afternoon meeting with the führer, Bouhler gesticulated toward the oval table centered in the room. "Sit down." The two guests moved toward the table, and both hesitated in slight turns as they looked back at the door that Bouhler had just bolted.

"What is so important that I must leave my medical practice in the middle of the day?" Dr. Brandt tugged at the hem of his lab coat while seating himself between the other two who were also taking seats at the table.

"We—you, Viktor, and me—we have been requested by the führer to formulate a plan for, shall we say, sludge removal—a cleansing of Germany." Bouhler's words and tone of voice were light though his proposal spoke of decimation.

"Do you mean we have the chance to rid the population of those who are unworthy of the Reich?" Viktor Brack spoke with no surprise.

"Yes. The führer faces murmurings of unrest with the economic struggles forced upon our country from the ravages of the war. Perhaps a little cleansing will put us back on our feet."

"So I suspicion that it's not our friendship but rather our practices that have called us to this table." Brandt turned toward the older scientist as he spoke to the young chancellor. "Viktor, have you any qualms with sharing your knowledge?"

A slow grin crossed the narrow face of Viktor Brack. "For years, I have believed Germany to be plagued with too many people who are parasites sucking the life from our country." He raised his eyebrows as he looked from Brandt to Bouhler. "Many nights I have sat at my desk at Tiergartenstrasse 4 drafting and dreaming experiments without subjects to prove my hypotheses. I have ideas, but first, Bouhler, what is it you ask us to do?"

"I have been commissioned by the führer to seek and pursue a way to purge Germany of the Jewish and Romani sludge. Can you help me?"

Dr. Karl Brandt stood as he nodded. "It is my right and my duty to use my craft for my country."

Pushing away from the table as he spoke, Viktor Brack also stood and turned toward the door. "Shall we meet at my office at Tiergartenstrasse 4 here in Berlin tomorrow morning at nine to formulate the conception of a better country?"

"The conception? Conception through killing . . ." The young chancellor stepped to the door and pulled open the heavy bolts. "Yes, yes. I believe the führer will be pleased."

By 8 AM Viktor Brack was in his office. The smell of strong coffee bubbled from the pot percolating on the corner cabinet. He needed time to organize his thoughts. This could be the chance to prove his scientific worth to Germany. This could be his opportunity to have full reign on experimentation that had only wandered in formulas and theories in his mind and in his books. "Patience, Viktor. Step by careful step. Today you propose. Tomorrow you prevail." The words he breathed aloud spoke to his calloused heart the scheming of a twisted soul.

By 9 AM Dr. Brandt and Herr Bouhler had taken seats with Brack in the back room of the office at the address of Tiergartenstrasse 4.

"I am commissioned by the führer to commission you, in the name of Germany, to develop a plan of action to rid this country of those who fail the Aryan rights of citizenship. As you know, we speak of action that is necessary but that must be handled in a manner as to set no alarm to other countries."

Bouhler nodded at Karl Brandt. "Dr. Brandt, you are the führer's own physician. He trusts your skill. As chief of the chancellery, I have been given the task of developing a program of euthanasia. Our führer has drafted a letter stating that you, Karl, will join me with the responsibility of broadening the authority of certain other doctors to help in this matter. Those persons suffering from incurable illness may be granted a mercy death."

"I understand." Karl Brandt nodded with a slow and deliberate movement, not taking his eyes off the chief chancellor. "I have the means for such *mercy* as needed. Perhaps you can assist me in finding the patients who are *in need*." With the exception of the punctuation of three words, Dr. Brandt's agreement was monotone and lifeless.

"Excellent. The führer will be most pleased to know your expertise in your profession is dedicated to the country." He swiveled in the wooden office chair. "Now, for you, dear scientist. How can I assure the führer that you have a most excellent plan?"

"For months, yes, perhaps for years, I have studied and contemplated ways to control men who do not wish to be controlled." A smirk complimented his narrow face, forming a nefarious expression. "The secret of control is not to let the subject know. So remind me, Philipp, what is the problem with a drop of—what was the term you used? Oh, yes. Sludge? Hmm?"

Willing to play along with the secret reveal, Bouhler grinned from his youthful face. "Besides the fact that sludge is worthless, it spreads and contaminates. What a pity."

"Indeed. And how well you answer. So, Philipp, and don't you agree, dear Doctor, that the sludge must be controlled in a way to prevent spreading?" The onlookers both nodded. "Then, Germany's sludge must be contained. We can't allow new sludge, and it seems the best means of control is castration."

"Forced population control! How brilliant but impossible to commandeer!"

"Ah, Dr. Brandt! Did you forget that I suggested that the subject is not to know." Viktor Brack's pleasure in his idea almost brought color into his sallow cheeks.

"And how can you take such measure without the subject knowing!? Surely, you haven't experimented with hypnotism!" Philipp Bouhler nearly laughed at the suggestion.

"Herr Bouhler, you have asked Dr. Brandt to have *mercy* for the ill. May I suggest we be merciful to those who are not yet ill and take every precaution to check their health?"

"I'm neither a doctor nor a scientist, but I am an intelligent man, and I know of no man who would willingly succumb to what you suggest!" Bouhler's patience in the game of words was wearing thin. "What, Viktor, is your experiment?"

"Very simply, Philipp, we check the health of individuals by applying excessive and concentrated x-rays. It is relatively cheap, can be carried out on thousands in a relatively short time, and the effects of sterilization will not be realized for weeks to follow. Thus, no alarms can be sounded to warn other sludge that their ability to spread has been blunted."

"Excellent, Viktor." Karl Brandt stood and slowly clapped his hands in approval. "Philipp, return to the führer with word that our country will address the needs of both old and new sludge. Viktor, as you try your sterilization experiments with adults, I'll begin my care plan with children." As if planning a pleasant outing, Brandt turned to the chief chancellor. "Do you know, dear Philipp, where we can begin our experimentation?"

"Indeed, we must find a location to begin . . . What shall we call this plan? It seems most uncouth to call these actions by what they really are. Besides, the world may not see the goodness Germany will reap in these actions. Whoever would have guessed the power of the minds and the formulated plan coming together at this address—Tiergartenstrasse 4?"

Karl Brandt returned to sit in the chair he had earlier abandoned. "Yes, the Tiergartenstrasse 4 plan. That's a rather innocent code name, isn't it? Suggest to our führer that T4 will initiate soon."

"For Führer and country!" Philipp raised his coffee mug in mock toast to the new plan. "Dr. Brandt, I'll inquire further as to where we shall begin."

Viktor Brack shuffled through a stack of notes on his desk. "Actually, I may have a location. Only recently have I begun correspondence with a nurse at the Hadamar Institute."

"Hadamar! The institute for mentally and physically disabled people? I know of the place." Dr. Brandt nodded in deep thought. "Is this one of the places you frequent, Viktor?"

"As I have been commissioned to begin camps to contain the Jews and Romani causing Germany's internal disruption, I have become quite familiar with both camp and institution. Moreover, I have become aware of those professionals in the field of health who, shall we say, think as we do."

"Hadamar has such an individual?" The chief chancellor picked up a pencil from the desk and began rummaging for a scrap of paper. "Viktor, share a name that I can take back to the führer with this report of T4."

"Irmgard Huber."

"A woman?"

"Not just a woman but a nurse with knowledge and skill but, moreover, with a heart of stone for mankind but yet a passion for country."

Bouhler jotted the name on a scrap of paper he lifted from the desk. "Do you stake your position on the probability of this woman's help?"

"I stake my life on it."

"And you, Viktor, you have your notes for the experiment with x-ray?" Bouhler tucked the scrap into his pocket as he stepped toward the door.

"Of course, he does!" Karl Brandt interjected. "I've worked with Brack on issues before. He keeps notes and has even coerced me into jotting notes in a leatherbound journal. That book is the brain that pulses outside of his skull! Show him the book, Viktor."

Viktor Brack clenched his jaw. "I don't have the book here, Karl."

"Where is the book?"

Viktor Brack dropped his head and his voice. "I don't know."

"You don't know? What do you mean you don't know?" Dr. Brandt swiveled back around to face Brack. "How do you know it hasn't been destroyed?"

"Don't speak to me like I'm a child, Karl!" Viktor stopped short when he saw his index finger only a few centimeters from the doctor's cheekbone. He lowered his arm and turned away. "It has not been destroyed."

"What makes you so sure?"

"It's in the hands of an American."

"An American?" Dr. Brandt's voice rose.

"It was stolen from an office where I worked at the *Justizpalast* in Munich before Hitler assigned Bouhler as chief chancellor. Bouhler summoned me to work under him here in Berlin. I've been too busy with this promotion to retrieve the book."

"So you know where it is?" Though exasperated that some of his own work lay in the hands of an American, Karl Brandt knew he wanted answers more than argument from a scientist who would clam up with secrets as he had done on occasion in the past. "I'll help you get it, Viktor. I have people who owe me—"

"It's not that easy!" Brack interrupted. "An SS officer and a stinking jaeger caught the American boy in my office. He had a girl with him."

"A boy? A boy and a girl?" Philipp Bouhler had sat silently as the doctor and scientist interacted, but this revelation appalled the young man of power. "It's no wonder Germany can't get her feet under her when she can't even take down a boy and a girl."

"Don't be ridiculous, Philipp. It's more than that. They were rescued from the jaeger attack. The man who rescued them had a triquetra on his forearm. The power of *the Watch*, though underground, is not to be dismissed without concern."

Dr. Brandt turned and reached for the door handle, looking back over his shoulder. "My sources tell me *the Watch* is busy with Russian issues right now. We can take them." He lightly brushed away a piece of lint from his shoulder. "For now, we have work to do. Come along, Philipp."

Though already pale, all color drained from the face of the scientist. Viktor Brack turned to face Dr. Brandt then riveted his eyes on Philipp Bouhler. "It was Möeller."

"Jahile Möeller? Why?" Bouhler secretly feared both brain and brawn of the man. He hesitated midstride as if fearful of taking another step.

"I don't know. I had him watched. It seems the kids live with him."

Dr. Brandt rejoined the conversation without the sense of alarm felt by the two chancellors of the SS. "It seems to me, Viktor, that your careless bookkeeping needs to be remedied as part of our new endeavor. We need the book. We need youths to begin our *cleansing process*." His voice tripped over the words as if they were naming a simple daily task. Without hesitation, he turned to Bouhler. "Philipp, how soon can you exert your SS power to send to Munich? One search of Jahile Möeller's home can give us a double reward—two youths for our experiment and one book of scientific notes." He swung open the door then clapped his hands together and smiled at the other two men. "We all win."

Viktor Brack returned to sit at his desk and rub his tired eyes as the door closed behind his two colleagues. Fatigue and pride fed the evil about to be unleashed to devour the innocent of Germany. A crooked smile crept across his face, allowing his breath to exhale a stench that seemed born from a rotten soul.

The Bait

OVER TWENTY-FOUR HOURS had passed since the T4 meeting of scientist, chancellor, and doctor had darkened the walls of the office at Tiergartenstrasse 4 in Berlin. Viktor Brack had scarcely left his desk for reason of eating or sleeping as he sketched details and plans to aid in the Reich's cleansing under the führer's command. Four solid fist pounds, followed by two staccato raps, brought the scientist's eyes back up to his office door just as it swung open.

"Brack! How long have you been in Berlin?" Colonel Wolfram Sievers tilted his head back in a half-inquisitive, half-taunting way. The heavy door closed behind him as Sievers waved his hand both to dismiss his crewman and to put the door into motion.

"Long enough to know I'm tired of waiting for these stinking jaegers to follow command and get back to me."

"What pot are you stirring now, Viktor? Still trying to butter the bread for the führer? You know that won't promote you in rank. That paranoid devil himself can't decide from one sentence to the next who is trusted to give rank or who is too close and must be, uh, set aside, shall we say?"

Viktor Brack leaned back in the swivel chair to wipe a drop of coffee from the armrest and set his cup on the desk before he returned Sievers' empty stare. "I couldn't care less about the führer right now." He leaned until his coat rested against the desk as he ran a hand through his unkempt hair. "I feel caught in a nightmare, Wolfram. I have plans." He let his hand fall from his head until it hit the desk with a fist. "*Auch!* Who cares about the führer? He has given full reign to the development of my camps for the filthy Jews.

I have a good mind to . . ." He looked up at the blank stare. "I even have henchmen to do my dirty work." Again, he sat back as the chair squeaked with the movement.

"It's a kid. One kid plagues my mind at night." Viktor inhaled and exhaled in tense agitation of soul. "I try to shake any fondness I ever had for this kid—or his father—but now I chase each shadow to get back from this kid a book, my personal journal."

"Viktor, that's a minor—"

"No!" Brack's fist pounded the desk then quickly withdrew from anger by flattening and smoothing the dust that lay on the wood. "No. It's more. I come here to work each day. I still take care of my day's work, but my mind continually churns trying to find this kid and get my book."

The dank air was silent except for the scraping of a wooden chair Wolfram Sievers pulled to the center of the room on the far side of Brack's desk. The weathered colonel twisted the ends of his groomed mustache. "Perhaps, Viktor, you should look among the pirates I've just been delivered. There's three boys, and they seem to be a spunky group. Too bad they're working for the wrong side. They might—"

"I don't have time or desire to check each rogue who runs through this town!"

Sievers lifted then dropped his open hand. "Suit yourself. It was just an offer." He crossed his arms then uncrossed them to smooth a wrinkle from his military coat. "But for today . . ."

Viktor Brack held an open palm toward Sievers when a heavy knock disrupted all thought and conversation. Both men stood and cupped a pistol in hand in a silent but practiced motion. Brack used his free hand to grasp the metal knob to open the door. "Yes, who is it?" He pulled open the door to see an SS officer holding an envelope. "Ah, yes, come in."

Brack stepped back, returning his pistol to the holster at his side, signaling to Sievers that the visitor was warranted. "Wolfram, we'll talk more later. This is the officer I sent to search Jahile Möeller's home."

"Möeller? What do you want with him? He is a powerful force against the Reich—a thorn in our side. We're better leaving him unagitated in Munich."

Brack turned to look at the officer. "What did you find?"

"Nothing, really. That man's good. He leaves no trail. We couldn't find any work of *the Watch* or any indication of their movement." The officer extended a bulky envelope toward Viktor. "I know they're just mindless brutes, Dr. Brack, but a jaeger brought this to me as we ransacked Möeller's cottage looking for those two kids."

Brack took the envelope and hesitated as he looked inside. "What's this? A picture?" He pulled a small frame from the envelope and stood without comment as he looked at the photo of a young Jahile Möeller with his arm across the shoulder of a beautiful young woman and a hand on the shoulder of a young girl. Brack made a clicking sound with his tongue as he walked to the desk and carefully laid the frame on a stack of papers lying in disarray. "A family. Humph. Strange that a man with his anti-Reich conviction and activity would leave a wife and child at home each day. I suspect they are dead—or in hiding."

Brack swiftly turned back to face the SS officer. "*Danke!* Heil Hitler!" A click of heels and an extended right arm let the officer know it was time for him to return the sign and leave with no further instruction or explanation. The officer closed the door behind him.

With a shaking finger pointing at the photo on the desk, Brack raised his voice. "That's it! Wolfram! That's it!"

"A picture? Have you gone soft?"

Viktor Brack leaned across the desk as both arms held him suspended above the small frame. "No! No, no, quite the opposite." Even in the small office where a single bulb hung from a cord above the desk, an evil grin brightened Brack's face. "A man with passion for a cause may have more than one passion—say, perhaps for a woman or, even more so, for a daughter. Wolfram, here's our ticket into *the Watch*. This is what you live for! The Reich is well aware that Jahile Möeller is an important cog in the wheel that runs *the Watch* and undermines the power of the führer. We've been chasing this elusive maverick to no avail. This, dear friend," Brack again pointed to the framed picture, "can bring an end to two problems. When my book was taken from my office, a man we are sure was Möeller came to the rescue of the boy who stole my journal. With the boy was a young girl. My guess, Wolfram, is, the girl is the tie that binds. You find this girl for me, Wolfram, and we have our bait for Möeller, the book, and the boy who has been the bane of my nightmares."

The air grew heavy and the light seemed to dim as Wolfram Sievers studied the faces in the picture before he tucked it in his coat and walked out into the misty morning.

Champion Prowess

No one saw the silhouetted man and boat drift purposefully and quietly up to a dock hidden under a waterway passage. No one saw, but a man named Peter watched, ready to unload his dear friend and ally in the fight against the evil of the Reich. Rarely did the Baron of Castle Eltz leave his fortress since being dismissed as the German director of travel. He had lost his position in a government job. As he stood against the führer, it was surprising he did not lose his life. He was wary enough to know that the Gestapo watched his every move, but that didn't shake him. He stood fast for God and for country and now was ready to stand for a friend. A smile softened the wrinkles of worry across his face as he stood in the lookout perched high above the waters surrounding the castle.

Since leaving Theo and Gracie on the docks of Frankfurt, the boat had become Jahile Möeller's hideaway. He knew the risks set in motion by showing his identity to the SS officer and jaeger during the attack in Brack's office. Jahile shook his head in reflection. *Ah, they're just kids. They're moved by their hearts to do what's right. Maybe it's best they didn't know the dangers they faced. If only I had the nerve to tell them that capture by the Reich would mean unthinkable horrors of . . . Well, they're safe for now. The Watch is unstoppable, but in the hands of my dearest—*

"Hello! Can you shine your light toward the edge of the dock? Terribly dark night. Best for travel." Jahile Möeller waved a mooring line toward the guard standing on the small wooden dock. Neither spoke further, but Jahile shone a light on his forearm, exposing the triquetra tattoo. He knew it was imperative for the watchman to see his identity. Seeing the well-recognized symbol, the guard released the grip covertly held on his luger and imperceptibly uncocked the hammer.

The watchman's light sank from a horizontal beam aimed between the night sailor and the pier. Swiftly, he moved and set down a lantern. Jahile could smell the light's kerosene waft across the water. The watchman knelt on one knee and balanced with an arm extended, waiting to receive the mooring line and secure the small boat.

"Many thanks, good fellow. Dark victory, eh?"

The watchman nodded in response to the code words and gripped Jahile's shoulder to aid a step up to the creaking dock.

Again, the silent watchman nodded and handed Jahile the pack he lifted from the small boat. Jahile threw the pack across his back and turned to walk to shore then up the steps of an incline. There was no need to look back through the hanging forest to ensure the watchman was securing the small craft that carried Jahile through river channels from Frankfurt.

"Poor soul." Words from Jahile's heart were hushed by the heavy night air.

The watchman wanted no sympathy as he did his work. He was eager to help in the underground cause of *the Watch* or anyone else who would stand against the Reich. His rough hands worked without anger that his heart refused to keep. Only briefly did he allow himself to remember a year ago when he protested the lies of a government. He had stood too close to a concentration camp guard named Irmgard. His insults of the powers of the Reich offended the nurse whose personal relationship with a Dr. Josef Mengele prompted the removal of his tongue. The watchman lost his speech but not the passion of his heart to help those who stood against the Reich. Tonight he smiled with sincerity as he helped dock Jahile Möeller, an intelligent and respected champion for right.

The sound of Jahile's pack dropping to the porch was covered by the stomp of a foot across the threshold of the castle door. His reach for the brass knocker was futile as the door swung out of reach, opening inward to expose the scent of piñon burning in a hearth across the interior room.

"Jahile! Come in!" the baron's voice boomed against the silent night promising a smattering of stars. A slender and almost-handsome man, whose smooth countenance belied his fifty-year-old face, stepped into the foyer that opened into the castle entry. "Your letter arrived last month. I was glad to hear of your possible visit and knew it would be useless for me to count the days before you arrived. We have watched diligently for your light in the shadows, hoping for a visit to come soon though we would have watched for you for a year."

The two men clasped right hands and clapped each other on the shoulder in a fond yet brief salutation. A third man, unknown to Jahile, was already whisking his pack to an upper room.

"Hello, Jahile." A soft voice pulled Jahile's face from his host toward the heat of the hearth. The fire dancing in the background silhouetted a stately and shapely figure of a beautiful woman. Blond curls swayed in the waves of the heat as she stepped forward to stand beside her brother. "Peter promised a visit from you. We are always honored to have you under our roof."

Save for the beauty of his own wife, taken from him too soon, he had always admired the heart and delicacy of feature of the Lady of Eltz Castle. "Elise, you bring excitement to this dreary castle, nestled so far from civilization. Surely, a jewel awaits your heavenly crown for the good you do. I know you certainly ease the strain on my weary eyes." He winked and gave a half bow as he lifted her hand to his lips in gratefulness for hospitality and in greeting.

Only the crackle of the hearth interrupted the conversation of the three sharing dinner and a few hours of laughter and memories. Jahile sat nestled in the overstuffed chair that held the welcome guest as if he were a child needing shelter from a storm.

"I'm afraid all this good conversation wearies my ears and eyes but never my heart, my loves. Talk of night should be reserved for the stout of heart, so I will take leave of you both until morning. Good night, my dear brother." The gentle woman walked to where Jahile sat beside the fire. "And good night, my dear friend." Elise's voice danced a soft ballet of sound as she moved from one man to the next, planting a soft kiss on the forehead with a lingering touch of hand on Jahile's cheek. "I'm afraid my beauty rest is waiting."

Jahile and Peter both jumped to their feet at the dismissal of the Lady of Eltz. "'Til we meet again, dear *Fräulein*." Jahile gave an almost-comical bow it was so low to the ground.

"I'll catch the baker before I go to bed, Elise, and make sure he knows to present a grand breakfast feast for three," Peter called out as the train of her dress flowed around the doorframe and out of sight. He treated his sister as highest royalty not by need but out of love. Years earlier, her dedication to family secluded her from education past gymnasium level as she cared for ailing parents while Peter traveled inland to study in the seminary. She supported his political activism though it prevented him from further studies in theology and nearly banished him to the remote hill where the castle stood so high that Peter teased that it was reverently knocking on heaven's door. By the time Peter had returned as baron of the castle, Elise's health had become fragile and threatened a shortened life. Her trips to mainland became dedicated to an orphanage where she educated the children.

"She's too good to you, Peter," Jahile noted her care.

"True. She's more than I deserve." The baron stoked the fire. "I don't tell her of my activities against the Reich. There is no need to flutter her delicate heart." He offered Jahile a thick-smelling cigar. "Now, my friend, what are you about these days?"

Jahile inhaled the sweet scent before he released the smoke of the cigar. "I thought my heart would never heal from losing my wife and daughter. I'm not sure it has." Silence hung between the men. Jahile inhaled the smell of the piñon playing a gentle chase with the wisps from the cigars. "I cannot forgive, Peter."

"But you must, my friend. It's not Christian to hold a hatred. That first year after your loss, I feared the devastation would destroy the man of strength I knew you to be. It's good to hear and see that you have a passion for the right and not a vengeance to retaliate against the wrong." The baron inhaled the sweet tobacco and continued through smoke wreaths. "What has renewed your passion?"

"A daughter." Jahile smiled and tossed his head against the cushioned chair. "Oh, she's not really my daughter and certainly not a girl I asked to have in my home. But in a favor to a friend, I have ended up keeping his daughter for nearly two years and also have become a home for a, well, a lost soul, so to speak, for the past year. Both are teens." He couldn't help but smile as he looked directly into the eyes of his friend. "Like you. Like me, Peter. They have a passion for the right, but they stand on the wrong side of the government."

Until the fire, stoked time and again, finally calmed into a shallow dance of firelight, Jahile Möeller shared his story of the recent years. Most of the events he told. Much of Theo's story of time jumping from the future and owning a robotic dog he neglected to reveal as it was too fantastical and a bit unnecessary to tell.

"There's a hope these youths carry. It has wrapped around my heart, Peter, and I'll do whatever it takes to help them," he locked eyes with his friend, "at all costs."

"It would be wrong for me to lecture you in any way." The baron tipped his head with a deep sigh. "In truth, I am half a breath away from telling you I'll join in your crusade. Do what you must, but be careful. You know, the Holy Scriptures state, *'The breath of the ruthless is like a storm driving against a wall.'* Be wary of the storm, Jahile. The wall to protect the good people of Germany must never break."

Though both men knew the storm of the Third Reich was threatening, neither was alerted to the silent porter standing and listening in a dark corner of the room, concealing that the storm had already penetrated the castle walls.

Necessary Journey

"FRITZ, OLD MAN, you're not one to sleep in. Must I rouse you from your beauty sleep? Rise and shine." TAR gave a gentle kick to the cushion under his friend's upper torso.

"I can't smell coffee, TAR. You'll do lousy as a housevife someday." Fritz couldn't help but smile as he rolled over, smacking his dry mouth and running his hands through his thick blond hair. "All right, all right. I'll rise, but I von't shine. I'm afraid my mind's a little dull. I spent a good portion of night pourink over Brack's book and tinkink."

"Thinking?" TAR wasn't ready to take a back seat to the teasing and let Fritz win the battle of the wits. "Who paid you to think? I thought you were the brawn of this little party. Nina is the one with the brains. I'm surprised Claus lets his wife get very far from his presence. He has quite a treasure in that one. She's the backbone of this Table and, possibly, of the whole *Watch*, wouldn't you say, Fritz?"

"Yah. I can't argue vit tat."

"Well, it's good to let her go to spend time with her husband before he sets out on his next, er, mission. Now, how about some breakfast, huh?"

Fritz looked around the room, still not quite awake or ready to spar with TAR in conversation. "Hey, vhere are der younk people?" He sat upright, rubbing the small of his back. "Ah, to be younk again and not be so stiff and sore in *der Morgen*—"

"Morning? I'm stiff and sore all day. It's called age, my friend. Well, age and lifestyle. Why do you think I leave the crawling through underground tunnels rescuing teenagers to you, eh? I don't quite bend like I used to." TAR handed Fritz a cup of coffee.

"Vhere did you get tis muddy vater? I don't see no coffee." Fritz grinned as he put the warm cup to his lips.

"Go ahead. Make fun. Who was the smart person who put that burner in here and stocked a few dry goods? I'll tell you who—Nina. I tell you, Claus has a good one," TAR spoke more to himself than Fritz and didn't bother to coax Fritz to the small table in the corner of the sparse room. "The kids? Oh, uh, they're out stretching their legs and taking care of 'necessary business' since this little cubby of a hideaway doesn't come with a *Garderobe*. But don't worry, Fritz. I told Theo not to pee on the trees, and I told Gracie they must stay hidden." He turned and glanced at Fritz, who was pulling a fist from the cereal container. "I tried to think of everything you would have told them." He guffawed as Fritz pelted the back of his head with a rounded oat.

"Just like you, Fritz, wasting good—" His rebuke was interrupted by a sound in the hall, followed by the metal door swinging into the room.

"Morning!" Gracie's voice sang into the air. Gracie and Theo stood all smiles and rosy cheeks from the cool morning. Murphy stood between the two and gave his body an all-over shake as if to shiver off the brisk air.

"*Guten Morgen!* And vhere have you two little chickadees been flittink? In de cover of de trees, I hope!"

"No worries, Father Fritz." The good rest and fresh air prompted Theo to tease his friend and mentor. "Don't worry. When Nina gets back, we won't tell her that you lost us during the night." They all had a good laugh, with Fritz laughing loudest.

"Okay, vise guy. As soon as TAR runs a few errands, ve'll head out. Until tat time, inside or out, remember, ve are not to be seen. So unless you vant to spend time tucked inside a vall again, you'll have to keep hidden."

"Where are we going? Do we have to leave already?" Gracie had a touch of disappointment in her voice. She didn't know the plan of *the Watch* or even of her guardians, but she felt comfortable and safe in their temporary hideaway and wasn't eager to give up the feeling.

TAR gave her a pat on the shoulder as he handed her the rolled-oat cereal. "Ah, my little spunky one. We too have enjoyed the rest and fresh morning air, but as the poet in Theo's country says,

The woods are lovely, dark and deep, But I have promises to keep, And miles to go before I sleep, And miles to go before I sleep.

"So it is with us, dear girl."

Theo looked at TAR with his eyebrows knitted and one eye squeezed shut. "Would that poet be Robert Frost?"

"Ah, good, my boy!"

Again, Theo smiled and thought how much he enjoyed his company of friends. He reached over and gave Murphy a quick head rub as the two of them plopped on the bed where Theo enjoyed a crunchy breakfast, and Murphy twirled three times before collapsing into a nap.

By late afternoon, a panel in the wall swung open with the outside push from TAR, returning from his day's activity. "Hullo, my friends!"

"You seem happy after being in der outside vorld, TAR! Ve have been vaitink vit longness."

"Longness?" Gracie wrinkled her nose. "You mean patience?"

"Yah, tat's vat I mean. I guess I don't have much need for it and don't know der vord."

Everyone in the small room laughed, while Murphy dropped his head to his paws and gave his best canine sigh.

"Ah, don't be too hard on me, my friend. I have a surprise for all!" TAR's voice had a happy tone.

Theo tried to peek out of the closing panel before it sealed again and became part of the wall. "Two questions, TAR. First, what tunnel is this you just came through? And second, how many more secret doors are in this room?" Theo only glanced at TAR before he started tapping the walls to find more secret passages.

"My young man, if I told you all of my secrets, they wouldn't be secrets, now would they, eh?"

"Who cares about tunnels?" Gracie stepped lightly and playfully tugged TAR's arm. "What's the surprise?" The cheerful sound of Gracie's voice caught Murphy's ear. He bounded to her side, giving a few leaps until she bent down and cradled him in her arms. "Murphy and I are ready for a surprise."

"Well, my little princess, I have procured a carriage to take you to Castle Eltz." TAR leaned against the nearest wall and crossed his arms to rest partially on his round stomach and partially against his chest.

"A carriage? Now this I have to see!" Theo's voice raised in excitement.

"Well," TAR tipped his head, "it's not exactly a carriage, but it will take the princess and all of us to the castle."

"Who cares how I get there! Do I really get to go to a castle?" The sparkle in Gracie's eye and the lilt in her voice brought a lightness to the air in the small room to make even the most doubtful believe a royal adventure lay up the road.

"All right, TAR." Fritz slapped both knees before standing and putting his hands on his hips. "Let's see this contraption of travel."

Half listening, half exploring, Theo was running his hands over the wall where the panel had opened when TAR returned. "So how do we open the panel?"

"Well, aren't you a curious vone? Ve vill leave by de same door you have been usink vhile you, Gracie, and Murphy have been runnink in and out all day." Fritz gestured toward the door.

"Unless it leads to the inside of the wall or a tunnel where I have to crawl like a snake, I was kinda hoping to use the secret passage," Theo dropped his arms down to his side and answered in a small pout. "Whatever."

"Vell, Teo, ve may make a tunnel man out of you yet! I can hardly vait to tell Nina the goot news! But for now, ve von't disappoint you. Ve vill access TAR's passage from der hallvay."

"C'mon, Murphy! Let's go see the surprise carriage!" Theo gave Murphy a quick head rub as he passed Gracie and headed for the door.

Falling in line, the four left the room through the door, where TAR took the lead. They had scarcely walked a couple of meters when TAR inconspicuously reached under a sconce lighting the hall. A gray section of wall opened to expose a hidden passageway.

"Cool! I love you guys!" Theo took no time plunging through the opening. Murphy barked and wiggled as Gracie set him down to follow along.

The short passage opened to a partially overcast day. Theo and Gracie looked around, wondering what surprise awaited, thinking it was hidden as nothing stood before them except a road-worn truck.

"So where's the surprise?"

"I'm not seeing my carriage."

TAR chuckled. "You're looking at it, my princess."

Fritz walked over to the 1930 Opel Blitz one-and-a-half-ton truck, clapping a hand on the front fender. "I suppose you didn't break into a bank to brink us tis jewel, eh, TAR?" He half grinned, watching the expressions on the teens' faces. "Ah, Gracie, tis is just your carriage in diskize. Ve can't very secretly roll up to a castle vit the sunshine of Deutschland shinink off a gilded carriage now, can ve?"

"Uh, I guess not." Gracie didn't turn her disappointed face away from the truck. She secretly hoped that enough blinking in the hazy daylight would bring a shinier vehicle into view. "But it's sure going to be crowded with all four of us plus Murphy riding on one seat."

Theo looked from Gracie to TAR to Fritz, waiting for a response.

"Oh, my princess, we won't be crowded into one bench seat. Only Fritz and I will be riding in the front. Here's where you, Theo, and Murphy will be riding." He stepped to the back of the truck to the wooden flatbed and patted the board slats that made up the sides.

Theo didn't understand the joke he was sure TAR was playing out in front of them.

"What?" Gracie reacted with such a quick gasp both men chuckled and Fritz winked at his older friend. "Why do we have to ride back there!" Her voice rose along with her raising arm and pointing finger.

"Vell, you see, Gracie, dis truck ist made to haul cargo, and . . . vell, you and Teo are our precious cargo." He paused long enough to wink at her as she turned to face him in disbelief. "Ah-ah, no arguments. Ve promised to take goot care of you. No vone vill see you. Ve vill be sure to hide you under a canvas tarp."

"You've got to be kid—" Theo thought the best he could do was speak up for Gracie. For as long as he had known her, she had proven many times that she was tough and could adjust to any situation. But once, just once, he would like to see that she was treated with the tenderness a woman deserved.

"Nope. No kidding, my young man," TAR interrupted before turning back to the door still opened behind them. "Now, we need to pack up and grab a bite before our journey. Fritz, you and Theo can bring a mattress to toss back here. The kids may have to ride undercover, but we'll make sure their ride is as comfortable as possible." Then he disappeared into the hallway, with Fritz following behind.

"You two comink? Ve'll give you a couple of minutes to admire der carriage, ten back to vork!" Fritz's voice came from the passage, while the two teens just looked at each other.

Inside the hall, Fritz whispered to TAR, "Vhere did you get dat jewel? It doesn't seem you vorked too hard to please."

"Actually, Fritz, I could have been back earlier, but as I was coming back with the car I had, er, borrowed from a drive, I passed a farmer driving too slowly for my likes. By the time I had thought a plan through, I had to back a half kilometer to get back to the farmer. I traded him the car for the truck. At first, he argued that a car would be useless, but I convinced him the car would bring good money to purchase a better work truck. The deal was sealed. By the time the Gestapo finds and traces the car, we'll be long gone."

"Gestapo?" Fritz raised an eyebrow. "Vhose car did you steal?"

TAR looked over his shoulder at his friend. "Whose? I don't really know. There were several lined up in front of the mansion of a government official. It was the last one in line, and the chauffeur seemed to be too busy snoozing under a tree to notice when I put it in neutral and rolled down the drive." He grinned at Fritz. "Nice guy. He left the keys in the car. Too bad it will cost him his job, maybe his life. Mean people, those SS officers."

Both men turned to look behind them as they heard the outside door click.

"All right, we haven't been pampered yet, so let's get this party rollin'." Gracie's voice seemed to brighten the passage just as TAR opened the door to their small hideaway. "When do we start?"

"Uh, 'scuse me. I'm a growing boy, and I'd like a little food before we go." Theo tried to sound serious, but everyone laughed.

Rode to Eltz

BY EARLY EVENING, the four patriots had eaten the last dry meal Nina had procured from a hidden pantry before she left to meet with Claus. A mattress had been loaded onto the flatbed of the Opel Blitz, and various empty canisters had been tossed in a fashion of disarray around the mattress. It would be as difficult to see the laden mattress surrounded by refuse as it would be to find an European castle covertly covered by a forest of trees. A canvas was haphazardly tossed across the pile to give the kids shelter from the weather and refuge from enemy eyes.

A few taps hit the heavy canvas above their heads as TAR drove to their next destination.

"Uh, Gracie, what's hitting the tarp?"

"Can't you tell by the heavy smell coming through? It's beginning to rain. Those are raindrops." Gracie pressed back and snuggled down as she lay on the mattress with the canvas tarp stretched about a foot above her head. She inhaled deeply.

"Won't the rain come through?" Theo's eyes scanned the dark canvas above where he lay.

"Not if you don't touch the canvas. The oils from your skin will weaken the fabric, letting the rain seep through." She turned her head and lifted it enough to see over Murphy, who had stretched out between them and rolled to his back, allowing four paws to flop loosely above his sleeping body. She studied the tense muscles in Theo's face. *Poor guy. He's lived in such a different, mechanical world that he's a foreigner to nature as well as Germany.* She allowed her thought to soften her heart. Again, Gracie's head pressed back into the soft feather mattress. Not knowing why but wanting to care, she moved her arm past Murphy until her fingers touched the back of Theo's hand that lay at his side.

"Just take a deep breath, Theo. The heavy canvas smell isn't one you'll forget. Believe it or not, I have some happy memories lying in the quiet alleys of Munich when I lived on the streets. The smell reminds me of warmth and quiet and times when I would dream and pray for the day I'll see my parents again."

Without looking, she heard a long, deep sigh from Theo. It wasn't an exasperated or anxious sound. It was a sigh of contentment. Gracie smiled as she felt Theo's hand turn under hers until his long fingers wrapped around her tiny hand.

"You can't listen to the patter of the rain without thinking happy memories." Even the hum of the rough truck engine seemed to agree with Gracie as it lulled the youths to sleep.

The jerk of the truck and the squeal of the brakes shook the stowaways awake. Murphy flipped to a crouch position. The hackles on his neck and his low growl justified the teens' suspicions of trouble.

"Shh, Murphy. Quiet. Stay down." After Theo's commands, no further sound or movement came from under the tarp. Theo raised one arm to cover the flashes of blue on Murphy's collar and to give the dog a reassuring pat. In the back of his mind, Theo wanted to be able to tuck his dog into his arms if trouble entered their hiding place.

"*Guten Tag!*" Theo could hear TAR's voice. He turned his head into the mattress to put pressure on the earbud so he could pick up the language translation from Murphy's collar.

"Heil, Hitler! What low card did you draw to get guard duty on this stormy night?" The teens could hear a guffaw in TAR's voice. "My partner and I thought we were the only ones being punished tonight. I hope our barrels of dung and desiccated body parts from the slaughterhouse don't slosh out during your road check. Rotten luck to work out in this storm and get your clothes smattered with cow guts. Here, we'll help you."

Gracie and Theo tensed as they heard the click of the truck door opening. The sound of a billy club hit the metal door.

"*Nein!* Stay in your truck and keep your sludge and refuse to yourself! Drive on!" The voice in the night commanded with another rap of the billy club against the metal truck door.

TAR and Fritz's voices shouted "Heil, Hitler!" into the groan of the truck engine as the Opel accelerated.

No more sounds interrupted the chugging roar of the engine but Gracie's voice whispering, "I bet they're smiling."

By late evening, the rain had given way to a vibrant moon commanding attention in the sky as the Opel pulled into a long drive that dived into a valley covered by a hanging forest, only to rise on the other side and come to rest at the foot of Castle Eltz.

"All right, my little stowaways. Come out of your canvas cocoon and meet someone very special."

Theo and Gracie took little time tossing back the cover that had sheltered them from the eyes of the Reich. TAR lifted a hand to help the teens dismount the flatbed. Theo accepted the balancing arm of help, but Gracie impatiently put a hand on Theo's shoulder to jump to the ground.

"Sure feels good to stand. C'mon Murphy." She had scarcely turned to face the bed of the truck before a flying beagle sprang into her arms.

"Looks like the pup's ready to exercise his legs too!" TAR started the laughter that drew all eyes to a robotic dog whose wagging tail and panting tongue accepted his brief moment of attention.

"Vell, ve can't—" Before Fritz finished his suggestion of going to the castle door to announce their arrival, a large hand clapped Theo's shoulder. The gloved hand smelled like new leather, causing Theo to throw an arm in front of Gracie in a protective reaction of alarm. Gracie grasped the arm in front of her as her wide-eyed stare matched the knot of terror in Theo's throat.

"*Guten Tag!*" Fritz looked from the kids to TAR. "My friends, meet Arnfried, a trusted friend of *the Vatch*!" He turned to the well-built and well-armed servant. "You've been a loyal servant to Baron

Eltz for many years, eh, Arnfried!" The burly soldier gave a nod, turning the grip on Theo's shoulder into a pat. He gestured toward an enormous door. In silent obedience, the travelers grabbed their packs and headed up the wide stone steps to the entrance of the castle. As if pressure of their footsteps on the stones triggered a reaction, the double doors opened to a stone walled entry where light from wall sconces exuded a warmth to match the smile of the castle's baron.

Murphy's collar flashed with intermittent blue lights as it buzzed to translate the cacophony of German words passing between greetings and introductions. Deciding to smile and avoid the confusion, Theo looked down and patted his thigh, signaling Murphy to jump into his master's arms. Just as Theo commanded "Roll," Murphy yapped and curled, bringing a short glance from Baron Eltz, who only saw a young man from America holding a silver ball. Theo returned his glance and smiled as he tucked the ball into his backpack.

"*Bitte, eine kurze Tour von euren Zimmern und etwas zum Essen, bevor ihr zu Bett geht.*"

Gracie caught Theo's look of confusion and reached up to unzip his pack enough to allow Murphy's language transmitter to aid Theo's understanding. She grinned at Theo, echoing the baron's words. "We would love to tour our rooms before we have a bite to eat!"

Theo lifted the corner of his mouth to give a half grin, half snarl to Gracie. *Again, she comes to my rescue! Someday I'm going to step in to save—* Theo's thoughts flashed into the vision of Gracie being pulled from his arms. He closed his eyes to block the premonition.

"Hello? *Hello*, Theo? You gonna stand there all day or come see your room?" The delicate face was gently and innocently turned up to look at her friend and companion. Theo glanced down and saw the tiny hand extended toward him. Shaking his trance, he accepted Gracie's hand of friendship and maybe even—

"All right, young people! Your rooms will be first. Here you go. Drop your bags while we wait here in the hall. You don't want to miss my tour. This castle has had three wings added, so it may be easy to get lost." Baron Eltz's voice continued in the hall as Gracie and Theo dropped their packs on two soft beds in adjacent rooms. Theo whistled, and Murphy unrolled and trotted out the door before Theo could change his mind. The three men had sauntered on down the narrow hall by the time the teens returned from their rooms. Gracie looked up at high ceilings rimmed with plaster friezes. The beauty of the castle reminded her of the luxurious room under the auditorium of the Alte Oper Haus in Frankfurt. *I'm going to memorize each millimeter of this castle!* Gracie's eyes widened with the promise she made herself. Two teens and their dog rejoined the men.

"To be honest, I've sent word for more security since Jahile's capture."

"*Nein!*" Fritz waved the conversation with his hand as his eyes swept from the baron to the young girl behind his right shoulder.

"Herr Möeller?" Gracie's eyes left the ceiling and danced to make eye contact with Fritz. "Are you talking about Herr Möeller?"

Fritz stopped walking long enough to wrap an arm around Gracie's petite shoulders and give a soft hug. "Ah, now aren't you de qvick vone. Baron vas just sayink tis room ist reserved for your dear Herr Möeller vhen he comes to visit." Fritz gave a wink toward the baron, who looked apologetic for his words.

"Is Herr Möeller coming?" Theo shared Gracie's excitement and was sure his heart skipped a beat with the exciting possibility of seeing their protector and friend.

"Well, not tonight, young man." The baron picked up on Fritz's cues and hedged the topic the three men had been discussing.

"Now how about we find our rooms." TAR glanced over his shoulder, trying to keep a lilt in his voice, but Gracie saw an intent look in his furrowed brow that she had only seen one time before—a year ago, at least—when TAR had held private conversations in Jahile's home. She walked past the door in silence, but her mind stayed ever active.

Dinner was filled with small talk about the beautiful castle that had been in the Eltz family for generations. An added surprise for Gracie was meeting Elise, the lady of the castle and sister of the baron. Gracie couldn't help but ask Elise an interminable number of questions to fill the silences. Until now, she hadn't realized how starved she was for feminine conversation. Elise too enjoyed the chance to talk and giggle with another woman, which prompted Theo to dismiss himself from their proximity and move his chair to the masculine end of the table where the topic of grouse hunting was taking predominance.

By nightfall, the chatter, laughter, guffaws, and even morsels Elise covertly tossed under the table for Murphy were all left behind. Elise properly dismissed herself with a humble air as if she were the guest and they were the prestigious owners of the estate. Neither Theo nor Gracie took the cue until TAR suggested they retire to find that their sleep would be most delightful without a canvas tarp over their heads. All laughed while Theo and Gracie offered their thanks for the warm hospitality and retraced steps from earlier in the evening.

Passing the room reserved for Herr Möeller, Gracie did not resist the urge to reach out and touch the doorknob as if a vibe from touching his door would waken the heartstrings tied to her guardian. Sounds hushed, and a blanket of memory fell in the ancient hall for a moment in time. A tiny rivulet of tears trickled down Gracie's face when she released the knob. Theo reached a warm arm around her and pulled her into his embrace. She let him, welcoming the chance to allow her soft femininity to unroll against his chest and in his arms.

Theo bent his head toward Gracie, causing a soft buzz to come out of his earbud. In reaction, he fell away from Gracie and cupped his hand over his ear.

Shocked and hurt by the sudden reaction, Gracie braced herself in a gushing wave of emotions. "What did—"

"Shhh!" Theo continued to cup his hand against his head and lift the other to silence Gracie.

"You can't—"

"Gracie! It's Murphy! We forgot he was sleeping under the table."

"So go get him. I'm glad to see *he* means so much to you!"

Theo missed her message of hurt feelings and shook his head. "No, no. He's probably still sleeping, but his collar is still recording and transmitting sound. I can hear what the men are saying." Theo's words dropped to a whisper, and his face seemed to pale. He squeezed his eyes shut, not wanting to believe the words he was hearing.

"What, Theo?" Gracie shook his arm. "Tell me! What do you hear?"

Theo swallowed hard. "Herr Möeller—he's been captured!"

"No!" Gracie's emotions soared out from under her control. "No! They need to tell me!"

Theo grabbed Gracie's arm.

"Let go!"

"No, Gracie!" He held against the strength of the distraught young woman. "Listen! Gracie, listen! Let's first hear through Murphy's transmitter. If we rush down there, they'll refuse to tell us anything."

"He's my guardian!" Gracie's voice filled the hall as she pulled away.

Theo tightened his grip on her arm. "But we're not part of *the Watch*! If we want to know what's going on, we have to listen through Murphy's transmitter!"

Gracie's shoulders dropped. She closed her eyes and tipped her head back, letting her muscles relent to Theo's hold. "Okay, but I need to listen too." She pulled Theo's arm as both teens hurried into his room. Theo removed the earbud, adjusted the volume, and held the tiny receiver between the two of them where they sat on the edge of the bed.

"How long was he here?" TAR's voice had a tense edge as if he spit the words in anger.

"He arrived almost four days ago."

Theo looked up at Gracie. "He must have come here after he left us in Frankfurt."

Gracie nodded in agreement and touched Theo's hand that held the receiver as a way to signal a need to listen.

Theo's words overlaid the more distant voice of Fritz.

"Last night? Vhen vas he discovered missink?"

The voice of the baron began talking as if going through a checklist of events. *"When Jahile didn't come to breakfast, Elise called for our house servant to check on him. The kitchen staff reported our* servant was missing. Elise and I both ran up to Jahile's room. I pounded on the door until my fist raps were covered by Elise's panicked yells for me to open his door." The baron paused and sighed.

Gracie and Theo locked eyes and held their breaths, afraid to miss the baron's next words.

"We've not touched his room since we found him gone. To think that we did not hear the bloody scuffle!" The baron's voice rose.

"There, there, Peter. Jahile's one of the strongest of the Watch."

"How can a man like that servant live under our roof for over a decade and be an undercover SS?"

TAR rubbed the whiskers beginning to show on his chin. "Doesn't make sense, Peter. Jahile's a bull ox when he's mad. It would have taken several to take him down and get him out of this house."

"Or one trusted servant who has muscle of his own—and a hypodermic needle."

"You found a needle? Where would he get a concoction to take down Jahile?"

"I don't know." The baron rubbed one hand across his forehead as if giving his mind a way to think. "He'd been going up to Hadamar, telling me he needed to see a doctor." The baron stood and walked to the sidebar to get a drink.

"I needed his muscle to keep this place going." He swept his arm through the air. "I never questioned what ailment he had." The baron slammed his fist on the sidebar. "*Sheish, Fritz!* I even paid for some of his medicine. I probably paid for the drug he used to stab Jahile and drag him out of here."

The room fell silent.

Gracie looked at Theo. "Where did he go? What's Hadamar? A city?"

Theo shrugged. "Until a year ago, Germany was just a place on the map in my textbook. I, for sure, don't know any cities."

"I have to help him."

"Gracie, we're kids. If *the Watch* can't even fight the Reich, what are we supposed to do?"

Gracie fell back on the bed and laid an arm across her forehead.

"Let's sleep tonight, Gracie. Tomorrow we'll let them know that we plan to help."

Gracie hesitated then responded with a faint smile and walked to the door. "G'night, Theo." Just as she opened the door, a small beagle trotted across the room and jumped up on the bed beside Theo.

"Good boy, Murphy. I sometimes wonder how much you know what you're doing." Murphy rolled to his back for a good belly scratch. In fifteen minutes, both boy and dog were snoring in a soft feather bed while the full moon peeked through the window slats, allowing a young girl to move through the dark halls to return to the room where her guardian had been.

Damsel in Action

GRACIE'S MIND COULDN'T compel her anxious heart to stay cooped up in her room. Did Theo honestly think she would be able to get any sleep knowing that Jahile was missing? The knob turned easily, opening the door to the unlocked guest room. An open window allowed light from a rising moon to crawl into the room and lie across the woolen carpet. Gracie slipped inside the room and closed the door behind her. She held stiff arms to her sides, but her legs threatened to buckle under her as the room told a violent story that weakened her heart. Signs of a struggle, indicated by an overturned chair and smashed vase, left little doubt in her suspicious imagination as to what happened. Mechanically, she walked to the open window and brushed aside the heavy drape hanging on either side of a thin curtain moving like a dancer on waves of wind. Outside the window, a rope and bedsheet had not been left behind to offer detail of how Jahile's drugged body had been wrapped and lowered from the window into the bed of a truck that left tracks too close to the castle wall to be a usual parking. Yet Gracie knew her guardian hadn't left on his own volition.

The idea of waiting for daylight seemed foolish to a girl who had spent months moving about the city of Munich like she was a shadow of the night. A lamp was still lit in Jahile's room—a clue that the attackers had not waited for the sun to shine on the castle before Jahile had been taken to whatever dark lair from which the enemy had come. She shook her head to block out thoughts of how she had first treated him and how relentlessly he had always come for her and protected her from the evil of the streets, of the Reich, and of creatures known as jaegers that seemed to crawl from the abyss of hell. Gracie looked around the dusk of her own room lit by a single bulb. *It's my turn to rescue Herr Möeller, my turn to repay his unwavering love and devotion.*

The Castle Eltz sat nestled in a valley, yet the stately castle rose defensively on a giant portion of earth that jutted up from the base of the valley. The small River Elzbach rushed wildly past the castle where the tributary had sprung from the larger River Moselle and wrapped three sides of the castle. Due to heavy rains and the last of the melting snow, the typically placid river was tumbling, sending lulling sounds up to most rooms in the castle. With determination in her heart, the young girl slipped into the deserted hallway, hoping the monotonous and continuous sound of the surf was muting the sound of any misplaced footstep.

She swiped underneath each eye with a shaking finger, convincing herself the castle dust irritated and caused tears. Wiping away the last droplet, she hesitated beside Theo's door. She wasn't afraid to go on this rescue mission alone, but she would like to have Murphy with her, and of course, that meant Theo too. She lifted her hand to tap on the wooden door, but something in her heart stopped her. It wasn't fair of her to expose them to possible danger or capture. Gracie lowered her clenched fist and tipped her head to swipe away another trickle from under her eyes. Again, she raised a fist to rap on the door, but before her tap could wake her friend, something or someone made a noise from a conjoining hallway. Not wanting to risk being seen or stopped, she sprinted in the opposite direction to face her venture alone.

Although Gracie's rush avoided detection in the night-darkened hall, her frustration was about to boil over into a scream of stress. In her attempt to leave the castle, she circled back to the same intersection just beyond Theo's room. The castle was massive. Three separate houses had been built and joined over its eight-hundred-year history. The island wrapped by the small river left three families of the Eltz name no choice but to build vertically into high towers. The high-ceiling darkness, hidden from the light of the night's full moon, made navigating the unknown hallways more like being in an architect's twisted maze.

Without knowing how or from which hall she had turned, she ran until she found herself in an open space not confined by hallway walls. Slants of moonlight proffered a dim lighting. Around the room hung beautifully crafted suits of armor from battles long past but polished and eager to reflect the moonlight. She remembered the baron's words as they had passed this room earlier—"the Knights' Hall, used for social events"—because even in passing, his words had enlivened her imagination. The castle tour had quickly brushed past the Knights' Hall, and her heart and eyes stole as much of a glance of the past as their fast walk had allowed. The beautiful suits of armor bore lifeless poses beneath massive ancient oak beams that ran the length of the ceiling, supporting the weight of the towers built above. The castle was symbolic of stability through battles of trade routes, as well as stability through political duress.

Well, thanks, Mr. Moon! I get out of the dark halls, and your pretty face tells me there's an opening—a way to reach the outside! Gracie's thoughts lightened her step as she rushed into the moonbeams to find an unlatched and slightly opened window leading to the inner courtyard of the compound.

The window gave easily to her push as she crawled onto the window ledge to slip through and hop down onto the soft dirt that had been sifted by the gardener. Pressed against the side of the building, she moved only her head as she scanned for possible sentries keeping watch in the night. Confident that she was alone at this late hour, she crept through shadows of the courtyard, staying along the walls to avoid detection as the full moon gave eyes to any passersby.

Her heart raced, but Gracie commanded her legs and feet to take time to stop every few steps to double-check that she was still alone and not secretly observed. As she stealthily tiptoed across the open courtyard, her eyes darted and pleaded to the darkness to reveal any hoped-for means of escape.

"Well, it's not exactly Cinderella's carriage, but I think this will take me away!" Gracie's whispers gave a smile and a wink to the moon before she gingerly walked over to the truck parked by an outbuilding.

Gracie sat with her hands gripped tightly around the steering wheel. She had never sat in the driver's seat of an automobile before, and she almost giggled with giddiness. She didn't care how silly it was to be excited sitting in an unmoving truck. She ran her hand down the steering column until she felt a key protruding from the shaft. Raised eyebrows showed that she even surprised herself to find the key. With only a half twist of her wrist, something inside of her caused her to freeze just before turning the key. "Idiot! Wake everyone up, why don't you," she scolded herself louder than she intended. Cringing as the door of the Blitz creaked into the still night air, she held the door and squeezed herself out through the small opening, not wanting to create any more sounds.

The bent grill on the front of the truck offered a crooked smile, too dull from age to reflect the moonlight. *Think this through, Gracie. Think how to move this dinosaur. I know how rattly you are, old boy. I can't take a chance on being heard. Think, Gracie. What's my plan?* She patted the hood of the truck as she bit her lip in thought. She nodded and breathed a quiet sigh. She noticed the truck was parked along a long cobblestone drive headed down a slight hill. Gracie walked to the back of the truck and put her shoulder against the raised bed, trying to push and get it rolling. The truck didn't budge under her weight. She stood back away from the truck, took a deep breath, then again used her shoulder to slam into the truck as hard as she could. She winced as the truck stood petrified and dumb in the moonlight. Exasperated, Gracie raised her foot to kick the bed of the truck and bounced backward and onto her bottom. "Ow," she moaned as she rubbed a sore spot and picked herself up off the ground.

She walked back up to the driver's seat and slipped through the partially opened door, sat down, and started to fidget with the steering wheel. *What are all of these knobs, levers, and pedals? Why didn't Herr Möeller teach me to drive? Ugh! This truck hates me or it would help!* Her hands moved from knob to knob and from lever to lever. Eventually, she wrapped her palm over the knob at the top of a long rod sticking out of the floor. She gripped the knob and wrenched the long rod back and forth. Caught up in relieving stress by punching and pulling knobs, she started stomping her feet against the multiple pedals sticking up from the floorboard. As she wiggled the long rod clutched by her left hand, she stomped against a pedal, and the truck gave a quick lurch forward.

"Uh!" Gracie sucked in the dark air. *Now what'd I do? Okay, old buddy. Did you really move, or did I just imagine it? How did I do that?*

Again, Gracie started pressing down on the pedals and jerking the long rod gear shifter until she popped the truck out of gear. Again, her stomping and bouncing made the truck hint that it wanted to roll. She quickly slipped off the seat and back out through the door still hanging open. She begged her eyes to see if the stony drive under the truck had changed. With both hands against the side of the bed, she tried to shake the heavy Blitz. *Okay, so it's heavy. C'mon, old boy, roll for me.* Gracie stepped to the back of the truck and pushed with her arms extended. *C'mon! Please! For Herr Möeller!* She turned and pressed her back and both shoulders against the high bumper of the bed. She felt it budge. With renewed vigor, she drove her weight into the truck until she felt the metal beast begin to roll down the gradual decline. Once the truck started to pick up momentum, she ran to the open door and crawled up behind the steering wheel.

Adrenaline pumped and heartbeat pulsed with exhilaration as the truck gained speed, rolling faster and faster down the drive. The young driver tightened a two-fisted grip on the steering wheel as she rolled under the arches of the guard tower and through an iron gate that had been left open when they had arrived earlier in the evening.

The rolling truck jostled over pebbles of the long drive and across the bridge spanning the Elzbach River until Gracie pressed the brake pedal to stop where the road divided. *Now the hard part.* She giggled. *Which way do I go?* She closed her eyes and said a silent prayer then fired up the engine of the borrowed truck. "Okay, Mr. Moon. You've been good to me so far. I can see the road better this way." She turned the wheel to the left.

I know which pedal is the brake so . . . She swung her foot to press the largest pedal until the engine roared, but the truck only slightly rolled. "Sheish!" She looked at the pedals on the floor then at the long lever sticking up in the middle of the floor. With a sigh, she cupped her hand over the ball on the stick, giving it a little shake. The truck lurched, and the engine stopped. "Oh, it's hopeless!" In exasperation, she started pressing the pedals with both feet as if she were dancing on springs. The truck rolled then stopped.

"Whoa! What caused that?" She started dancing on the pedals again with both feet. Again, the truck rolled and stopped. "There must be something about the pedals, but this one stopped, and this one killed the engine." Deliberately, she talked to the night air and put one foot on the outside pedal. The truck began to roll. She raised her foot off the pedal, and the truck stopped rolling. She gave a determined sigh as she started the engine again, pushing on the outer pedal. So far, so good. Again, she pressed the big pedal and heard the engine roar. At the same time, she began trying to move the ball in her hand and push the outer pedal. Suddenly, the night air was filled with a terrible sound of metal grinding. The truck lurched forward.

"I'm moving! I'm actually moving forward! Thank you, Lord!" Gracie was unsure of what combination moved the truck, but she sat straight up in the seat and put both hands back on the steering wheel of the moving truck. "I'm driving! Herr Möeller, I'm coming for you, and I'm driving!"

Gracie rolled down the window, allowing the cold night air to brush her face. She had been alone before, so she felt no fear driving through the dark night. The moon lit the road for several kilometers, promising his part in the journey, but at times, the road ducked under cover of ancient trees where arching limbs touched in a web of branches above the road. It was at one of the dark times she began turning and pulling knobs until the truck's dim headlights popped into the thick darkness. Adrenaline bounced with the rumbling, dark country road. She didn't know where she was or where she was heading, but with hope against hope, she prayed she would go where she needed to be and that she wouldn't be too late getting there.

Mental and physical energy drained as the hour and road passed into nothingness. The moon abandoned the old truck and its passenger. Heavy rains from earlier in the day had changed the dirt roads into ribbons of thick muddy ruts. Too often, the truck would pull left, and as soon as she could get the vehicle corrected, another rut would yank the truck to the right.

An ancient stone bridge narrowed the road to only wide enough for a single vehicle. Gracie tensed her grip and her focus to keep the truck sides from scraping on the stone walls of the bridge. Barely across the river enough for Gracie to release a sigh of relief, the truck shuddered then lurched ahead again. *Now what's wrong? What's the matter, old truck? Did the cold water under the bridge give you a shiver?* Her thoughts were filled more with curiosity than fear.

Scarcely had the truck made progress than it shuddered again, this time with clanking noises. The truck slowed to a jerking crawl. Gracie looked at the gauges, understanding and seeing nothing in the night. A red bar on a gas indicator meant nothing to the young girl. The truck jerked to a stop in the middle of the tree-covered road.

"What was that?" She turned the key on the column, but the engine only growled. "Ugh! Some friend you are!" She grabbed the door lever and used her foot to shove open the creaky door. Sliding to the ground, she pounded her fist into the seat before she slammed the door shut behind her. "I don't need you anyway!" Gracie kicked the side of the truck and turned to jog in the direction she had been heading.

To Gracie's tired legs, one kilometer felt like a hundred. Without the protection of the truck, every shadow and tree loomed a threat along the ominous road. Just over a year ago, she had spent many nights in the dark streets and alleys of a city, but this was different. Night in the city wasn't this dark; a streetlight or glow in a window could always be seen from wherever she was hiding. In this forsaken countryside, the tall forest trees blocked out all light from the heavens. The darkness had been her friend and protector many nights on the streets, but here she could not control or escape the dark. A chill shivered down her spine and started to crawl back up again. Every sound and scrape bellowing from the depths of the forest caught in her imagination as made-up monsters from her father's stories of dragons and monsters of the Third Reich invisibly hid behind every tree. Gracie fought with herself to stay calm as she walked the narrow twisting country lane and focused on the road beneath her feet.

The thought of a jaeger hiding in the woods terrified her. She had no weapon but the strength of kicking legs to defend herself. She wouldn't be able to escape a terror of the night if she was too tired to run away from her attacker. Her heart pounded in her chest, and despite the cool night air, a bead of sweat rolled down the side of her delicate face.

"Stop it, you silly girl, stop it now!" she loudly ordered herself.

"Stop what?" a voice spoke in the darkness.

Gracie froze in the dark, muddy road, swallowing a scream of terror. She scanned the woods, trying to see who or what interloper spoke out in the night. Small, quiet breaths begged her ears to hear and her heart not to explode. The cool air bounced a curl against her cheek. She waited in the empty, dark night.

"Silly girl," she whispered, "get control of yourself. How can you help Jahile if you can't even walk through the woods?" She took a few timid steps before stubbornness kicked in and she started walking down the road at full stride, refusing to give in to her childish imagination.

"Thank goodness I didn't ask that silly American to come. He would never let me live this moment down."

Though Gracie tried to walk briskly with brave determination, weariness slowed her pace after a short time. Her mind bounced between fear of the unknown in the forest and scolding for charging off into the dark night in a land she didn't know. "Okay, Gracie, keep your head. How stupid am I to take off by myself? I can't help it. No one was looking for Herr Möeller. Morning might have been too late. I had to come. I had to come. I had to . . . Where is he? What am I even looking for? What'd I expect to find? Do bad guys post signs for their secret lairs? Do bad-guy places stink like jaegers? What if a jaeger finds me? Oh, what if I don't find Herr Möeller? What if someone finds me dead instead?"

Gracie felt a swelling of tears pushing against her tired eyes. She shook her head and stomped her foot in determination to keep control. "Stop it! I will find him!" she shouted to the empty road.

"Stop what?" again, a voice spoke from the dark forest beside the road.

"Who's there?" Gracie glared into the darkness, standing with feet planted and fists balled, ready to strike.

"What does it matter? You don't know us," another voice came from the opposite side of the road.

Gracie gasped and twisted back around.

"You don't even see us as human." The voice was accusing and rough.

"Don't be mean!" the first voice scolded. "Not everyone is so mean as you."

Gracie stood speechless, listening to the arguing voices from either side of the road. Her mind whirled. *What's happening? Maybe I should run. I'm surrounded! How many are in the trees? What if I can't outrun them? What if I can't escape? What kind of demons are after me?* A heavy silence filled the woods and interrupted Gracie's thoughts.

"Do you have a knife?" the first voice broke the silence.

"Like she's going to tell you that. You silly girl!" retorted the deeper voice.

"She doesn't seem dangerous. Do you see a star on her collar? I don't," the softer voice spoke in a hopeful tone.

"A star? What in the . . ." Gracie spun in the road, trying to see both sides and catch a glimpse of someone, something. "And yes! I have a big knife, so stay away from me!"

"No, you don't. Don't lie." The deeper voice laughed with a resonance that bounced off the trees.

The rough laughter made Gracie's fear begin to boil into defense. She pretended to reach for something under her coat, trying to prove her lie was truth. "You wanna bet your life on it?" A twig snapped. Gracie swung around, ready to face her attacker. A shadow disappeared behind a large tree.

"Nice, Zuza. Way to be quiet. I knew I shouldn't let you come with me," the deeper voice complained to the moving shadows.

"Shut up, Hezekiah. I'll tell Papa, and you'll get whipped!"

Gracie recognized the tone in the softer voice. It sounded like her scolding Theo. Gracie stood a little straighter, relaxing her shoulders a bit. *These are just kids. Maybe they're not dangerous. Maybe they are, but if they're kids, they're probably not the worst thing in these woods.*

Gracie convinced herself to take a chance. "Zuza, that's a beautiful name. Um, Zuza, can you help me?"

"Don't do it, Zuza!" her brother yelled from the other side of the road.

"You're not my boss!" the childish soft voice yelled back.

Another snapping noise from behind the large tree caught Gracie's stare. She slowly sidestepped to the right side of the road, fists still clenched in case of attack. She stopped near the tree, doing her best to slow her heart rate and keep her breathing under control. Without warning, she lunged around the tree with her fist raised and her voice screaming a war cry, trying to catch the girl off guard.

What? Nothing but darkness stood behind the tree. Gracie lowered her fist and turned back to the road. A scream caught in her throat. Standing in the middle of the road where she had been was a young girl. She wore a long skirt made from many squares of fabric. Her shoulders were draped with long hair that hung below a patchwork scarf covering her head. The moon that earlier refused to show his face on the forested road now gently dropped beams around the child, lighting the ground where she stood.

Gracie relaxed her tight fists and stood with her head tilted as she looked at the small vision in the road. *Who is she? She looks delicate. I bet I could break her in half.* Though her mind raced, only Gracie's eyes made any perceptible movement. *She looks almost familiar. I don't know her. Maybe someone like her. Where? Where before? This girl or . . . or someone like her. She looks . . . No, it's not her. Her clothes . . . She looks like . . .* Gracie straightened her head on her shoulders and gasped. *She's dressed like a photograph of Mama as a young girl! This girl—is she?* Unintentionally, Gracie's thoughts gently fell from her tongue. "She's Romani!"

"*Sastipe!*" A very long time had passed since she spoke to Papa and Mama in their native tongue, but Gracie's soft *hello* in the Romani language had the effect she hoped.

"*Sastipe!*" The girl in the road tipped her head and smiled.

Gracie stepped out of the forest and up to the side of the road. Air that had been veiled with fright lifted between the girls, allowing them to chatter and trip over words that danced between them in the Romani tongue. "My name is Gracie. Are you Zuza?" The wide smile of the young girl was caught by the moonlight and sent back to Gracie with nods and giggles.

More cautiously than his young sister, the boy called Hezekiah emerged from his hiding place among the trees. "How do you know our words?" He tried to keep a firm tone to express displeasure in talking to the stranger, but his curiosity created a lilt to his question.

"She's one of us, Hezekiah." In the moonlight, the girl was visibly younger than the boy who looked close to Gracie's age.

Shuffling through the drying mud, the girl moved closer to Gracie. In the silence, three beating hearts could almost be heard. Zuza extended an arm and stepped to where Gracie stood until her forehead was close enough that had she nodded again, she would have touched Gracie's chin. Wiggling fingers touched a curl hanging across Gracie's shoulder. At first, Gracie stiffened and squinted at the little girl. The delicate curl was pleasant to Zuza's touch and beckoned her to reach higher and run her palm down the side of Gracie's head.

"Puha és gyönyör," Zuza whispered her reaction to the soft and beautiful hair, not to Gracie, but to her own heart and the moonbeams that scarcely carried the sound beyond the two standing at the side of the road.

In a move as quick as the smile that broke across Zuza's face, she swung both arms around Gracie, pressing her head against Gracie's chest. *"Lánytestvér."*

Zuza's gesture and endearing word of *sister* gave Gracie comfort in the dark and lonely night.

Matriarch

Hezekiah and Zuza spoke in their native language, eager to help their new friend. Gracie used her active imagination to create a believable story about sneaking away from her mean uncle. She felt a slight pang of guilt for lying to her new friends; their expressions exposed their good souls.

Grunts of pushing by the two older kids and luck of steering by the tiny Zuza aided the trio in removing the disabled truck from the middle of the road. The abandoned truck was the only sign of humanity on the road once the Romani children pulled Gracie into the dark woods.

Gracie had no idea where they were or how her two new friends could navigate the forest so easily. She wondered if they could see through the impenetrable dark of the forest. She had heard stories about magical powers of Romani gypsies, but she wasn't sure what Mama created from her imagination and what was a memory of her childhood.

Time passed with the swift movements of her light-footed friends. The full moon swam in and out of clouds and finally froze in the sky, allowing half an hour to pass before sounds could be heard bouncing through the wooded land ahead. Gracie heard the Romani caravan long before even the dancing firelight flashed through the dark trees. Sounds of laughing, singing, and lighthearted talking overtook the quiet night, pulling the trio toward the vortex. Their pace quickened until the campfire's light flamed in the darkness—a beacon guiding the youths to safety.

Standing on the edge of dark forest, Hezekiah and Zuza stopped before emerging into the Romani camp in a clearing of tall trees. Gracie turned to the boy, waiting for an explanation. In the shadows, Hezekiah tipped back his head, facing toward branches overhead. She heard him whistle like a bird. Impressed by the bird call's pure tone, she smiled and tilted her head. The tall, skinny Romani removed his hat, wiped his sweaty brow, and waited. The silence hung undisturbed. Gracie waited, not knowing what to expect to see or to hear. She jerked her head around and kept her ear tilted toward the night sky when the same bird call fell back down from where a sentry sat hidden in the canopy of trees.

Zuza understood Gracie's surprise. Her childlike features hardened for a moment when she whispered, "We can't be too careless... Not safe for anyone who isn't pure."

Gracie nodded, letting them both know she understood all too well about dangers that lurked in the dark and now in the sun of the daytime too.

"There's no sympathy for anyone who dares to try to penetrate this area," Hezekiah spoke without joy in his voice, sounding like more of a man who had been at war than a child. He turned a complete circle without taking a step as he glanced through the trees surrounding the campsite. Then, with no further talk, he stepped out of the cover of woods and into the field. He never looked back to see if the girls were coming.

Laughter and music called the young trio into the realm of warmth and safety. Horses tethered together on the outer rim of the caravan circle formed a maze entrance. Gracie walked between her two friends through a layer of circled wagons until they stood in a core area, bustling with life and energy. Gracie couldn't move her head and eyes fast enough to take in all the action happening around her; there were so many wonderful distractions.

For once, the skip of her emotions was from amazement. Two men engaged in a heated knife-throwing contest backed up so far that the target was scarcely visible, yet both split the bull's-eye with not enough space to determine the winner. The men looked at each other, lifted flasks to their lips, and pulled long swallows of something stout and satisfying. As each lowered his drinking vessel, a smile spread across his face. The contenders clasped each other on the shoulder, giving vigorous shakes in celebration of their ability. Their voices were hearty as if all energy poured into creating a memory. The men retrieved their handcrafted knives before disappearing into the mob of people celebrating life.

"That was amazing!" Gracie's excitement was not held back.

"They do this every time they see each other. They always tie." Zuza's matter-of-fact explanation was laced with pride.

"Wow, how can they throw like that?" Gracie shook her head, letting her eyes follow where the men disappeared into the crowd before she turned back to follow Zuza. "Where are we going?"

Zuza pointed to the far side of the festivities surrounding the large communal campfire. Gracie wasn't sure she had ever seen such a large flame. Past flames dancing to tunes of jubilant music, she noticed a large wagon that sat out of place and alone but still inside the perimeter of the circled caravan. A small campfire glowed at the base of three stairs dangling from the back of the wagon and leading up to canvas pulled tightly to form dutch doors. The top canvas was tied open, allowing air to flow through.

"Whose is that?" Gracie sensed the inside wagon belonged to someone important. Why else would it stay inside the circle of wagons forming a wall of protection from outsiders?

"Mama Vertina," Hezekiah paused and lifted his chin as he added, "our matriarch." He hadn't looked back at the girls since they crossed the threshold from the wooded darkness, and he answered, still not looking back. Hezekiah raised his arm in gesture while weaving through the revelry sprawled in front of him. "Stay close!" he ordered.

"Who's Mama Vertina?" Gracie's mind was spinning. The laughter, music, and dancing blended into one large symphony. Each sound played off the other in an intoxicating rhythm that radiated from each of the gypsies yet none at the same time. Mesmerized, for the first time, the young *Mischling* understood the longing in her parents' eyes when they told stories of the great caravan celebrations.

Unexpectedly, a nervousness crept into Gracie's soul as the three friends neared Mama Vertina's wagon. The commotion and celebration had captured her attention since they had stepped out of the cover of forest. She began to lag, getting a slight tug on the sleeve from Zuza, whose gentle smile had the tilt of a sneer in the shadows of the firelight. Gracie gave her head a quick, subtle shake. *Get it together*, she silently reprimanded herself. *Jahile would be brave—you must be brave!*

In signal, Hezekiah's uplifted arm dropped to his side. The trio halted near the small fire burning beside the matriarch's wagon. Gracie's eyes moved from two men appearing in the shadows to Hezekiah, whose cocky confidence wavered in the presence of Mama Vertina's guards. The curious *Mischling* shifted her eyes back to the staunch shadows again. Two men, wearing only vests over flannel shirts, stood motionless on either side of the small set of stairs. Each looked like a chiseled marble statue better fitted to be on display at the *Louvre* in France than in a dirt campground hidden in a German wood. If their intent was to intimidate, it worked to perfection; even Zuza let out a small gasp at the sight of the two stoic guards.

"Be gone from here, children. This is no place for you." A guard half turned from the stairs, shooing them with his hand. "Go play with the rest!"

Hezekiah shook a chill from his body and glanced back at his sister, who nodded in scared encouragement. He turned back to face the guard as he sucked in a deep breath and stood up as straight and tall as he could. "We seek audience with Mama Vertina." He willed his quivering voice to be confident in front of his sister and the pretty girl he had rescued from the empty road.

A glance between the two guards showed they were impressed, still slightly annoyed by the boy's bold request. The guard who had not yet spoken began to cross the distance between himself and the young boy.

"Loiza! Stop!" ordered a soft yet powerful voice. The man stopped midstride, bringing his foot back to rest on the soft earth. He turned and, like the rest of them, saw a visage of wrinkles partially hidden from view by the cowl that fell over the matriarch's face.

"Yes, Mama Vertina." The guard back stepped in two motions to his post beside the staircase.

The lower half of the canvas dutch door rolled open, revealing folds of fabric skirt worn by a frail and hunched woman. A soft thud of her cane brought down on the top step steadied her descent and interrupted their pounding heartbeats. A guard reached to assist the elderly woman covered in a heavy cloak despite the heat radiating from the two campfires. In a swift reaction, she slapped his hand away and glared at him.

"If I can't walk down a few stairs, you should just put me down, Loiza." She glanced up at the man whose hand hung suspended in midair. Light from the small fire danced where wrinkles on her cheeks deepened as her lips pulled into a grin. "Quit trying to coddle me." She winked, pulling a very rare smile across the teeth of her most trusted protector.

"Sorry, Mama Vertina." He lowered his head and hand to give her space, though he kept a close eye, ready to jump if she should falter.

"I'm sure you are," Mama Vertina added lightly. "As a baby, young man, you wanted freedom from those who hovered over you to protect you from hazards of life. But then, how did you learn to pick yourself up, Loiza?" She paused and gave the cane a quick rap on the step. "You had to fall down first," she answered with a smile. "I am old, no longer a baby, but I'm still determined to learn."

The guards and the youths waited in silence as the elderly woman steadily lowered herself down the steps then made her way to the fire. She lowered herself to sit on a tree stump that had been hewn into a perfectly formed chair and allowed the fire's heat to warm her cold old bones. "Come here, child," Mama Vertina ordered in a caring and soft voice, without taking her eyes from the center of the small fire. "Come, child, I am not getting any younger." She laughed.

Zuza pushed the stunned Gracie toward the fire and took a step back from the dancing light, while her brother stepped up by his sister.

"Come, come. You are safer here with us than you were on that road," Mama spoke loudly enough for even Hezekiah and Zuza to hear. Gracie turned in shock to see the same look of surprise on the siblings' faces, each one wondering how the old woman knew where they met.

Mama Vertina was inwardly pleased at the expressions of surprise and wonder. She knew the children would tell their friends how she had mysteriously known about their excursion on the dark road of the forest beyond their camp. Her legend grew stronger. "Pull a log and sit beside me, child." She spoke to the girl without turning her head, allowing the flames to dance in the reflection of her eyes. "Gracie is it?"

Gracie hesitated so suddenly in hearing her name that she tripped, stumbling against the woodpile. *She's a witch! What now? Will she turn me into a small animal or take my soul?* She hadn't grown up among her parents' people, the Romani, but she had seen a few travelers in her town and had heard rumors of witchcraft and other unnatural powers possessed by the Romani. Fear began again to bristle up her spine and linger at the base of her neck as it wrapped around her throat. Gracie would rather face the gangs of Munich than a witch. Too frightened not to obey, she grabbed a log from the woodpile and set it down where Mama Vertina had motioned with her walking cane.

"Don't be afraid, child," Mama Vertina whispered just loudly enough for Gracie to hear. "Leave us!" she ordered guards and the siblings with a wave of her cane as if to sweep them away. The old woman waited silently as the two guards returned to the wagon and the two children fell back into the chaos of the celebration. She rubbed her hands near the fire, warming them, patiently waiting to be alone with the girl beside her. She bent over and grabbed a long branch lying beside the stone ring of the firepit. With poking and pushing motions, she began moving the burning logs, making circles in the red-hot embers. Tongues of fire lapped up the darkness and danced high into the night sky.

"Are you reading the flames?" Gracie blurted out, immediately sorry she hadn't been able to control her curiosity and fear.

A soft chuckle joined the dancing flames. "Something like that, child." Mama Vertina continued to push the burning wood, allowing for better airflow, earning in return stronger flames for more heat. The Romani matriarch never turned her face from the coals she stirred. "What do you seek, Gracie?"

"How did you—"

The old woman interrupted, "How did I know you were looking for something? Child, why else would a young girl like you be driving around the countryside at this hour of night?" She tapped the long branch on the stones ringing the fire before she sat back and looked directly into Gracie's eyes. "Beyond dangers that hunt beautiful young girls like you, you also must be wary of those who do not like people like us. That list is growing longer every day, child." Again, she tapped the branch against the fire ring of stone. "Dangerous times we live in, Gracie. Dangerous times." Her eyes and voice drifted back to the fire.

Gracie shuffled her feet, squirming against the log seat. "I'm looking for," she paused not sure what she wanted to say next until her thoughts, words, and heart poured into the fire-warmed darkness, "my friend Herr Möeller, my parents, my life."

"Jahile? Yes, Jahile."

Gracie leaned forward to rivet her eyes on the old woman's face. Confusion and question covered her countenance.

"Where Jahile is, you cannot go."

"I don't understand. How do you—an old woman—how do you know all this? My name, Herr Möeller . . ." Gracie shook her head at the fire. "If you know so much, where is he? Where is Herr Möeller?" Gracie could feel a fire in her soul being kindled and turning her face red as her voice leaped with the flames of emotion. "Tell me where he is. I'm not afraid! Tell—"

"No!" The matriarch sat up and tapped the stick against the stones so forcefully that it broke and dropped into the fire. "Your Herr Möeller is in a dangerous place. Once, it was an institution to heal people with insane minds. Now it is controlled by dangerous people with depraved minds. Life has a strange way of twisting and turning."

As if a door of her mind had shut out the sadness of her thoughts, a deep inhale lifted her shoulders, and her countenance seemed to lighten. "Go ahead, ask me!" Mama Vertina laughed, breaking the seriousness of the conversation.

"Ask you what? I just asked you my question."

"Dear child, ask me what you are afraid to ask." Mama Vertina turned her eyes from the flames, staring into the young girl's eyes, seeing a fire burning in them too. "Ask me!"

As Gracie stared into Mama Vertina's eyes, a youthfulness and a sadness seemed to be struggling for control. "Are you . . . Um, are you . . . a . . .," she hesitated, afraid to ask, afraid a magic would come to life from the stories she had been told, "um, a witch?"

The hunched-over, wrinkled matriarch let out a fierce laugh. She stamped her wooden cane into the soft dirt at her feet and continued to laugh for so long she began cough. "Didn't your parents teach you anything about your heritage?" Mama Vertina slowly calmed herself and motioned for Loiza. He disappeared into her tiny home and emerged a few moments later, bringing her a steaming drink and offering another cup to their guest. Gracie watched as the woman sipped on the concoction until her coughing and breathing came under control. The warm wooden mug felt amazing in Gracie's chilly hands, sending a warmth up through her arms and into the rest of her body. The warm sensation subduing the cold made her body react with a fierce shiver. She sipped on the warm liquid.

A few minutes passed in silence between the two. Loiza stood over the matriarch until she handed him her wooden cup and shooed him away again. "I really should be nicer to him," she broke the silence. "He is a great man. I don't know if I've ever trusted someone as much as I trust him."

Gracie didn't say anything; she could see through the man's overbearing demeanor. He reminded her of the expressions her father and Herr Möeller had when they looked at her. She felt almost jealous, watching the man devoted to Mama Vertina and feeling the pull on her heart, knowing she didn't have her two special men to care for her. That feeling raging through her body helped her refocus and gave her the strength she needed. "Mama Vertina, where is Herr Möeller? I need to find him. I'm afraid, but I have no choice." She paused and looked at the embers glowing under the fiery logs then back to Mama Vertina, who was waiting, the smile gone from her face. "I owe a debt to him. I must repay it!"

The old woman stared back at Gracie, measuring her, then retreated inside her own thoughts and memories. As her gaze returned to the fire, she stoked, causing air to encourage the flames to burn hotter and brighter. She began to speak, unwilling to divert her eyes from the flames. "I owed a debt once." Her lips opened to speak, but her thoughts kept her silent until the words formed in her mind. "But I did not have your conviction to repay it. Even to this day, I am troubled by my choice of inaction, and it happened so many years ago. You think I should have forgotten by now, but I haven't."

Mama Vertina looked into Gracie's intent stare. "Now, I struggle with a very difficult decision, Gracie." Her voice dropped so low that Gracie wasn't sure if the old woman wanted her to hear. "I truly don't want someone so young to go through life bearing guilt as I have, but do I deepen my own guilt by sending someone so young to a certain end." The old woman's words and thoughts blew away in silence with the ashes of the burning fire.

Instinctively, Gracie placed her hand across the blanketed arm of the old woman. "Please, Mama Vertina, please. I *need* to go. At least point me in the right direction."

"It's late, child. Your body and mind are exhausted." Mama Vertina used her cane to push herself up from the log seat and moaned as her tired bones protested the movement. Gracie pulled her legs under her to stand, but the matriarch placed a hand on her shoulder and looked into her eyes. "I will give you my decision in the morning. A few hours of rest will do you good."

Determined, Gracie tried to stand but found herself unable to push against the pressure the hunched woman had on her. She tipped her head back in shock. "Let me up!"

Mama Vertina held firm and never broke eye contact with Gracie as the teenager struggled to stand. "Sleep now, child."

"But I'm not—"

"Rest."

"But I—"

Mama Vertina leaned down and whispered, "Sleep now, child."

"But . . ."

The Romani camp smeared in Gracie's vision while she fought with all her willpower to keep her eyes open. She felt herself succumb to being gently laid on the earth. Soon, the chill of the late-night air was doused by a heavy quilt covering her body.

Touching the Future

As if someone captured billowing clouds from a night sky and encased them in soft linens, Theo sank into the softness of the bed and slept soundly at first. He rolled on the soft mattress and felt his companion Murphy snuggled under the covers near his ankle. Theo blinked in the brightness of the full moon that shone across the bedroom floor. "So, old man moon, you're sportin' your stuff tonight. I guess you're awake and think everyone else needs to be awake too, huh? I thought you were off hiding your face behind a bunch of clouds."

The young man cupped his hands behind his head cradled in the feather pillow and looked around the guest room of the castle. Moonbeams competed to find the best places to reflect in the room. A dressing table's three-way mirror, dark in spots where the silver backing had oxidized, reflected the beams that became animated when Theo rolled his head from side to side in his cupped hands. A light bulb overhead was scarcely hidden behind a square piece of opaque glass that took on a frosted appearance. Even in the corner where a castle servant had forgotten to pull a drape across a closet-like niche, a strange pipe and bag figure huddled in the corner, exposed by the beams that bounced off the silver skeleton that held the bag.

Hmph. What the heck is that? He stared and decided he saw a cord wrapped over the silver pipe. *Man, that looks like a golf bag on a weird base and pole.* Then, as if the moonbeams lit up a dark corner of his brain, he raised his eyebrows. *Cool! I bet that's what was used as a vacuum. I'm glad I live—uh, at least in my real time—when all I have to do is flip a switch and let all dirt and dust from inside the house be sucked out through vents. Our house dirt collects underground to refurbish the earth. What would these people do with a bag full of dirt?*

Theo grinned at the moon then tossed and turned for several minutes before he lifted the soft cover to the side, exposing a robot dog curled and recharging at the foot of the soft bed. "Hey, Murph! If I can't sleep, you can't either!" Theo gave the dog a quick head rub before swinging his legs to the side of the bed. He sat in the stillness and glanced over his shoulder at Murphy, who was reluctantly stretching paws and legs.

"Don't you miss home, Murphy?" The young master looked down at the muzzle still planted in the bedcovers, barely exposing the dog's eyes. "I mean, except when I'm getting beat up or having the crap scared out of me, this has been fun and all, but . . . Oh, I dunno, I just sometimes miss home." Theo looked down at his wrist propped on a pillow. The dark screen of the wrist computer stood out from the white pillow. "You know," he swung his arm over to pet the ears of the beagle wiggling through the blankets, "technology. Sure, I have you, but kids here don't even have video games or music pods with earbuds." He knitted his brows and looked at his robotic dog as if he could understand and give him an answer. "What do teenagers do here for fun?"

Murphy took advantage of his master looking to him for answers and rolled to his back with all four paws hanging loosely in the air.

"Oh, I see, you think a good belly scratch is the answer for everything, huh, buddy?" Theo couldn't help but laugh as Murphy's back leg reacted with the usual "air kicking" from having his stomach scratched. "I don't care if you are a robot. You're fun!"

Much to Murphy's disappointment, the belly rub stopped abruptly when Theo jumped out of bed. "Hey, I'm a scientist like Dad. If I'm missing technology, why don't I just make some? Whaddaya think, huh, Murph? I mean, I can't sleep anyway, right?"

Theo walked to the window where the moon had made its entrance. Clouds were sweeping through the night sky, beginning to obscure the full light of the moon. As billows rolled across the face of the moon, glimpses of moonbeams jostled through the dark layers providing temporary light. Theo could see outlines of niches and bulges of the massive castle. He tipped his head to follow a tower that spiked into the night sky. "Look, Murph, that tower seems to rip up through the sky. I wonder how tall it is. You know, maybe this would be a good place to try our radio transmission again. Whaddaya say, boy?"

Theo turned to question his robot friend, who was lying with his head hanging off the side of the bed. "Really, Murphy? You're too tired to get up? May I remind you that you're a robot? Robots don't need sleep, but I thank you for your drama." Theo reached for a light on Murphy's collar. "Looks like you're recharged. How about we see how high that tower really is? Maybe we can have a midnight conversation with IRIS." Murphy raised and cocked his head. "I know, I know. I bet it's been a long time since you've heard me say I miss IRIS. Pretty crazy that a nearly eighteen-year-old guy would want to have his integrated robotic information system around, huh, Murphy?"

Murphy wagged his tail and tipped his snout toward Theo to encourage him to continue the head-and-back scratch. "Well, give me a minute to dress, and then maybe we'll find a tower. Everyone's asleep, so we won't have to explain what we're doing. They all seem so smart here. I can't believe they haven't figured out our technology. It's like they enjoy living in . . . in the past!" Murphy sat expressionless as Theo enjoyed his own private joke about the differences between his world of mid twenty-first century and the world of 1937 Nazi Germany.

In stealth, the young man and his robotic dog pulled open the door and took a glance into the hall. "Looks pretty quiet around here." Theo and Murphy turned into the hall and walked to Gracie's door, where Theo paused and Murphy pressed his snout to the bottom of the door.

"What are you saying, boy? Do you think we should wake Gracie and see if she wants to go to the tower?" Theo lifted a fist and started a light tap on her door. Something inside of the teenager made him hesitate in the middle of the rap, causing him to pause with his fist on the door. *Maybe she needs to sleep. Besides, I'm just going to the tower to try some technology. Gracie would never understand, and I'd have to answer all kinds of questions and never get anything done.* Dropping his fist back down to his side, he glanced down at Murphy, whose rump was stuck in the air and whose nose was pressed into the crack between floor and door.

"Murphy, what are you doing? You usually have more patience than to stick your nose under the door. Maybe the full moon is making you act weird." Murphy looked up at Theo then pressed his nose back to the floor again. Theo didn't notice that Murphy's tail wasn't wagging but instead was pointed straight out behind him as it did when the computer chips were in warning mode. Nor did Theo notice a red blinking light on Murphy's collar that signaled danger.

A pat against the master's thigh motioned for the obedient dog to follow. Theo reached the end of the long hall before Murphy left his post at Gracie's door and caught up to follow his master.

"How can the moon be so bright outside and the halls of this castle be so dark inside?" Theo shivered and rubbed his arms to fend off the cold air. "Murphy, I need your collar light to help us—or at least to help me—see where we're going. How 'bout it, huh, pal?" Theo reached down and pushed a small button on Murphy's collar, causing a blue light to give a soft glow in the ancient walkway. "Whew, much better."

At the end of each hallway, Theo looked for a window to find the looming tower and figure the direction of winding passages to reach the elusive edifice. Twice, Theo looked out a window and realized he had wandered in a curving hall and taken a wrong turn leading him away from the tower. Too often he grumbled for not being able to see the compass dangling from the strap of his backpack. Too loudly he stomped his foot when he found he had gone a wrong direction. Too impatiently he wanted to reach his world of the future.

After a fifth time of taking a wrong turn, Theo glanced out the window to see neither full moon nor looming tower. He noticed Murphy had returned to a hallway they had passed in the darkness. The small dog stood with his back toward Theo and slowly wagged his upright tail like a metronome keeping beat. The blue light on his collar dimmed in the nearly hidden hall. Theo knitted his brow and followed Murphy, who was already padding down the darker passage. "Man, I didn't see this hall at all! Hey, Murph! Wait for me!"

The hall offered no windows. Theo felt his breathing heavy and tightening in his chest. "Hey, Murph! How about we slow down a little, huh?" In truth, both boy and dog were slowing in pace, but the heavy atmosphere and his increased pulse gave Theo the impression that they were hurrying into the dark.

Suddenly, the light on Murphy's collar raised in the darkness. Theo looked down and noticed Murphy's front feet were standing on a stone step. Theo caught up to the trailblazer pup and looked up the stone staircase. The shadows of darkness gave the perception that the steps were twisting upward.

"Wow. This is cool, Murph! I can almost see swashbucklers standing and swinging their swords as they fight on these stairs!" Imaginary shadows that came straight out of a novel of long ago replaced the smothering darkness.

"Well, up we go!" Theo stepped past Murphy and lead the trek up uneven stone steps that spun from a solid post on the right side of the stairs. Panting and lifting up his hands, he stopped on a stone landing where a wooden ceiling covered with bolts and metal plates hung above the top step. A grin broke across his face as he stood and pressed upward, feeling the heavy ceiling lift.

Huh! A half year ago, I would have been prying this door open or been waiting for Gracie to come rescue me. Maybe I've built a little more muscle while running from the bad guys of Germany.

The moon bolted into the opening, causing Theo to squint as he looked up into the heavily lit night sky periodically agitated by clouds. Theo pressed the door in the ceiling until he could spin it enough to create an opening large enough to move through. He stood his full height, allowing his upper body to feel the night air. It took several hits of a small robotic dog against Theo's shin to realize Murphy was on the step below, wanting to be lifted. "All right, all right, here you go."

Theo bent down and lifted Murphy through the opening, setting him on the rooftop. He laughed as he watched the blue light on Murphy's collar run and stop, then run in another direction and stop, turn and run and stop—over and over. "Guess it feels pretty good to exercise in this good night air, huh, little buddy?" Theo tossed his backpack out to the rooftop and used the strength of his arms to lift his lower torso and legs through the opening, where he sat absorbing the freshness of life that the moon offered.

"Now, where is my other new invention—the radio?" Theo smiled at his modern-invention joke as he rummaged to the bottom of a second compartment of his backpack. Murphy ran and jumped a few twirls in the air. "At least you're taking in oxygen to clear the channels of your processors, huh, buddy." Murphy stopped briefly but continued to pump his legs in his jumping recharge motion when he saw that his master wasn't paying attention.

"Ah, here it is. I guess a few wires need reattached since I haven't looked at it for a couple of days. IRIS always harped that I am too careless with my technology. I wonder if she had any idea that I'd be stuck in the past without any way to hear her robotic lectures." Theo tried to make himself grin, but the reality of living in a world without technology for work and games and even everyday activity was starting to wear on him. He dropped his shoulders with a heavy sigh and leaned against the wall of the roof.

Theo looked down at his hands and turned over the handcrafted radio a few times. Two of the wires had come loose from their connectors, and one of the foil liners from the wrapper of a nutrition bar was missing from where it had been squeezed and flattened to connect the wires with a paper clip. "Zikes, how do these people live?"

Murphy was standing on his hind legs with his front feet propped against the tin flashing rain gutter on a short wall that bordered the roof. "Whatcha lookin' at, Murph?" Theo crossed the tower's roof to lean against the wall with his robotic friend. "Sure looks pretty out there, doesn't it?"

Again, Theo looked down at the radio in his hands. "Talk to me, IRIS. Don't leave me here. If I were at home, I'd be just a kid playing games and being lazy." The breeze touched his face with a clash of warmth and cold. "If I were a bird, I'd fly this coop and glide from the top of this tower down across that valley." Theo rested his chin on his hands crossed on the wall. "With my luck, I'd get caught in the branches and flip over into the river down there." As if to add his two cents, Murphy tipped back his head and gave a soft howl to the moon as it watched the two time travelers stuck in a culture unfamiliar, a world that had been left behind.

Murphy ended his howl by nudging his nose under Theo's arm. "Well, we've got each other." Theo gave a good scratch to the furry head lying next to his chin. "So whaddya say we find something to do? What can we do that's fun? Fly?" Theo laughed again at his own joke and rubbed the soft fur under Murphy's collar, causing the dog to point his nose into the air to stretch out his neck and enjoy the massage. As if touch was controlling his thoughts, Theo's fingers moved from Murphy's neck to the tin flashing.

"Aha!" Theo ran his hand along the tin flashing. "Lightweight, bendable, strong enough to carry some weight—yep. Okay, Mr. Moon, you can't tell Peter that I'm taking a piece of his roof for my new plane!" Forgetting it was the middle of the night, Theo began digging through his pack for anything he could use as a tool as he popped rivets holding the flashing to the roof.

"Hey, Murphy. We can do it. Let's build a bird. I mean, really, what would we do if we were back home?" Murphy cocked his head, confused by Theo's need to talk. "We'd be playing with technology, right? And how would we get something to entertain us? We'd build it! C'mon, Murphy, let's get these treasures back to the room!"

Confused and disappointed that the rooftop excursion had ended, Murphy waited for the bedroom door to be pushed open before he took a flying leap onto the bed and turned three quick circles before he collapsed onto the feather comforter with his muzzle resting across his tail and hindquarters.

Ignoring Murphy's body language of disappointment and boredom, Theo set his pack down beside his dog. "Okay. You rest, but I'm going to build a drone. Well, I doubt if I can find motors or balanced propellers or circuit board or speed control and flight controllers." His chest constricted and pushed the air out in a huff. "But I'm gonna build something. You'll see." The excitement in Theo's voice didn't transfer to Murphy.

VIGILATUS

"Thank you for the gifts, Baron Eltz. Why, yes, I think I will help myself to a little fun." Theo dug in his backpack for his all-purpose tool. By the end of the next hour, the archaic vacuum and the light bulb that had been secured in a ceramic plate on the ceiling had been taken apart. Motor, cords, tungsten coil filament from the bulb, motor blades, tin roof flashing, even the aluminum beater bar from the vacuum had been reassembled and held in place with the pull chain from the light fixture, cord from the drapery, and wire from a lamp cord.

"There." Theo held a hollow aluminum tube with propeller-like motor blades and wings cut from flashing and a bedside book cover. "So it's not the best-looking plane in the world, but maybe we can help this baby fly."

The plane was rough and looked more like scraps for the trash than a flying toy, but the mental exercise of creating something gave Theo a good feeling.

A snoring muzzle suddenly started to wiggle as all four of Murphy's legs began pawing the air as if he were running while stretched out sleeping on his back.

"Hey, Murphy . . . Murph! Wake up! You chasing rabbits in your sleep? You're making my nightlight shake, and I'm just about done. I'm about ready to attach my radio to give it some power. It was falling apart as a transmitter, anyway." Theo tilted his head and examined his work. "I need some way to communicate with the drone if we're going to fly it."

The fact that Theo was talking aloud was lost in importance as Murphy stilled back into his snoring sleep. Theo glanced at Murphy. "Fine. Chase your rabbits and then torture them with your snores. I don't need your help anyway. I just need your collar for a little light to see . . . Wait a minute! Murphy, you're a genius! Your collar! That's the trick! This will be just like programming a computer!" A renewed energy surged through Theo's body as he began rebuilding the radio transmitter into a device to communicate through the computer chip in Murphy's collar.

The moon had left his place of watching Theo work and had moved across the sky by the time a weary young man sat back against the bed, satisfied with his new creation.

"It's too dark, and I'm too tired to try this now, Murphy. Tomorrow we'll see if the drone can be controlled by your collar. This is great, but I'm ready to pack it in." Theo carefully secured the drone to his backpack with the straps that had held his driftboard when he lived in a different century, in a different land. "Let's call it a night." Theo stretched both arms and legs, not even aware of how much he had physically grown in the year since he had time traveled to Nazi Germany.

Suspicions of Heart

THE BED FRAME became Theo's backrest as he leaned back and looked at the makeshift drone suspended on the backpack. "Sure makes me miss where we lived, Murphy." In empathetic reaction, the beagle jumped down from the bed and crawled on his stomach with his legs splayed behind him until he could prop his jaw on Theo's leg.

Just as Theo turned his head down toward Murphy, a flashing image caught somewhere on the path between his brain and his vision. Theo sat up and glanced over his shoulder. Nothing. He saw nothing but the blanketed bed. "Weird. Sorry, Murphy," he apologized as his quick jerk had rolled his leg out from under the dog's resting muzzle. "Maybe this old castle just makes me jumpy." Theo softly but deliberately petted Murphy's back.

Again, he saw an image flash. This time, it was on Murphy's back. He froze, denying any movement. Something about the image was disconcerting, but strangely, he couldn't identify or clearly see the image. He closed his eyes, trying to force the image to appear again, but even the darkness behind his eyelids projected nothing. He opened his eyes and resumed petting Murphy.

At first, his mind didn't confess that he was seeing the image again until Theo noticed Murphy's fur seemed to change. His hand stopped halfway through a stroke down Murphy's back, but only seconds passed before Theo continued his slow petting motion, determined to see the illusive vision. *Don't lose the image. Don't lose the image.* His mind chanted with each beat of his heart as he willed his mind's eye. Then as if caught in a state between wakefulness and sleep, Theo watched as one of Murphy's spots on his back seemed to peel off, leaving only white fur beneath. Slowly, Theo blinked as he moved his hand along Murphy's fur. He saw his fingers touch the light-brown spot. Again, the spot curled and peeled away from the dog's body. Theo lifted Murphy to his lap, hugging both arms around the dog as if to hold in place the beagle's spots.

A breath caught in Theo's throat as the brown spot changed until it was no longer an irregular shape of a spot but rather the shape and appearance of Gracie's face. In the mixture of moonlight seeping through the drawn curtains at the window and the light of the bedside lamp, the image of Gracie's face began to peel away from Murphy's soft fur.

"No! No!" Theo opened his arms, dropping Murphy down from his lap. "No! I don't know what I'm seeing, but stop!" Theo jumped to his feet and screamed to the air.

Murphy cocked his head and looked up at his agitated master. He didn't know what took hold of Theo, but he let out a whimper.

Theo looked down, fearing the vision would come again. He patted Murphy's head to reassure the dog he had done nothing wrong. "I just . . . I can't think right now, Murphy. I just . . . I just need some sleep."

Theo didn't even undress as he collapsed onto the bed and tugged the covers around his body. As much as he wanted to block out what he saw, he knew the disturbing vision could be a precognition. He never asked to have the visions. Sometimes they came true in future events that passed nearly without notice. Too often, however, they were omens of dreaded darkness.

I have to see her. Theo knew he couldn't sleep with the unsettled image of Gracie's face. *I won't wake her, but I have to see her.* With his mind made up, Theo slung on his pack and crossed to where the hall opened into her room.

The round glass doorknob was cool in the palm of Theo's hand, sending a shiver through his body. *Okay. Get a grip or you'll wake her.* Theo scolded the fear crawling beneath his skin. *I'll just quietly walk to the bed, see that she's fine, and leave. I can tell her about it tomorrow morning and let her call me a silly boy.* Under the twist of his hand, the doorknob clicked as Theo held his thoughts and his breath and entered the room.

The lace curtains undulated in the soft wind that swirled through the window that was opened just enough to let a line of moonbeams dance in with the drifting air. *Oh, so, Mr. Moon, you beat me here. What, are you jealous that I have Gracie and you don't?* The faint smell of Gracie's powder wafted on the breeze and lightened Theo's thoughts as he tiptoed toward the plump feather bed. *If she wakes up, she'll probably tackle me and punch . . .* Theo's thoughts broke off abruptly as he looked over the undisturbed covers on her bed.

"Where's . . . Gracie?" At first, Theo's reaction poured out in whispers, but as he ran his hand over the quilted cover, the realization that she had not slept in the bed grabbed at his voice, making it spring to the surface as if gulping for fresh air. "Gracie? Gracie, where are you?" He moved with agility in search of the caramel-skinned girl.

Where? Think! I gotta find . . . Gracie, where are you? Theo's mind raced with unanswered thoughts. He returned to the hall and glared into the dark passage as if an answer would be illuminated on the wall. His eyes dropped to the crack between door and threshold at the closest room begging a light to show, but opening his door, he knew the darkness within had only been disturbed by him and Murphy since they returned from the tower.

Theo leaned against the doorframe and ran a hand through his hair; his tired eyes searched each darkened door along the corridor. "Herr Möeller . . . of course." Theo sprinted to the door that had welcomed their guardian just days before. He knew a knock on the door was unnecessary as Herr Möeller had left before they even arrived. He hoped to find a sleeping Gracie, who was determined to be back with her guardian, even if it meant to linger in a presence held only by some spirit world left behind.

The knob turned, allowing the door to sigh across the woolen carpet in the quiet night. This side of the hall was hidden from the light from the presumptuous and prying moon, but Theo's eyes adjusted to searching in the black velvet night. With a step inside the door, Theo grabbed his T-shirt hanging between the front straps on his pack as if to prevent his heart from escaping. Even in the darkness, the room screamed of disarray. Any sign of life was gone and had been strewn across both floor and furniture. The upset of the room was more than Theo's heart or head could understand.

Answers. I need answers! Theo lunged back through the open door and stood in the middle of the hall, letting his pounding heart surge with the anger he felt. *Who will talk? Somebody knows, and somebody . . .* In anger, not caring who heard him, Theo began pounding his fists against walls and doors.

"Talk to me!" Theo's screams echoed back in the chilling quiet of the hall. Ahead of him, he saw light from a room roll into the hallway as a door creaked open. Theo stopped in his tracks, fearful—not of what would happen, but of not hearing the truth. He stared into the darkness as a flowing gown billowed into the hall on the waves of moonbeams. The beautiful woman who lived in the castle with her brother stood staring at Theo.

"What do you know?" Theo didn't care how gruff his voice sounded. "Elise, what do you know?"

Whether the cool air in the hall caused her gown to shimmer or whether her frail body shook from the aggressive voice, Theo perceived a shiver shake her tiny frame. "I'm sorry. I don't mean to frighten you, but I need to know. Where's Gracie? Where's Herr Möeller?" He patted his leg to command Murphy to stay by his side. He needed the German language to be translated by Murphy's collar. He needed answers. He took steps toward the lady of the castle as he spoke.

"I . . ." Elise shook her head as she spoke. "I don't know. I truly don't know."

Theo stood looking down at the petite woman. "Maybe not, but you know more than I do, and you're going to tell me."

Elise shook her head. Confusion and panic mixed in her expression. "No, I don't—"

Theo grabbed and held both of Elise's shoulders as he gave a slight shake. "Yes, you do know something, and I need to know!" His breath was warm against her face in the chilled hall. "Now, where's Gracie?"

A tear streamed down Elise's soft cheek. "No . . ." She shook her head and hesitated. "Come in. I'll tell what I have overheard."

Before the quarter hour had struck on the clock in Peter's study, the frail mistress of the castle lay in a heap on her bed. Tears poured from her eyes as her heart feared for her brother, who stood against the evil power of the Reich, and hurt for the man viciously kidnapped from her home and whom she secretly loved.

Theo followed Elise's direction to the kitchen, where he removed a key from a set of hooks beside a door. Once outside, a motorcycle balanced on a kickstand at the end of a rocky path, reflecting a ray of moonlight that pointed as if it knew the young American needed direction. Theo's jog toward the motorcycle slowed as he approached. He knelt beside Murphy and typed a word into his watch screen. Within seconds, Murphy's collar lit up in staccato flashes.

"Now, little buddy, let's mix some twenty-first-century technology into our new world of the past." Turning the drone over in his hands, Theo connected wires between drone and radio transmitter. The propellers began a soft buzz while he spoke to the robotic dog sitting patiently, wagging an arc into the dust on the stone pavement. The flashing lights on Murphy's collar settled into a pattern. "So far, so good." He held one hand on the drone and one hand on his dog. "Here's the plan, my little friend."

Theo looked between Murphy and his wrist as he made last-minute connections. "I need to you find this place that I've typed into your computer system. It's called Hadamar. I know you can find it. Problem is, I'll be on this ancient transport machine, and I'm afraid I'll lose sight of you when you run in and out of the shadows." He held up a finger as if he had made a discovery. "But never fear, my little guide! I can still follow you—in a way, that is. The drone is programmed to follow your collar. I've attached a small light, so I can see the drone even though the sound of the motorcycle engine will probably keep me from hearing its buzz. So I'll follow the drone." He scratched Murphy's head between his floppy ears. "Whaddaya think?

Ingenious? Maybe for the twentieth century. For now, we better get going. I'll command you through the voice transmitter. According to Elise, we have a ways to go." He gave a final pat to Murphy's back as he stood and walked to the waiting motorcycle.

"Okay, little dinosaur. I'm not sure what you're about, but if you balance anything like my old driftboard, we'll both be able to make some progress." Grabbing the handlebars, Theo hoisted one leg over the machine until he sat comfortably on the seat. *Not too bad.* Theo raised his eyebrows. *This may not be too hard.*

He twisted the key in the ignition and quickly released it, surprised by the loudness of the engine turning over. "Zikes, wake the neighborhood!" He shook a little to adjust the pack on his back. "Okay, Murphy. We'll need to take off as soon as the machine starts his roar." Again, Theo turned the key, this time prepared to hear the loud motor. Pressing up with one leg, he kicked the stand balancing the motorcycle. His eyes searched the handlebars. "How the heck does this thing move forward?" Theo ran both hands along the bars that stretched out from the core of the bike. He pushed and twisted every button he could find. The motorcycle sat motionless, roaring into the quiet night.

"C'mon!" In exasperation, he leaned his locked arms against the handlebars. The end of one handle turned under his pressing palm, and the motorcycle jumped forward, causing Theo to lean backward and the bike to tilt toward the ground. "Whoa!" He stared at the end of the handlebar that turned under pressure. "Okay. I get your game." Slowly, he pressed his right hand in a turning motion, and the bike under him spun in the rocks, rolling forward, this time with balance that Theo would have used on his driftboard.

"I got it, Murphy! We're moving! Woohoo! We're off to find Gracie! I'll see you on the flip side! You're my navigator, Murphy. Lead the way. The drone will follow you, and I'll see and follow the drone!" Theo pointed forward, while his little companion from another century turned and headed down the road. As if tied by a string instead of by radio technology, the makeshift drone lifted and flew with its own set of flashing lights that became a beacon in the night.

Though sometimes wobbly and too often roaring in a wrong gear until Theo found his feet could control the gear changes, the road offered a chance to find at least one of his missing friends, if not even more. Only the silent stars sitting atop moonbeams watched two centuries converge as a dog bolted into a run while connected to both a drone and his master by a flashing collar. With motorcycle pursuit, a young man headed for someplace he had only been told, someplace he had never been, and someplace he would never forget—Hadamar.

By morning, Elise had dried her tears and stepped boldly to breakfast. At first, she was frightened of her brother's scolding reprimand for not waking him in the night, but her words were met with too many questions. Fritz and TAR reacted without finishing their meal.

"It's a tough vorld ve live in Elise. The burden ist not to be yours." Fritz glanced at his host. "Peter, vhy didn't you tell me vhere you suspicioned tey took Jahile—a prison for Jews?"

Fritz whirled around to follow his friend, who was already headed up to the rooms where they had slept and left their belongings. "TAR, ve must hurry. I've only heard about nightmares of Hadamar, but I've seen maps, and I tink I know how to get tere."

The dining room was left quiet except for the weeping that came again from the frail sister being held in the arms of her brother, baron of the castle and friend to *the Watch*.

Darkness

Begging, nearly to the point of fit throwing, Hezekiah and Zuza finally convinced Loiza to let them go with him as he led Gracie to a place where he both faced and fought his fears. As brave as his birth name (meaning *famous warrior*), Loiza rarely backed away from the devil himself, but he knew that with no Aryan resemblance, a man would write his own death warrant by walking into this devil's lair. Nonetheless, the *Mischling* who fisted her hands and stood demanding direction personified the heart of the gypsy camp threatened with annihilation by the Third Reich. Loiza knew she would delve into the forest on her quixotic quest with or without direction. Truly, it was a fatal journey, but he felt he could at least give the young martyr a safe head start and a hope of survival. So it was that Loiza stepped up to Mama Vertina and volunteered to guide the half-breed to where her abducted guardian had been taken. "In morning, Mama Vertina, I will lead her. In mourning, Mama Vertina, I will return."

Without waiting for daylight, four shadows left the warmth of campfire and Romani camp to journey through a forest of shelter. Never would they have approached Hadamar had it not been for the demands of a determined stranger on a quest to find family. For over an hour, their journey passed through the heavy forest. Beginning a new journey with new friends at first lifted Gracie's spirits. She smiled to think how they joked and laughed with one another. With no one to notice in the dark forest, Gracie rolled her eyes in thought. *At least Zuza and Hezekiah have laughed with me. Loiza acts like a standoffish old man. He hasn't even talked just to me since I woke up by the campfire.* As if to hold conversation with her thoughts, Gracie shook her head. *I don't know what Mama Vertina slipped into that warm broth to make me sleep so deeply. Whew. But I have to admit that this walking is helping me shake off the grogginess. You better watch out, world! Here I come, and I'm feeling stronger than ever!*

The travelers' footsteps fell silently as their feet sank into the cold, damp earth. A storm from the previous night had done its best to upset the forest; branches had been ripped from the trunks and laid strewn about the ground below. They passed massive trees that had been uprooted or torn in half by fierce wind and dangerous lightning strikes. An uneasiness stirred the back of Gracie's mind with the anticipation of running into someone—or something—in the deep forest.

Loiza stopped midstride and threw his fist into the air, signaling to the three behind him to stop and make no movement. Gracie rested her weight on the hand that was firmly gripping a large sapling that had survived the treacherous storm. From the past two years, she had experience in keeping still as danger passed during the late nights she had spent running and hiding from thugs and drunks wandering the streets of Munich. This was different somehow. She was at home in the streets, brick and mortar being her jungle. Here, in the matted woods, the shadows and animals moved in ways that she hadn't been able to grasp. For the first time since they stepped off the dirt road leading away from the camp and plunged headlong into the portentous and thick forest, her heart began to labor under a veil of nervousness.

Gracie watched intently as Loiza pulled his fist from the air and pushed a flat palm toward the damp forest floor, signaling the group to hunker down behind anything that would hide them from an unseen enemy. She glanced over her shoulder just as Hezekiah, who had been acting as the rear guard, shrugged and disappeared behind a large tree trunk. A shiver ran down her spine. Hoping to become invisible, she slipped into a small group of pine tree saplings. Gracie quietly lowered herself down until she felt the cold earth soak into her bones. She took a long, deep breath, exhaling slowly, begging her anxiety to exit with the warm air from her lungs.

She scanned the forest in front of her, trying to locate Zuza. The gypsy girl was a few years younger, but she moved skillfully through the woods. Finally, Gracie spied Zuza where she had burrowed herself into the side of a tree stump that had fallen a long time ago.

Gracie sniffed the cold air and winced as a familiar, potent smell stung her nostrils. Her mind went immediately to a dark place: the smell recalled a terrifying memory she didn't want to relive. The forest disappeared as she witnessed Theo pulled back into the underground tunnel between the opera house and the Kaiserdom. In a vivid memory that passed through her mind, she again saw a warped hand reach out from the abyss of an underground tunnel and grab Theo's ankle to pull him back into the darkness.

She shook the nightmare vision from her thoughts. *No. No. This is a different smell. No way that devil creature survived the cave in.* She commanded her thoughts to bolster her. Nina and Fritz had pulled Theo to safety and collapsed the tunnel with a large explosion that would have stopped any man in his tracks. Then again, she wasn't worried about any man. The creature was worse, much worse.

In a whirlwind of panic, Gracie's eyes jumped from one tree to the next as her imagination and fear began to win the battle in her soul, creating trouble in places it did not exist. Her eyes came to the stump where Zuza had hidden. The air sucked from her lungs when she realized the younger girl was gone. Gracie frantically scanned the forest, looking for signs of the tiny girl. Not wanting to make any noise, she twisted herself around as much as possible without moving her feet. She wanted to cry out for Zuza and Hezekiah. She focused on the tree trunk where she had seen Hezekiah duck for cover. She waited, willing her eyes to see even the slightest movement. Time stopped along with her breathing, as the longer she stared into dark stillness, the more fear gripped her heart with icy, smelly tendrils.

Where are they? Did they abandon me? They promised. They promised to take me to Herr Möeller. They promised! Gracie's pulse pounded against her temples, pounded against thoughts that swirled in her mind.

A snap of a twig pulled her eyes while an inhale prepared to let out a scream, but a dirty hand clamped over her mouth before the noise could escape.

"Mulani," Loiza breathed a barely audible whisper.

Gracie shook her head from side to side, not comprehending the word.

"Mul—" Loiza stopped and closed his eyes for a moment, searching for the translation. "Ghost."

Gracie understood that word perfectly, and her earlier fear was confirmed. He might not call it a jaeger, but it was. She preferred a ghost, remembering the devastation these beasts could inflict.

"We won't make it if we stick together," Loiza explained, worry heavy in his voice. "The other two have obeyed my command to retreat." He put a hand on her shoulder as he looked directly into her eyes. "I will allow you to leave if you still insist on a dark destiny." He dropped his hand from her shoulder to point behind where they stood. "I'll wait farther back in the woods and come for you if you change your mind."

"Yes," she answered firmly, deliberately turning to face the edge of the forest that lay ahead. She did not allow his words to weaken her heart.

Loiza's frustration at Gracie's stubbornness came out in a heavy sigh. "Child, please come back with me."

Gracie shook her head and kept her eyes on the woods in front of them.

"As you wish." Loiza's eyes and voice dropped. He knew her upbringing had woven determination into her blood. Loiza motioned up into the sky with his eyes. "Head for the smoke."

Gracie followed his gaze and, for the first time, saw smoke wafting upward through daylight, breaking above the forest. "How will I know when to—"

Before Gracie could finish her question, Loiza sprang up and let out a ferocious war cry that echoed through the forest, waking animals that had been bedded down since the storm. The once-quiet forest woke with a flourish of noise. Gracie sat stunned for a moment then bounded up and began to weave through the trees, looking up every few steps to make sure she was following the smoke. She ducked low-hanging branches, vaulted over fallen trees, and lost her footing a few times but managed to keep stumbling forward at the breakneck pace she was forcing out of her body despite her brain's protest.

She never looked back, even when another terrifying shriek cut through the air—more disconcerting was that it was answered with another of Loiza's battle cries. She wouldn't waste this gift of the distraction he made. With heart pounding, she weaved away from one evil in the forest and ran blindly into another, ready to pounce on its unsuspecting prey.

Again, Gracie found herself heading into the unknown by leaving warm hearts behind. Again, Gracie felt determination to right the wrongs of the world. Again, Gracie's eyes and heart promised to search for someone she loved though the quest was laced with danger and no promise of finding her guardian. Gracie turned from the world that held Hezekiah and Zuza and Loiza. She squatted at the edge of the lush lawn that surrounded a looming stone building with the name *Hadamar* etched in stone over the double doors.

Once a place where Germany had tucked away victims of mental disability, a place reserved for the mentally insane, real or assumed, Hadamar itself had been stifled with change brought on by the German Reich. The fine line between handicap and health became a justification of government to allow unstable minds to be the materials deemed "subhuman" and suitable for exploration of science.

The stone walls of Hadamar stood as a two-story asylum holding secrets of the demon-possessed minds of scientists and doctors who performed experiments in the lower region. Signs posted along the road to Hadamar warned travelers of an epidemic, ensuring that no one approached unless it was someone involved with the T4 euthanasia program or an innocent victim believing he would be healed. Sick rooms used for the mentally insane of earlier days of Hadamar were converted into quarters for the staff.

No one, however, could disguise the stench and horror of the basement of the facility, for it sat in the depths of the earth as a chamber of an abyss too dark and too horrible to be conceived from any mind capable of human compassion. A shower room converted into a gas chamber stood starkly beside yellow tiled rooms with drains in the yellow tiled floors that carried away fluids that both held and sucked life from the emaciated bodies lying cradled in cement beds. Even the lights suspended above the cement beds emitted a yellow glow—not a yellow of sunshine but a yellow of bile and pus—unwholesome, contagious, repulsive.

Gracie shivered as she looked up at the stone building. The fragile rays of daybreak were denied as the stones sucked the light from the sky. With a glance back over her shoulder, she gave a nod. She hoped Loiza and the kids returned safely back to the camp. She couldn't handle the guilt if something bad happened to them.

This place gives me the creeps. Maybe we should've come in bold light of day. I'm such a silly girl to let darkness play with my imagination. She tried to convince herself that the building was void of meaning, but the touch of her hand upon the cold stones warned her to withdraw and run from terrors that even made the air of dawn shudder in cold waves.

I can do this. Good riddance to the forest. Her thought propelled her. Time on the streets of Munich had trained Gracie to move in stealth under windows exposing secrets of the inside. Inching along the cold stones of the fortress, her tiny footsteps called no attention to the muted movement and snaps of mulch beneath her feet. Periodically, she hesitated under a window, straining her ears to hear a sound, a hint of life, a word that would expose the location of her guardian. *Herr Möeller, I'm coming for you. Let me hear your sigh. Laugh for me. Tell me you're okay in there. Please, Herr Möeller, please.* Relentlessly, she crept around the building.

Gracie's shoulders dropped as she rounded the fourth corner, knowing she had circled the building and returned to the side where steps and a porch led to the double-door entry. She slid down the side of the building and sat in the damp mulch. Dropping her head onto her arms propped on her knees, Gracie wavered between wanting to sleep and trying to think of a plan for finding Herr Möeller. With her head lying on her arms, she watched the gentle sway of her long curls cascading toward the ground. Unintentionally, she began humming a soft lullaby that her mama had sung many nights as they lay in the quiet darkness of a place they called home.

> *Sleep, little babe, in the arms of the night.*
> *Sleep as the angels hold you so tight.*
> *Dream of parents who hold you in their heart.*
> *Dream of the love that will never depart.*

As she softly hummed the tune and let her lips whisper the words, she swayed back and forth, watching her dangling curls lilt with the tune.

Over and over, she hummed the tune, accepting the time of quiet rest. Under her arm as she watched the gentle swing of a lock of hair, a light popped into the darkness.

"Uh!" Gracie sat up straight against the wall and held her breath. In her search for a window above her head, she didn't notice the barred rectangular windows below, not even as high above the ground as her knees. "A light."

Gracie pressed her head against the building and tipped it enough to see a window where the light escaped and split the darkness. In a quiet unfolding, Gracie moved from her sitting position to lying with her stomach against the cold ground. She kept her body close to the building, allowing only her eyes to pull her face close enough to see into a corner of the lit room. *Underground.* Gracie mouthed the words to herself but did not let even a breath of sound come from her lips.

Darkness.

The light that offered a glimpse of the lower region recoiled into the darkness, giving Gracie no visual of what lay inside. *So there's a level below ground! Maybe the only people awake are in the underground rooms. Ah! Herr Möeller, did you send me a thought? I bet I can move around on the first floor and try to find you in the darkness if the people who are awake are downstairs!* If the eyes of predawn could have seen the small teenager sitting in the bleak and empty flower bed, they would have seen a smile break across the delicate face, hidden between hands clasped as if celebrating a discovery.

Gracie stood and brushed away the dirt hanging from her clothing. She began to move then froze midstride and knitted her brow. *No. Not the front door. I must keep my head and think wisely. I must make Herr Möeller proud of me.* Gracie scanned the asylum wall. *There it is.* In her earlier trek around the building, she stopped for a lengthy time under an open window where no sound had come from inside. She thought the window was to be avoided, but now she welcomed the open mouth of the window as entrance into the quiet ward.

The rough stone wall of Hadamar was enough to give toeholds to Gracie as she climbed for the window. Her hand felt the smooth surface inside of the sill after she worked the toe of her heavy boot into a crack so she could hoist herself up into the open window. She braced both elbows on the stone sill and started to wiggle her way to the brim of the opening when an agitated reflection on the windowpane caught her eye. She turned her head just in time to see a giant of a man come storming from the treeline, straight for her. She doubled her efforts to crawl through the window and into the room. She pulled her upper torso onto the ledge and pushed off with her foot. The weight shift caused her foot to slip, and she fell back toward the ground, catching only the edge of the windowsill with one hand. Unable to hold her weight, each finger lost its grip, forsaking her to tumble down the stone wall.

Though she hit the earth with both feet, the momentum dropped her down to the ground. Like a frightened animal, she rolled and bounded onto her feet, facing the oncoming threat with just enough time to duck the gigantic arms that swung out for her. She dipped down to sprint for the woods, getting only three strides into her run before she was hit from behind, harder than she thought was humanly bearable. The blow tumbled her facefirst into the ground with such force that her body bounced, and her face smashed into the unforgiving earth. Scrambling onto her hands and knees, she shook the blur from her eyes, spit grass and dirt out of her mouth, and began a crawl for survival. Determined, she stood to run, but another massive blow sent her sprawling out of control back down onto the hard terrain. Her head slammed into a rock, prompting a gush of blood to spray against the earth. Heaving, she rolled to her back and instinctively kicked both feet out toward the blur of a mountain reaching down for her. Unimpeded blood flow flooded her eyes from the trauma to her head. *No! No!* She blindly and wildly kicked her legs, trying to fend off her attacker.

No! You can't . . . Like a blinded animal in a trap, Gracie instinctively fought to survive. She felt a few kicks connect with the man towering over her. As he reached to grab her ankles, she pulled back hard then exploded out with both legs into his chest. He didn't budge from the blow as she slid away from him. He grunted angrily and knocked away her second attempt like he was swatting an annoying fly. The force of his hand spun her halfway around. She flung her arms and tried to roll over to her stomach to spring up and escape, but his foot planted into her stomach and rolled her, thudding to her back.

"Bad girl," the brute of a man growled and slapped across her face. He bent over the unconscious girl, bracing his hands on his knees to catch his breath. The pretty girl's breathing slowed. His rough visage softened as he tilted his head to look at the tiny figure on the ground. The moonlight lay against her caramel skin, giving the barbaric man a glimpse of an angel from a realm far from his own. Without permission, he ran the back of his huge hand over her soft skin and smiled, letting his thoughts beat with the slowing of his breaths. *So pretty.* He squatted, enveloped in darkness, admiring his captive.

"Where's your mother, little *Fräulein*? You're not like my usual fare of hikers and people who get lost in the canopy of these woods. No, you're much too pretty and young." A half grin that broke from a demon's countenance widened across his teeth. "I'll take good care of you." His words dangled between realms of soft reasoning and sinister repulsion.

Bondage

Where? Loiza? The tiny frame ached and tried to move. *Loiza? Arms. I can't move my . . . Where am I?* Gracie's mind told her to call out, but her face ached as she parted her lips without sound.

Gracie tried to open her eyes, unable to move her pounding head. Her left eye showed nothing but blackness. A bloody gash from falling against a rock widened when the fist of her attacker bashed against her face. Blood dried, welding shut one eyelid. Gracie willed her confused mind to make sense of being unable to move. She rolled her arms only in slight movement against rough leather straps. In the blur, she squinted through one eye. Her wrists were tethered by something bulky. She pulled against the bondage, but even slight movement lit fireworks of pain.

My legs are strong. He can't keep me! She rejected the truth. Both legs were bound to something hard, something unyielding to her body, something cold.

Dim and naked, a bulb hung from a cord, barely exposing the mold-covered walls and filth that had accumulated on the partially stone, partially dirt floors. The yellow light penetrated her eyelids and left in her mind's eye a man standing in front her. She could still feel his hot, stinking breath on her face. She willed herself to slow her racing heart. *He beat me. What does he want? What's he going to do?* Another breath was pulled out of the stale yellow air. Gracie tried to calm the pounding in her brain. A pain pulsing behind her eyes made focusing her thoughts nearly impossible. *I'm alone. No one is coming. No one knows where I am. I don't even know! Please, please, dear God. I need someone. Tell Herr Möeller I need him.*

A tear trickled and pushed against the clotted blood until it was able to roll from her eye socket and drop to the concrete bed. Gracie knew no one was coming this time. She had put her gypsy friends in enough danger already. A lump of guilt was building in her chest. Maybe she should have listened to Mama Vertina and Loiza; they had pleaded with her not to come.

She willed her mental toughness not to scream from terror and anger. *No! No, don't start thinking like this. You'll figure a way out of this. Breathe. Breathe. Focus.*

The sound of a bolt clicking bounced off the walls of her tiny prison. Heavy air pressed against her ears as she heard two more bolts snap into place, sealing her in. Gracie winced at the finality of the sound. The dull thud of the locks sent a shock wave through her soul, threatening everything she struggled against. She refused to be a victim. Fear could not take her; she had come too far.

Stale air seeped thickly into her throat, leaving a cough where uninhibited oxygen should have passed. Gracie wrinkled her nose at a stench she pushed out through her nostrils. This was no time to admit the throbbing in her head; she lay paralyzed. Sitting or rolling was impossible; she lay fettered to a rocklike surface. Only her head could pull away and raise to allow her to take in her surroundings with one slightly opened eye. The putrid colored room was scarcely visible in front of her face. As she squeezed her sore eyes shut, her heart fell, and she laid her head back down to the hard bed. Again, she tried to move, but only her arms rolled where they were tied.

Gracie's fingers became sensors to touch and to understand the hard surface. She could only guess that the brute who knocked her unconscious had carried her there and strapped her to a cement slab. The back of her head found no comfort. She forced her arms to pull away from her body against the restraints wound around her wrists. Rough leather dug into her soft skin. She fought the feeling of bondage that warred against her natural instinct of free will.

Who wants me tied up? Her thoughts and the restraints kindled a fighting anger within her. Pain in her body from the man's assault drove her to her boiling point. Gracie squirmed and tugged against the restraints. She jerked her fists upward as hard as she could, feeling the coarse bindings cutting into her delicate skin. Warm blood trickled down her wrist, making thin streams along fingers until, at her fingertips, it balled up and, like thick raindrops, fell to splatter on the concrete.

Gracie tipped her head and cringed at the thought of bloody wrists. Determined, she would not give up. *If I can squeeze my hands through these stupid* . . . The leather strap bit deeper into the fighting flesh. The writhing smeared slick blood over her hand. She winced but gave a small gasp and pulled her bloody hand upward. Gritting her teeth, she twisted one wrist, feeling her skin tear but fighting to be free. She grimaced and bit down hard on her lip to keep the pain from exploding from her mouth.

Impatiently, she pumped her fist to encourage the blood. With each twist of momentum, she pulled harder against the strap until her hand stuck at its widest point. She squeezed her thumb to her pinky finger, continuing the painful jerks to pull her bloodied hand until it escaped the bondage of the leather strap. A small sound escaped from Gracie's throat. She leaned her head back against the concrete slab. She started to bring her hand up close to her face to examine the damage but stopped, fearful that the sight of her bloody hand would weaken her.

The blood-covered hand lifted and reached across her body to where the other hand was still firmly strapped into submission. Mechanically, Gracie fingered the strap to find a cold metal buckle. Frustration growled in her soul as her bloody fingers slipped on the metal surface while she fumbled with the clasp. Young fingers worked quickly, determined to do the work she visualized through limited eyesight until a metal tink came from the buckle hitting the concrete bed.

Thank you, Yahweh! Gracie pulled her hands to her body and sat upright with her legs still pinned to the table. She flexed her fingers against biting needles of pain. She bent to her ankles and worked with both hands to unbuckle the restraints. *He took my boots! I gotta find my boots!* Gracie swung her legs from the concrete slab and moved in the yellow dusk away from the center of the room. *Breathe. Take your time. Stay sharp.* Her mind had not forgotten her mission, but finding Herr Möeller had become challenged by her own survival.

Pressing her body against a wall, Gracie inched to a doorless opening, where she tilted her head just enough to peer into a connected room. A simple desk and chair sat against a wall. Just inside the opening sat a metal table that stood high on wheels. Gracie stepped into the room until she stood beside the high table. Curious, she lifted her hand to the metal table, not caring that she scraped her wrist against the edge and restarted drips of the coagulating blood.

What? She lifted one after another of the cold metal pieces that lay on the table to better see through her less swollen eye. *What? These look . . .* Gracie's hand shook as she tried to focus her mind on the surgical tools on the high table. She dropped the cold piece onto the tray of scalpels, clamps, forceps, and scissors.

She turned and stumbled to the desk, where both hands caught and stabilized her. A small mountain of dirty rags lay heaped on the desk; folded cloth hung across the back of the wooden chair. Her body and head hung over the desk. *Why would . . . ? What would he do with . . . ?* Rationalization wouldn't come. Without warning, a cramp in her stomach caused her to turn and fall to her knees beside the desk while she vomited on the floor.

An empty stomach had little to give, but the retching relieved a pressure building inside of her. Gracie cupped her hand around her hair to pull it back from her sweaty face. Her eye caught sight of the bloody wrist. *No . . .* She tipped back her head to let curls fall back from her face and resignation to fill her mind. *No! Not Li'l Grey!* Determination of heart lifted her from the floor. She scooped a folded towel from the back of the chair and ran back into the shadows of her holding cell.

Hidden in a dark corner, Gracie squatted and used the towel to wipe her eye. Crusted blood flaked into the towel. Pain from her touch jabbed back into her skull, triggering a soft cry. She paused. Again, dirty fingers tapped and scraped against the matted eye. Gracie knew her own tears could moisten the sealed eye. *C'mon. I gotta see to get outta here. C'mon!* Her thoughts prompted her fingers. The gentle scraping against the matter and dried blood continued until her fingers forced the eyelids apart. The swollen flesh denied much vision, but the matted blood no longer sealed her eye.

Vision in the wounded eye adjusted to the bulb hanging motionless over the concrete block where she had been fettered. She stood, pressing into the corner. "Oh." She couldn't stop the cry as her body screamed with pain. "Come on, Gracie." Sound barely escaped from her gritted teeth. "You've been in worse spots than this." She wrapped the thin towel around her lacerated wrist, tying it off with her free hand and the help of her teeth. "That'll hold." Through swollen eyes, she searched from the shadows. "Even the fires of hell have more light than this place. I gotta get outta here."

A solid door without a handle did not beckon Gracie to escape. Li'l Grey did not realize how tightly she clenched her fists while her swollen eyes glared angrily at three brass locks separating her from her freedom, holding her hostage against her will. She examined the keyholes of each one. She stepped back and exhaled heavily. "Great." A shudder crept down her spine as she forced her legs to return to the outer room. She paused before the instruments cluttering the tall metal table.

Gracie's head swam as it hung over the tools used for unimaginable evil. "Were these part of your plan, evil man?" She lifted a scalpel, which barely reflected light from the opening in the wall. "You can beat me, but you can't crush my spirit, you stinkin' . . ." A dull clang caught her breath when the scalpel dropped back down to the metal table. "Not gonna make this easy for you," she murmured. She stared at the door, horrified to think a door to escape could put her face-to-face with the monster again. The tender girl ran her fingers over the instruments of death, looking for just the right one. "My enemy, my friend." Gracie again lifted and turned the scalpel in her hand before she tucked it into the pocket of her coat. "Now for the lock." Blood-crusted fingers searched through narrow blades, hoping for something to slip into the lock mechanisms. She knew her life depended on how the next few moments unfolded. She had to get this right.

Click. The top lock snapped open, breaking the silence, but the silence didn't wait before being subdued by muffled shuffling noises.

Gracie stood motionless with the small tool hovering beside the second lock. The shuffling noises grew louder then stopped on the other side of the locked door from where Gracie stood.

Metal... scraping... Frozen with fear, Gracie's eyes dropped to the second lock where sound was seeping through from the outside. Instinctively, the pointed tool shifted into the palm of her other hand where she wrapped her fist around it, letting only the blade stick out. Calmer than her pounding heart suggested, she reached into her pocket and pulled out another scalpel. *C'mon, Li'l Grey. Take the challenge. Take the stinkin'...*

A jingling abruptly cut off with a clank, and a muffled voice interrupted her thoughts. Words were unintelligible through the thick door, but the voice was rough. *Keys... dropped... Gotta move.* Gracie's fists tightened as she bit a swollen lip. She looked down and watched her own shoeless feet as she carefully lifted and planted each foot in a backward motion until she stood away from the door. *Do I hide? Run? Gotta think.* The yellow light from the connected room exposed only shapes. Gracie's eyes crossed where the wooden desk chair cast a dark shadow.

Jingling keys returned to locks, snapping first the bottom then the middle. A double thud, combined with more mutters of someone questioning why the top lock had not been secured. The doorknob turned. Light from the hall rolled into the room. Compared to daylight, the light was dim, but in the dark underground, competing with the yellow bulb, the brightness forced Gracie to squint her sore eyes. A darkness moved into the center of the doorway, lessening the light. The monster had returned to claim his prize.

A large man stepped through the door. The distorted smile on his face was covered by the darkness. Nurse Irmgard praised him when he found and brought in the girl. He was eager to get the pretty girl prepped and ready for the procedures to start. The simple-minded brute loved watching Nurse Irmgard work. *This will be a wonderful surprise. Nurse Irmgard will be happy. Sometimes she lets me help—when she's not mad. Maybe today! Maybe today!*

Alvar knew in his constricted heart that he needed to make the head nurse happy. His own parents were never happy with him, and at a very young age, the uncontrollable child with an untrainable mind was brought to Hadamar. Once they brought what they called their monster child for treatment at Hadamar, they never looked back and never came back. The mountain of a man clenched his fist in anger, thinking about his parents and being raised in the prison walls of Hadamar. His wandering thoughts settled too long on his rejection, allowing his happy emotion to turn to anger.

Without stepping out of the funnel of light, the brute in white nursing garb entered the room. Alvar began to pound a fist into the open palm of his other hand. The tempest in his heart swirled as he writhed in small circles, tipping his head first to one side then the next. "Why did they leave me? I'm good. I'm good. I help Nurse Irmgard. I know. I know how to make her happy. Nurse Irmgard likes me. I'm good. I help her." A sadistic smile opened to a blackness of missing teeth between others crooked and yellow. "Alvar, not a monster," he slurred.

Alvar moved with his swinging head, walking deeper into the darkness of the room. He patted the desk with an open palm, beating a rhythm that matched his swaying back and forth. His large hand moved across the desk, fingering surgical tools, towels, and straps where they lay waiting for use. Half out of habit and half out of agitated soul, the brute began circling the desk.

"I get things ready for Nurse Irmgard. I make her happy. I get, uh, I get . . ." Again, the large head tipped to the side, confused by something out of order. "Where chair?"

"Here!" Gracie screamed and lunged from the shadows, aiming at her attacker's head.

The wooden chair crashed against the back of his head and neck just as Alvar's attempt at a quick turn threw him off-balance. His heavy body betrayed him, joining the momentum from the blow to smash his face into the desk with a dull thud. The legs of the chair shattered in the blow against his shoulders. Gracie stood holding what was left of the chair, hovering over the disoriented man. In reaction, she took a step backward and lowered the chair. Her eyes were riveted to the face lifting off the desk, the face of her attacker. Adrenaline mixed with fear gripped her heart.

Impulsively, the petite girl swung the chair in an arc from where she had lowered it to her side. It contacted the tottering brute, forcing his head back down to the wooden desk. Fueled by anger, Gracie pounded the chair against the neck and back of the man before he could rise from where his legs had dropped him across the desk. Viciously, the pounding continued from the force of the hurt she held inside. She did not notice his strong arm lift against her attack. She did not notice his head turn her direction as she pummeled his face. She only knew that when the mass fell to the floor, she had to run, run for her life.

Gracie glanced back over her shoulder to see the giant stumble out of the doorway, holding his head in his hand. She ran knowing to be caught would not be with a second chance of escape. The cold yellow floor sent pangs of ice up her legs. *Faster! Run!* Her mind pulled every nerve of determination from her body. A tin plate with an arrow drawn across it hung from the ceiling ahead. *Arrow. Out maybe? Please, Lord.* Shoving open the steel door, Gracie jumped to the stairs, where she ran, hitting every step for fear of tripping and falling. Even when she left the stairs and turned into the upper-floor hall, she continued to run on her toes. Speed without noise was a must for her escape. Blood pulsed behind her swollen eye, but the other eye searched for another arrow pointing out of the building.

"Yes!" A breath of hope came with a pant of air. The ceiling of the hall ahead offered another small tin arrow. Without breaking stride, Gracie rounded the corner. A smile crossed her dry lips at the sight of double doors with a sign labeled Ausgang nailed above. "Exit!" Her heart jumped as she gave a last kick of speed. *I have to get through those doors! I have to . . .*

Breath was ripped from Gracie's lungs. A door near the exit opened, where a tall, skinny man dressed in a white uniform stepped into Gracie's path. His expression turned from shock to anger at the sight of an inmate trying to escape. Trained as an orderly, he had dealt with so many of these futile attempts. He prepared himself by pulling a baton from his belt and widening his stance, waiting for the blow. *They always try to knock me over. Simple minds, simple plans.* He smiled. This one would be no different.

Gracie didn't slow down, even when she saw the man pull his club and set his stance in the middle of the hall. The doors were too close. Her mind couldn't form a plan. Her limited eyesight didn't offer another exit. She hoped the grinning face would weaken him with overconfidence. Hope faltered. She leaned her shoulder forward and never stopped running.

"Ahhh!" A war cry ricocheted off the walls. The orderly flung arms wide, ready to grasp his prey. One last step, he snapped shut his arms, but she wasn't there to be captured. He missed his chance to see the runner fall to the yellow tile and slide through his wide stance. He twisted his upper torso to face behind him but didn't see her fist pump upward to catch him in the one place she knew would send him crumbling to his knees.

The orderly screeched at the instant pain, and his baton slipped from his hands hitting the floor before he fell to his hands and knees. Gracie jumped to her feet and spun around to snatch up the baton before he could recover. Still in motion, she moved swiftly behind the wailing man, and before he could turn to see her, the baton repeatedly swung down across the back of his head. The once-confident orderly crumbled in an unconscious heap onto the cold, ugly tile.

Gracie stood looking down at the man, waiting for him to move. In the stillness, she lowered the baton. Wasting no more time, she searched his utility belt and pockets. "Yes!" Her hand closed over a metal ring filled with keys.

"Hey! There!" bellowed a deep, angry voice.

The gruff voice was too expected. She didn't need to look. She knew if he caught her again, horror would take her. She turned, refusing to show the fear he would see in her eyes. The monster rumbling toward her roared as she slipped through the double doors.

The barefoot girl ran with speed, seeing only a gravel path ahead and feeling a mass of keys in her hand. The forest stood with its shadowy arms, welcoming back the *Mischling*. Gracie stumbled and fell into the matted overgrowth. Neither the curious squirrels nor chirping birds could do anything to calm the heaving sounds of sadness coming from the girl curled into a ball.

She had escaped. Escaped. Terrors lay in the room that became her prison. Capture was the intent of all who saw her. But now she was safe on the outside of the evil edifice called Hadamar.

Gracie cried for the terrors. She cried for the battles she had been forced to fight. She cried for the what-ifs that never took place.

Gracie cried because she knew she had to return.

A ring of keys lay on the matted ground beside Gracie. Nearly an hour had passed since she escaped. She sat up and leaned against a tree hidden from the eyes of Hadamar, yet it loomed in the vision of her uninjured eye. *Oh, evil place and people. What have I done to you to make you hurt me?* Tears coursed until they dropped from her tender face to where they were absorbed by her woolen coat. She pulled her stocking feet under her legs as she leaned to pick up the keys.

"I hate you. I hate you all." She moved keys around the metal ring. "But I have to go back. I need my shoes. I need," she sniffed and looked up at the cloud-covered sky, "to finish why I came." Her hand brushed back hair that had fallen down over her temples then moved to wipe streaks where tears had soiled her face. She looked at the name etched in stone and yelled from the woods. "I'll return for my boots, and if he—that man, that monster—if he locks me up again, I'll get out and I'll find you, Herr Möeller. I'll get you out too. I'm coming back for you, Herr Möeller! I'm coming back! I'm coming . . ."

Sobs robbed her of voice, but the keys in her hand gave back her confidence.

Unexpected Danger

"Don't lead me wrong, Murphy!" Theo leaned forward over the gas tank of the motorcycle as if to push it to run faster. The military machine was twice Theo's weight. He knew he needed to keep an eye to the uneven ground, but his hope to find Gracie would depend on his ability to keep the drone in sight. His pulse kept a rapid beat as an out-of-place smile broke across his face. *Finally! Finally, I'm the one leading the rescue! We can do this, Murphy! We can find Gracie and Herr Möeller and show these Germans what they're missing by living a hundred years too soon!*

"Yawww!" Impulsively, Theo let his emotions escape in a yalp covered by the roar of the machine and stifled even more by the thick night air.

Three hours passed by the time Theo slowed the motorcycle and tapped his wrist computer to voice command. "Murphy! Murphy, heel. Slow down, buddy. Stay on the road where I can find you. I see a building way up ahead. Stay where you are. I'll catch up and shut down the drone."

Over a kilometer ahead, the robotic dog picked up the voice command and slowed to a trot until his internal drive wound to a stop. As if by instinct instead of programming, Murphy trotted to the side of the road and turned to face where he had come so he could see his master's approach. Only seconds after Murphy's slowing to a stop, the drone hovered above the dog at the side of the road.

"You two are the best!" Theo slowed the motorcycle and turned off the engine. He tapped his wrist computer. Murphy stood by his master to watch the drone drift down to the road while propellers buzzed slower and slower until all power had shut down. Theo picked up the drone and noticed that one of the thin metal propellers was missing. Another was bent. "Wow, you must have led this ol' guy through some branches, Murphy. I'm surprised it kept aloft. But hey, you two got me here, so I'm not complaining." Theo looked down at Murphy, who had lost control of his wildly wagging tail.

Pointing ahead, almost to the sky, Theo continued in conversation as if Murphy were a speaking companion who could help him scheme. "I guess that may be where we're headed. That's what we're looking for. Elise said it's a stone building off by itself." Theo let his eyes search the horizon while he planned his next step. He sat down beside Murphy and held the drone on his lap. Murphy took advantage of the nearness of his master and rolled belly up for a belly scratch of thanks.

"Seriously? We're here in the middle of nowhere, trying to find our friends, and you think it's time for a belly rub?" Theo laughed at Murphy rubbing the back of his head against the ground, causing his snout to sniff and snort into the air. "I guess you deserve some pampering after a marathon of running." He moved his hand up to the collar that had fewer lights blinking. "Actually, I guess we better stop and rest long enough for your internal system to recharge before we go on. Looks like the drone could use some rest and repair too. Ugh. Your collar lights are dim, but my wrist computer flashlight can give me enough to see."

Theo dug into his backpack for his all-purpose tool and scraps of tin from the castle roof. He didn't mind taking the time to repair the drone. In impulse, he had taken off with the hope to find Gracie and maybe even Herr Möeller. He hadn't considered any dangers or problems that would keep him from walking right into Hadamar and taking his friend—his girlfriend—home. "I need some time to think, anyway." He grinned at Murphy, who had rolled to his side with both eyes closed, unconcerned with what Theo was doing.

By the time the drone had new propellers and the radio wires had been checked and tightened, Theo's eyes were feeling the sting of a sleepless night. He scooted off the road into a soft pile of leaves and pine needles. Pulling his backpack under his head so the sweet-scented pine sap wouldn't stick to his hair, Theo set the drone on the ground at his head and patted the middle of his soft wool coat. "C'mere, Murphy." Obediently, Murphy snuggled against Theo's stomach, where they lay under the brush. Within minutes, both boy and dog were snoring, and the night air lay still.

Had a squirrel not scolded and woken the interlopers for invading his tree territory, Theo and Murphy could have doubled their four hours of sleep. "What's that?" Theo raised on one arm, thinking he was lying in a bed somewhere. "Oh yeah. I forgot we're on the side of a road. No wonder my nose is so cold." He rubbed the tip of his nose with one hand and the tip of Murphy's nose with the other. "Your nose is cold too. See? You're a regular dog, not a robot." Murphy's tail gave a few happy wags as if he understood.

"Man, I wish I had some of those snack bars that IRIS used to make me put in my backpack. Actually, I wish I had IRIS. Don't get me wrong," Theo looked down at the dog who cocked his head as if trying to understand, "the drone and radio are cool, and at least some functions of my computer watch still work with your collar, but it would be nice to hear the robotic voice of my integrated robotic information system telling me what to do and giving me a map to do it." He sat up with his arms across the knees of his bent legs. "I guess I can learn to do whatever they did in 'the good old days'—kinda." Theo leaned across Murphy and picked up the drone, moving a small lever to an unmarked "on" position. Instantly, Murphy's blue collar lit up in a wave of staccato flashes. "Great! Looks like all systems are connected and ready to go. I guess there's no reason to stay here any longer." Theo stood and swatted the pine needles from his coat and jeans as he hoisted the backpack across one shoulder and carried the drone toward the motorcycle.

Murphy trotted to the middle of the road and let out a series of short yaps that made it look like he was jumping with stiff legs. "Hush, Murphy. Whaddaya want?" Murphy trotted forward, turned and ran back toward Theo, then turned and trotted forward again.

"I *am* coming, if that's what you mean." Theo gripped the motorcycle handlebars, and again Murphy began the pattern of run, bark, and run, even nipping at Theo's pant leg as he bounced close to Theo. "What? You weren't excited about leaving a few minutes ago. Whatza problem?" The beagle tipped back his head with his snout in the air as a half growl, half howl came from his rounded mouth before he took off running down the road.

"I just don't under—oh! Duh! Murphy, you're so right! It's the motorcycle, isn't it? You don't want me to turn on the noisy motorcycle. Is that it?"

Murphy did a few fast spins in the middle of the road as if chasing his tail before he turned and trotted back to Theo and sat down in front of him.

"Sorry. I guess I just wasn't thinkin'. Okay, little buddy. It doesn't look far. We'll walk to this Hadamar place. They'll probably give us something to drink when we get there. How bad can it be, right?" Theo strapped the drone to his backpack. Again, boy and dog began their trek to find Gracie.

"Whoo." Theo gave a soft whistle. Even with cloudy skies, daybreak didn't afford much stealth when the stone edifice labeled *Hadamar* came into view. Murphy plopped his belly down to the earth and pushed himself forward with paws gripping the earth and legs extended. Taking Murphy's cue to be careful, Theo lay on the ground beside Murphy. At least a half kilometer back, the dirt road had narrowed to a gravel drive. Theo couldn't read the German words on the sign warning stray travelers to stay away, but Murphy's growl and hackles standing on the back of his neck warned of unfriendly territory. They moved to a hedgerow bordering a lush lawn and circle drive leading up to stone steps that ended in a surprisingly small porch for such a large building.

"I don't get it, Murph. This place doesn't look any different from the other big buildings and castles we've seen, but it gives me the creeps. Maybe I should just grow up and quit acting like a kid scared of ghosts and things that don't exist. I'm going to knock on the door and ask."

Theo pulled one leg under him to push up into a standing position, but when he drew up his other leg and tried to stand, Murphy locked his teeth around Theo's pant leg. In backward hopping motions and growls, the dog captured his attention. "What now?" With a mix of instinct from his own gut and reaction to Murphy's attempt to pull him down, Theo squatted back to the earth. "So you don't like this place?" Murphy lay down and planted his snout into the spring grass. Without hiding disappointment, Theo let his shoulders drop as he lay quietly looking up at the institute, quiet and stately against the gray morning sky. Theo took several minutes to formulate a thought before he deferred to his robotic best friend with an apology and a plan.

"Okay. You win. I won't just walk up and go inside, but look at all of those windows. We can at least *look* inside." He paused and squinted his eyes. "Zikes, all of the windows look kinda high for a first floor. Maybe we can find some lower windows at the back of the building." He jostled the backpack to the middle of his back as he rose to a crouched position and swung an arm toward the hedgerow. "Let's stay in these trees. It looks like we can get to the back without coming out of cover."

Perhaps it was the crisp air, or perhaps it was the lack of sleep in a good bed, but scanning the back of the structure gave Theo a boost of courage. "We can do this, Murph. Look at the windows. All the shades are down. No one will see us, and no one would expect visitors at the back, anyway. We're not going to find Gracie by standing in these trees. C'mon. Let's do this." Theo looked like a poorly postured Neanderthal man as he squat-trotted with long strides across the lawn from trees to building. Murphy shot out of the woods and passed Theo, not stopping until his side hit the stones of the building. By the time Theo reached the wall, Murphy had dropped his snout to the ground and was nearly digging a path with it as he ran along the wall sniffing with hackles raised and tail pointed straight out.

"They must be scared of people getting into the basement. Why else would they have bars on the windows?" Theo crouched beside Murphy, who had started a low growl and stopped with his nose against a cold and clouded windowpane covered with a yellow shade.

A click from a back-porch door at the top of steps a few meters away warned Theo and Murphy to squat under the cover of the wooden porch and stairs. No voices were heard, only a raspy cough as someone tossed the contents of a pan, water perhaps, down the side of the porch. Theo turned his face away to prevent being splattered by water or mud. Another click followed the steps that retraced back inside.

Silently, Theo reached down and rubbed Murphy's neck. Content that no one else was at the door, the curious youth stood out from under the porch and craned his neck. "I can't see anything from down here except some boxes hanging off the wall. I need to go up and look in." He started to move away from his dog but suddenly turned back and knelt down. "Wait, let's connect. I need your eyes, Murphy. My watch computer will be able to use your vision. Keep a good lookout so I can see what's going on in two places. Okay, Murph. It's spy time." Theo touched his watch screen until he could see the lawn in front of Murphy's eyes, then put his hand on the dog's head, and gave him a quick rub between the ears, grinning at the smiling pant Murphy offered back. "You stay here. I'll be right back."

Theo slipped the backpack off his shoulders and set the pack and drone against the wall under the porch where he had hidden moments earlier. Murphy sat against the backpack as if to show Theo he would guard it, then he watched his master climb the porch steps. Exploring Germany's streets with Gracie had given Theo skills he had never learned from his sofa in America where his biggest threats were apocryphal assassins in his HoloGames. More times than the fingers on his hands, Theo realized the false realism of the games and how disgusted he had become with his shallow understanding of war and what it meant to be a hero.

Once his master was out of sight, Murphy moved along the ground and the lower windows. His senses were heightened, causing his usual blue light color to change to the word *danger* displayed in red. Programmed to protect, the canine became more robot than companion as smells and sounds began to record on an internal chip. The system Theo and his father, Luke Marshall, had created was to aid scientists conducting research or to aid rescue workers in disaster situations. The robotic sensors could record video and register dangerous chemicals to keep humans further out of harm's way. Theo and Dr. Marshall had earned recognition for their creation, and it had been successfully used to keep people safe. Now, in Germany, over a hundred years prior to its creation, the scientific technology was an anachronism—yet still a lifesaving device. Oblivious to what or why, the robotic dog paced along the building until his impulse was to stop and look into a window where the shade hung partially ripped, exposing a gray room with concrete beds and yellow lights dangling from the ceiling.

Creeping up the steps and across the porch, Theo sidled up to a window not far from the door. He pressed so flat against the building that even a ray of sunlight, if it did decide to peep out from the clouds, could not pass between his body and the wall. He turned his face toward the window, but like the others, it prevented any view to the inside due to a yellowed shade suspended from top to windowsill. The stone exterior ruffled his hair as he turned to look toward the door. Two small boxes on the wall disrupted his sight. Curiosity prompted Theo to lift his head away from the building far enough to identify the boxes.

"Hey, Murph," he whispered down to his dog, who was busy with curiosity of his own, "I'm not moving to the door until I know if these boxes are some kind of laser alarm . . ." The sudden realization that he put twenty-first-century technology into 1937 Germany gave him a nervous snigger. "Oh! Duh!" He held his finger to his lips in the gray air as if to scold himself with a reminder to stay quiet. "Sorry, boy. I forgot these old guys don't even know what lasers are." He inhaled a breath. "Okay. Carry on, Murphy." The robotic canine paid no attention to his master's break in concentration.

Theo leaned around the boxes hanging by the door. "Really?" He forgot his vow of silence and walked to the railing around the porch to send a gravelly whisper down to Murphy. "These people must be a little like us. These are only a thermometer and a barometer! I wonder if they like how cold it is outside?" He grinned down at Murphy, who lifted his head when he noticed his master leaning over the porch rail. "What? Oh, right." He spoke to a dog who only returned a blank stare. "Outside. Right. I'm supposed to be going inside. Got it!" Theo returned to the wall, but this time, he stood under the metal boxes. *Good thing they use these old doors with clear glass windows. Bad thing they like window shades.*

Theo pressed the side of his face to the stone wall where he could see inside through a gap between the window shade and the wooden frame. A light exposed a porcelain sink holding scattered dishes. He held his breath as a woman dressed in white and wearing a white cap and white shoes came into his line of sight, set a coffee cup on the sink, then turned, and walked away again. He listened for sounds of talking or movement. The light went out, giving Theo a chance to exhale. *Must be a kitchen. Glad they're gone.* Mentally, he made note of every movement and sound so he could know just the right time to go into the building. He gripped the doorknob and slowly turned.

The click stopped his turning, but he held the knob in position until he was certain no one heard the noise. No light came through the window, promising an empty room. With a deep breath and a smirk of success, Theo raised his hand eye level to push the door open just enough to fit through when the sight of a man's face appeared before his eyes. He gasped and spun back and away from the door. His quick spin countered his balance, sending him backward over the porch rail. The drop was only a couple of meters, but the tumble hadn't given him a chance to get his legs under him before he hit the ground.

"Umph!" The wind was knocked out of his lungs. Theo winced in pain that shot up his leg. He grabbed and looked down where his hand held the aching shin. Again, he saw flashes of yellow and dirt, causing him to draw back and look up in terror at the porch above him. The porch was silent and empty.

What? No one. But there was . . . Theo shook his head trying to make sense of the vision in his mind. *I know I saw someone.* He grimaced and looked down at his leg. Again he noticed the flash of putrid color, but the colors were coming from his watch. Jerking into a sitting position, he deliberately looked into the face of the watch.

"Murphy!" Theo's voice called in out a raspy whisper. "Murph! Where are you? What are you seeing? I saw a face on my watch!" Before he called out again, Theo pulled himself back under the porch where he had left his backpack and dog. "Murphy! Come!" Theo scanned the area and prayed the leg he was rubbing would show knots and bruising without broken bone. He bent his knee until he could rest his head and fight the dizziness from the upset and pain of the fall. With his eyes closed, he pumped his foot to reassure himself that nothing was broken. A cold touch made him jerk his head, but the touch was followed by a whimper.

"Murphy! Where have you been? I saw something. You saw something. Man, that about killed me with fright. I thought someone was coming to get me, but it was you. How'd you get in someone's face like that? Where were you?" The questions rolled as quickly from Theo's mouth as the tail that wagged in response to the quick hand petting his back.

Again, Theo jerked as a pain pierced his shin. "Man, I hope I can walk. I need a minute to get my leg to stop hurting. Where were you, buddy? What'd you see?" The questions brought the vision of the man's face back into Theo's mind. He needed to rest. He needed to walk. Without understanding why, he knew he needed to find Gracie. For now, he pulled Murphy onto his lap, petting and holding him tightly as he tried to think of his next move and convince himself to make that move on a wounded leg.

Long minutes passed before Murphy's vision detected a light snap on through a nearby basement window. With the stealth of a wild animal approaching its prey, Murphy slid from Theo's lap and moved toward the low window.

"What's up, Murph?" Theo knew to keep his voice low, but he didn't want to waste energy if Murphy was chasing imaginary rabbits. "Do you see something?" He watched his dog press his nose against the window where the partially ripped shade hung inside. Curiosity encouraged Theo to roll to his stomach and do a one-legged push of an army crawl to Murphy's side.

"Dang. How'd you find such an ugly room? I can hardly see. It's like the room's in a fog or something." Theo squinted his eyes as he lay on the ground next to Murphy, who had lain down but kept his snout pressed to the windowpane. "Okay. Now this is making sense. When I was on the porch, I saw a man's face. Actually, I didn't see it—you did, didn't you? Did you get caught looking in this window?" Theo's questions were not for Murphy's response but were more so he could mentally piece together the puzzle of sights. "Murph! What if that man comes looking for you?" Theo half rolled so he could look over his shoulder where he saw nothing but stone wall, a suspended porch, and the dark blue-gray sky that was becoming agitated by a resurgence of storm. He rolled back to his stomach for another look into the window.

"I'm not seeing much, Murphy. What I really want to see is Gracie, but we're not finding her by lying outside all day." Theo pushed up to a sitting position and rubbed his leg while his face grimaced with pain. Again he scooted on his rump until he was sitting beside his backpack, half sheltered by the overhanging porch. "C'mon, Murph. We need to plan." Theo dropped his head into his hands and rubbed his eyes with closed fists. He hadn't realized how dirty his hands had become through the night's trek and how much his head ached.

Murphy gave a low and muffled bark to leave a warning to any goons who wanted to appear at the window before he trotted to Theo's side.

"We've got to get inside." Theo rested his arm on his backpack and mindlessly twirled the drone's new propeller on a scuffed wing. "But I don't know how to . . ." He stopped and looked at the drone. *Okay.* He shook his head in agreement with his thoughts. "Okay, Murph, I think I have a plan." He looked at the dog sitting with his head resting against Theo's leg. "Well, not exactly a plan, but at least I have an idea."

Theo picked up the drone and began a series of back-and-forth movements of touching the screen of his computer watch, moving tiny levers on the plane, and adjusting buttons on Murphy's collar. "There, let's check. Hey, Murph, look out there." Theo pointed toward the hedgerow and looked down at his wrist. A crisp picture of the trees appeared on Theo's watch. "Nice. Now, for the drone."

He poked the face of his wrist computer and Murphy's blue lights began a sequence of flashes. Intermittent green lights popped, and the propellers of the drone started their bee-hum turning. "Excellent! All systems are 'go.' So it's time for us to do the same." Theo looked up at the porch over his head.

"Ya know, Murph, I'd like to think I can just hobble in there, find Gracie and Herr Möeller, and let them tease me about hurting my leg as all three of us leave this spooky place." Theo glanced at the darkening morning sky. "Yeah. That's what my mind says." He put a hand on Murphy's back and gave several long petting strokes before he put his fears into words. "That doesn't seem to be the pattern of getting things done here in Germany, though." His eyes moved back to the wall boxes over the porch above him. "We don't have any way to protect ourselves, Murph. I need to think like Dad and let scientific knowledge help us out." He momentarily lifted his hand from petting to point to the boxes before putting his hand back down to Murphy's back.

"Listen, Murph. I saw a woman dressed all in white with a funny little white cap. I've seen old pictures, and that's the way nurses used to dress. If there's a nurse, this must be some kind of hospital or something. So see the mercury in that barometer? I may find something inside that I can mix with the mercury." He paused long enough to look out across the lawn as his mind looked into his memory. A grin skipped across his lips. "I remember one time at Dad's lab, I mixed mercury, nitric acid, and alcohol. The next day, I tried to move my experiment to another table, but I dropped the petri dish. Man, did that thing explode! I thought Dad was going to come unglued!" Theo stopped talking and looked back up to the porch. "Maybe we should borrow the mercury in case we need it later." He nodded to no one. "Won't hurt to be overprepared."

"Looks like my leg is swelling." Theo gently rubbed the bruised shin. "This is not the time to be a softy, Theodore." He allowed himself a slight grin as he chided himself. "Well, Murphy, I might be a little crippled up, but I have to remember why we came to this creepy place. We gotta get Gracie and Herr Möeller." He rolled to stoop over with most weight on his good leg. Determined to be a hero, he slipped first one arm then the other through straps on the backpack with the drone attached. "Okay, little buddy. Lemme carry you to the porch. I've already been there." Theo knew Murphy would have no trouble climbing the back steps, but there was just something reassuring in wrapping his arms around his best friend.

On the porch, Theo set down Murphy and studied the boxes on the wall before he tipped his head back. *Oh, Gracie. What would I do without you?* His thoughts made him smile as he reached inside his coat and pulled out the lanyard necklace that held the metal driftboard charm. Again, the charm that represented his former passion became a tool to remove screws securing the barometer to the wall. Theo laid the barometer in his backpack and squatted beside Murphy to review their game plan.

"We can go in through that door. I think it's a kitchen. At least it has a sink and a coffee cup." He grinned at the dog who sat staring at his master. "We'll go in, but there's too much building and at least one mean-faced-looking guy inside, so we'll need to split up. For now, I'll keep the drone on my pack. Keep lookin' around so I can see through my watch." He wrinkled his forehead. "Ya know, Murph, I better make sure the sound transmitter is turned on. I may need to hear if you come face-to-face with that goon again." He squeezed what looked like a rivet on Murphy's collar, then gave him a quick pat. "No, just a pat won't do." Theo pulled Murphy into his arms into a tight squeeze that buried his face into the soft fur and sighed. "Here we go again, buddy. We can do this."

Murphy wiggled his snout between Theo's chin and the woolen coat. If a stranger had seen the robotic companion, he would have claimed no greater love between the boy and his dog.

Watch of Two Worlds

I N THE DARK kitchen, a shaft of light fell across the porcelain sink. Though hours on the clock showed it to be day, the promise of a storm kept agitated winds pushing thick clouds across the hazy spring sky. Theo and Murphy stepped through the back door of Hadamar, secure in the darkness and begging their steps to be silent so they could move in stealth. The linoleum floor only belched a few squeaks from Theo's shoes, but it threatened to expose them by magnifying the clicks of Murphy's paw-steps. Lengthening his stride and holding to his straps so the pack and drone would stay centered on his back, Theo moved swiftly across the kitchen to an open doorway connected to a narrow hallway. After a quick look into the hall, he turned to Murphy and gave a soft pat to his thigh as a command to follow.

The kitchen floor flowed into the hallway with periodic cracks and buckled patches where the linoleum had worn thin and left divots of exposed subflooring. "Which way?" Theo mouthed the words to Murphy and held a hand suspended as if uncertain. Murphy wagged his head both directions and turned where he could trot into a doorway a few meters down the hall.

"Ah, good choice." Theo bent down and patted Murphy's back after they stepped into another doorless small room. He noticed a desk in the room across the hall. "Stay." Theo held an open palm in front of the dog's face with the whispered command. "Stay until I get back."

Murphy squatted on his haunches, showing he would not leave the room, but his eyes never left his master as Theo took three long strides across the hall. He turned and placed an index finger across his lips to remind Murphy to stay quiet. Without moving his feet, Theo turned to visually scan the room and think about his next step. *I'm not sure what I'm looking for.* He slipped behind a wooden desk that faced a wall. Papers across the desk seemed to have no order or filing system, and nothing that looked like a name popped out of the German handwriting.

Well, this does me no good. With a sigh of exasperation, Theo turned back to the door just as Murphy tensed up and the blue lights of his collar started to strobe. Quickly, Theo motioned with his palm down and lowered his hand. Murphy obediently followed the cue and lay on his stomach in the darkness so the lights would be covered by his ruff and not be detected. In the same second, Theo hid behind the door that swung into the small office, held his breath, and prayed that whoever was approaching had no interest in stopping.

Through the narrow slit between door and doorframe Theo heard steps bring voices closer. The voices stopped in the hall on the other side of the wall from where he hid. A woman was wearing a white uniform and a white nurse's hat. The man with her was much larger and was wearing dingy white pants and top. Theo couldn't see higher than halfway up the back of the woman's head, but one thing was obvious on both. The man and the woman both wore armbands with a red circle filled with a black swastika. Theo knew this was not a sign of friendly territory.

Hoping his pulsing blood was making no noise, Theo looked down at his wristwatch. As if reading Theo's mind, Murphy stayed flattened against the floor but kept his eyes open and riveted on the hall. By the time Murphy's eyes scanned upward enough to show faces, the people had passed his doorway and only blond hair beneath the backs of their caps could be seen.

Hearty laughing broke the silence, propelling the walkers on down the hall. Theo forced himself to count to twenty before he slipped from behind the door and motioned to the dog flattened across the hall. "C'mon, Murphy. I don't know where they came from, but we're going to find out."

He didn't need to signal again. Theo and Murphy were in a fast tiptoe trot up the hall before Theo hesitated and reached down to scoop Murphy into his arms. He held the dog close to his face. "Murphy, roll into your ball. I can't lose you now, and I have to be ready to turn and run in an instant."

Obediently, the dog rolled into a silver sphere that Theo tucked under his arm as if carrying a football, sliding with his back close to the wall but not close enough to scrape the painted plaster wall with the drone hanging from the backpack. A snap of a light stole Theo's next breath. He tipped his head backward as if it would make him invisible if he touched the wall. Again, loud laughter and a cacophony of voices floated out of the kitchen. Theo turned and exploded into a sprint down the hall away from the kitchen. As he ran, his head turned from side to side for quick glimpses into rooms. He didn't know what he wanted to see. He didn't know where he was running, but his blood pulsed in urgency. *Please, God, help me. I don't know. I don't know. I don't know.*

His first awareness that he was not alone was a waft of flowery perfume that his nostrils sucked in. The pungent smell intersected a swallow, causing him to cough before he could catch himself and cover the sound. He caught sight of a shapely figure in a white dress, a white cap, and white shoes standing with her back to the door he passed. Colors flew beyond the whiteness of her form, showing that she was arranging flowers on a small table in the center of the room. Quickly he ditched into a room with no light except the filtered daylight determined to peek past storm clouds and window shades.

"Viktor? Viktor, is that you come early?" The nurse's soft voice was lilting and filled with high-pitched expectation. Theo heard the twisted squeak from one of her white shoes as she spun in place before taking steps to the doorway. From his position between half-opened door and wall, Theo had a limited view to the door only a few steps back. He saw half of the white dress and cap lean into the hall, suspended by a slender arm that held to the door facing. Again, he heard the inquiring voice, "Viktor?" The only sound to follow was the pop of the slender arm dropping against the side of the white dress and the shuffle of the white shoes as the figure disappeared back to arrange the flowers.

Theo was thankful that the pounding in his ears didn't end in the explosion his body threatened, for he was sure the pulsing blood would have easily caused a great puddle on the floor. *Breathe. Get control! You've been in worse situations, so settle down!* He mentally reprimanded himself and denied his feet the chance to move until he could regain the calm he would need to search for his Gracie. He rubbed his hands across the silver sphere in his hands. *I need a plan. This is crazy.* Theo crept from behind the door and again peered into the hall before he crossed deeper into the room and pulled aside the window shade enough to look out into the misty gray morning. Nothing in sight was moving outside besides the spiny tree branches showing hints of green against the brown of the front circle drive. He pressed his forehead against the cool glass and turned to look up and down in an attempt to see the outer walls.

"Well, Murphy, it looks like we're on the first floor, but we're high enough that there must be a pretty tall basement." He gently patted the silver ball. "There must be stairs somewhere. Let's explore the basement where there may not be as many people." Theo set the ball on the floor. "Okay, Murph. Unroll. I think I have another plan—at least for the next few minutes."

Before he finished whispering, like an armadillo awakening, the sphere turned into a dog with stretching legs. Murphy stood on back legs with his front paws reaching up to the shoulders of the boy squatting beside him, tail wagging in unalarmed happiness.

"Ya ready for some more action, little buddy?" Theo looked over his shoulder toward the silent hallway. "C'mon. Let's find some stairs."

With only a moment's hesitation at the doorway and a quick turn of two heads to look one direction then the next, both were in a fast trot down the hall until Theo swung an arm to the side, signaling that a heavy metal door promised access to another floor. Theo fell with his shoulder against the door to allow an opening large enough for his backpack laden with the drone to follow him through.

Murphy was through the door and down a switchback flight of stairs before the door whooshed and clicked shut behind them.

The woman in the white dress cocked her head at the noise in the dark but disregarded it as she crossed the hall. For the moment, she desired a view of the front drive and pulled back the window shade that, just minutes earlier, had been moved by the hand of a young man.

Evil Intentions

R IPPLES OF LIGHTNING exploded, illuminating thick storm clouds and exposing a fast-moving convoy weaving toward a destination. Thunder shook the elements as the sky collapsed into darkness, causing the driver of a matte black Mercedes to jerk the wheel, careening the car to the right. He regained composure and glanced in the rearview mirror, fearing his passenger would spit a diatribe for his incompetence in driving. For the duration of the drive from Berlin, the irritable passenger had complained.

What error had he made? The driver wasn't sure what he had done wrong to have prompted this assignment. His commander assured him this was a promotion. He would escort a brilliant scientist named Viktor Brack, the real brains behind some of Hitler's whims and now an SS officer on his own fast track of promotion. The driver nodded to himself without notice from the back seat. He had heard rumors. This same man would soon head up a program so important to the Reich that only a handful of people knew about it. Who was this obscure scientist whose notoriety developed out of the thin air before he was pulled from a small town and given rank and power in the powerful Nazi SS?

Against the voice of reason in his head, the driver tried to sneak another look but quickly averted his eyes. "Maybe if you look at the road instead of that blasted mirror every five seconds, my paperwork wouldn't be strewn about back here!" the officer growled in his graveled voice. "One more time and you'll be driving that supply truck on the return trip. Keep your eyes forward!"

"S-S-Sorry, sir. W-W-Won't happen again." Fear gripped the driver's throat, causing him to stutter over his words. His knuckles turned white from the grip he held on the steering wheel.

"For your sake, boy, I hope not." The passenger resumed collecting his papers from the seat and floor.

The young driver breathed a heavy sigh when the next flash of lightning revealed that the motorcade was nearing its final destination. The Hadamar Institute loomed menacingly on the Möchsberg hill, yet it stood partially hidden by large trees standing as sentries around a fortress, leaving the small town below wondering if indeed it even existed. Another shattering lightning strike revealed a thick cloud of smoke billowing from towering chimneys jutting up from the destination—an asylum for the mentally insane. A shiver ran down the driver's spine while rumors and stories too horrible to believe wove through his mind. He squeezed the wheel even tighter, determined not to give the doctor in the back seat any reason to leave him at this location.

Rain pelted the windshield, threatening to shatter the glass. Roaring car engines jostled with the sound of the wind and rain moving the caravan through a long sweeping bend in the road that sharply swung into a reverse hairpin curve exposing a little-known gateway at the top of the hill.

Two motorcycles with armed submachine gunners seated in the sidecars pulled past the unloading area. Drivers and passengers were off the motorcycles and standing guard as a half-track vehicle pulled up, dismounting three rows of troops to set up a perimeter to protect Victor Brack. Brack's driver stopped in front of concrete steps leading to a small porch attached to Hadamar's front entry on an elevated first floor. A short young woman in nurse's uniform stood with three men directly behind her waiting to attend to her orders.

Brack waited impatiently in the back seat of the Benz while the troops created a corridor between the black Mercedes and the waiting staff members of Hadamar Mental Institute. Once the troops were all in place, Brack angrily cleared his throat.

"S-S-Sorry, sir," the nervous driver stammered as he slammed his shoulder into the door in a rush to get out. He shoved the door open using a boot extended with a kick of his leg. In his hurry to circle the car and open the reverse door of the vehicle, he slipped in the mud but recovered as he swung an umbrella overhead.

Brack ran his fingers over the new insignia on his left collar, intending the German Army—and soon the world—to see his promoted status. His mind promised that the Germans would not lose next time. Emblazoned on his right collar was a silver SS shaped as two lightning bolts. For those chosen and pulled into the Nazi party, the emblem was a badge of honor and power. For anyone else, it was a symbol of respected fear. He stepped out of the car and stood under the waiting umbrella held by his incompetent driver. Water dripped from the umbrella and beaded on his wool uniform before it oozed down his woolen sleeve. Lieutenant Colonel Brack ripped the umbrella out of the shaky hand. He glared down at the driver and dismissed him without a saying a word.

The young nurse pulled her long trench coat tightly around her body and walked down the few steps to greet her guest. She didn't seem bothered by the rain as she walked out from under the overhang of roof. Intentionally, she flashed a sensuous smile to welcome the man instrumental in what the Reich believed was purifying the German race. Briefly, she had met him months before in a meeting called by the führer. This time they met—and would work—on her grounds. The largest of the three male orderlies, who was as thick as a tree in both physical and mental quality, followed her down the steps and covered her with his umbrella. She abruptly stopped as an armed soldier stepped between her and Brack, protecting the Nazi officer.

"Fool, get out of her way," Viktor Brack ordered firmly and raised his arm to push the soldier out of the way. "Can't you tell she is just excited to meet me?" he quipped scarcely over a whisper with extreme pride, his own legend building his ego.

"Sorry, sir." The soldier stepped aside, lowering his head in embarrassment and concern for repercussions for such a mistake. Brack's notoriety was still new to most, but word had spread that he did not give second chances for any mistake—regardless of how simple or innocent. Even a soldier's mispronunciation of Dr. Brack's name had ended with permanent removal from both military and social circles.

"Lieutenant Colonel, Doctor, I hope you remember me. My name is Irmgard." She lifted a soft hand and placed it atop Brack's leather-gloved hand before he could extend it even halfway between them. "It is an honor to have you at our modest institute. We can ensure that the lower level has all of the structural and surgical needs your work requires." A soft smile turned away from Brack with a swivel so close that her hair pulled back into a tight bun brushed against his coat buttons. The nurse motioned for Brack to follow her out of the weather and into the facility. "I believe you will be pleased with the progress we've made so far."

"I'll be the judge of that," he replied sternly, not wanting to give the nurse an inch of confidence. He thrived on control of everyone and everything around him. He yearned to be like a puppet master, tugging on the strings of his many marionettes. His plan was moving smoothly; he was manipulating from the highest level of the regime through lower people like the nurse, moving them in any direction he wanted, making them do exactly what he wanted.

At the top of the steps, Brack spun in a turning stomp, raised an arm toward the ominous sky, and shouted, "Heil Hitler!" Before his arm had relaxed back to his side, the standing troops repeated the salute, and with eyes riveted on the lieutenant colonel, they saluted Brack through his command of "Dismissed!" and held the pose until the newly promoted leader turned to walk through the doors of Hadamar.

Only out of unfamiliarity with the institution and not from order of rank, Viktor Brack smirked an evil smile as he followed Nurse Irmgard through the heavy steel door that clanged from the swinging chains of multiple locks built in for extra security.

The procession stopped at an intersection of gray walls inside the first-floor foyer. A flick of Nurse Irmgard's wrist toward her personal entourage dismissed all but one orderly, the largest man in the group. She responded to Brack's gaze. "This was once a prison for people who could not function in society. We converted it into an institution per the führer's command." Brack nodded in understanding and waited for her to take the lead. "This way, Doctor," she offered, slipping around the tall, slender scientist and heading down a dimly lit corridor.

Brack turned and mumbled a few orders to one of his lieutenants. "I understand a prisoner has recently been captured and brought from a castle where it's known the proprietor does not support the führer's command. Find where the prisoner has been locked and we shall soon prep him for, ahem," Brack intentionally cleared his throat, "his therapy, shall we say?" A sinister chuckle caught in his throat as he punctuated the word *therapy*. "Irmgard, where is the electroshock therapy corridor?"

The shapely nurse stopped and faced Viktor Brack with a sadistic expression that slowly morphed into a large smile. "That's in the east wing, Doctor Brack. If you would like, I'll have Alvar take you there after I show you your office."

"Perfect!" Viktor Brack tilted his head back as he made eye contact with the nurse's assistant as if he were looking down upon the man, though the orderly was sizably larger. "Alvar, show Lieutenant Higgins the location of this room." With scarcely a breath of pause, Brack snapped the lieutenant into his vision while continuing his orders to the orderly. "From now on, Lieutenant Higgins will personally deal with the security in that wing. Is that understood?"

Though Brack's eyes never left the lieutenant's face, both men snapped heels and voiced an obedient "Yes, sir."

"Of course, Doctor." Irmgard smiled, sensing a darkness in him—the same that pulsed through veins beneath her hypocritical soft skin, kept hidden for fear of retribution and disgust. She waved the behemoth orderly named Alvar to her side; he leaned down so his ear was close to her. The nurse whispered then patted him on the cheek, like one would touch a small child needing encouragement. "Go, Alvar. Show our guest the way," she ordered loudly for the waiting lieutenant and the two soldiers who flanked his side to hear.

Alvar looked at her like a child admiring his mother, nodded, then clumsily turned and headed down the east wing of the institute. Every few steps, he looked back to make sure the new guests were following. He wanted to show them the special room and watch the new prisoner receive his treatment.

Over two decades earlier, Alvar had been left as a patient in Hadamar's psychiatric asylum. Irmgard came as a nurse to Hadamar when Dr. Karl Brandt convinced the führer to use the institution for studies in experimentation. Through her adept medical knowledge, Irmgard determined the oversize oaf just needed a firm hand and a caring word. By the passing of only half a year, she had turned Alvar into a heavily muscled security guard for any prisoner or patient who would require restraint.

Brack watched as the giant led soldiers down the hall and disappeared behind double steel doors. "It's hard to find a good assistant." He chuckled with cruel sarcasm. "Which way, Nurse? Delay does not amuse me."

"Yes, Doctor. Follow me." Irmgard admired Viktor Brack, but her terse words intimated her refusal to submit to rank. With a graceful swing of her body, she started down the west wing of the facility to offices used by the doctors and other scientists.

The three-leveled facility was larger than Brack envisioned. Halls seemed to flow into endless darkness. Pounding of boots and muted squeaking of rubber-soled shoes bounced off the walls of the narrow passage. A feminine voice disrupted and stopped the sound of footsteps. "You may use this office as you wish, Dr. Brack." Viktor Brack crossed the threshold of the dimly lit room. Irmgard backed into the hall, closing the wooden door behind her.

A metal file cabinet stood like a sentry beside a bare desk that absorbed most of the space in the room. Brack cleared his throat while he walked behind the desk and sat in a chair that complained its own remarks with a creak of springs beneath the leather seat. For a moment, he closed his eyes and remembered a similar chair in another country and another time. His thoughts commanded his attention. *Odd, the future holds so many advances in technology, but office chairs haven't changed much in comfort or form. If I shut out any sounds or smells, I may just forget I'm not Viktor Brack, the scientist with modern towers of the twenty-first century bearing my name. I may forget that I spent over two decades of my life building and perfecting a machine that could bring me back to the homeland and year of my ancestral heritage. I may forget . . .*

He leaned back in the large handcrafted office chair and ran his hands along the smooth armrests, enjoying the coolness under his open palms. He noted the attention to detail and skill that the carpenter put on display, creating the claw handle armrest. He placed his hand over the claw, mimicking its posture. Again, his thoughts captured the direction of his mind. *Quite a craftsman, eh, Mr. Chair Carpenter? What were you thinking when you carved these clawed armrests? Did a picture of a writhing soul get caught in your mind to be released in the carving? Mr. Chair Carpenter, did you plan that your chair to be left in this place where the devil himself lives?*

How can you, or anyone else in this backward time, understand the technology I created and harnessed to make my time jump to my great-grandfather's military career? Thoughts of self-promotion and pride caused Brack's chin to lift, tipping his head against the back of the chair.

Brack ignored subliminal thoughts gnawing with a twinge of guilt for causing injury to his fellow scientist, Dr. Luke Marshall. Luke had been a good friend, not in the traditional sense, but in the way he had dedicated himself—unknowingly—to Brack's plan.

What happened in the future does not matter! I must reshape the past! A tight fist slammed down on the desk, scolding and snapping his thoughts back to his plan. *Luke Marshall tried to stop me. He got exactly what he deserved for trying to prevent me from reaching my goal. My goal, yes, and that of the Society—yes, the secret backbone of the Reich who trusted my family for years. No! No Marshall will interrupt my plan—not Luke Marshall from the future and certainly not his punk kid, Theo. Who cares what happens to that kid! It was his choice to follow me in the TimeWorm and jump into the past. I'll show him and that group of the Watch. I'll get my book back from that kid and not look back on whatever happens to him or any of his people. That book is filled with my life's work, and no stinking kid will keep it from me!*

Scientists who focused on controlling the future seemed so "accidental" to him. Even as a youth, his mind was tantalized by science. Brack gritted his teeth in memory of the ridicule that came from his own father—a nobody on the streets but a genius in the science workshop where he and his father before him whittled and wasted hours creating but suggesting nothing to society. Thoughts were stunted with his father's voice of rebuke in the memory of his mind: *"Viktor, stop your foolishness. We hold our ideas because the world doesn't understand. You threaten mankind. You threaten powers when you use science as a toy and wag it in the faces of men who have spent their lives studying."*

Even now his father's voice slashed at his heart. For years, the young Viktor Brack kept sketches and mathematical studies of a time machine hidden in pages of a journal. It wasn't until his university studies that he read the research of another young scientist on campus and knew his dream could become reality. Viktor looked down at his large hands gripping the claw-shaped armrests. In the dark room, he could scarcely separate what was hand and what was wooden claw. *Calm down, ol' boy.* He relaxed his hands but kept them cupped on the armrests.

Being raised in the future, he knew exactly what was going to happen, and with knowledge of the world's history, he could assume the power and recognition he deserved. He drummed fingers on both hands while arguments of right and wrong churned in his mind.

How do I slip through time, until just the right moment and then—his slow breathing whistled through his narrow nose—*and then change the fate of the world. No! Who cares about the world? The devil may care, but I do not. I'll change the fate of me! Yes, that's it! I'll have absolute power so nothing will disrupt my plans! I'll create change until . . .*

A light knock at the door jerked the twenty-first-century scientist turned twentieth-century Third Reich militant from the recesses of thought.

"W*hat?*"

A woman's dispassionate face that distorted any sign of previous beauty peered past the opening door. Brack stood abruptly and furrowed his brow in reaction to the physical change. He was certain it was the light from the hall that swirled with the darkness of the room causing disfigurement to a soft face that he silently admired. Without tenderness or expression in her voice, Irmgard stood with her shadow named Alvar looming in the hall behind her. "We are soon to administer a treatment on a most deserving patient. I am hoping you will join us. The procedure promises to follow some of your own recommendations for—what is the term?—*cleansing?*"

Both nurse and orderly waited patiently for a response, showing no sign of irritation or nervousness. "Do you doubt my formula, Nurse?" Brack chose words and tone of voice to intentionally make the lead nurse uncomfortable. He liked to make people uncomfortable. It kept them vulnerable and easier to manipulate.

Not even a raised corner of her mouth betrayed Irmgard's stoicism. "Of course not, Doctor. I simply hoped you would like to witness your genius at work." Her heart skipped a beat and prompted her to stand in a beckoning pose silhouetted by the yellow light in the hall. Life at the institution could not fulfill the sphere of her world. Enticing through flattery denoted a shallow man, but the demons that filled her soul allowed no tenderness to touch her heart.

Viktor Brack's egotistic reaction gave her a foothold of control before she took the risk of introducing him to her own private area of the institution.

The Abyss

"Well, this looks like your typical old stone German building basement." Theo snorted in an attempt to deny his heart a chance to skip a beat as he felt a cold chill hit his face and trickle down his spine. Murphy stood motionless against Theo's pant leg. His robotic programming, cued from the intensity of the heavy darkness, began a nearly silent whir of conversion to heat vision. Without reason or alarm, both youth and dog checked their emotions and never turned to look as the steel door made a dull click and sealed behind them.

Hearing Murphy's collar switch to heat vision, Theo looked down at his wrist computer and pressed a button to sync with his dog. "All systems go, Murphy." Theo stared up the hall. "Okay, Murph." He squatted beside the dog, who only glanced up at his master then resumed a watchful eye to the empty darkness in front of them. "We can do this. We have to find Gracie, but those happy people aren't going to stay happy if they find us down here. We better divide and conquer. I'll take the rooms on the right. You take the rooms on the left." Theo stroked Murphy's back with one hand while he pointed down the hall with the other. "About halfway down, we'll compare notes."

A low growl let Theo know that Murphy was ready for a challenge, but when he glanced down at Murphy, he jerked his hand away from the dog's back. Murphy cocked his head and sat down. Theo rubbed his eyes with a fist before he looked back at the dog. His confidence took a hit as a chill spread fingerlike tingles up the back of his neck. For a second time, he had seen a vision of Gracie's face in a spot on Murphy's back, and for a second time, he caught a glimpse of her face peeling and rolling away.

"Man, I gotta get a grip on myself. I've a strange feeling we better hurry." He shook his head. "I don't know why." Theo hadn't even finished talking before Murphy jumped to his feet and trotted up the hall and dipped into the first room on the left.

Theo jogged with crooked strides from his wounded leg and with his wrist extended in front of him so he could be alerted by Murphy's heat vision. With the exception of an occasional blip of red, the face of the watch remained an ebony field of inactivity as he turned into the first room.

Murphy jolted to a stop. The smells of the lower level were strong, but there was a familiar scent that made the robotic dog turn with his nose tipped upward toward the door of the room he had just entered. A smell, a powdery scent that Murphy liked hit his sensors, but by the time he trotted back to the doorway to peer down the hall, he missed the sight of a girl running in stocking feet to find her boots, slipping into a room that had been her prison. Logging the scent on his internal memory chip, the dog returned to look for signs of life in the tiny dark room.

Theo intended to take a quick look into each room and move to the next, but the first room captured his interest. He stood with his back to the hall as he extended an arm to push a half-open metal door. There was no resistance and no sound. The windows on the opposite wall rested just below the ceiling, allowing only vertical shafts of gray light to enter at the sides of shades that hung down and lay awkwardly on the windowsill. The hazy daylight was enough to give a slight perspective of the room where two concrete islands protruded from the floor. One wall was vertical steel bars.

Impatiently, Theo waited while his eyes adjusted in the limited light. He moved to one of the concrete islands, but it made no sense to him. He ran his hand along a narrow rim of concrete that bordered the stone table. The table lay at an angle where anything set on it would roll to one end. He ran his hand down the table but jerked his arm back when he realized a metal drain was at the lower end. *Gross. I wonder what they wash in such a shallow table.*

He stepped back with his thoughts as he turned and saw an odd shape on the floor. Even with the shafts of daylight sneaking into the room, his eyes couldn't create an identifiable object out of the small mass on the floor. At first, he wondered if it was a miniature broom or mop with an end in wispy knots. He bent over and grasped the handle, lifting it from the floor. It wasn't until the odd object was pulled close to his chest that he saw it wasn't a mop at all but rather a small hand and arm that had been amputated just below the elbow.

"Augh!" The scream came from Theo's chest and plummeted into the nothingness of the room while the severed arm dropped back down to the floor. He fell backward against the vertical bars. Icy fingers grabbed his neck from behind, threatening to crush his Adam's apple and puncture his throat. Instinct for survival made him pull the icy hand from his neck and lunge for the door. A glance over his shoulder from the hall showed him an arm silhouetted against the dusky light, suspended in midair.

Back in the empty hall, Theo's body trembled with a blending of fear and confusion. The watch on his wrist remained blank. *What is this—a house of horrors? What just happened?* Theo replayed the episode in the room against the wishes of his heart. *What grabbed me? What if I couldn't get away?* He kept his shoulder against the wall and peered back into the dim room. He listened for any noise but only heard a light shuffling sound like a mouse scurrying across the floor. *I gotta get out of here.* Before he had time to consider the room again, he turned and headed for the next room.

The wall was interrupted where a steel door was sealed inside its metal frame. *Maybe I'll skip this one.* Theo considered avoiding the closed room. *No. No, I can't take a chance on missing Gracie. Ugh, I hope she's not in this creepy basement. Please, please, please, Gracie, please be somewhere else.* He gave a slow blink to bolster his courage as he wrapped his fingers around the metal knob on the door. His mind wandered with the shape of the small doorknob in his hand. *Wow. I wish I could see this doorknob better. It's sure different from the keypads at home. Didn't people get tired of turning knobs in the old . . .* A click from the turning knob made Theo's wandering mind stop short. He listened for a response from inside the room. His own slow breaths filled the silence in his ears. Without releasing the knob, he shoved the door that opened easily and quietly.

The structure of the room with a yellowed window shade at first seemed to copy the other room. It wasn't until he breathed in that Theo realized this room had a distinct odor, one that almost stung the inside of his nostrils. He remembered wincing at an odious smell of rot and filth in the first room—almost the opposite of this pungent smell. As he took slow, deliberate steps farther into the room, he swung his arms in case the poor lighting failed to show him an obstacle in his path. But nothing, no tangible object rose from the floor or suspended from the ceiling.

Almost gingerly, Theo turned as he stepped, begging his eyes to reveal any hidden secrets of the room. He stopped and tilted his head as he had seen Murphy do so many times before as curiosity prompted his thoughts. *Okay, so the floors upstairs squeak against the sole of shoes, but I've been able to move pretty quietly on these concrete floors without worrying about my shoes making sounds.* He took deliberate steps as he walked in a tight circle. *Here in the center of the room I hear a difference when I walk. Not squeaky. Not a tap or click. Just different.* With his arms hanging loosely at his sides, he squatted until his fingers touched the floor. *Huh, some kinda tile floor.* He remained in a squat and swung his arms, dragging his hands across the floor. *Weird. Another drain? Makes more sense to have a drain in the floor than on a table.* He stopped swinging his arms and, in one movement, stood and walked to a wall with his arms extended in front of him. At the wall, he began the arm-swinging movement just as he had done on the floor. *Yep, just as I thought.* He fingered the metal pipe coming out of the wall. *A shower room, well, whaddaya know. Well, I guess I'm done in this room. Now on to find Gracie.*

Using his hands to propel himself along the wall, Theo confidently walked back to the door and swung it shut behind him as he mentally checked off another room. *One more before I compare notes with Murphy.*

Theo's watch rested blankly on his wrist as he followed the door's inward swing prompted by his shoulder and stepped into the third room. *Okay. Two rooms connected. Looks like I'm coming in through a back door. Maybe this small room is a dressing room or something.* Theo pushed the door closed behind him but rolled his head to scan the side and back walls from where he stood.

An opening in the wall of the small room showed two concrete islands jut up from the floor in the middle of the next room. A torn yellow shade let dreary daylight into the adjacent room. He was relieved to see a difference was that this room had no vertical bars, only solid walls. In a reflex action, he put his hand on his neck, trying to brush away the memory of the icy fingers at his throat.

What's with the concrete tables? He shook his head, welcoming an assessment of the two rooms as a way to keep his mind busy.

Ugh. First things first. Theo stepped farther away from the door. He continued to scan the small room, where he noticed a desk and pieces of a broken chair scattered on the floor. One wall held rows of shelves. Theo turned his head away but snapped it back as something clicked in his mind. Dozens of small glass bottles lined the shelves.

Look at all of those little bottles. That lady I saw was a nurse. Maybe all of those little bottles are medicine or something. I'm going to need some nitric acid. Oh yeah. Maybe I've finally run into some good luck.

He took long, slow strides until he stood in front of the shelves. Daylight that struggled against the storm brewing outside and against the heavy darkness of the basement room did little to help Theo as he squinted and turned bottles to read labels—some typewritten, some handwritten. Carefully, he lifted and gave a soft shake to several bottles, collecting three as possible winners in his quest. Bottles with liquid were returned to the shelf. He needed a saltlike powder to give power to his drone.

Too bad I can't find something to stop the pain shooting up and down my leg. Theo set his mind into his science mode and stepped to the small room's window with the three bottles. One by one, he held the brown glass bottles to the side of the shade. The second bottle brought a nod and a quickened limp back to the shelves to finish his work.

Mortar and pestle dishes were stacked at the end of the bottom shelf. Theo took the top dish from the pile with only a slight tink when the ceramic dish touched against another dish. In the scant light, he nodded to himself, allowing a smile to turn up the corners of his mouth. He almost felt as if he were back in his dad's laboratory having fun with another experiment. Another quick tap against the ceramic dish, and the mercury from the broken barometer tube dropped onto the powdery nitric acid.

One more ingredient. Theo moved a finger along the rows of bottles as if he could read by touch. *Ugh. I'll just have to take more bottles to the window to find some alcohol.* He started to reach for the top shelf. *No, Theo, think. Alcohol would be used for a lot of things, so it will be in an easy-to-reach spot.* He let his eyes wander the shelves until they landed on some larger bottles sitting on the bottom shelf. *I wonder.* He carried both bottles to the shaded window but took little time returning to the ceramic dish with a grin on his face and a brown bottle tipped to pour the clear alcohol into the nitric acid. *Now, make me some crystals!* Theo rolled the pestle in the dish to allow air to crystalize the new mixture of mercury fulminate.

Ah, step 2. A gentle shrug of his shoulder dropped Theo's backpack until he could slip one arm out of the shoulder strap and swing the bag around to his chest. He grasped the homemade drone strapped to the pack. He had loosened the bungee straps a million times to pull off his driftboard when he lived back in America. Theo softly snorted to himself. *America. Wow. The explosion in Dad's lab and getting catapulted back to this ancient time in the TimeWorm machine seems so long ago.* He shook the thoughts from his head for fear that dwelling there would make him sad and distract him from his plan to find and take Gracie out of this hellish place.

Theo set the drone on the narrow table under the shelves of bottles and petri dishes. Steady hands. Theo wasn't nervous about making mercury fulminate, and he was sure it was still pretty safe in this liquid state, but he wanted to be very exact and have the outcome he expected. His hands pushed down along the sides of his coat until his arms were fully extended, and any sweat from his hands had been left on his coat and jeans. With gentle precision, he lifted the ceramic dish and let the liquid mixture run into the hollow wings and fuselage of the drone. *Okay, now dry so I can use you!* He adjusted his backpack, being careful not to knock into the drone left sitting on the table.

Theo mechanically moved to the opening in the wall and peered into the next room until his eyes stopped at one of the raised concrete tables. Some kind of straps or rope hung off the sides. He studied the dangling forms. Above the table, something was suspended from a long cord connected to the ceiling. He studied the suspended shape until he realized it was old-fashioned lighting—a chain hanging from the metal base of a glass bulb.

Maybe I can see better if . . . Theo noticed something had been tossed in a bulky pile against the back wall. In the darkness, he stood unaware that it covered a frightened girl huddled under a blanket. Theo stepped to the empty table and reached up. Just as he gripped the chain to pull and light up the room, he saw the face of his watch computer glow red from Murphy's heat vision.

Murph! Theo dropped his arm, and in a few long strides, he rushed into the hall just as Murphy slipped out of a partially opened door and bolted into the next room. He followed the robotic dog into the unlit room across the hall where they hid behind the open door. In a chill of darkness, he pressed his face to see between the wall and cold steel door.

Murphy pressed against his master's legs. Theo could feel a slight vibration. *Strange. He's a robot, so he can't be shaking from fear. I wonder why . . .* He listened for a low growl that sometimes came as if a motor were idling and causing a vibration, but just as he looked down and cocked his head to listen, Murphy's blue language transmitter lights flashed in intermittent procession and voices from the hall filled the silence.

"Grab her!" Viktor Brack's voice resounded off the cement walls of the cold lower region.

An icy hand grabbed Gracie's throat, alerting fear in every fiber of her being as she tried to escape. She kicked forward with her thick boot and upset a silver cart, sending metal tools of surgery across the hard floor. She knew to survive meant to think clearly and fight relentlessly, but the pressure on her neck sent a pain and fear of losing all means of breathing. Backward she kicked with one foot as she tried to stomp with the other, but her foot only swung loosely above the floor. With both hands, she grabbed and pulled the hairy hand and arm that lifted her by her neck. It was impossible. The grip of the big man was too strong to be affected by the pull of a sixteen-year-old girl's hands. Instinctively, Gracie balled up one fist, while the other hand kept its grip on the arm that threatened to strangle her. With a swinging motion, Gracie punched backward. Contact with the face behind fueled the pumping action of her arm. Backward punches of her fist exploded as her kicking legs pummeled her heavy boots into the legs and torso of the large man holding her.

"We . . . caught . . . a bit of a . . . devil with this one, Dr. Brack. Had to knock her out in the forest," Alvar grunted out words while Gracie dropped from his grip.

"How could you let her escape? What kind of facility do you run here? Perhaps you are softened by the girl. Do you forget your position and duty to the Reich? To *me*?" The uniformed man turned his face to spit the last two words into the face of the orderly who stood in the doorway of the room. "Perhaps you lose your touch and need to be demoted." Red with anger, the officer stormed out of the room to pace in the hallway.

The shouting of men's voices was as dark and blurred as the putrid yellow glow coming from the bulb dangling above the concrete slab standing like an abandoned and broken pillar in the middle of the room. Gracie scooted backward, away from the man who had earlier beaten and tied her to a table and now tried to strangle her. She pulled her legs, ready to spring into a run from where the release of the hairy arm had dumped her onto the floor.

Get behind . . . Gracie searched with wild eyes to find a place to hide, but she was caught off guard when two more men in laboratory scrubs grabbed her arms and legs. "Ugh. No! No! No! No!" She tried to pull her arms and legs back as the men flattened her against the floor. Her head hit against the concrete floor. "No!"

"Get the needle!" This time, the voice of a woman yelled above the scuffles and grunts.

"No! No! No!" Gracie continued to pull and wrench her body, fearing her life would be left as a lifeless form if she didn't fight. "No! No!" A sting in her shoulder sent an icy chill down her arm. "No! N-n-n-o . . ." Gracie forced her eyes to see through the blur that was numbing her body. Her brain voiced the word *fight*, but her muscles refused to obey as they contracted into useless flesh that she saw but could not feel. She looked through the blur and wondered why the voices had become slowed and distant though she could see forms standing around her.

The crack between door and frame limited Theo's sight, but he could see from the gestures of a swinging arm and pointing finger that the speaker was a man in a gray-green uniform that formed upward out of knee-high leather boots that looked scuffed from wear but not rough to suggest combat exercise. Theo's eyes caught a glimpse of a skull patch on the collar of the uniform.

The shouting continued. Theo put his hand to his neck, fearing the sudden knot in his throat would strangle him if he didn't get it swallowed. He pressed the side of his face into the wall to see through the crack behind the door that concealed him. The face of the military uniform, even in the dim basement lighting, was Viktor Brack.

He lifted Murphy into his arms to pet him and prevent the dog's instinct to growl at the evil whose stench filled the air. Even with each petting stroke of Theo's hand, the hackles on Murphy's back refused to relax back down into the soft fur. Together, they listened as the concrete walls magnified the voices in the room he had hurriedly left.

The nurse spun on her heels to face Dr. Brack. "I cannot tell you how, but I know she's got a live spirit in her. We've given her a heavy injection of veronal to sedate her. She's as helpless as a rag doll."

"A heavy dose?" Veins created ridges in Brack's neck that were visible from where the teen and his dog peered into the passage.

"I don't want her dead—not just yet! She's my weapon against *the Watch*, against Möeller! Who do you think trained her wild spirit? If she's his daughter, she has no other blood than that of a warrior. I want him tortured, and seeing his dead girl is not enough! I want him to pay for being an enemy of the Reich, and that payment will be the peeling of her skin!"

"Besides," Viktor's voice dropped in intensity as he walked into the room to squat beside the girl lying in a heap, "I need some leather for a new book cover as I seem to have lost my old journal." He let the tips of his fingers glide down Gracie's soft arm as she lay unflinching on the concrete floor.

A sound from the room across the hall, much like a sob from a tightened chest, made Irmgard hesitate and glance at the door that stood slightly ajar. Without notice, she slipped up to her private quarters to change into a crisp uniform and pull tight the strands of hair that hung loose from the scuffle.

"Bring in our guest. I believe we have something Jahile Möeller should see," Viktor Brack spoke with too much enthusiasm inside the hazy, cold room.

Torment

A BEATEN MAN STOOD strong and stoic though he was hit with a club and shoved into walking down the gray-black hall. Iron chains suspended from shoulders and snaked down arms and legs into shackles at wrists and ankles of the man as two orderlies goaded him into the concrete room.

"So you thought you'd keep your treasure a secret, did you? You're good with secrets, but unfortunately, you are an enemy to Germany's Reich. Tisk, tisk, tisk." Brack clicked his tongue against his cheek as if scolding a schoolboy. "Too many secrets, but we've found one," Brack spoke slowly as he walked toward the body lying on the floor. "Set our little secret up on the surgery table, men. I don't think she will cause any more problems, and we want to be sure everyone gets a good look." He turned and sneered at Jahile Möeller, who stood with his jaw set and his eyes trying to search every inch of the dungeon room.

Gracie's long hair fell down toward the floor as Alvar lifted her shoulders not caring that the drugs that had put her into a stupor caused her head to drop back. She turned her head to look through the dizzying yellow air as the chained prisoner lunged against the chains and men holding him. She blinked to see through the fog in both her eyes and her mind as the orderly laid her on the table and carefully, perhaps too carefully, adjusted her arms and legs as if to lay her in a comfortable position.

Voice? Whose voice? Gracie's thoughts were as suppressed as her vision by the thick drugs pulsing through her body. *Whose . . .*

"Gracie!" Jahile's voice was scarcely recognizable as the concrete chamber echoed back his half yell, half cry. "Brack, release her! She has nothing to do with you!"

Voice . . . "Help . . ." Gracie's slurred plea surfaced from her thoughts. She couldn't see what wrapped her guardian's body, but she knew his voice, knew he had come to save her again. "Help me . . ." Her words were lost in the shouts of the chained man's voice as it threatened the mad scientist, who stood with a half smile across his fiendish face.

"Did you think, Jahile, that we would not find your daughter? No wonder you hid her from us." Brack pulled the back of his hand down the cheek of the girl lying on the table. He turned to the large man whose hairy hand held a scalpel that glinted in an eerie reflection of the yellow light. "Shall we start with an arm, Alvar?"

"No! No! Enough of your sick evil! Do what you want to me, but leave her alone!" Jahile's words fell between the chasm of yelling and pleading.

Irmgard stepped into the room, dressed in white, the color of purity that was so out of place in this dungeon of hell. "Dr. Brack, surely you wouldn't begin without me." Her soft voice belied her calloused heart. She kept her eyes on the evil scientist as she walked to the table. "Ah, such a pretty one, such a perfect one." She held out her hand to Alvar, who obediently laid the scalpel in her hand. Had a light been shining in this den of death, any onlooker would have seen her countenance harden and wrinkle though her demonic eyes looked out of a stoic expression. She began cutting Gracie's jacket and the shirt underneath, pulling fabric away from the body that lay unable to react or even move on her own.

Nurse Irmgard drew an imaginary circle then tapped against the soft skin below Gracie's neck. "Oh, please, Viktor. May I have this pretty piece of skin? I need a new cover for my favorite book."

"Oh, no. No, no. It's not right that you keep this beautiful skin to yourself." Brack turned his eyes toward Jahile as he bent his face down within inches of Gracie's blurred vision. "Is there anything you would like to say to your father, hmm?"

"Fath . . . ?" Gracie couldn't form the word with her lips any more than the word could form into sense in her brain.

"For the sake of all the evil in your heart, Brack, leave her alone!"

Irmgard tugged and threw fabric of Gracie's clothing, exposing the delicate caramel skin of her arm and waist.

"Such beautiful color of skin, wouldn't you say, Jahile? But it's all wrong. It doesn't fit the laws of the Reich now, does it?" Viktor Brack let his voice move as slowly as he pulled, never lifting, his index finger from her shoulder down her arm until he stopped against her hand.

Against all reason of hopelessness, Jahile lunged against the chains that held him as he tried to reach the table where Gracie lay. His screams emerged from depths of hatred against the government that had destroyed his own wife and daughter and against the demon who had slithered from the Third Reich abyss preparing to destroy the child he promised to guard and grew to love.

Brack stepped back in reaction to the bloodcurdling yells of the guardian whom he mistook as Gracie's own father. His own heart settled only after realizing the chains and guards held Jahile from any attack. "Well, I was going to offer you a piece of this lovely flesh as a memento, but your useless yells are beginning to irritate me. I'll just have to keep her flesh myself to replace something she stole from me." Even the putrid yellow light could not have made Viktor Brack's face look more diabolical than the sneer that distorted his countenance. He gestured toward the guards. "Return this man to his cell." He bent down until his hot breath covered Gracie's face. "Tell your father goodbye, my dear. He'll not recognize you once we peel off your beautiful skin."

Straightening to his full height in a feeling of power, Dr. Brack looked around the room until his eyes settled on the young nurse standing beside him. "Irmgard, let's first celebrate with a bite to eat. This procedure always takes so long and makes me terribly hungry." The evil scientist motioned to the orderlies as he turned to walk out of the room behind the yells of the tormented guardian being dragged back to his cell.

Alone in the cold and heartless room, Gracie's head rolled to the side, unable to fight the stupor that commanded her eyes to close.

Action

IN THE SILENCE of the concrete basement, Theo was sure he could hear hoarse screams from someone who had been dragged away, screams that sounded familiar. He heard Brack's threats across the hall, but he knew Gracie's father would be far from this place. Who stood in Gracie's room tormented and threatened by Viktor Brack? His ears could not prove, but his heart was never more sure—this was the voice of their friend, Gracie's guardian, Jahile Möeller.

A pulsing dagger of pain shot through Theo's head. The dark and silent room where he stood could not assuage the screams of terror and the words he heard from across the hall. He held Murphy and, with an arm, wrapped the dog's neck to keep the collar lights from being seen. With Murphy's head close to his own, Theo heard the cries, the shouts, the pleadings of voices he knew and loved interspersed with conversations that boiled up from depths farther below the basement where he stood.

An eerie cold crept down Theo's back. He didn't need Murphy's collar to hear screams, boots scuffling, and even a calm and determined walk retreating down the hallway, leaving a hollow shell of quiet. For what seemed an eternity, neither boy nor dog made any sound after footsteps of the scientist and his henchmen could no longer be heard in the basement hall. He bent to set Murphy down on the concrete floor and winced at the pain that shot through his leg.

"Augh." With both hands grasping his shin, Theo slid down to the floor. Like Murphy's growls and hackles, even his own body had gone on defense and had tensed every muscle. Now, as he fought to be calm in the face of fear, the pain from injury exacerbated by muscles held taut for too long sent spikes of nerve endings to the surface. He slumped over to rest his spinning head on the cold floor, unsure if the pain or the thoughts of horror would overtake his mind first.

Murphy paced between open doorway and master sitting behind the door. The red staccato flashing lights on his collar warned of danger. The uncanny loyalty of even a robotic heart told him to stay with his wounded master. The click of his agitated paws in incessant motion tapped against the pulsing throbs in his master's veins.

"Murphy!" Theo's harsh whisper came out with more force than he intended. "Please, just stop!"

The clicking paws stopped, while a cold muzzle pushed and licked the master's face. Between the cold floor and the comfort of a friend who lay down beside him, reason began to push past pain, and Theo rolled to his back. His eyes focused on the rough ceiling.

"Okay, Murph. Sorry. I'm fine." Theo turned his head toward the dog beside him. "Really. At least I'm fine enough to know that we've gotta get Gracie outta here. Man, with my leg hurting so much, I need to buy myself some time." He sat up and looked around the dark room as he gave a brisk rub to encourage circulation in his aching leg. "How the heck am I gonna get her out of here?"

Murphy's head popped up just as his tail lifted and started a steady wag. In a movement that made his head jerk upward and lift his whole body, Murphy was on his feet and clicking around the room, standing on back paws, craning his neck as if trying to see the tops of the counters that lined the room.

"I'm not sure what you're doing, but you're right. I need to get up and start looking for . . . Oh, I don't know what I'm looking for, but . . . Augh!" Theo couldn't help but react to the pain in his shin. "Mind over matter, mind over matter. There's no bone sticking out, so surely I can stand a little pain." The last few words came out with a grimace as he pushed up with one leg until he was standing. Carefully extending his hurt leg, he began with a few slow steps that rolled into a rhythm as he moved across the room. "Walk it off, Theo. Walk it off." He could hear his old driftboard coach in the back of his mind. "Yeah, right. I've had worse tumbles from airs on a half pipe when an ollie took my board a different direction from my body. Surely,

I can stand to get one tiny girl out of a concrete torture chamber." Although his voice was a mixture of pain and sarcasm, it was enough to invite determination into his spirit.

"Murphy, let's set your vision on my wrist computer. I need you to check the halls to be sure everyone has gone upstairs." He glanced at Murphy while he tapped the face of his watch. "C'mere. Let me see your collar." A touch to the collar filled with chip technology, and Theo's watch displayed the sights through Murphy's eyes. He gave a quick rub to the top of Murphy's head, making his ears shake up and down before the obedient robot gave a quick yip and headed out the door.

Little time passed as Murphy made a quick circuit of the hall with zigzags in and out of doorways. Theo kept his eyes glued to his wrist screen and his legs ready to bolt if face or demon showed through the dog's vision. The storm brewing in the skies outside made each yellow-shaded room a little darker with Brack's sinister plan hanging in the basement air. Murphy returned to his master, seeing no other people in the empty basement rooms.

"They're not just evil, Murphy," Theo whispered into the soft ear of the dog whose collar not only translated but also recorded every word. "They're monsters. No, they're not unthinking monsters. They're demons with dangerous minds. But they can't have Gracie. Dear God in heaven, they can't have an angel!" His clenched jaw was set with the determination in his soul. Without a sound, he motioned with an open palm to Murphy. "Stay." In three strides, Theo was in the room across the hall.

Not until he reached out and let his fingers touch Gracie's face did Theo let himself make a sound. Overwhelmed and uncaring that he allowed his emotions to be exposed, he bit his lip, holding back all but a slight cry of anger and fright. "Gracie. Gracie. Wake up. C'mon, Gracie. Wake up." He shivered to think this was the room where he had earlier seen something against the wall, but the noise in the hall had stopped him from pulling the chain on the light above the bed. "I didn't know, Gracie. I didn't know you were here." He frantically looked around, trying to channel his thoughts.

"I have a plan, Gracie. I don't have it all thought out, but this is my turn, Gracie. I'm going to save you, Gracie. I'm going to save . . ."

The scant light filtering in from the torn window shade tormented him as his mind's eye made it look as if Gracie's skin was pulling from her face. "My vision!" He jerked his hand away from where he was smoothing a lock of hair that had fallen across her cheek, and he ran from the room.

Unwilling to distract himself from a plan, Theo dropped to his knees. "Murphy, Dad always said science should be used for good. We have work to do." His voice commanded full attention of the dog, who paced back and forth from Theo to the doorway in a mixed attempt to help and keep watch at the same time. "C'mon, Murph! We need the drone to get Gracie outta here!"

They returned to the room where the drone was left, filled with crystals of mercury fulminate, waiting like a cocked gun. "Stand, Murphy. I need the light." Theo held the drone and squatted by the table, using Murphy's collar to see. "If I drop this drone, we won't have to worry about saving Gracie because we'll all die in an explosion." Whether or not Murphy understood Theo's words, he knew his master's tone of voice was stern and needed to be obeyed. Theo set the drone on the floor beside his backpack and leaned back on his haunches, wiping his palms against his jeans.

"Okay. Murphy, on impact, this drone will become a destructive device." Theo swiped his arm across his brow. "Ugh." He closed his eyes while he moved from a squat position to where he could extend his wounded leg. "Now, what's the rest of our plan?"

He rubbed his calf and shin to ensure circulation. "Buck it up, Theo. She's saved you enough. This ain't no HoloGame. It's time to save her. Quit whining and get busy."

Murphy tilted his head from one side to the other, causing the light from his collar to move back and forth across his master's face. The words recorded into the robotic dog's computer chip, but he was not programmed to understand why the youth was talking to himself or what his words meant.

Theo dropped his head into his hands and rubbed his forehead as if to clear thoughts and make room for more. "Murphy, I don't know what to do. I mean, I know I need to get Gracie outta here. She's knocked unconscious, so, umm, I, uh, so I'll have to carry her out of here. Yeah. I think my legs will be stronger if I use my quad muscles more than my calf muscles—thanks to this stupid injury." He looked at Murphy for inspiration but only saw a dog with his head cocked sideways. "So, uh, so, I'll put, no, I'll . . . Oh, I know, I'll carry her across my shoulders. Okay. Yeah, so that'll work." He glanced at the makeshift drone with the makeshift mercury bomb.

"As soon as the drone crashes, there will be one heck of a boom. That thing'll explode enough to bring down some of these concrete walls." This time, Theo was the one to cock his head as he looked at Murphy. "First, we need to get out of here. Problem is, I don't know how to make it fly so it can crash." He rubbed his forehead again and sat with his head in his hands. "I can't think, Murph. It flew before because it was programmed to follow your collar." Murphy walked to the drone and picked it up in his mouth, while Theo reached for the backpack. "Well, I better strap this on before I forget it holds Brack's book."

Theo clasped the front strap of the pack as he stood and looked down at Murphy. "You're right, Murphy. If I'm busy with Gracie, you better hang on to the drone so it doesn't get damaged. Let me set the program so it will fly." Theo bent down to manipulate small wires and buttons on both the drone and Murphy's collar. A barely perceptible whirr began inside the drone. "Okay. We're all set." He rubbed the top of Murphy's head as the dog with the wagging tail gently picked up the humming drone. "Try not to let go of the drone. If we need an explosion, we can throw it into a wall or something and not even need to set it off with your collar. Maybe we won't need the distraction to get outta here. I just don't know." He stood and looked down at Murphy. "One thing I do know, I need to get Gracie outta here. So let's get her on my back and start down the hall. C'mon, little buddy."

Determined in heart and mind, Theo paused in the doorway only long enough to be sure the halls were still dark and empty before he lunged into the next room.

As if Gracie were in on the plan, her limp body draped across the shoulders of her friend, who lifted her from the table and held her legs with one arm and her shoulders with the other. Theo was sure he felt a calm sigh from where her stomach rested against the back of his head.

"Skin. Murphy, I feel her skin against my neck. She'll need cover." His eyes searched the room. Nothing. "No coat. Ugh." He saw the wool blanket by the wall where Gracie had earlier hid. "I dunno what evil deed this has covered, but we have no choice." In a balancing act, Theo wiggled the blanket through the straps on his pack.

In a half limp, half jog, the rescuer returned to the hall. "Murphy, I'm pretty sure their voices didn't stay down here for long, so they must have taken the closest stairs. We'll just have to play it safe and take the long way around." With Murphy trotting at his ankles, he headed back toward the stairs at the far end of the dark passage.

Imagining that he looked like a hunchback, Theo's confidence increased as he bore up under the weight of the girl and the pain of his injured leg. With a puff of air boosted by pride in his plan, he focused on a shadow that promised to be the end of the hall where a stairwell would lead the way out.

Voices from behind interrupted his thoughts.

"Hallo! Halt! *Wie heissen Sie?*"

Without looking down at Murphy, Theo was sure he heard voices calling him to stop and give his name. Pleading for the end of the hall to come to his rapid feet and heartbeat, Theo knew to look back would slow him down. "We've gotta get outta here, Murphy! Run! Run, Murphy!" He knew the sounds pounding in his ears were the pounds of heavy boots that chased behind him.

To his right, Theo saw the door opening to a stairwell. He released his grip on the legs of the girl slung across his shoulders just long enough to turn the cold metal knob and push open the door. "Run, Murphy! Run!" Quad muscles built with driftboarding skills in another century had missed too many workouts, and the fibula wrapped in muscle on his lower leg was threatening to break under the pain and pressure. Dauntless and determined, the unwelcome noises pressed Theo forward.

Imprinted memory gave Theo an automatic impulse to turn back up the hall when he reached the open doorway at the top of the stairs. This time, the pounding was his own feet bearing the weight of his burden and the increased weight of his year of growth since he had left the twenty-first century. His vision was more sure in the main floor hallway, though lights were only what seeped from rooms farther down the corridor. He was sure he saw something white, maybe a ghost, standing and yelling with extended arms. He didn't care. He grunted and panted forward with his elbows held out from his body when he crashed into the white form that attempted to stop his progress. The impact was real, the high-pitched scream was real, the sound of a head being thrust against the wall was real. His ears told him a watermelon split open, but he shook the sound and ran until he could turn and run down the steps that led out of Hadamar and opened onto a lush green lawn shadowed by thunderclouds overhead.

Unknown to Theo, his robotic dog had turned in the lower region of Hadamar to face the demons wrapped in surgical garb, standing at the far end of the long hallway. Where he stood near the stairwell, Murphy heard the voices of prisoners crying out from where they were locked in the cages of the first room.

Although Murphy was a robot without a heart and without a command, his internal intelligence programming connected him with duty and with the drone. He looked up the stairs where Theo had run on the mission of escape. Then, he turned and gently released the grip of his mouth setting the drone on the concrete floor, facing the length of the corridor.

Without Theo's knowledge and without hesitation, Murphy took off in a full-speed run. The drone lifted and increased in speed as it held a course of flight two meters above the floor, just a step behind the charging dog. Murphy's internal radar detected the approach of the men. Computer chips inside the small dog reported converging air currents of life-form, robot, and drone. Programmed instinct gave Murphy the knowledge that his wounded master with a load on his shoulders needed more time to escape. Murphy ran away from the stairwell, with intent to run headlong into the wall at the opposite end near the yelling and confused men.

The impact of the drone hitting the wall caused the mercury bomb to detonate, sending concrete shrapnel from basement and first floor in all directions. A quick spin and roll of the robotic dog catapulted a silver sphere through a vacant space in the exterior wall where Hadamar secrets lay exposed to a storm-crested sky. The sphere, propelled as if shot from a gun, lay battered and lifeless at the back of the lawn.

Theo was halfway to the road that bordered the forest when an explosion behind him thrust him from his feet, tossing both youths into the gravel drive. Slowly, he pulled to his knees, shaking his head to make sense of what happened. In an instant, realization shot through his mind, and he lunged for the unconscious girl lying several feet farther.

"Gracie! C'mon, baby, I'll get you to safety." He squatted to lift and cradle her in his arms. "C'mon, Murphy!" The young man, bent on rescue, never looked back. He knew the drone had done the work it was fashioned to do. He didn't care how it happened as long as his dog and his girl were safe.

Branches from cedars and tree roots reaching upward created a web of foliage. Theo hung his head across the body carried in his arms. He pulled his arms in toward his body to fold the girl inside his head and arms to protect her from the scratches of brambles and limbs. He didn't stop his headlong rush into the woods until the darkness of the stormy skies had been darkened even more by the cover of the forest.

"Here, here we go." Theo let his legs collapse under a pine where the winter shed of sweet-smelling needles had created a soft mat. "There you go, sweetie." He lifted her shoulder enough to pull his arm from where it had cradled her head. "Just rest. Here, stay warm." With gentleness she did not feel, Theo cocooned her in the wool blanket. He collapsed beside the sleeping girl and dropped his own head to his arm resting on his knees, allowing fresh air to calm his rapid breathing. Minutes passed before he raised his head.

"Murphy?" At first, he spoke just above a whisper. "Murph?"

The sounds of the forest did not return with the pant of his companion. Theo pushed himself to his feet, bearing heavy on his uninjured leg. He tugged at the tangle of branches that had broken in their escape.

"Murph!" Theo barked the words through a choke in his voice. "Murphy! Where are you?" He pushed back through the web that stood between their safety and the smoldering and crumbling walls of Hadamar.

"MURPHY!" Anger, pain, and fright mixed into screams answered only by a roll of thunder from oppressive storm clouds lowered from the heavens, promising to bury the gateway of Hades below.

"MURPHY!" The scream came from the depths of a shattered heart as the scene before him touched every nerve feeding his mind. He knew the drone was powerless without the movement of Murphy's radio collar. Unless thrown, it could not move or crash without the lead of the dog. The boy who had grown into a man in a century brutal and far behind his own collapsed just inside the roots and briars of safety, drenched by rain and tears.

Wandering

Theo's thoughts tangled in a pulsing headache, but the sweet smell of pine prompted him to open his eyes. He could hear rain hitting the matted web of branches above where he had collapsed several hours before. He propped up on an elbow and stared where Gracie lay at the base of large pine tree. He rubbed his stiff legs demanding attention before he rolled and crawled from under the brush to stand and gather thoughts of Hadamar. Craving a deep breath of the rain-soaked air, he placed his hands with fingers interlocked on the top of his head to open his airways while he paced nervously and searched the forest for any threats.

Fresh air began to clear the fog of memory. He turned in place, looking at the sleeping Gracie and forcing his eyes to find any other movement in the undergrowth. *Please, please . . .*

"Murphy." Theo begged a furry head to pop up in the forest shelter.

"Murphy?" The young man who had come so far refused to believe he was separated from his robotic friend, his best friend, his piece of life from home. "Murphy?" His soft calls of the dog's name brought a vision of the robotic face holding the drone softly in his mouth. *No! Please! Please, God, bring him back!*

"Murphy?" The air answered in silence. Theo walked to the edge of the forest. Smoldering smoke was rising in wisps where walls of Hadamar lay crumbled and people in military dress and white uniforms were descending the front steps, loading suitcases into cars, and driving away.

A heaviness of spirit overwhelmed Theo. He turned and crawled back under forest protection where he could lie next to the sleeping girl. He lay in the silence, seeing visions of his dad bringing a dog with floppy ears up the steps of their home, visions of Murphy rolling down the steps and rolling into a ball to ride in a backpack, visions of Murphy standing on point searching for Viktor Brack in a smoldering laboratory, visions of Murphy pressing a wet nose against his hand and begging for a good belly scratch, visions of Murphy that continued until his bursting heart gave way to exhaustion and sleep.

Daylight passed and temporarily took the rains of storm with it while the teens slept. Theo rolled against the girl beside him. He lifted a hand to pull the curls back from her bruised face. Gracie's eyes squeezed tighter in reaction to the touch.

"Gracie, are you with me?" Worry hung heavily in Theo's voice.

A long silence allowed Theo's fingers to caress the cheek and neck of his friend. Matted branches of their shelter were less dark than when he had first laid Gracie under the protection of the foliage. A thin ray of early evening light shone through a pinhole left in the storm clouds that held back any rain remaining in the threatening skies.

"I, uh, I think so." Soft murmurs moved across the pine needles as Gracie rolled her head toward his voice.

Theo looked down at the struggling girl, and in the silence interrupted only by the rumble of thunder, he watched her without moving or speaking. A massive weight evaporated from his mind when she looked up and smiled. The young man turned his face away from her and tipped his head back. An unrestrained grin formed—a reaction from his heart, relieved and happy to have her back again.

A noise uncommon to the wilderness erupted and stripped the smile from Theo's face. He moved into a squat and watched the trees for a possible assailant. Without looking down, he scoured the ground with his hands feeling for a large stick or branch to use to defend Gracie and himself.

Unexpectedly, Theo's thoughts catapulted back to the Jump Station at his father's science laboratory. He could almost feel water creeping up his body, trying to slow him down, trying to drown him. The eerie sense of *déjà vu* crept over him and stole his focus from the present threat. "Focus," he heard himself whisper. "She's counting on you."

The rough ground littered with matted pine needles gave up nothing to become a suitable weapon against attack. He raised his hands and clenched them into fists, ready to punch out with scared rage. He opened and closed his fingers a few times, preparing for the worst. He forced his eyes to see into the impenetrable darkness of the trees to see the enemy—*Hadamar nurse, Nazi soldier. Come on—SS officer, stinkin' jaeger.* "Uhh!" He sucked in and pulled back a fist. *Squirrel!* "Oh! Huh!" He blew the air out of his lungs at the sight of the four-legged critter searching for a late day snack.

Theo sat back down beside Gracie and nudged her with his shoulder. "Gracie, how far is sixty kilometers?" He wanted to make conversation and keep the girl from falling asleep—the effect of drugs Brack's goon had injected.

"Umm, it's ten kilometers farther than fifty." Sarcasm came in a whisper.

"Thanks, you're incredibly helpful." Theo sighed, feigning disgust, but he knew it was a good sign that she was joking with him.

"It's between thirty-five and forty miles," she sat up midyawn, "I think." Gracie laid her head against Theo's shoulder. She looked up at him and watched his eyes dart from tree to tree. "Do you think they followed us?"

"I don't know for sure. There was so much goin' on, so much chaos. I think maybe we slipped away unnoticed, but I'm not taking a chance." Theo looked down with a reassuring smile. The chill of evening air warmed a little when he looked into her eyes. "Either way, we gotta figure out where in the world we are if we're going to get to Frankfurt in time for our flight to America."

Theo and Gracie turned with their backs to each other and did their best to stay awake as evening hours crept past. They both watched the forest around them, not sure what they would do if someone came for them. Gracie was still reeling from the effects of the drugs the evil of Hadamar had pumped into her; Theo was still hearing the sounds of explosion at his back. Neither said a word as the sunlight sank from their world and the moon rose into the encroaching darkness. The night air dropped daggers of cold around them. Without speaking, they moved closer to each other. Their shared warmth gave them temporary protection from the cold, but even as Gracie snuggled into the arms that wrapped around her, they both nodded into an unrestful sleep.

An hour or so passed in silence. Theo jerked awake as his mind warned that he should not sleep. Disoriented and panicked, he scanned the area around them then looked down and saw Gracie's curly locks lying on his chest and his arms that held her. He carefully pulled one arm away and used the free hand to wipe the sleep from his eyes and reposition himself to a slightly more comfortable position. He looked around then up to the moon that was now at its zenith. "Oh man, how long?" he whispered.

The teenage boy's stomach cut into the silence of the still woods. *When was the last time I ate?* He reached out toward his backpack with his free hand and desperately swiped at the air. Again, he willed his arm to stretch just a bit farther. *If I move, I'll wake Gracie. If I sit still, I'll starve.* He gave one last swipe toward his pack but realized his arm wasn't going to grow any longer. In disappointment and slight frustration, he sighed and put his arm back around the *Mischling*, determined to keep her safe.

Slowly, the moon drifted toward the western world, sporadically slipping behind then reappearing through suspended storm clouds. In contrast to the white slice of moon, angry clouds threatened to break at any time and unleash their power. Gracie shivered involuntarily as the fingers of cold worked through Theo's embrace.

Morning came with shivers through Theo's body. His clothes were soaked through to his skin from the fine mist that started late in the night when exhaustion finally won. "Gr-Gra-Gracie," he forced out through involuntary shivering and chattering teeth. "You . . . you . . . up?"

"Freezing," she whimpered. The only dry part of her was where Theo's arms had firmly held her against him. Gently, she wiped the sleep from her swollen eyes and pushed her head back to look up at the boy who held her close. "What time is it?" She didn't try to lift her aching head from his chest.

"Not sure. I think almost daylight," Theo spoke quietly as if he were afraid of waking the forest. "Maybe if we start moving, we won't freeze to death."

"Okay." Her head wanted to argue, but her heart knew Theo was right. She crawled out from under the bushes at the base of the tree. A stretch gave her good reason to move her head and look around from where she stood. "Where are we headed?"

Theo didn't answer. He stood, stiff from the cold and mist, again moving close to Gracie in case she was weak from sleeping for two nights and a day in between. He shook his head and looked in all directions. "I've no idea. I just want to start moving, warm up our muscles, and figure out our next move. Maybe we'll stumble onto a town that's not full of psycho nurses and SS."

"Good plan. I hope it doesn't rain any harder." Gracie's extended hand shivered while they watched the mist collect in her palm. She peered intently through the trees, hoping for anything that would remind her of a path used by Loiza when he led her to Hadamar. "I think if we head through these trees, there should be a village." She waved an arm to the south, praying for a familiar sign. "Maybe we can dig up something to eat outside a bakery or something."

"Maybe."

The duo headed out, making their way deeper into the unknown, neither eager to begin a new journey, both fearing danger waiting behind every tree or in every shadow. Stumbling through the unforgiving wilderness, their unspoken worry and thoughts shifted back and forth from Murphy to Herr Möeller. Neither wanted to say aloud what hearts knew to be true: Herr Möeller was there in Hadamar with them. They had been just steps from being reunited. The *Champion of the Watch*, as Fritz called him, was there. But thoughts were kept unspoken because to speak the words would make them true. Their dear Herr Möeller was willing to take to his death, and possibly did, his promise to protect them. He was more than a protector. He was more than a friend and guardian. He was part of the beat in their hearts.

Despite the sun's unsuccessful struggle to pierce the dark clouds and heavy foliage with a few warm rays, the forest began to wake and come alive. Gracie stopped and knelt at the edge of a fast-moving stream. She cupped her hands together and lifted the icy water up to her lips, sipping at first. Her lips were cracked, and the coldness soothed them. She lifted more to her mouth as she bent closer to the water and let it wash away the dryness of her mouth and throat. She tried to remember the last time she had been given a drink or anything to eat. With a hand on her stomach, the emptiness and pain affirmed that it had been too long. "Do you have any food?" she whispered desperately, knowing the pounding in her head was partly due to hunger. "I haven't eaten since I was with Mama Vertina."

Theo looked over his shoulder from where he knelt farther down the bank. "Who?"

Gracie sighed and gave a crooked grin where her lip was still swollen and split from the hand of Alvar's beating. "Oh, a woman . . . uh, a woman I met when Zusa and . . . Oh, honestly, I have a lot to tell you, but I'm too tired and hungry to talk."

Theo walked up the bank and knelt beside his friend and put his hand on her shoulder, rewrapping the blanket around her. "I'll figure something out."

Gracie looked at their reflection in the water then up to Theo. "I know, I'm sorry."

"You have nothing to be sorry for." He wanted to admit to her that he hadn't eaten since dinner at the castle. Maybe a year ago, he would have whined and thought of his stomach first. Not now, though. Now he had the chance to step up and be the leader, to be the strong one, and he wouldn't let Gracie down. "If we had Murphy, we could use all kinds of modern technol—um . . . no. I'm sorry. We need to eat if we're going to survive out here. It'd be a shame to go through all of this just to die from starvation and hypothermia." Theo reached over and patted Gracie's hand. "I'll take care of you."

Gracie nodded. "Can we rest for a bit?"

"Sure." Theo stood and looked around. Excited to find the running stream, he hadn't noticed how the tall trees had branched out far above the ground, leaving them open to sky and to earth—open to anyone or anything that crawled upon it. The lack of cover would make it hard to hide from patrols or wandering hikers. Theo tensed as he realized how exposed they were by the side of the stream. His eyes followed the stream to where it split the top of the steep valley. Either side of the valley offered pine trees clumped together. "There." He pointed toward the largest grouping. "We're not safe in the open." He sighed to convince Gracie that he, too, would rather have stayed where they were. "We need to find cover. Those trees are still near the stream. We can climb to the top of this valley and then rest with water nearby." He held out his hand. "C'mon. I'll help you, Li'l Grey."

Never had the boy from the future recognized her by her name of the streets—the name of her father, the name given to her by other street urchins for her strength in defending herself. She knew she was nearly too weak to walk. She was certainly too weak to fight. *Li'l Grey, huh? He knows my heart will fight. He's sweet to encourage me.* Gracie reached for Theo's hand.

Hand in hand, the lost and beaten-down teenagers slowly made their way up the steep valley wall, using smaller saplings to help pull themselves up the hill. Theo put a hand on Gracie's back to steady her as she slipped on a wet rock. Beside the rock, he noticed the grass was laying over. He let his eyes follow the depressed ground cover down to the stream.

"Hold on a minute," he whispered, keeping his hand on her until she had firm footing. "A small game trail." He pointed down at the ground. "It goes down to the stream." He traced the path back up the mountain with a pointing finger. "And it weaves toward that large group of pines where we're headed!"

"Why don't you rest a few minutes. I need to dig a cord out of my backpack. I kinda borrowed it from a vacuum I found in the castle." He glanced over at Gracie, who was staring at him. He laughed when he saw her brows were wrinkled in question. "I made a drone."

"I don't know that word." Gracie didn't understand what was so funny.

"It's from the future." He smiled sweetly so she wouldn't think he was being haughty. "It took me quite a while to remember what the vacuum was. It kinda scared me at first. See? That's why we need each other. I'm confused without you." Though he spoke in a light-hearted way, he hoped she would hear the truth of what he said. He stopped digging in his pack and looked into the dark eyes looking back at him. "Really."

Purposefully, Theo let the silence hang between them before he winked and returned to his search for the cord. "Aha! Here we go!" He explained as he worked, "I'll strip out a few feet of wires from inside the cord."

After a few minutes of planning, a crudely created snare was dangling inches off the ground. Theo placed pieces of rock and broken limbs on either side of the trap, to help funnel the unsuspecting creature into the long looping wire. "I hope this works," he mumbled under his breath.

"Have you done this before?"

"No, I've built snares before but never used one to actually trap anything." A hint of sadness softened his voice. He picked up a stick and poked at the snare.

"So what's wrong?"

Theo stopped swinging the noose of the snare with the stick and looked at Gracie. "I dunno. It's just that I've never had to kill my food before—not a hundred percent sure I can do it." He stood up beside the dangling snare and looked up at the trees. "It doesn't feel good, but I don't know if we have another choice."

Gracie didn't answer right away. She looked up at the pines that would be their shelter for at least the remainder of the day then back down at the ice-cold mountain water running through the basin of the valley. "It's too early in the season to forage for nuts or berries." She followed Theo's gaze around the mountain and gestured with a wide sweep of her hands. "This is our only option. It's how life works. The strong devour the weak." For the first time since they started the hike up the mountain, she looked at Theo and smiled.

"At least we're doing it to live, not just because." She paused. "That makes me feel better about it."

"Yeah, good point. I'm better too." Theo looked up the mountain and pointed to where the ground wasn't as steep. "You take this side of the pines; I'll take the other. We can make a wide arc and come in from the other side. Hopefully, that'll scare out whatever's in there. If it stays on the path, it'll get funneled straight into the snare."

Gracie nodded and turned to climb the mountain.

By late afternoon, Gracie and Theo sat huddled under the low-hanging pines where rabbits had earlier nested. Gracie collected some fist-sized stones and made a makeshift fire ring. Inside the ring, she leaned small twigs into a tent shape with a small opening at the bottom. A few small pine knots were piled at the side, and a hard piece of pine sap was placed in the center of the twig tent. She wrapped the cord from the snare around two ends of a stick and spun with another stick in a back-and-forth motion. Theo helped her make the bow drill and explained how to press down on the vertical stick, the spindle. He warned her that the bow action would take a long time and a lot of stamina. At first, he was overprotective and afraid the physical exertion for over an hour just to start a small flame would be too much, but Gracie insisted that trekking up the mountain and snaring the rabbit had renewed her energy. Though her face was still cut and bruised from Hadamar, Theo noticed that she looked happier and stronger than two days earlier when he first laid her under the pine tree in the forest. Grinning in agreement, Theo picked up the rabbit and limped down to the water to skin and clean their dinner with a shard of rock he fished out of the stream.

"Weird." Theo picked up a thin branch too long for the fire ring and jumped on it until it broke in two.

"Who?" Gracie picked up scraps of rabbit and tossed them into the fire.

"What, not who. By the way, that rabbit fur stinks."

"Okay, what's weird? And I'd rather have stink than an animal smelling fresh rabbit and inviting himself to join us."

Both teens laughed. It felt good to laugh. It felt good to know their rabbit dinner would give enough protein to boost their mental alertness as well as satisfy their hungry stomachs.

"Oh, I was just thinking how picky I was when I lived in America. Man, I would love to have some good ol' American food, or a German pastry, or some porridge that you made at Herr Möeller's, but now I feel like a king after eating a little fried bunny."

"Have you ever eaten a rabbit before?"

"Nope. The desire hasn't even been on my radar."

"Theo, what are you talking about?" Gracie picked up a small rock and threw it at Theo.

Arms swung open in a wide expanse, the lanky teen jumped toward Gracie. Screams and laughter rolled from the hearts of the teens as they did their best with a beaten body and injured leg to run and jump in a game of chase. Days of intense and frightening circumstances had physically stifled their emotions, breaking them mentally. In the depths of a forest, lost and weary, a little food allowed them an outburst of voice and soul.

"Get off me, ya goon!" Gracie purposely rolled down an incline until she lay on her back, looking up at the afternoon sky. She turned her face uphill, enjoying the sound of laughter from the boy from the future. "Do you have forests in America?"

Theo propped himself up on one arm where he sat on the hillside. He took time to take in the mountain view, shaking his head before he answered. "No. I mean, yeah." He returned the smile of Gracie's expression. "Where I live, there are buildings and roads and, you know, city stuff. Oh, we have a city park, but it's nothing like this." He lifted his chin to gesture toward the mountain valley. "There are places in America where there are beautiful mountains. I've seen them in pictures. Some are in the next state over from where I live, but since my dad's a scientist, we don't travel far from a laboratory. My mom always wanted to travel, and they made plans, but the wreck . . ." He felt a knot catch in his throat. "Well, plans change."

Gracie shook her head, but her eyes never left the American who had entered a different century and a different world. "I'm glad you're here."

Theo slapped his thigh. "Well, we better not let a good thing go to waste. Let's get the fire a-blazin' so we can have a little warmth after the sun sets behind that hill. How 'bout you stoke the fire and I'll prop up some pine boughs to give us a little hut for protection tonight."

With renewed energy, the two kindled both fire and friendship.

"I . . . I'm . . . I'm freezing," Theo forced out through his chattering teeth.

"Me . . . me too," Gracie stuttered, cold and delirious from days of wandering through the woods with next to nothing to eat. The storm had made wildlife scarce after their first and only successful snare had awarded them the small rabbit. "I can't feel my fingers. We need another fire."

"No, Gracie, we need to get out of this forest and find a town. If we keep stopping to build a fire or a shelter before dark, we give up time when we could be walking. I don't know my way around Germany, and I sure don't know how to get outta this dark forest. It's not my fault we're lost."

"It's not my fault either!"

"If we hadn't tried to find some old woman who sedated you to make you sleep and then sent you to Hadamar, we wouldn't be so far into the forest!"

"If I hadn't gone to Hadamar, you'd have had a hard time finding me!"

"Who said I wanted to find you?" Theo stood with his back to Gracie, but he could still hear her sobs. "Look, Gracie, I'm sorry. I'm just a little testy." He turned and limped toward her with his arms out, but she walked away and kept her back to him. "Hey, I said I'm sorry. We're lost. I know that. Murphy's gone. Honestly, I'm struggling to admit that." He paused to rub his forehead. He sat on the ground and held his head in his hands. "Sorry. So very, very sorry."

Minutes passed before the sound of Gracie dragging pine boughs into a pile broke the silence. Neither of them spoke as Theo picked up boughs and added them to Gracie's pile. By dark, both teens had crawled under the makeshift shelter and curled up in each other's arms. Warmth was shared, but neither spoke until morning.

The sun and mist rose at the same time, giving hope to the spring ground. By the time Theo crawled out from under the pine boughs, Gracie was standing beside the shelter.

"I walked to the top of that hill over there." Gracie swung an arm in gesture. "When light hit the horizon, I saw something that looked like smoke, lots of it, in that direction. Maybe it's a town." She looked out over the valley. "At least it's downhill."

Unseen Paths

Recent storms had forced most of the inhabitants of the quaint town to seek shelter from the dismal weather. The deluge of water had slowed over the last hour into a steady drizzle, making sure that everything remained soaked and miserable. The people on the streets hurried to get out of the wretched weather, uncommonly cold for this time of year. Theo and Gracie watched from the alleyway as the few brave souls made their way about the town, heading in all directions.

"We aren't getting any warmer waiting here," Gracie grumbled.

"I know," growled Theo. "I gotta make sure it's safe. You wanna get caught by *Hitlerjugend* so they can stomp us both again? I can barely stand on my sore leg, let alone fight a group of hate-mongers!"

Gracie looked at her exhausted friend. She could see he was truthful. Rings below his bloodshot eyes reinforced the fact that he had gotten little restful sleep since he rescued her from Hadamar. She patted his shoulder, nodded, and slipped behind him into the alley. She leaned back and rested her head on the cold, wet wall. Instinctively, Gracie's eyes and mind scanned for escape routes, places to hide, and places to sleep. The street layout seemed similar to those of Munich, where she had gained reputation among the street urchins and the name Li'l Grey. Days in Munich felt like a lifetime ago. Heavy thoughts jumped from days on the street to escape of Hadamar to days in the rain-soaked woods and then settled on Jahile.

Where is he? Did I risk my life for nothing? Have I let him down again? Gracie shook her head in frustration. Her gaze scrolled toward the other end of the alley where she and Theo had slipped in undetected from a small park at the north end of the town. A half cry caught in Gracie's throat before sound hit the air. "There's something there."

"What?" Theo spoke but didn't turn to look at Gracie as she slid farther into the alley. "Gracie, what?" He spun around when a glance over his shoulder caught sight of Gracie moving away from him. "Where the heck are you going? I thought we were doing this together?"

"Shhh. Look." Gracie stood in a half squat with a finger pointing at a lump, visible in the shadows. "I saw it move."

"Really, Gracie. I thought we were trying to avoid problems, not identify every little bump in the night that—"

"Someone's hurt!" Gracie fell to her knees and pulled locks of blond hair from where they lay across a girl's face. "You're okay, sweetie. You're okay. Trust me."

"Gracie, let's worry about saving ourselves before we start saving every street urchin we fi—" Theo's words were interrupted by moving shadows that sprang from the end of the alley.

Theo stood tall as he faced the oncoming threat. "This way!" Reaching down, he grabbed Gracie's hand and pulled her into a dead sprint, heading straight toward the oncoming shadows. He surprised her with a quick right turn down a small side street. Rains had caused the packed earth to turn into a slush of mud with pieces of broken rock strewn about. The mire stuck to their shoes, causing them to slip as they ran.

"We . . . gotta . . . woods," Theo called out in staccato breaths. His energy level was already dangerously low. The fear of capture was the only thing keeping him upright and moving forward. He knew, though, that Gracie's body was more taxed than his, and he ran with the intent of carrying her if needed.

Three teens lunged from the next alley, tackling both Theo and Gracie. "Watch your—"

"Fight, Gracie!"

"Stop! We're not gonna—"

"Umph. We're not the—"

Shouts and grunts mixed with words tangled in the bodies rolling in the muddy pathway.

"Jakob! Jakob! Listen! I've got one." A strong teenager sat straddling Theo's back, pulling his arms behind until any movement caused Theo to wail in pain.

"Get away from—"

"Adalric! Come help me! This one's a bit wild to hold . . . Ouch! It bit me!"

A boy lunged across Gracie's flailing legs, pinning her to the ground. Someone grabbed her wrists and pulled her arms over her head as if to pull them out of their sockets.

"Talk to them, Jakob! Calm them down!"

"Listen. Listen to me!" the boy named Jakob yelled over the screams of Gracie still encouraging Theo to get up and fight and threatening to beat up her attackers.

Gracie felt a hand rub across her forehead and down the side of her face. Then again. Then again. Then the words "You're okay, sweetie. You're okay. Trust me."

The words—her own words coming back to her—confused thoughts and sounds. The touch on her face continued. "No!" The yell coming from Gracie's lungs gave her the power to lunge into a sitting position, but something stopped her body from moving forward and standing to run. *What? Move my . . . feet . . . Get out . . . Theo . . .* Her thoughts pounded in her mind, but the restriction holding her body even prevented her from unfolding from where she sat on the ground.

A hand then an arm circled the back of Gracie's neck. Surely, surely she was yelling against an attacker, but her heart and mind played evil tricks, and only the soft cry of a tired and wounded animal came forth. Tears erupted in the silence that fell. She could fight no more.

"Gracie."

A familiar sound interrupted the *Mischling's* heartbreak of giving in to whatever was holding her.

"Gracie." Again, the sound. Her name? "Gracie . . . Okay." It sounded so familiar, but perhaps she was only dreaming. Something or someone held her arms at her sides. Something was wrapped around the back of her neck.

The touch again—only different, a bigger hand, not rubbing, just holding, holding the side of her face just beside the bruised cheekbone and eye, her reminder of Hadamar.

"Gracie." Warm breath washed down from her forehead. The hand rubbed across a tear.

"Who? No! Stop hurt—"

"We're okay, baby. We're okay, Li'l Grey." The words were distorted by a voice filled with its own tears, a voice of a young man who had been challenged beyond any dangers he had ever felt, a voice of a struggle that had survived. "Gracie, it's me. It's Theo. And look . . ."

The arms that had wrapped around to hold Gracie's body and head released her to Theo's arms to allow a small beagle to crawl onto Gracie's lap and snuggle a muzzle under her chin.

"Theo?" Gracie's body relaxed into a heavy slump that was welcomed into her American friend's arms. She lifted a hand to the bundle on her stomach and felt the soft fur. "Oh, Murphy? Murphy? Is that you? Oh, Murphy!"

Three teenagers, strangers to what they witnessed, stood back in a huddle and wrapped arms around one another as they silently watched a youth whose long arms held a girl and a dog while they cried and wept without shame.

Spring sunshine wedged its way into the narrow alley where homes lay outlining the city of Wiesbaden. Unafraid of the daylight but determined to help a pretty girl with caramel-colored skin, a tall boy with wide shoulders, and the dog they had found a day earlier, three teens convinced the travelers to join them in a nearby home.

"There's plenty of porridge and warm milk." Minne pointed to a small wooden table flanked by chairs and a wooden bench that showed wear. The small kitchen offered warmth and food. She knew her parents would share with the young travelers as they had been known to open a back door and a hidden room her father had crafted between the wallboards. She would give explanation to her parents later, after the teens were fed and after she could contrive an excuse for bringing them to their home.

Minne bustled around the kitchen. Gracie looked out of the tops of her eyes and watched the girl, probably a year or two older than herself. There were questions of who they were and why such a strange rescue, but she dare not stop the spoon moving between her mouth and the hearty porridge that warmed her inside. "Who held me?" Words passed across the spoon as the porridge met Gracie's lips. Her eyes followed the busy young hostess. "Was it you?"

A short laugh came from a handsome youth who sat in a chair and leaned his arms on the table, though he had nothing to eat. "Yes, it was Minne, but I dare say that if we tumbled in the alley again, I'd rather hold you in my arms than take another swift kick from your boot!"

The other boy laughed and rubbed his shin. Theo looked up from his porridge bowl with a blank expression. Physical threats had been laid aside, but something about the kind words and actions of the teens who laughed with Gracie made Theo uneasy. He paused in eating and raised the warm milk to his lips to give his eyes an innocent chance to look around the table and judge the looks passed among the three young people. A hesitated glance at the well-built older boy caught a wink toward Gracie. He wanted to glare to warn him about flirting with Gracie, but a freshly healing scar and bruise from forehead to cheekbone beside the boy's winking eye caught Theo's attention.

"Uh, we're . . . uh . . ." Theo wanted to break the attention given to Gracie, though he had no plan of intelligible thought. "We . . . uh, yeah . . . We know how to fight."

The smiling eyes of the oldest boy danced in friendship to Theo. "Indeed, my friend, and good for you! I can't imagine what you've been through, but it looks as though you two have survived quite an ordeal."

"Jakob, let's not remind them of anything unpleasant." Minne's hand found a resting spot on Theo's shoulder as she spoke to her brother across the table. "My guess is they would like to finish eating and have a chance to clean up in a warm *Badezimmer* before we remind them of anything unpleasant.

Aware of the soft hand on his shoulder, Theo looked at Gracie, whose eyes riveted to his own before they fell back down to the bowl of porridge. A slap of a hand on the table shook Theo's attention back to the muscular boy on the chair.

"So right, Minne! C'mon, Adalric. Let's give them some time before we decide what needs to be done." Scarcely had the handsome young man finished his thought than all three youths were standing and walking to the kitchen door. The oldest of the three gave a quick squeeze to Gracie's shoulder as he passed beside the bench where Murphy had found friendship and petting from the youngest boy. The youth named Adalric bent face level with Murphy.

"So now the puzzle pieces almost fit, eh? Found your family, did you, ol' boy? Must say I'll miss you even though I don't understand your ways. Must like the varmints from outside better than biscuits, but I like you anyway." With a rub between Murphy's ears, Adalric gestured to a bowl of food left on the floor to feed the hungry dog who could no more enjoy a savory meal than a mechanical toy could intake a morsel.

Stepping back out into the warm sunshine, Minne encouraged her two new friends to enjoy the porridge and freshen up with pump water she had warmed and left in the *Badezimmer* and with fresh clothes she and her brother offered. The door clicked lightly behind her.

"They're so sweet," Gracie spoke to herself but let her words be heard by Theo as she finished the last helping of porridge in her bowl.

"Too sweet." Theo's retort was meant to be under his breath enough not to be clear but enough to make Gracie know he was uneasy.

"What?" From the sink where she set her bowl, Gracie turned to look at Theo. She was sure he had spoken, but his words were too soft to understand.

"Nothing."

"Okay. Well, I think I'll take up Minne's offer and go wash up." She slightly smiled at Theo. "I'm half scared to see myself in a mirror."

"You're beautiful." Theo looked at Gracie and spoke from his heart. He returned her smile before she turned to walk into the next room.

Taking his bowl to the sink, Theo picked up Murphy from the bench and cradled him with one arm. "What in the world is happening, Murph?" A muzzle nudged against Theo's shoulder. "And how'd you end up at this end of the forest? Man, are we gonna have fun replaying your internal recorder." He pulled Murphy up to his chin. "But for now, I think I'll find a sofa to collapse on and wait for my turn in the washroom. Shall we?" The long-legged youth hadn't noticed that he had grown several inches in the last year since the TimeWorm had spun him back a century, but he knew the dirty shoes by the back door would be replaced by the bigger boots of a young man.

By early afternoon, three youths of Wiesbaden sat on the floor in a tight circle with Theo and Gracie where all could ask questions and Murphy could wander from lap to lap enjoying a good back scratch or belly rub.

"On the streets—Munich, where I lived with my guardian—I heard about pirates, but I didn't really understand or pay much attention," Gracie spoke boldly.

"We're part of the society of *Edelweiss Pirates*—"

"Not really a society, actually—"

"No, but we really are an organized group. Difference is—"

"We're kids."

"The opposite of the *Hitlerjugend*—kids who act for Hitler."

Theo raised his eyebrows. "Do they like working for Hitler?" Everything his history teacher, Mr. Medi, had said about Hitler made him think it would be crazy to want to be a part of the Nazi regime.

Jakob sat a little straighter before he answered. "It's not a choice. Perhaps youths in America get to choose whether or not you follow your leader, but here, it's the law."

"If you want to survive, you're two things." Adalric held up a finger for each point he made. "One, you're Aryan. Two, you're a *Hitlerjugend*."

"Don't you have the right not to be a part?"

Gracie looked at Jakob, but she already knew the answer to Theo's question. Before Theo could ask the next obvious question, Gracie chimed in, "But you're not a *Hitlerjugend*. Isn't that risky?"

"Of course, but we still think we're lucky. Jakob and I," Minne gestured from her brother to her friend sitting beside Theo, "and also Adalric. We have parents who believe in the good of mankind, regardless of skin or blood kindred." She smiled at Gracie. "They allow us to think and believe of our own minds."

Theo looked around the circle. "Aren't you, aren't your parents scared to stand against the government?" In his mind, he understood the words they spoke, but he had never considered acting on belief rather than what every other teen was doing.

"Scared?" Adalric spoke up. "Sometimes, but proud that we have learned deeply and believe even deeper that what we say and do can make a difference. Besides, we don't see it as standing against the government. We see what we do as taking a stand against evil, for good, you know, for the good of the people—today and tomorrow." Adalric's voice punctuated the phrase "today and tomorrow." "No one will ever take a child from me with the brutality I've seen on the streets!"

Minne put a hand on her friend's arm. "Our passion always seems to come out in Adalric's words." A pause followed. "Now, about you. You don't wear a star, but you don't wear a swastika. Where do you stand, and why are you running?"

Theo's eyebrows raised as he gave a slight shake to his head. It wasn't that he didn't want to talk; the three new friends seemed trustworthy. He just didn't know where to start or how much to say. He looked at Gracie and grinned in reply to her wink.

With a pat on her leg to call Murphy to her, she was confident she could tell just enough yet everything the *Edelweiss Pirates* wanted to know. "C'mere, Murphy." A loping beagle crossed the space faced by all teens and plopped on Gracie's lap. "This is Murphy."

Everyone laughed at the panting dog with his head tipped back accepting Gracie's rub between his ears.

"Looks like he's laughing, so he must be your dog." Jakob grinned at Gracie.

"Actually, he's Theo's dog. Murphy, Theo, and I met during the winter when Theo came from America to Munich where I lived with my guardian." She hesitated. "Theo was roughed up by some *Hitlerjugend* and rescued by my guardian, so he and Murphy came to live with us. My guardian—well, I guess I should say *our* guardian—is a member of *the Watch*, a society against the Third Reich and their efforts to annihilate anyone who is not Aryan. Long story short, some of the people of *the Watch* have helped my guardian and us. For our safety, my guardian wants to get us out of Germany, so arrangements have been made for us to go to America on the next flight of the dirigible called the *Hindenburg*. We had a short stopover on the way to Frankfurt, and uh, we kinda got tangled in some bad plans at a place called Hadamar." She put her hand on Theo's knee without looking up at him. "Theo rescued me from Hadamar, but we got lost in the forest several days ago. We wandered here, and you found us."

A long, soft whistle from Adalric was the first sound anyone made in response to Gracie's explanation.

"Sounds like you met up with some people on the government's *Most Ruthless* list." Minne shook as a shiver ran down her spine. "I thought being kidnapped by the *Hitlerjugend* was bad."

"You were kidnapped? How'd you escape?" Theo's questions stacked on top of each other before anyone could answer.

"We were at a rally in a town where a member of *the Watch* was performing acrobatic tricks from a rooftop, and he saw the *Hitlerjugend* jump us and drag us into an alley."

"Unfortunately, our rescue didn't come before we nearly lost Jakob," Adalric finished Minne's sentence, causing silence to suffocate the lighthearted conversation. Theo swallowed hard when he noticed the older boy had tilted his head so the vivid scar on his face was away from the eyes of the circle.

A slap of hands on his thighs made everyone jump as Jakob moved attention from himself. "Hey, how about we show a little

German hospitality and let these two enjoy what our town has to offer." A smile filled the young man's face as he stood and offered Gracie a hand up. "We have just the perfect remedy for tired travelers—hot springs!"

"Hot what?" Theo thought he had heard the phrase before, but he had learned a change of century and country could mean big changes in language.

"Springs!" Minne laughed. "Jakob, what a perfect idea! I'll get some water clothes for Gracie, and I'll get some of yours for Theo!"

"Is it like a resort?"

"Well, American friend, I'm not sure what you mean, but Jakob and Minne's parents built this house around a spring." Adalric pointed to a hallway.

"So it's in the house?" Theo's voice sounded unsure. He thought a spring was like a river. "You mean something like a hot tub?"

"Tub?" Adalric laughed loudly.

"Adalric, don't be rude. Maybe they don't have hot springs come up from the ground in America." Minne's voice began with a scold and softened with a smile to Theo.

"Yeah, we have water springs, just not in houses." Theo returned her smile but was anxious to reclaim his relationship with Gracie. "Whaddaya say, Gracie? I'm game if you are."

"Minne, you help them get what they need to relax in the hot springs. Adalric and I will find Joseph and ask what he knows about a dirigible flight out of Frankfurt." Jakob spun and was walking toward the door before anyone could respond. "C'mon, Adalric. I think I know where to find Joseph. He said something about getting a crate for his dog or something like that. I want to find him before he leaves town."

Less than half an hour passed by the time Theo and Gracie lowered themselves into the therapeutic hot springs. With Murphy contentedly following Minne around the house, Theo and Gracie were left to relax.

"You'll have to go to Frankfurt alone. I don't think I'll ever get out of this warm water," Gracie spoke with her eyes closed while she half sat, half lay in soft sand that lined the effervescent spring in the enclosed room.

At first, Theo only smiled in agreement, but the jealousy of his heart began to bubble with the warm waters. "Really? You think I'd leave you here with Jakob so he can wink and flirt with you? Hmph. I don't think so."

Enough water splashed across Theo's face that he snorted some up his nose. "Hey! What was that for?"

"You don't own me, Theo!" Gracie kicked her feet in the warm water. "You can't say who can or can't like me. Besides, he's just being nice."

Theo wanted to respond, but he couldn't think of anything to say. He plastered a grin on his face just to irritate her in case she opened her eyes and looked at him.

Water still churned where Gracie couldn't sit still. "You sure aren't having any problem being nice to Minne." She glanced at Theo before closing her eyes tightly to squeeze back any emotion. She hoped Theo would think the warm springs had reddened and moistened her eyes and face.

"Minne?"

"Quit yelling!"

"I'm not yelling, and I'm certainly not making goo-goo eyes at Minne like Jakob is making with you."

"You think I don't see her pawing all over you every time she gets a chance?"

"Oh, forget it." Theo had noticed Minne's softness and gestures of touch. "These are just nice people, that's all."

Both teens sat quietly and relaxed both body and soul until nearly an hour later when Minne came with warm towels and told them the boys had returned with exciting news and a friend they knew.

Gracie and Theo walked closely, though not touching, from their separate dressing rooms to the place where they had earlier met with their new friends. A woman's soft voice beckoned and welcomed their curiosity as they approached the kitchen. Scarcely had they stepped into the doorway than a woman stood and turned to look at them with outstretched arms.

"NINA!" Theo and Gracie lunged into her arms. Tears welled up in Gracie's eyes as she tiptoe-hopped, refusing to leave Nina's embrace.

"How did you . . . Wait, where did . . . When . . . ?" Theo wrapped his long arm around Nina to pat her back.

Minne clapped her hands in happiness, while the boys grinned and Jakob stood with his arms crossed against his chest.

"You were right, Gracie. You and Theo do have guardians!" Adalric's excited voice was happy for them being back in the arms of a protector and dear friend.

"Ah, we have been so worried about you! Fritz and TAR followed you to Hadamar, but some of the walls of Hadamar had crumbled in an explosion or fire. Our best guess was that you died in the explosion or had been taken by those who fled Hadamar."

"Oh, Nina. We're fine. Theo rescued me. It was horrible, but Theo took me away." Gracie put a hand on Theo's arm in a silent gesture of fondness.

Hearing the name Hadamar brought visions in bits and pieces into Theo's mind. "Nina, did Fritz or TAR go into Hadamar? Did they find—" He caught his words, unsure if Gracie remembered Herr Möeller was captive in the abyss of Hadamar. "Uh, was anyone there?"

Though she didn't know the story of their travels, Nina's wisdom guided her words. "The only souls left there were a few who were scarcely alive." She gave both teens a final hug and stepped back. "Now, let me look at you! Joseph told me these Pirates found you and have taken good care of you. We've hit a bump in the road, but it's time to finish the plan for getting you to America. The *Hindenburg* takes flight in three days. You've just enough time to enjoy this beautiful town of Wiesbaden and your new friends. You'll be safe here. I'll make arrangements to get you to Frankfurt in time to return to your homeland, Theo. Gracie, you'll enjoy America until we can call you back to Germany in better days."

A hit against Nina's legs nearly knocked her off-balance, but she laughed louder than any of the teens as a whirling Murphy came racing from where he had been curled up by the stove snoring through a warm nap.

"Oh, Murphy! Who could forget you! You'll get your spot on the flight too! For now, Theo, your dog has the right idea. Enjoy the time to relax. I'll come for you tomorrow. Fritz, TAR, and I will work on a plan with Joseph. Until then, hugs all around!" Nina threw open her arms again and held the *Mischling* and the American in an embrace that was sealed with her private prayer for their safety.

PART IV
The Hindenburg

Special Delivery

THE WIND WAS dancing across the open field. It grabbed at loose pieces of earth and moved them through the patches of sparse grass strewn about the airfield. The sun was generous, and the air was not as heavy with humidity as it had been the past few days. The sixty-person crew, along with the extra SS officers and militia provided by the Nazi Department of Security, scurried about the base, each seeing to flight day agendas and preflight checks.

Erich Spehl made his way to the hangar from his room in the soldier barracks that had been built at the far end of the airfield. Once the führer had pulled the airship's construction and navigation under the Reich's Luftwaffe command, all persons associated with the airship fell under the German military. An increase in funding helped create larger and more impressive airships, including the *Hindenburg* itself, just over eight hundred feet long. Upon completion, the dirigibles flew over every single German city and dropped pro-Nazi propaganda from the windows as a show to the German people of the Reich's power. Recently, the *Hindenburg* had been fitted with rooms to nearly double her occupancy, allowing fifty-six crewmen and thirty-six passengers to make the flight from Frankfurt to the American naval base at Lakehurst, New Jersey.

Erich rubbed his temples, his mind still foggy from the events of last evening. He had left the pub early but not soon enough. His head thumped mercilessly. Swastikas that had been freshly painted on the rudders of the silver airship loomed over the young-looking rigger who would help prepare the zeppelin for flight. The emblem of Hitler's power made Erich's stomach turn with disgust. He had heard the rumors whispered through the hangar—rumors that the US sale of helium to Germany had been denied. The *Hindenburg* would be flown with hydrogen. Erich knew a fine line between political and commercial ventures was volatile as the Reich grew in power.

Now, however, politics were not consuming his thoughts. Last night's conversation with his girlfriend, Keila, and her words whispered into his ear continued to swirl in his mind. She left this morning before he had a chance to see her.

"Erich, you are late young man! Don't make me regret sticking my neck out for you to get this job," a stern yet caring voice half-heartedly reprimanded him. Ludwig Knorr, the chief rigger on the *Hindenburg*, smiled as he could see the headache in Erich's eyes. "You'll need to learn how to drink better if you want to be a good German."

"Sorry, Herr Knorr. It won't happen again," Erich whispered.

"What won't happen again?" Herr Knorr smiled with a silly look of confusion on his face. "You'll not be late again or drink again?"

"Right now, neither."

"Of course not!" Knorr laughed. "We will be up there." He pointed to the sky above. "You will have nowhere to hide that I can't find you." The chief laughed out loud at his own joke, which was something he did often. "Get to your station, boy. These SS officers are watching for any reason to ground this bird from taking off."

"Yes, Herr Knorr," Erich replied to his senior officer's words of warning and made his way into the hangar. His breath was taken away when he turned the corner and the full view of the heightened security measures came into view. On top of the increased presence of the security detail, it looked as if the hangar had been invaded by a miniature army of German officers. Some two hundred young boys and girls were snooping around as well. He had not been aware so many students from the local Hitler Youth Military had arrived. No crew talking or orders from those in command—nothing—had clued him of the presence of the *Hitlerjugend* near the ship or even at the airfield. In Erich's head, he could hear his father quoting Hitler, his hero, whom he believed to be the savior of Germany: *"The weak must be chiseled away. I want young men and women who can suffer pain. A young German must be as swift as a greyhound, as tough as leather and as Krupp's steel."*

Erich's father had insisted the entire family listen to the führer when he addressed the German people on radio broadcasts. Never did Erich and his father see eye to eye on the right direction for their beloved Germany. His love for his father had weakened and even been replaced with a love for his uncle, Jahile Möeller.

Jahile Möeller also struggled with his brother's blind following of the führer. He had sensed his nephew's rebellion to the Reich and had secretly supported Erich as he matured. Erich's separation from his father was eased by his love for his uncle. In addition, Erich didn't dislike his stepmother, but she never accepted him as a son, and he found himself lost amid eight other siblings. He had left the house as soon as he found his first apprenticeship as a leatherworker. Erich never found working as a saddler as invigorating as working the world's largest airship, and he often thanked God that Herr Knorr found him and saved him from that dreary existence.

Without drawing attention, Erich looked to the far corner of the hangar where the freight boxes should be waiting for him to load onto the airship. He began to sweat a little as he noticed a few SS security officers looking around the boxes, trying to decide whether the cargo boxes had been opened or not during the previous day's inspection. Erich saw his window of opportunity and hustled over to the three officers and the *Hitlerjugend* who were following the SS officers as if they were superheroes.

"Excuse me, gentlemen. Herr Knorr has just finished chewing into my backside about having left these boxes to the last minute. He's going to make me work the night detail if I don't get these on board immediately." Erich controlled his voice to sound like a penitent dockworker.

"Hold up, boy." The tallest of the three SS security officers stepped toward Erich and put an outstretched hand in the middle of his chest. "Who do you think you are, boy?" he asked with a snide hint of superiority in his voice.

Erich risked a quick glance up at the man who had just laid a hand on him. He was a massive man with piercing blue eyes like a hawk that glared down at him. His long black leather coat and hat were covered with marks of a low-ranking member of the *Schutzstaffel*, but the Nazi military always took advantage whenever the opportunity presented itself to bully those beneath them.

"Beggin' your pardon, sirs." He gave his best performance as a low-level member of society who was totally in awe with being so near Hitler's military officers. He hoped stroking their egos would get him out of this situation and get those freight boxes loaded into the cargo hold before any of the crew started poking around. Their egotism would make it almost impossible to get the extra cargo stored without incident. These SS men were more interested in checking their appearances in any shiny object that would reflect what they thought of as German perfection.

Erich swallowed a laugh, despite his nervousness and the real danger of the situation as a whole. He knew he was a right judge of character. He just had to play the role of a humble servant. "Would you like me to open any boxes for you, sirs? Maybe seeing the contents of Herr Späh's performance props would set your minds at ease," he offered, taking a huge leap of faith that his willingness to open the freight would ease their suspicions.

The group went silent at the mention of Späh's name. *This is it*, he thought. *I am busted and will get sent away to one of those camps where no one ever leaves again.* He wanted to scream. He wanted to run, but he was paralyzed with fear and just stood with his head down, waiting for the ruse to get sniffed out.

"This stuff belongs to Joseph Späh?" the plumpest of the three officers remarked inquisitively.

"I . . . I . . . I believe so, sirs. Herr Späh has paid quite a lot to get the extra cargo on the ship due to its weight. He already had his dog crate and many suitcases loaded yesterday. Seems a bit excessive for one man to have so much . . ."

"Let the boy do his job, Ekhard. Can't you see he's in hurry? Always trying to harass the help," the SS officer barked in a gruff voice though he had stood quietly watching with narrow eyes up to this point.

Erich didn't get a look at him. He kept his head down, trying to play up the pathetic-servant routine. *Come on*, he thought. *Listen to your friend. Let me take these crates.*

The tall officer named Ekhard stared at Erich, judging him as he did everyone. "Fine. Boy, go do your job and get out of my face." With a half turn, he spit, "Albrecht! Hans! Help this rigger. Get these boxes loaded for the cargo hold as quickly as possible." Two wide-eyed *Hitlerjugend* jumped at the chance to do something that might gain them favor in the eyes of any member of the SS, no matter how low on the totem pole.

"Boy, fix your cover!" Ekhard snapped back around to face Erich before he spun and staccato marched away.

"Yes, sir!" Erich obeyed, quickly straightening his army-issue hat that never sat properly on his head. He took careful measure not to bump or even come close to the three officers as he grabbed a dolly from one of the small storage sheds spread throughout the gargantuan hangar. He lost little time moving away from the SS officers and toward the special freight. The two youths asked no questions. Scarcely had they hoisted the boxes onto the dolly before Erich thanked and dismissed the *Hitlerjugend*, who were eager to receive a new command from their SS leaders.

Again, Erich adjusted his hat to be sure not to give the arrogant officer another reason to detain him a second time. He shoved his body weight hard into the dolly to get it moving. It eventually picked up momentum and became easier for Erich to push over the rough concrete floor. *All that money spent on the airship, couldn't they have made the floor a little smoother?* He strained his body to keep the cart rolling while keeping a watchful eye for any more SS who might stop him and ask more unnecessary questions.

Erich rubbed the sweat from his brow. The *Hindenburg*'s lift was located halfway down the ship's keel. He hoped the loading platform would still be lowered from yesterday's massive security inspection. The SS security detail had stripped the zeppelin down to the bare bones of its structure then left it to the crew to put back together. The arrogant officers and enlisted troops had even gone as far as to try just enough food that the kitchen staff had to return to market and restock the ship for the upcoming voyage to the United States.

The crew had worked most of the previous evening to reset the zeppelin to flight standard. By nearly midnight, Captain Pruss ordered the men to finish reloading the following morning. He laughed out loud to himself. The captain had erroneously assumed the extra work duty would send them back to the barracks for some shut-eye, allowing no energy or time for drinking at the pub.

"Thank goodness." Erich sighed at the sight of the cargo elevator still resting on the hangar floor. He pushed a little harder on the cart as he saw his chance—it might evaporate if he didn't hurry. Stress was building, but the rigger was bolstered by the importance of his task in helping *the Watch*. He knew getting the cargo on the ship was just the beginning. The next few days would be equally, if not more, dangerous for everyone involved. The travelers who just wanted a luxurious way to travel to the United States had no clue of lurking danger. They would be innocent bystanders.

Good or bad, war has unintended consequences. Erich had fallen in love with a woman whose age passed his by several years. Even now as they were apart, Keila's voice of reason resonated in his head. Often, perhaps too often, Keila would shrug a cold shoulder and repeat the reasoning when he complained about dangerous outcomes of her role against the Reich. Moreover, she made the same stoic response when he argued for innocent people. It was more than her pat answer. It was her belief.

With a quick shake of his head, Erich blocked dwelling on the never-ending arguments with his Communist beloved. Focus was necessary to complete the task of getting the cargo on board the dirigible. Without stopping the rolling momentum, he swiveled and backed toward the elevator until he stopped with cart and cargo propped on the platform. Though he did not quite understand the science behind the elevator system, mechanically, he reached for the heavy thick rope looped through the intricate pulley system. It had taken his muscular strength from his slender frame to push the cart filled with the heavy freight boxes, but with the pulley, both himself and the cargo could smoothly be hoisted up to the storage chamber of the *Hindenburg*.

The cart started to roll as the platform jolted off the ground. Erich coughed a nearly silent gasp at his forgetfulness. His emotions were getting the best of him and affecting his efficiency. Any time lost getting these crates loaded was time that someone could notice his blunders and start asking questions. Checking his actions, he set blocks behind the wheels of the cart to keep it immobilized then yanked hard on the rope to resume the lift. The platform and its contents smoothly rose off the ground with each downward pull on the rope. Moving hand over hand in a controlled rhythm that he had practiced many times, the rigger relaxed into his usual flight routine.

Less than a meter from elevator platform meeting the cargo hold, Erich felt the pulley tug backward just as two hands grasped the edge of the platform. *What now?* Erich leaned over to see the unfriendly face of a mechanic for the *Hindenburg*. He cringed at the sight of the other crewman. In previous flights of the airship, the two men had had crossed paths and not seen eye to eye. It didn't help that the mechanic, Robert, was convinced that Erich had cheated in a game of poker and taken most of a month's earnings from him.

"Robert, let go!" Erich ordered. "I will lower when I get this cargo loaded."

"I want my money, you crook," Robert growled angrily.

Offended by the accusation, Erich spit back at the man hanging from the platform. "I'm not a crook! I've told you a dozen times, I beat you fair and square, Robert. You just need to deal with the fact that you're a lousy card player."

From physical exertion and embarrassment, the mechanic's face reddened. He swung his legs to pull himself up onto the platform. The additional weight shook the platform, causing the thick rope to pull backward through the pulley and tear against Erich's palms as the elevator lowered toward the hangar floor. He knew the aggressive mechanic had nothing to hide and would think nothing of causing a scene in front of the *Schutzstaffel*. "I said let go, Robert! I'll file a complaint with Captain Pruss if you don't get off this platform and let me work."

The mechanic laughed at the idle threat. "You're all talk, Spehl. I'll see that you don't file a complaint!" With a final grunt, he lifted the upper half of his body onto the platform.

Erich hesitated, muscling his full weight on the rope inching backward through the pulley. The mechanic's aggressive behavior was untimely and uncharacteristic. He had made idle threats before, but his words had never ended in a physical attack. "Robert, I'll return your money."

"Too late. I'm gonna take it outta yer hide," the mechanic furiously spit back, throwing a leg onto the elevator platform.

Erich held tight and pulled against the rope until he could lunge to the platform edge. He kicked the heel of his boot against the mechanic's chest before he stomped down hard on his hand. A scream of pain and anger exploded from the mechanic, who swung backward unbalanced but held on to the jolting platform with his other hand and leg. In fury, Erich kicked at his attacker's face, but in quick reaction, Robert ducked the blow, causing Erich's foot to miss its target and knock him off-balance. Erich's back hit hard against the platform. He realized that he had wrapped his forearm with the rope and had kept his grip. He reached up with his other hand and pulled himself up. The counterweight against the pulley again lifted the platform.

Erich held his weight with both arms and slid his feet under him as the mechanic pulled his body onto the platform. "Sorry, Robert."

"For what?" the suspended man bellowed. "Cheating me outta a month's salary?"

"No, this." Erich gave a quick and measured release of rope. The elevator plummeted in a brief free fall before he recaught and stomped on the rope, causing the platform to jerk to a hard stop. The unexpected drop caught the mechanic off-balance, causing a backward fall. Catlike reflexes broke the mechanic's fall and left him again hanging from the edge of the platform, holding only by his hands.

Still with rope tethered around his forearm, Erich pulled enough slack to launch himself into the air to push his boots downward and land with a crunch onto his enemy's unprotected hands. Erich's feet pinned the dangling mechanic to the raised platform.

Erich squatted, leaning heavy on his heels while lowering his face. "Our discussion of your problem is over!"

The mechanic's mouth opened in a speechless grimace as he hung from the platform unable to block the pain. He let out a cry as Erich twisted his heels one last time before stepping back to release the crushed hands, letting his nemesis fall to the hangar floor.

Erich refused to look below him but looked at the rope wrapped around his throbbing arms. He set back to lifting the platform to the dock of the cargo hold, where he tied off on the anchor. From the elevated height, he scanned the loading bay, looking for anyone who might ask questions. His glance saw no one. His heart prayed the fight had no witness. He heaved his body weight against the cart, this time to move it into the open airship. The iron wheels thudded as the cart dropped down from the platform to the lower wooden floor of the cargo hold. A low growling noise came from inside one of the freight boxes.

"Sorry," Erich whispered as he leaned against the box.

"For what?" a voice came from behind a large stack of burlap bags labeled with styles and brands of coffee. A fourteen-year-old boy emerged from behind the stack of coffee, stuffing something into his back pocket.

"Werner! Where did you come from?" Erich snapped more from surprise than from anger. "What do you have in your pocket, Werner Franz?"

"Don't tell, Herr Spehl!" the young cabin boy pleaded. "I . . . I can't lose this job! My parents depend on me!"

"Relax, Werner! You just scared me, that's all." Erich replaced his scowl with a smile to ease the young boy's fear. "That's quite a hiding spot you got there. So this is where you go when no one can find you."

The young cabin boy kept his head down. "Please, Herr Spehl, don't tell the captain. He already caught me reading the comic pages and scolded me. Told me to get my head outta the clouds and focus."

The rigger looked at Werner for a moment then walked over to stand in front of him. Erich kept his roughened hand curled as he placed his fingers under the boy's chin, giving a lift to look him in the eyes. "Next time someone tells you to get your head out of the clouds, you need to remind him what we do for a living!"

Werner laughed and looked gratefully at the rigger.

"One more thing, uh, Herr Franz."

"Yes, Herr Spehl?"

"Call me Erich. You make me feel old calling me Herr!" A smile broke across his face as he added, "And that's an order!"

"Yes, Herr Sp—I mean, Erich."

"Good, now run along before someone who isn't as nice as me finds you. Plenty of work to be done before we take off this evening," Erich said in his best Captain Pruss voice, making Werner laugh as he turned and ran down the large loading dock and disappeared like he did so often.

He probably knows the ship better than anyone. Erich watched the boy vanish. *I—we—may need his help the next few days.* Thoughts began to swirl into plans in the rigger's mind as he returned to pushing the dolly, looking for an inconspicuous place to hide the cargo.

Arrival

E RICH SLAPPED HIS hat off his leg in impatient bewilderment. *Where is he? I hope something bad didn't happen. What if the SS or evil jaegers and Brack got to him?* Erich hadn't seen Joseph Späh since the night at the Kaiserdom when he had come storming in with those filthy, smelly hunters hot on his tail. *The Watch* had barely gotten away in time.

Erich and Keila had taken every back road and hiding spot he had previously mapped out before they were finally able to lose the bloodthirsty minions of the Reich. Since that night, Erich couldn't shake an eerie feeling of exposure like someone or something was watching him, and he avoided going anywhere alone. He did not like to admit it to himself, but he was terrified that they would capture and torture him to get to the rest of the *Table* members through him.

Loyalty to *the Watch* remained a precedent to every move. A plan had been determined, and it was all the rigger could do to hide impatience for each step to be set in motion. Erich watched the crowds of people gathered at the Frankfurt Airfield to watch the magnificent silver airship take flight yet again. For all outward looks, this flight should have been one of his easier trips; the passenger list showed only half the occupants that could be accommodated and twice as many crew as needed. That should have meant half the work, but the sweat running down his back and soaking his hair under his hat said otherwise.

From the appearance of stiff-backed youths swarming the airfield, the *Hitlerjugend* must have gone home and polished their boots and medals over dinner in an attempt to return and impress the older guard. The SS officers were in top form too, as the arrogant SS embroidered on collars of black shirts caught attention regardless of the cloudy skies hanging overhead. Erich shook his head in unspoken disgust. It was hard to believe that Claus was one of them. Whether working beside his wife, Nina, or on a lone mission for *the Watch*, Claus gave his heart to his countrymen. Sometimes Erich had to remind himself that not all men in Nazi uniforms were truly the führer's pets. Some of them still had a soul hidden under those long black leather dusters.

The tarmac was teaming with heightened security and Hitler's bodyguards. To appease the führer and keep him from directly entering the town, the city bused half the city's population to the airfield to watch the Nazi Party's show of technical prowess. Although hidden from the masses of common people, the US government had refused the Reich access to the helium they so coveted. Flights of the massive airships were at the mercy of the Americans. It was a critical time to save face in the eye of public opinion. The lack of helium, the airship fuel, threatened for the first time in thirty years to ground the German pride of the skies. Thus, the crew was ordered to fill the ship with hydrogen. The crew and captains had argued furiously against adding such a flammable material and almost boycotted the flight.

The crew had been reassured numerous times by the experts that the *Hindenburg* was perfectly safe. Erich's heart doubted the reports, but his loyalty to carry out his duty to *the Watch* trumped all reasoning. *What do scientists know? Zeppelins are designed to fly with helium. Just because the führer threatened the life of a few scientists, should that really outweigh the lives of all the people flying on the airship?* He struggled with the knowledge since he had been informed of the switch in gases. The German government had convinced the flight superiors that this was an opportunity to throw America's embargo of helium right back in their faces. The German people were proud of their countrymen's advances in the aeronautics field. Zeppelin flight was amazing, and each flight was another way for Germany to show the rest of the world that they had bounced back after the vicious Treaty of Versailles had crushed them and ended the First World War.

"Erich! Erich!" a familiar voice yelled over the commotion and pageantry surrounding the launching of the voyage to the United States.

From where he stood, Erich anxiously searched the crowd for Keila's face before he locked eyes with the beautiful woman of his dreams. He glanced around to ensure none of his officers or the SS were watching. His earlier encounter with the mechanic put him on high alert for anyone who might still be observing him. He slipped through the crowd unnoticed. The public wanted to see or talk to engineers and pilots. People were there to watch the air show, not some low-level rigger of the crew. He was glad to have the protection of anonymity as he walked swiftly toward Keila.

"Where did you go this morning?" Erich held his face close to her ear as he kept an eye on the crowds around them.

"I had some business in town, my love," Keila's voice lilted sweetly.

Erich turned his eyes to meet hers. He knew the implication of her coded words. He knew there must be members of the Communist *Red Peace* in Frankfurt. "What are they planning, Keila?"

"I don't know who you mean, Erich." Keila feigned watching the crowds around the airship.

The rigger turned his back to the crowds, allowing his voice to get louder and angrier. "There are almost a hundred innocent people aboard that ship, Keila. They don't deserve to be caught in the crossfire between two radical idealist groups! How can you justify working in both German and Russian undercover societies?"

Keila narrowed her eyes at his words and almost imperceptibly pursed her lips. "Choose your next words carefully, my love! *Red Peace* is present and disguised on this flight. They're not unaware of the covert work of the secret *Society* of Germany. *Red Peace* knows that half of those civilians wandering around here are actually SS spies. The Reich's power is reaching beyond this country, Erich. They cannot be allowed to destroy the country from within. They won't stop on German soil! The Nazis aren't the only ones who can sneak someone on board in disguise."

Erich clenched his jaw and hesitated before he spoke. "I don't like what the Reich is doing either, but it's not fair to those people on board to be hurt—or worse—because of a difference in political opinion. There are more than just men aboard that ship—innocent women and children could be harmed!" He grabbed her hands in his and looked into her eyes to soften the pounding in his chest. "Keila, dear, tell me what you have planned with them."

Keila dropped her eyes away from his. She couldn't look into his eyes, from soul to soul, knowing what she had done. She leaned forward, offering a gentle embrace. "Erich, don't go on that ship." Her whispering lips brushed his ear. "I have taken advantage of your kind and tender heart, my love."

"What does that mean?" Erich's heart sank into his stomach.

She started to answer then stopped and began to sob.

"Keila, you must tell me the plan!"

"I don't . . . I don't know who is a spy or even how many may be on the airship. *Red Peace* doesn't trust me any more than the *the Watch* does now." She pulled her hands away from Erich and covered the tears that streamed down her face. "I've made a real mess of things, Erich. I told them about the boy."

"Are you insane? If the *Table* finds out you've betrayed us, they'll not stop until you're dead. Why would you do such a thing?" Erich fought to contain his anger and to avoid a scene. "Tell me what *Red Peace* has on you that you would put that poor boy's life into more jeopardy than it already is!"

"They have my daughter, Erich! They have my daughter!" Her outburst shook her entire body as she fell weeping into his arms.

Erich looked down at the broken woman he was holding in his arms. As he lifted a hand to cradle her head, he began to notice looks and comments spawned by reaction from the curious crowd around them. Erich placed a strong arm in the small of her back to lift her up as straight as he could while he leaned his head to her ear. "My dear, I beg for our safety that you pull yourself together until we can get to a more private place. There are eyes and ears everywhere, my darling. You know this best."

Without another word, the mystery and danger that had surrounded Keila most of her adult life helped her instincts kick in. She brought her white-gloved hand to her face to tap the moisture from her eyes then gently wrapped her wrist through Erich's waiting arm. He leaned down and kissed her on the forehead and guided her toward one of the parking areas. He continued to scan the crowd for intense looks or suspicious onlookers. The young man hoped they could talk a little more openly without so many Nazi ears around.

Once Erich thought they were out of danger from being overheard, he stopped and leaned his distressed love against a car. "What do you mean they have your daughter?" Erich believed her only child lived with the father from a previous relationship.

Keila crumpled from her usual composure of a strong-willed woman. Though she tried to contain her emotions, they escaped as small hiccupping outburst of tears. "A few years ago, I was approached by a member of *Red Peace*. She told me they knew I was part of Fritz's *Table* and they had news of my daughter that would interest me. My love for my child overrode my common sense, and I went with her to a *Red Peace* meeting and have been working for them ever since. Last night, I was told that my child has been found and her father has been disposed of. You cannot blame me for my hopes of getting back my little girl."

Erich stared at Keila, unsure what to say to her. He could see the conflict churning inside of her. Her love for her daughter, her love for him, her dedication to *the Watch*, and now the fear of losing it all were tearing her apart. "What are they going to do to her, Keila?" He paused as worry built a lump in his throat that gave his voice a guttural sound. "What does *Red Peace* have planned for my ship?"

"Last night, they told me they have a plan to bring down the airship." Keila's eyes pleaded as she looked up at Erich. "They said if I tell you anything, I will never see my daughter again. Erich, please understand! I believe she is being held and indoctrinated somewhere in Stalingrad." Keila's hands reached up and tightened on the lapels of his coat.

"Why didn't you tell Fritz? He would have helped you." Exasperation forced him to talk in a rough whisper, realizing it was too late to do the right thing. "He has many friends in and out of *the Watch*." He sighed and turned away from Keila to scan the airfield activities before turning to face her again. "I must see that Gracie and Theo make it out of this country to the safety of America. We will be coming back in a few days with a full ship. This is our first flight this year, and people are eager for the crowning of the new king of England. I'll ask for a few days' leave. I'll go with you. We'll find your daughter, Keila." Erich searched her eyes as if to read her thoughts. "Don't do anything until I get back. Can you promise me that?"

Keila's soft hair draped across her soft features as she nodded and buried her face in Erich's chest. Her tender "yes" was barely audible over the commotion coming from the crowd.

Erich placed his hand tenderly on her chin to lift her face until he could see into her eyes. "Keila, my love, I want you to promise me you will wait until I return."

Again, she nodded without speaking and sank into the arms of her younger companion. Erich didn't say any more; he just held her. He knew that their complicated lives were about to become dangerously more complex.

"Spehl!" Herr Knorr's voice could be heard across the tarmac. Erich looked up to see Knorr making exaggerated arm gestures to signal Erich back to work.

Erich loosened his embrace with Keila. He spun to face the airship as he reached into his vest pocket and pulled out his watch. "It's 6:55! Where is that man?" He cursed aloud, not caring who heard.

"My love, I'm sorry, but I must go. Are you okay?"

"Yes." Keila grabbed his arms. "Do you have to go?"

"You know I do. This is bigger than us all. We have to get those kids to the States. Captain Pruss will not wait for Späh." Erich sighed loudly. "A week ago, Joseph missed the naval ship he was to take to America. If he doesn't make this flight, for whatever reason this time, then I'll be alone with the kids." He hesitated for a moment. "I mean, I'll be alone to deal with Nazis, SS, *Red Peace*, and quite possibly, members of the *Society*. He gave a slight smile as he stroked Keila's hair and gave a light kiss to the top of her head. Slowly and reluctantly, he pushed her away from him and leaned in for a long kiss, the last kiss for what seemed like an eternity.

"Remember, do nothing until my return." Erich studied her eyes. He wanted to see the truth in them, but unease made him suspicious. He had many questions bubbling beneath the surface, but he thought it better to hold his tongue and avoid leaving with harsh words.

Keila—girlfriend, mother, and Communist loyalist—did not answer right away but turned her head toward the people crowding to the airship. Without looking at her young lover, her voice held a note of determination. "I will do nothing until your return."

"Promise me!"

Keila's eyes flashed back to Erich with a smile. "I promise, my love, that I will wait patiently for my knight in shining armor to come home from his adventure and save the day." Playfully, she raised up on her toes to brush his cheek with her lips. "I should keep kissing you until that overglorified balloon lifts off and leaves you here by my side."

Erich grinned to see the sly smile on her lips. "That might be worth getting fired for!" He leaned in and stole one more soft kiss then ran toward the *Hindenburg*. He knew he was in trouble. He was in trouble with his chief rigger, the engineering wrench heads, and most importantly, he was in trouble with Keila because he knew she had his heart in her hands, which trumped his ability to reason.

Through the cars flooding the streets leading to the airfield, he saw a taxi speeding and blasting its horn.

"About time! That better be Joseph!" Erich yelled over the commotion as he ran back to his duty. He picked up his pace and fought the urge to look back at Keila.

The driver of the taxi hit the horn repeatedly, threatening people and objects to get clear of his path. The passenger in the back seat with his dog had promised a very handsome tip if he drove right up to the hangar. The driver was sweating as the swastikas painted on the rudders of the awe-inspiring silver bullet came into his view. The sheer size of the ship took away his breath. His eyes widened and his mouth fell open as he neared the silver pride of Nazi Germany that blocked his view of the sky.

A loud "woof" escaped from the black Mercedes-Benz cab and broke the driver's daze as he screeched to a halt. Men in black uniform standing guard at a gate across the entrance to the tarmac glared, causing the driver to fear for his life. Through his rearview mirror, he saw that the small-framed passenger only seemed concerned with the gigantic dog that would join him in boarding the airship.

The cabbie rolled down his window as two SS officers approached either side of his car, machine guns in hand. "*Guten Tag*! Passenger for the *Hindenburg*!" the driver announced to clear himself of wrong.

"Who is he?" a guard asked gruffly, holding his machine gun at his hip, ready to fire.

"Herr Späh, the famous acrobatic performer. You've heard of him, haven't you?" The driver hoped his passenger's prestige would support his attempt to drive up to the heavily guarded *Hindenburg*.

From the back seat of the car, a voice spoke boldly to the guard peering through the cab window. "They are waiting on me, boy, so I suggest you let us through immediately." The passenger appeared irritated to be delayed by unnecessary questioning.

The guard cocked his head, stooping to look through the window at the passenger with one arm draped over a large dog. Few people would dare speak to an SS officer with such tone. The guard released his machine gun and let it hang with a strap across his shoulder. He reached inside his heavy leather coat and pulled out a folded manifesto of the ship's cargo and passengers. He searched the list and eventually came across Joseph Späh's name. "Yes, here you are, Herr Späh. You are late."

"Obviously, my good man, hence the speeding cab and all the honking of the horn. Now, if you're ready for your next move, it should be to lift the gate so my driver can take me to the airship."

The officer swallowed down a retort and anger at the demeaning tone of the passenger. He slowly refolded the manifesto, slid it into his interior pocket, then motioned for the gate guard to lift the barrier. With the barrier gate raised, the guard gave a "move along" motion with his hand, wanting rid of the little man's sharp tongue.

"*Danke!*" the taxi driver shouted, rolled up his window, and slammed on the accelerator. "Are you insane? Do you have any idea what happens to people who talk to a member of the *Schutzstaffel* like that?" he questioned but allowed no chance to respond. "They usually disappear right from their homes in the middle of the night along with their family members, never to be seen or heard from again!"

"He was nobody of importance," Joseph scoffed. "He wouldn't be at that piddily gate if he mattered or knew anyone who mattered. Probably, just some bitter man trying to gain his future as the führer's personal envoy."

"You are a very small man to be speaking so boldly." The driver was amused by the small-framed man in his back seat.

"Are you trying to lose your tip?" Joseph spoke shrewdly, letting the driver know he had overstepped his bounds by calling him small. The driver stammered, trying to get back on his passenger's good graces.

"Enough," Joseph ordered. "When you pull up, don't say a word. Just get out and quickly unload my luggage. Think you can handle that?"

"Yes, sir. Sorry, sir. I did not mean to offend." The driver offered more apologies while looking in his mirror, trying to read Joseph's face for any clue as to whether or not he would be getting the large tip as promised. The cabbie slammed on the brakes as more SS officers and *Hindenburg* crew members rushed toward whoever had the bold recklessness to drive onto the loading hangar.

"You cannot park this car here!" ordered a rather tall and handsome SS officer. Behind the officer, Captain Max Pruss, the ship's commander, made his way while pulling out his flight manifesto. Chief Steward Kubis, a few years the captain's senior and close personal friend, stayed step in step as they hurried toward the cab.

The taxi driver jumped out of the car before the approaching men could get to him and make him turn around. He ran and opened the trunk, doing his best to hurriedly unload the passenger's luggage. Why one man needed so much luggage was beyond the driver's understanding. He heaved and strained to unload the travel trunk first.

Joseph Späh made no hurry to get out of the car. He leashed a beautiful German shepherd and drew her from the car. Her ears were perked high as usual, and her dark-brown eyes seemed to notice everything around her. "Come, Ulla. We are late," Späh spoke lovingly to the dog, almost as if she were his child. The giant dog stood beside her master, alert that he argued with the officers of the Reich and commanding members of the flight crew.

"All passengers were to be picked up and have *all* luggage and property checked at the Frankfurter Hof Hotel by this afternoon," the tall SS officer explained, putting emphasis on the word *all* as he watched the sweaty little cabdriver pulling piece after piece of luggage from the trunk of his car.

"Ah yes, the Frankfurter. I was unable to get into the city until very late this afternoon and missed the inspection." Joseph reached down and stroked his dog's ears. "I do apologize for any inconvenience to the führer and his stooges."

"Watch your tongue, Herr Späh! You have very little room for mistakes on this flight." The officer used Joseph's last name to intimate that the performer was known by him and, most likely, by people higher up the chain of command. "We wondered if you would show."

Joseph looked up to the SS officer towering above him and cocked his head to the side. "Here I am! Now, if you're finished trying to intimidate me, may I head to my cabin? I've had an awfully long day, and my Ulla needs to be fed immediately." He shoved a bag of dog food into the arms of the officer.

"How dare you talk to me—"

"Ah, Herr Späh! We've been waiting for you. You nearly missed your flight!" Stepping up to the men, Captain Pruss removed his hat and placed it under his arm, revealing a mass of slowly graying hair. With a glance at the SS officer, he grabbed the dog food from the officer's arms and handed it to a boy waiting with a luggage cart. Erich approached the group of men huddled around the taxi. With a gesture and a whisper, he dismissed the boy to return to the ship for his duties.

"I do apologize, Herr Späh, but all of your luggage will need to be thoroughly inspected by members of the SS. This is an order from the top of German command. You must understand with the rising tension in the world, the führer wishes to keep his people safe from harm." Captain Pruss winked and grinned at the smaller man.

"I expect nothing less from the man." Joseph nodded sarcastically with a sly grin. "Feel free to dump my undergarments all over this filthy tarmac." He used the end of the dog leash to gesture in a sweeping motion.

The SS officer nodded for the young rigger to load the luggage onto the cart and bring it to him. Erich avoided making eye contact with the late-arriving guest in fear he would start laughing at his spunky little friend who seemed undaunted by the power of the Reich. Erich pushed the luggage cart to the waiting giant of a man, who was eager to find something in the contents.

"Sir." Erich gave a slight tip of his head.

"Open them, boy." The officer ordered Erich as if the task was beneath him.

"Of course, sir." Erich deliberately opened the smallest suitcase and set it at the feet of the officer. He pursed his lips to prevent a grin as he stood back and waited.

The officer stared down at the tiny suitcase then kicked it with his foot, dumping the contents on the ground. Erich shot a quick glance at Joseph and imperceptibly moved his head slightly back and forth, warning the acrobat against lunging at the arrogant officer. Joseph unclenched his fist and puffed out his cheeks to slow his tempered breathing. Erich was right. He needed to regain his composure and refuse the officer what he wanted—a reason to keep Joseph Späh from making the flight.

"Clean this up, Erich," Captain Pruss ordered. He did not approve of the Reich officer's bullying tactics, but he could not argue and give them a reason to ground the entire flight. The flight was delayed already. Pruss was anxious to get all passengers boarded and get his beloved ship into the sky where she belonged. This was her twenty-eighth flight and the first of eighteen scheduled flights for the year. National tension had crept into airflight. He was exhausted and stressed from the extra security and nonsense that had led up to this day.

"I trust you can handle the inspection. I need to make few preflight checks so we'll be ready to lift off." Pruss replaced his captain's hat and spun on one heel to walk away.

Although he had warned his friend, Erich, too, was steaming. He repacked the small case and grabbed another. With each piece set before him, the officer stared then kicked the luggage or flipped it over with his hands. Erich seethed with the rude tactics—bag after bag.

After repacking the last suitcase, Erich hesitated as he hoisted a large trunk from the cart and set it on the tarmac. As with the others, the contents of the trunk were haphazardly spread across the ground. The SS officer had searched but not found anything to prevent this insolent man from boarding the airship. Again, Erich began systematically repacking the trunk when the officer angrily shoved him to the ground.

"Hey!" Erich's temper flared. He scrambled back to his feet and stepped instinctively toward the officer. Another officer stepped up and grabbed Erich's arm. Erich swung his head around and looked into the older officer's eyes.

"Be smart, boy" was all he said in a low and warning fashion. "Not that one."

Erich was taken aback by the officer's warning, trying to decide how to interpret his words. The officer released his arm and shook his head only once with another warning not to tangle with that member of the *Schutzstaffel*. The older man bent over and picked up the young rigger's hat that tended to slip more than sit on his head. He dusted it off and handed it back.

"*Danke.*" Erich intended his thanks more for the warning than for retrieving his hat. His attention was turned back to the aggressive officer who had pulled a large knife from a hidden sheath in his black leather duster.

"What do you plan to do with that?" Ulla sensed her master's mood change and stood with a low warning growl exposing her large teeth. Joseph caught himself. "Easy, girl."

"This!" The officer laughed and dug the blade into the lining of the travel trunk, slashing a large gash in the fabric. He did the same to the bottom of the trunk then, in one fluid motion, swung the large knife around in his hand so he was holding it blade down and, without looking, stuck it back into its sheath. After securing his blade, he bent down and tore at the lining of the trunk. He was desperately searching for anything the Reich could consider to be contraband—anything from a weapon to a book—deemed hostile to the government. A list of books was growing larger every day, exposing the clouded truth the führer was using to cover Europe.

Joseph stood with a red anger radiating from his face, but he kept his mouth and mind in check. "Are you satisfied that I am not some evil mastermind on a mission as a saboteur?"

The officer motioned for Erich to return the contents of the trunk after shredding the liner. "Not quite yet, Herr Späh." He flashed a sinister smile. In a quick move, he stepped up and grabbed Joseph by his shoulders and viciously spun him around. Joseph would have lost his balance if not for his years of tumbling and intense gymnastics training.

"Whoa, what are you doing?"

The officer did not reply to Joseph but began a pat-down starting at his legs and working his way up. Joseph's anger was supplanted with discomfort and embarrassment as people who had gathered to watch the ship set sail were watching him be harassed.

"Aha!" the SS officer shouted in victory as he felt something large on the inside of Joseph's coat pocket. He took a step back and had his Luger pistol out and pointed at the acrobat before anyone had a chance to respond. "Take it out nice and easy. No sudden movements or I will shoot." The officer's order was calm and eager.

Without moving, Joseph looked at the man holding the gun then at the gun pointed at him. Turning his head, he stared down at Erich, still gathering contents of the trunk. With a further turn of his head, he glimpsed over his shoulder at the older officer, who had not reacted as quickly but did have his pistol in hand at his side.

"Be calm, sir." Joseph slowly reached into the inside pocket of his coat jacket. He pulled out a surprising large package wrapped in newspapers.

Before Joseph had opportunity to remove the wrappings, the SS officer seized the package with his free hand and began tearing away the newspaper. He looked in shock at what he held in his hand. He looked at it for a moment, turned it around in his hand, then raised his eyes back up to the small-framed performer who was smiling. The officer looked down again where he held a doll in a pretty dress. He tilted the doll and lifted the dress, desperately searching for an infraction.

"It's a girl, *Dummkopf*." Joseph laughed at the expression and disappointment on the officer's face. "Really. Must you check under her dress?" Muffled laughs from the onlookers quailed as the member of Reich High Command shot them all evil glances.

"Get him loaded and see that he makes it to his cabin. This animal will not be allowed in the front of the ship. Keep it back in one of the storage areas!" the officer shouted commands, trying to save face in front of the large crowd and for his own mental composure.

Joseph turned to walk away when he heard the taxi driver loudly clear his throat to get attention. The agile performer turned and looked at the cabbie then to the officer who had kicked and strewn his private property all over the tarmac. "My good sir, would you mind? Seems with all this repacking, I've misplaced my wallet." Without waiting for the officer to refuse, he turned and followed Erich to the ship.

Family in Flight

Passengers began filing into the *Hindenberg*. Though most of the passengers were single men, many of whom had an assigned job on the dirigible; passenger age and gender had no stipulation for the flight to America. The Doehner family was awarded a newly built family cabin with floor windows, which promised a splendid view. Young boys, Walter and Werner Doehner, were anxious for the flight to begin. To them, the massive dirigible was an incredible adventure waiting to mix with their imaginations and play.

"Really, brothers," Irene dropped her shoulders, "you have time to set your luggage before you run off to play. Right, Mother?"

With a sweet expression of understanding how her fourteen-year-old daughter was assuming her role as a young lady in the well-to-do family, Matilde Doehner paused before she responded.

"Irene, I'm needing a little time to gather my wits about me and settle my thoughts. Why don't you go to the promenade across from the dining room and draw a picture of the beautiful view? I'll join you with the boys in time for the takeoff. We'll have plenty of hours to tidy the cabin once we are in the air. Go along now. I need some quiet for my prayers."

"You really treat me like a child, Mother. I am fourteen and too old to play silly games. I think I'll go in search of Father." Irene spun around, but not too fast to seem impudent or disrespectful to her mother.

In truth, Irene was caught between two worlds. As the eldest Doehner child on the trip to America, she had outgrown the antics of childhood, which she tolerated as little as possible from her younger brothers. At home, she had two other grown brothers who were busy with work and school and could not join the family for the flight to America. She loved her older brothers, and they loved her with a tender simplicity as the only daughter in the Doehner household. She admired their freedom, and she envied them for their ability to sit around a kitchen table and discuss life and politics with Father and make Mother laugh. Obediently, Irene left the family apartment and began to see all the dirigible had to offer in way of entertaining sights and ways to escape her brothers.

Matilde Doehner was truthful in wanting a moment of rest. "Walter, why don't you and Werner go on an adventure to find the dining room? Surely, you'll be able to stay out of the way as most people are watching out the windows of the promenade.

The two boys were out the door before their mother could change her mind. The dining room lay to the front of the dirigible, and the boys were skipping up the hall with their treasured freedom.

"Walter, let's play tank!" Werner was eight years old, and although he was curious about the flight, he and Walter had already done much walking around the airship. He was ready to play with the new toy their great-aunt had given the two of them before the family left on the trip to America. The lounge floor was carpeted and had ample room for the boys to roll around playing war games. Twice earlier, the boys had been shooed away from loading docks and cargo areas where their exploring adventures had caused them to be in the way of preparations for flight.

"All right, Werner, but first, we need to make some hills and a ramp so the tank can blast right through Russian lines." It seemed the ten-year-old's imagination was ever brewing up new scenarios for play. Soon pillows from chaise lounges became mountains, and a nearby magazine rack became a ramp that led to a hanger for the tank's hiding. Over and over, Walter and Werner ran the tank across magazine enemy lines, but the most fun was working the tank through the tundra of carpeting. "Aunt Nancy sure knows how to pick awesome tanks!" Walter was commandeering the tank as the tracks and wheels rolled across the new carpet, leaving small sparks that the boys referred to as firing on the enemy. Both boys had come to play equipped with extra toys in their pockets, but the excitement of the new tank made play even more fun.

"You boys don't need to make so much racket," Irene commanded in her most grown-up voice as she passed through the lounge on her way to find their father. Neither Walter nor Werner paid attention to the advice from their older sister as they were too busy building a path of obstacles for their tank encounters. Truly, they were playing out of the path of the hustle and bustle of passengers loading and getting settled. Besides those passing through the lounge area, most passengers who had found their quarters were busy with their cameras and finding the best seats at the observation windows with expectation of the takeoff. Few took more than a glance at the two youngsters playing on the soft carpeted floor.

"Perhaps boys should be in the promenade looking out the window for an experience of a lifetime!" The stern voice of an older gentleman seemed a contrast to his kind face.

"Oh, Otto," Elsa Ernst scolded her husband, "you sound as if the past fifty years have made you forgotten what it was like to be a boy! Never you mind his growl." Elsa turned to the boys who had paused and looked up at the passing couple. "He's just admiring your toy and longing for days when he could roll around on the floor." She slipped her arm through Otto's and gave a pat to his forearm as they strolled on through the lounge.

Werner turned his attention back to rolling the tank, enjoying the sparks from the friction against the carpet. An airship steward passed through the dining lounge and paused to watch the boys play. "Has Captain Pruss seen your toy?"

Werner was younger than his brother, but he was first to pull the toy off the floor and hold it behind his back. Walter shook his head. "No. Mother told us to stay out of the way."

The steward turned briskly and walked back in the direction from which he had come. "Are we in trouble, Walter?" Werner didn't know what they had done to have an adult, especially one who worked on the airship, stop and talk about their new toy.

"No, silly. He probably just has a boy at home and likes our—" Walter didn't have time to finish before the steward stomped back into the room and held out his hand.

"You must give me the toy!"

At first, Werner sat quietly, biting his lower lip and holding the tank behind his back. Walter reached behind his brother and eventually pried the tank from Werner's grasp.

"No! My aunt—"

"Hush, Werner. Father will be furious if we get into trouble." Walter leaned against Werner to calm him and to comfort even himself by hugging his younger brother.

"*Danke!*" The steward did understand the sadness of the boys, but safety was foremost in his mind. He knew the *Hindenburg* was taking flight with seven million cubic feet of hydrogen, a more flammable gas. A quick conversation with another crew member assured him that a spark could be dangerous and even fatal if the gases that held the airship aloft were ignited. Thus, any spark, even a small one created by the friction of a toy on carpet, was a potential risk. The steward just shook his head in worry as he passed the smoking lounge encased behind an airtight double door, created and pressurized to keep out any gases.

Werner couldn't hold back the tears, and Walter's sniffles were smothered in the shoulder of his little brother. Neither boy understood what had just happened, but both boys were reluctant to tell Father in case they had done something wrong.

Secrets

"Where's the cargo, Erich?" Joseph kept his voice low as Erich led him to the private cabin with *Joseph Späh* printed on the placard beside the door. He squeezed through the narrow hallway with a few of his packages clumsily tucked under his arms.

"Still in the cargo hold." Erich pushed the luggage cart specially crafted for the slim hallways of the airship. "I had a spot of bad luck when I was loading the boxes and didn't have time to get them relocated." His mind drifted to the repercussions that were undoubtedly going to occur after his brawl with the mechanic.

"Anything we need to worry about?" Joseph knew this flight was going to be dangerous and challenging enough on its own. They didn't need another distraction to redirect their mission.

Erich acted like he didn't hear the short man's question and pushed open the next cabin door that he came to. "Here is your room, Herr Späh," Erich spoke loudly, adding a low bow to his sarcastic tone and began casually tossing luggage onto the small bunk in the room.

"What are you doing, *Dummkopf?*" Joseph shrieked in mock horror then pushed the young man into the room and shut the door behind them. "You didn't answer my question, Erich. Did you think I didn't notice?"

Erich sighed. "I had hoped." He flashed a slight smile while organizing the luggage in the room and tidying up the blanket. "I had a bit of a scuffle with a mechanic who's convinced that I cheated him in a card game last season."

Joseph helped organize his bags by putting most of them on the top bunk in the five-by-eight-foot cabin. "Well, did you?"

"Did I what?"

"Cheat him."

"No!" Erich exclaimed passionately. "He had the worst poker face I've ever seen at a card table."

"Amateurs." Joseph chuckled as he set down packages and began rummaging through the luggage as if looking for something particular.

"What are you looking for?" Erich watched the tiny man throwing his well-organized piles back into chaos.

"Ulla's dog food." He continued to dig without looking up. "She hasn't eaten since this morning, and she will be very grumpy with me if I don't feed her soon."

"You already—hey! That reminds me. The captain has denied your special request for admittance into the restricted area to feed Ulla. You'll need to let one of the crew feed her. I'll try to do it myself as often as I can, but Chief Knorr will keep me busy. Besides, I need to avoid the mechanics' quarters."

"WHAT!" Joseph stopped his reckless search and stood up. He wasn't a tall man, but he carried himself well, and the lean muscle on his body gave the very real impression that he was not a man who liked to be told what to do. "Ulla will only eat if I feed her. I will forget that you told me about this. I'll deal with consequences." He paused and put his hands on his hips. "I'm more convincing when I ask for forgiveness than permission." He couldn't prevent a sly smile crossing his face.

"Well, just don't get into any trouble. I found out last night your name is on the security detail's 'persons to watch' list. They'll be watching you. I know for a fact that we have at least two SS in uniform and maybe up to four who are disguised as passengers." Erich paused and looked at Joseph. "There's another problem, Joseph."

"What else?" Joseph held little focus as he was impatient to find his prized dog's food and feed her before takeoff.

"There are members of *Red Peace* on board as well. I have no idea how many or who they are, but they know about the cargo."

Joseph, who had turned away, stopped, paused for a minute, then slowly swiveled to face Erich. His crimson face exposed the anger of hot blood coursing through his veins. "How is that possible, Erich?"

Erich removed his cover that had once again tilted to the side of his head. He made a mental note that he must get a new hat once they got back—one that fit. He'd steal it if he had to. He ran his hands through his hair then rubbed them on his trousers. He looked over at his red-faced companion. The room seemed to shrink as he began to sweat from anxiety. "*Red Peace* has Keila's daughter, Joseph. They tricked Keila into the group and then wouldn't tell her much. All she knows is that they want 'the cargo,' and they plan to make an example out of this airship."

"What does that mean, 'an example'?"

"She doesn't know. If I had to guess, they want to bring this symbol of Nazi power crashing down." Erich waved his arms to emphasize the ship. "It would be a spectacular act of defiance and monstrous embarrassment to the German government."

"I see." With his foot, Joseph slid a suitcase that was blocking his path to the bunk then sat in silence for a few moments. He looked up at the boyish man in front of him. *Too young to be wrapped up in all this danger.* Joseph's thoughts were for the young man as well as for the situation. He patted the empty space on the bunk, motioning for the young man to sit. "So should we help them or stop them?"

"They will not be concerned about civilian casualties, Joseph. I am all for throwing mud in the face of the Hitler's Reich, but I don't believe innocent people should be hurt in the process. I won't be surprised if they try to blow up this ship during takeoff or landing. We have to be diligent to find them and stop them. We must keep the cargo safe until we arrive in America. Then, it will be Amelia's problem to protect them once we land."

Joseph gave a low whistle. "That is a big problem, Erich. We must get the cargo to Amelia and her people. Hopefully, she knows that we're coming. I haven't had any contact with TAR since we split up on the road a few nights ago."

"I've only had contact with Keila." Erich sighed and looked Joseph in the eyes. "Things were not going well at that meeting before you burst in. I'm almost glad you came in that way. TAR and Fritz were really upset with Keila, and I am not sure how that meeting would have ended for . . ." Erich fidgeted and reached up to swipe imaginary lint from the bedcover.

"And?" Joseph knew the scuffle would cause the mechanic to keep an eye on Erich during the flight, hoping for a time of revenge, but Erich's continual setting and resetting of his oversize hat showed an agitation beyond a scuffle.

Erich tried to hide what further bothered his soul. "And? What? Do you think there's more?"

With an eye roll and crossing his arms across his chest as he turned to face Erich, Joseph needed only to chastise with few words. "Out with it. What else do I need to know?"

"The hangar was crawling with *Hitlerjugend* during preflight checks."

"So does that surprise you? They're all wannabe SS minions. Tell me, Erich, what else. Did you know any of them?"

"No." The young rigger wiped the sweat from his forehead with the back of his shirtsleeve. "No, but I kept an eye on them all day for fear that they had seen the scuffle and would somehow call me out in front of an SS."

"But no one did?"

"No—at least not that I'm aware."

"So why the worry? You must be open with me, Erich. We have too much at risk to play games."

"Sorry. Yes. Yes, I know you're right. One of them—one of the *Hitlerjugend*—he's on the flight as a cabin boy."

"Well, certainly no harm in a German boy working for a living, eh, Erich?"

"No. But I've seen him twice—once passed him in the hall—seen him talking quietly to a man in an American raccoon-fur duster and tan fedora." Erich removed the slipping hat and held it in both hands. "Don't you think that's odd, Joseph? Why would an American have such secretive talk with a *Hitlerjugend*?"

"Ah, good question. Erich, your sleuth senses will make *the Watch* proud." The small man placed a hand on the rigger's shoulder. "For now, I've got some unpacking to do."

Joseph Späh succeeded in passing a calm expression to ease the worry in the young rigger's mind, but he promised himself that he would keep diligence in his unspoken role of guardian of the two teens and fulfill Jahile Möeller's plan to save them from the Reich.

A loud horn blast filled the air and echoed throughout the hangar, even resonating inside the *Hindenburg*. Erich jumped up like something bit him. He put on his hat and spent more time than most trying to get the cover to sit properly on his head.

"What the heck was that?" Joseph growled, annoyed by the deafening intruder.

Erich, with his hat sitting sideways on his head, stepped three quick strides to the door. "We're ready for takeoff. Chief Knorr will throw me overboard if I am not at my station," he blurted back as he was running out the door.

Passengers

A HORN BLAST SIGNALED the five-minute warning for the crew and heightened the anticipation for both passengers and the large crowd that had gathered to watch the LZ-29 zeppelin lift off for America. The inside of the dirigible resembled an ant colony as crew members scurried about the airship in a pattern that most could do with their eyes closed.

Outside the *Hindenburg*, the crowd displayed a fervor of excitement. A band was playing, and all the pageantry that had been ordered by the führer was having its desired effect. The control car operators began the difficult process of hooking up to the ship, preparing to pull it to the zone designated for liftoff. Even before the passenger loading door was sealed, travelers swarmed out of cabins where they left their numbered luggage and moved along the window ledges in the promenade with anxious hearts.

Erich busied himself in moving, stacking, and securing luggage and crates. The rigger concentrated on his work of reorganizing and placing the late luggage of Joseph Späh—a welcome cover-up and excuse to be in the cargo hold when time had come to get the stowaway teens from crate to cabin.

A click of a door caused Erich to turn and rush to what he thought was an empty aisle.

"Joseph! what are you doing in here?" Erich spun in a full circle to see if they were alone in the cargo hold.

"Be calm, my friend! I remembered the goon loaded Ulla's food with my luggage. Perhaps you can help me find it if my presence makes you a little jumpy, huh?" Joseph ran his hands along the sides of the crates as if his fingers could help him read the names written across crates. "Dunn, Doehner, Schmidt . . . Is there any order to the stacking of these crates?" Joseph did not worry with quiet voice as he questioned without looking at Erich.

"*Nein!* They're stacked by size—large on the bottom. The weight of your trunk makes it easy to figure out. It's on the bottom across that aisle." Erich pointed to a black trunk nestled among shipping crates. "But don't make a mess! I'm tired of stacking and restacking."

"Then get a different job. Ah, here it is!" Joseph flung open his trunk and held up a small bag of dog food.

"Joseph," Erich's voice softened, "truly, I never know when you're teasing. You know this isn't my standard job. You can't imagine the talking I had to do to convince Chief Knorr that I felt a little nauseated and wanted to work away from other crewmen in case I was coming down with a flu." Erich's crooked smile gave way to a chuckle. "When I told him I thought I had caught something contagious and hoped it didn't delay the flight, he couldn't assign me into the cargo hold fast enough. Ol' Hans was thrilled to trade places and go work in the engine room pulling the securing ropes."

Erich looked up to see Joseph grinning and holding a bag of dog food in his crossed arms as he leaned against a shipping crate. "Joseph, for a moment, I thought perhaps you forgot." With one hand, Erich reached and caught his hat as it slid off as he tipped his head toward a crate marked *Späh*.

"Forgot? How could I forget my love for my dog? My love for my family? My love for my country?" He paused with each question to allow passion and mystery to roll from his words. "Perhaps as you are a little short on help, I can assist you in opening one of my crates that arrived before I did. I'm sure I'd like to check what's inside." Joseph gestured toward the crate and bowed at the same time. "After you, my friend."

"All right. But let's move quickly." Erich pushed the toe of his boot under the crate and kicked a metal bar from underneath. "Ah, this should come in handy." He grinned at Joseph as he picked up the rod. "Joseph, stand and watch the aisle for unruly passengers who may be lost or searching for dog food." He raised an eyebrow and turned the side of his face to the crate after his eyes scanned the cargo hold.

His voice dropped in volume and in pitch. "Once this top lid is pried off, I need both of you to crawl out and quietly move to the corner behind me. You'll need to squeeze along the side. I've left a small open space that I've walled with crates. It's the best I could do to create a hidden room in this dirigible." Both Erich and Joseph listened until they heard a double rap from the inside of the crate.

"Good. They understand. Now!" With swift silence, Erich slipped the rod under the top panel of the crate. In a single agile move, Joseph pulled himself to the top of the crate where he balanced on side panels to give an arm to aid the climbing teens. From inside, Theo bent on one knee to allow Gracie a step for climbing out the top. He looked at Murphy and commanded "Roll!" then tucked the sphere into the front of his hoodie. Theo's long legs were ready to stretch to his fullest height as he stood and pulled himself out last. By the time Theo's feet hit the floor, Gracie had already spun through crates to reach the sidewall and was disappearing. Lid and rod were replaced as both men arrived in the secret meeting spot even before Theo had time to turn and squat next to Gracie.

Erich coached the kids on the importance of intermingling yet staying out of the way once the *Hindenburg* was aloft. He didn't look as young to Theo as he had in the hidden room of the Kaiserdom. Theo wondered how wrinkles and taut skin could take over a young man's face in a matter of days. Erich, too, felt he was older. He laid a hand on each of the teens' hands as he spoke. With a final pat, he stood and warned the teens not to recognize him during any part of the flight. Then he turned and vanished from the cramped hideaway.

In quick fashion, the teens followed Joseph to the door leading to the hallway. Without talking, Joseph led them along a back hall where small cabins were reserved for crewmen. "These are double bunk cabins. This last one is yours. Restrooms are down the hall. Separate when you're not in your room. Unless you're in the workers' dining room, stay out of the way or stay in your room. If you need me, I'll feed Ulla at 8 and 3. Otherwise, we'll disembark in Lakehurst. Look for me on the tarmac. I'll introduce you to Amelia.

She's a wonderful person; you'll love her. Until then . . ." Joseph tipped his hat as he opened a door to gesture them into a small cabin and turned to walk in the direction they had just come.

"Well, here we are." Theo looked around the cabin. "I get bottom bunk!"

"Yeah, and here I go." Gracie grinned and assured her friend. "I'll see you around out there. Remember, we're to eat in a separate dining room for the crew. For now, I'm missing a flight of a lifetime." She was out the door before Theo had a chance to wish her luck and to remind her to stay out of the way.

"Well, Murph, just stay curled up inside this hoodie, and we'll both be fine. I'm ready to do a little exploring myself!" For the first time in months, Theo had an indescribable feeling of happy anxiety. "We're headed home, buddy. We're headed home." With one last glance around the room, he closed the door behind him and started down the hall.

Theo knew Gracie would have no problem using her street-urchin ways to become invisible. *She's probably been all over this ship by now.* Theo grinned as he pictured Gracie's head popping up in pillows in the lounge chairs or standing beside a post looking like an art decoration. He coached himself in being careful not to forget his stealth as his attention was drawn to the amazing dirigible.

Indeed, the giant airliner was impressive from the ground, but the inside was nothing like Theo imagined. *I guess jumping back in history gave me the impression that the people would be jumping backward in civilization. Whew. I haven't seen this much fluff and decoration since I stepped foot inside the Alte Oper Haus!* Theo's thoughts could hardly stay ahead of his eyes. The furnishings made him feel as if he had stepped into a luxurious hotel, not an air balloon. He wanted to take in every detail of the dining room, but he knew the best way to stay out of sight was to find people and blend in with activity. Fortunately, Erich had given both kids a drawing of a bird's-eye view of the interior of the dirigible. Most guests had a similar sketch showing the floor plan to help them navigate the vessel. Erich's version was a little more detailed, showing the extended areas of flight control rooms and cargo holds.

"You lose this," Erich had warned, "you'll have a hard time to come running to me because you'll be lost. You may never need all of these rooms, but for now, every nook and cranny is your possible hiding place. I can't tell you who's a good guy and who's a bad guy. Stay alert. Memorize the map. Remember the name Werner Franz. He's a kid, like you, and he knows every inch of this ship. Don't acknowledge me when you see me. Uncle Jahile said you two are smart and you're survivors. Do this for him." Erich ended abruptly to hide the quaver in his voice that came when he thought of his dear uncle. The shake in Erich's voice matched the sudden lump in Gracie's throat. Against all truth, she loved Herr Möeller and wanted to believe the reports of his disappearance were wrong and that he lived in a cabin tucked away in the beautiful mountains of Germany.

Theo inhaled a deep breath and shook his head. "For you, Herr Möeller. For you, Dad. For you, Germany."

"*Verzeihung?*" a light voice behind Theo made him jump.

"What?" Theo pulled his arms just below his chest where they held a round ball against his stomach. He spun around to the voice behind him. His need for Murphy's translation collar had become such a part of his life in Germany that he knew he needed Murphy tucked close enough to hear yet exposed enough to translate.

"I said, 'Pardon?' I didn't mean to frighten you, but I heard you talking and didn't see anyone. So I thought perhaps you said something to me." The young girl's sincerity was innocent, but she blushed as the seventeen-year-old stood with his mouth gaping open.

"Oh! Uh, I'm, uh, I mean, I was just, uh, no! I mean, yeah, I was just talking to myself," Theo stumbled over his words. He half felt like a schoolboy seeing a beautiful girl and half felt a wave of relief to see another youth. "Sorry. I'm Theo." His words were scarcely spoken before Murphy pushed his nose out the bottom of Theo's hoodie.

Murphy's surprise entrance hadn't been detected by Theo until the girl audibly sucked in her breath and looked with wide eyes at Theo's waist.

Instinctively, Theo put his hand on Murphy's head to shove him back into the hoodie as he covered, "Oh, sorry. I have a mechanical *toy dog.*" Theo spoke his last words with intensity, hoping Murphy, who seemed more human than robot, would remember his command to stay hidden.

Thoughts spun in Theo's mind. He knew the old adage "safety in numbers" would be even better as "safety with other teens." "Again, I'm Theo."

"I'm Irene. I'm here with my par—" The soft voice spoke a little bolder but was interrupted just as two sobbing boys rushed up to her trying to speak as one and trying to hold back a gush of tears.

"Irene, they took—"

"We weren't doing any—"

"We were just playing with—" Werner's sniffles were louder than his words.

"We don't know that man, but he scared us and—"

"Don't tell Father! He took our—" Walter's voice became louder as it mixed with Werner's crying.

Theo was curious about what had happened to the boys, but he became uneasy with their wails drawing attention. He reluctantly stepped away from the children and the nice girl and walked from the dining room into the promenade to look out of a nearby window where he could see ropes being pulled up into the engine compartment to stow in preparation for the airship's launch. He kept close to the edge of the viewing windows to prevent being seen from either inside or out. The voices behind him were a mesh of German words and tears. "Stay," he commanded the squirming dog wanting to emerge from the sweatshirt. "This is not the time to be caught with a dog. If they catch you, you'll be put in the animal cargo hold, and I'll have a lot of explaining why you're here and why I'm here!" His voice was firm but soft, and the wiggling stopped. Theo was sure he heard a soft whimper.

"*Es tut mir Leid.*"

Theo looked over his shoulder, turning enough for Murphy's collar to pick up the sound just as Irene repeated herself.

"I'm sorry. Those were my brothers, Walter and Werner."

"Werner?" Theo interrupted with a rushed voice. "Werner Franz?"

"What?" Irene knit her eyebrows in confusion.

"Is Werner's, I mean, is your last name Franz?"

Irene's look of not understanding did not change. "No. Our last name is Doehner. Why do you ask?"

Theo tried to not sound discouraged. He remembered Erich's advice in becoming acquainted with a cabin boy named Werner Franz. "Oh, I was just confused. I'm sorry. Go on."

"I was explaining that my brothers are upset because they had a toy taken away. Before we left Germany, our great-aunt gave them a toy tank. Some man said they couldn't play with the tank and took it from them. They're sad for losing the tank and frightened Father will be angry with them. I think I calmed them by convincing them to look out the windows as we launch. That should distract them for now." Irene's control over her brothers made her seem much older than her fourteen years.

Even at seventeen, Theo could remember the fun of playing with a new toy, especially an air car or old-fashioned road truck. He grinned at Irene, who looked prim and proper and probably didn't understand how heartbroken the boys must have been. "Poor kids. That's rotten luck to get a new toy and barely get to play with it before it's taken away. Why was it taken?"

"Honestly, I have no clue. The boys were blubbering so much and so frightened that Father would be mad. You'd think they were playing with a bomb or something." Irene grinned and leaned in to casually put her hand on Theo's arm as she lowered her voice to say the word *bomb*.

Her proper behavior made Theo forget about the toy and return her smile. He wondered about her age and would have asked, but just as Irene leaned in and touched Theo, Gracie came around the doorway from dining room to promenade.

"Uh-hum," Gracie cleared her throat half due to interrupting and half due to wondering how Theo managed to find a young female passenger so quickly. "You certainly seem to be mingling with the passengers." The cold in Gracie's voice matched the cold stare that contacted Theo's startled look.

"Oh, uh, hi, Gracie. This is, um, Irene. Um, sorry, I've forgotten your last name. And this is Gracie, my, uh, my . . . my friend,"

Theo stammered and gestured and looked back and forth between girls. He crossed and uncrossed his arms against his stomach as if to prove to Gracie that there had been distance between himself and the other teenage female passenger. Murphy took advantage of the movement to again begin working with his nose from under the bottom of the sweatshirt.

Gracie made no move and did not change her glare in Theo's direction.

"Hello." Irene's pure innocence did not detect the thickness in the air.

"*Guten Tag*," Gracie's words were jumbled in Theo's ears as he turned his back and walked a few steps away. He needed to focus on moving Murphy into a ball again to move him farther up under the hoodie. Theo hoped his busy attention to Murphy might buy him some time to think about what had just happened.

What was that all about? You would have thought Gracie had told me I couldn't talk to another human being. Why would she be so upset? What does she want anyway?

Theo twirled around to see if Gracie needed anything or if she was just passing through. They had agreed to separate and walk around the airship to get a feel for the layout before they joined up again to make a plan. He hadn't even moved his hand from the ball on his stomach when he spun around. "Gracie, did you need—" Theo's words dropped as quickly as his hand felt the ball unroll again.

"Well, Murphy. What do ya think of that? First, I'm talking to two girls, then I turn around and they're both gone. Go figure. I don't understand girls." Murphy just let out a sigh as he took the opportunity to stick a black nose out from under the hoodie again.

Passenger Problems

Gracie turned and nearly ran from the promenade. She didn't want anyone to notice the heat rising from her chest to her face. *Augh! I have been in tight spots a million times and handled myself just fine. So why do I feel like I need to throw up! I don't have any special rights to Theo. Just because he's been by my side for most of a year and is my partner on a mission. What makes me think he might think I'm the only girl alive? Since when did I need a boy anyway? I don't need him. I don't need anyone. I can . . .* Gracie's thoughts moved as swiftly as her legs until she hid her face in a curtain to pretend to watch the takeoff and to stifle her uncontrollable tears.

"Are you okay?"

Gracie squeezed her eyes shut to rid them of any moisture and in hopes of even blocking out any sound interrupting her thoughts.

"Excuse me. Are you okay?"

It's her! Can't she just bug out and go find a window to look out of? She better not push me. No. No. She can't get the best of Li'l Grey. Gracie talked herself down from her hurt and anger. With control that came from the depths of Li'l Grey, she turned and calmly stood face-to-face with the girl passenger. "Oh, hello again. I guess I didn't catch your name." Gracie dropped her voice to just above a whisper in an attempt to control any quivering that might be detected.

"Oh, sorry! My name's Irene. That sweet young man was so kind when my broth—"

"Sweet young man?" Gracie was too quick to interrupt. She tried to cover by turning to walk farther back in the airship in the direction of the sleeping rooms.

Irene didn't hide her blush, and the color gave a soft compliment to her blue eyes and chiseled features. She walked and kept pace with Gracie. "Well, he was so understanding when my brothers had their toy taken away. He seemed to understand their blubbering even better than I did, and here he is—a perfect stranger."

Gracie looked down at her shoes as she walked and secretly wished her scuffed leather boots looked a little more feminine. Her eyes couldn't help but see the tiny red satin slippers that almost skipped beside her. Gracie had a secret war going on in her head. *Do I just pound her now, or do I act like I don't care? No, I have shared times with Theo that she's just too young to understand. I do care.* Gracie's breathing became accelerated.

"Is he?" Irene stood with her head cocked at an angle, waiting for a reply from Gracie.

"Is he what? Sorry. I guess I was lost in important thought and didn't listen to you." Gracie intended a little bit of a dig to see if she could hurt the girl with insult.

The red was gone from Irene's face and had been replaced with a friendly smile. "Oh, I didn't mean to come in and interrupt you."

There was nothing fake in Irene's voice or words. Her sincerity and innocence seemed to come from deep inside, perhaps rooted with her soft skin and delicate features. Gracie felt her stomach begin to knot and her heart begin to pound with a beat to match each heavy, booted footstep. Without realizing, Gracie quickened her pace, trying to get to her sleeping cabin. She wanted to be alone. She wanted to be rid of this pretty girl. She wanted Theo just to walk up and call her—only her—by name.

"Well, I'm busy."

"I was just wondering if the young man is your brother. I think he's handsome and I—"

Gracie exploded before Irene could finish her thought. With one hand turning the doorknob of the first passenger cabin and one hand grabbing the bodice of Irene's dress just under the neckline, Gracie pulled Irene inside the empty cabin in a swift and forceful move. "No! No, he's not my brother. He's my boyfriend, and if you know what's good for you, you'll learn to keep your distance from here on out!" Gracie's fist had closed around the fabric of the bodice enough to pull Irene toward her as her words spit out with anger before she huffed, released Irene's dress, and was out the door before Irene could react.

Sweet Irene crumpled into a ball where she cried for her misunderstanding. She allowed herself only a few minutes of self-pity before she dried her tears and stood to smooth her dress and step back into the hall. Irene was determined to let nothing shake the pleasure of her flight as the blue skies accepted the *Hindenburg* lifting from the ground.

Discovery

GRACIE STUMBLED INTO the sleeping cabin she would share with Theo for the duration of the flight. The size of the small cabin made it easy for her to take few steps from door to bunk ladder. She climbed and fell onto the top bunk. The heavy boots kicked the mattress to fight the embarrassment, anger, and new feelings—feelings of wanting a boy to be more than someone from the streets, feelings of wanting a boy to be a friend, a boyfriend.

"Simmer down!" Theo's voice came from the bottom bunk. "What got into your beehive? I've never seen you act like th—ouch!" A heavy boot followed by a second catapulted down from the top bunk.

"*Dummer Junge.*" Gracie's words were muffled from under the pillow she used to cover her head as she lay on her bunk.

"I don't even need to have Murphy out of my backpack to understand that. I guess I'm getting used to the German language." Theo lay on the bottom bunk, looking up at the board that held the mattress above him. "So now what have I done that I should get a title of *stupid boy*? You know English. Why do you insist on speaking another language when you get mad?" Theo's voice had a little too much lilt and teasing.

"Leave me alone. I didn't know you were in here."

Both teens lay quietly for several minutes as the fans in the engine pod could be heard through the muffled distance.

"Your voice sounds funny. Gracie, are you crying?" The tease in Theo's voice was replaced with an honest sound of concern. "Did someone hurt you?"

Theo's questions were answered with silence. In the dark room, Theo thought about his time in Germany. *So many things have happened. I think I've changed since my struggle in the lab. I've seen so much painful truth that I treated like fiction in a boring history book. I've felt the pain of losing family, losing a dad I took for granted, losing so much that kids in Germany can't even fathom. I've learned to realize Murphy is more than a computerized dog. I guess I'm pretty bonkers to love a robot dog. Oh well, I'm not the only one to love Murphy. Gracie loves him. Silly dog. I have to watch or he'll love Gracie more than he loves me.* Theo's thoughts made a chuckle pop out into the darkness. *I better be quiet or I'll get clubbed again! Good thing she only has two feet. Those flying boots are deadly!* Theo rolled to plant his face into his pillow to stifle another chuckle. *Gracie. Li'l Grey. Hmph. She's quite a girl. Man, without her, I'd probably be dead already. I guess maybe Murphy's not the only one who loves her. I wonder if we'll ever stop fighting long enough for her to love me back. Sigh. For now, I'll just have to share Murphy with her. Good ol' Murphy. He's been a good dog for time trav—*

"That's it! That's what we need to do!" Theo broke from his thoughts, nearly yelling into the quiet air. He jumped up from his bunk and put his face close to the mattress above. "Gracie! Hey, Gracie! I have an idea. Do you know where the two little boys went?"

"No! Go find them and play cars with them and leave me alone." Grace lay with her face to the wall.

"That's just it! The boys can't play cars because they got their toy tank taken away!"

"You sure sound happy about it. Leave me alone. I couldn't care less."

"No, I'm not happy they got their toy taken away, but it helps me. I mean, it helps us!" Theo paused long enough to put his hand on Gracie's back. "Look, Gracie. I don't know what upset you, but I want to talk to you. Will you come down and sit on my bunk with me so we can talk?" Again, he was met with silence. "Please?" Theo plopped down on his bunk. He knew he had a plan, but even as a young man who had witnessed a meeting of *the Watch*, he knew that communication was not just important; it was a must.

The steps of Gracie's socks on the ladder didn't break the silence, but seeing her coming down made a smile break across the face hidden in the dark of the lower bunk. Gracie swiveled from the ladder and sat on the edge of the bunk beside Theo. She didn't lift her head as her eyes stayed riveted to the floor.

In a tender move, Theo slid his arm around Gracie's shoulders. "You okay, kid?" He pulled her toward him but said no more as he felt her head tuck against his neck and nestle against him. With his other arm, Theo wrapped Gracie to him. He envisioned himself a cocoon holding a delicate butterfly. Neither rushed the moment or spoke.

Afraid she would drift off to sleep in Theo's arms, Gracie eventually broke the silence. "So what's this great idea of yours?"

"Well, you know how we have to stay out of sight?"

"Yeah."

"How can we know what's going on?"

"I dunno. I'm pretty good at spying. I haven't really worried about that, yet."

"Oh, I'm sure we'll have plenty of spy time, but I thought of a good way to hear what's going on even when we're not around."

"Is this another of your science inventions, or does this have something to do with your weird ear things?"

Theo laughed at her skepticism of science. "Well, yes and no. Yes, it has to do with science, but no, it has nothing to do with my earbuds. We can use Murphy to—"

"Lemme guess—are we going to use him to record and send us conversations again?"

"Transmit—yeah. And I know just the innocent way to do it! Irene, the girl you met, has two little brothers."

"Ugh. I should have figured it would have something to do with her. Count me out!"

"No, listen. We won't plant Murphy with Irene. We'll give him to her two little brothers, Walter and Werner. They were upset when their toy tank was taken away. I'll, I mean, *we'll* cheer them up with a toy ball to play with. Murphy will love the attention. If Walter and Werner are typical young boys, they will play all over this ship.

They've already lost one toy, so they'll keep a close eye on the toy ball and take him everywhere. All we have to do is keep our ears open and listen to conversations Murphy's transmitter collar sends to my watch."

"I still don't understand all of this science stuff, but it sure helped us the night of the meeting of *the Watch*. I'm game as long as I don't have to deal with Irene."

"What's with you and Irene? She's such a sweet—" Theo felt Gracie's body tense up and pull away from his side. "Oh, nevermind. Let's just focus on what we have to do. Right now, that means rolling Murphy and letting the boys play with a new toy!"

As if aware of his part in the new plan, Murphy snorted in his sleep and extended his legs with a stretch before he curled up again to finish recharging at the foot of Theo's bed.

Theo gave Gracie a quick hug and turned to dive under the bed, searching for his backpack. He knew he could tuck Murphy into his pack with a quick zip and carry him to the boys like an innocent toy. Just as Theo extended his arm under the bed, a knock on the door stopped him from reaching any farther.

"Who knows this is our room?" Theo put his face to Gracie's ear to question her.

"How am I supposed to know? I can hardly find it myself! I haven't even talked to anyone besides your new sweetheart, Irene."

"Oh." Theo reacted just as the door knocking started again. He turned toward the door until Gracie grabbed the back of his T-shirt with enough force to bring him back against her.

"Oh? Oh what? Who have you told?" Gracie's voice was terse and suspicious.

"Gracie, settle down. Lemme answer the door." Theo pulled away from Gracie as she stepped into the corner behind the door just as it was opened.

"Irene!" Theo tried to sound surprised.

"Hello. I was bored, and I remembered you said your room was the last one on this hall. My family has an apartment on the lower level. It has a nice view with observation windows in the floor. I just thought I'd go crazy if I had to spend one more minute with my brothers. Besides, if Mother asks me to take charge of them again, I'll just explode!" It was as if a cork covering Irene's emotions had been popped, and the usually quiet girl couldn't stop talking.

Theo stood with a half-pleased, half-confused look on his face, not knowing how to stop the girl talking in the hall or how to stop the other girl glaring at him from behind the door. In his wildest dreams, he had thought of being surrounded by girls, but he knew this dream could quickly turn into a nightmare if the two girls crossed paths with him caught at the intersection.

"Um, I was just, um, hey, um." Theo refused to look over at Gracie standing rigid in the dark corner. "I was, um, just going to the observation windows. Wanna go?" He started to move into the doorway.

"No!" Irene threw up both hands as if to hold him in place and keep him from stepping into the hallway. "Sorry. I thought, well, I just had an unpleasant experience with another passenger, so I don't care to go back that direction."

"So you want me to walk you to your room?"

Gracie kicked the wall with her heel. She couldn't help but make a sound to send a signal to Theo to let him know she was not pleased. Theo tilted his face away from her to send a reply signal that he would make his own decisions. He intended to step into the hall, but Irene stepped forward toward the open door at the same time.

"I want to get away from my brothers too. Can I just visit with you awhile? In here?" She swung her arm toward Theo's shared cabin.

Had Gracie not been so mad at Theo at that moment, she would have laughed aloud at the expression on his face. Truly, she thought Theo's mouth opened wider than the door that had swung open with a push from Irene's gesture.

"Uh, sure. It's kinda dark in here. I'll switch on the light." Theo used the chain hanging from the bulb suspended from the middle of the ceiling as an excuse to move away from the door. Irene stepped in and closed the door behind her. The click of the door and the click of the switch on the hanging light were the only noise for a moment as the dainty young girl, *Mischling* in the corner, and teen boy swallowing his guilt for who-knows-what were all bathed in light.

Theo started talking and backing to the other side of the room to prevent Irene from seeing Gracie in the corner. "Look, Irene. Um, Captain Pruss and crew don't know that I'm on this flight without my parents. They, uh, they were caught up with a lot of government work, and at the last minute, they couldn't get away. Please promise you won't tell anyone that I'm here. I know they can't kick me off, but I could be locked up during the flight, and I haven't done anything wrong."

"I'll promise, Theo, but why—" Irene's innocent concern was framed with a wrinkled brow expressing confusion.

"Just promise and don't say anything!" Theo stepped forward and took Irene's delicate hands into his own.

"I promise, I promise. But once you get to America, what will you—"

Theo wanted the deceptive conversation to end. Thinking on his feet and creating a rational story was not his strong point. "Don't worry about me, Irene. I'll be fine. My sister and I—" Theo released Irene's hands as he gestured toward the corner.

Gracie couldn't help but inhale deeply until it brought on a cough.

Irene spun around to face the corner behind the door where Gracie stood with a smirk on her face.

"Oh!" Irene gasped and wished she could melt into the carpet. She spun back around to look at Theo, who was still standing with his eyes and mouth wide open. "Sorry, Theo, I thought, I mean, I didn't mean to interrupt you and your sis—I mean, your girlfr—I have to leave!"

Irene lunged for the door and pulled it open without moving out of the path of the swing of the door as it caught her in the forehead.

"Oh." Her cry of pain and embarrassment was soft and innocent.

"Irene!" Theo wasn't sure what he wanted to say or do, but he knew the tension in the air didn't need to hurt an innocent girl. "You don't need to leave. We were—" His words were cut short with the click of the door latch.

"Smooth move, Romeo." Gracie smirked and stood against the wall with her arms crossed across her chest.

"She's just another passeng—Gracie, did you do something to Irene? Why was she so frightened?" Theo didn't sound angry, but he returned Gracie's questioning smirk.

"She's probably a nice girl. Let's just say I just had to clarify a few rules of ownership during this flight." Gracie stepped out of the corner toward Theo with a matter-of-fact demeanor.

They both collapsed on the lower bunk beside each other and just lay in silence for what felt like an eternity. "Do you think she will keep her promise?" Theo asked with concern thick in his voice.

Gracie rolled slightly to her side so she could look at Theo. "Probably. She wouldn't want to upset her perfect little Theodore now, would she?" Gracie tried hard to keep from laughing.

"You're such a jerk," Theo replied, still concerned about Irene's quick departure. "Not my fault!"

"Whatever. She was pathetic. I would never drool all over some stupid boy like that."

"You wouldn't have to," Theo responded without thinking and immediately regretted his words. He could feel the blood rushing to his ears and cheeks as his feelings were evident in the red tint covering his face.

Gracie rolled to her back and stared up at the top bunk without saying anything as she was too busy trying to hide the huge smile on her face. "Well, since we should land Thursday morning, after tonight we only have two more days to lie low and stay out of trouble. Think you can handle that?"

"I'm not the one trying to beat up other passengers, am I?" Theo shot back. He sat up and looked around their shared cabin. "Where's my backpack?"

Gracie sat up. "What?"

"My backpack. I didn't feel it under the bed. Where is it? I want to use it to give those kids the 'silver ball' to play with. I need my pack. You know it has my book!" Theo jumped up from the bunk and started searching the tiny room. He looked under the sink and dropped down to his hands and knees again to look under the bottom bunk. He pushed Gracie's feet out of his way with protest from the young girl.

"Whoa, what do you—"

"I gotta go get my backpack and my book," Theo started talking faster and pacing around the tiny room faster and faster. "I can't believe . . . I can't . . . I think I left it in the crate!"

Gracie stood up and grabbed Theo's shoulders to look him in the eye. "Let's go get it. We need to be really careful. But first, just calm down and breathe." Gracie tried to soothe his anxiety.

Theo closed his eyes, knowing he should take Gracie's advice. He had lost the book before, but still his concern tensed his muscles. "I can't believe I left it. Do you know what will happen if they get the book again?"

"We were both barely awake when Erich moved us here. We were both exhausted. Don't feel badly, " Gracie explained patiently. "You need to focus so we don't get into any trouble."

"I know. I just feel . . ." Theo could only shake his head as words refused to form.

Gracie kept her grip and gave his shoulders a firm shake. "Focus! You can feel however you want and consider all of the what-ifs after we get it back."

"Okay," Theo blew short puffs into the air, trying to regain his composure. He glanced at his watch. "We gotta go to the cargo hold—only not right now. It's getting late. In a little over an hour, it'll be time for the meal to be served. Most passengers and even crew will be busy at the front of the ship in the dining lounge. We can sneak to the cargo hold."

"It doesn't sound like a sure bet, but since the dining room is in the opposite direction from the cargo hold, it may be our best chance." Gracie turned and put a foot on her bunk ladder. "For now, we need to stay out of sight. It could be a long night. I suggest we take a nap." She was on the bunk and crawling under the woolen blanket before she even finished talking. Theo knew her suggestion was not up for discussion. Besides, when plans were made that involved danger, Li'l Grey had good common sense. Theo kicked off his shoes and crawled under the blanket on his bunk. Just as he was setting the alarm on his watch to ensure they wouldn't oversleep, his arm was bumped from behind.

"Fine, Murphy. Just don't hog the bed. I hardly have enough room the way it is." His words made no impact as the robotic dog was already spinning three times on the pillow at the head of the bed. A slight hum of his internal computer system was a comfort as Murphy lay against Theo's ear.

The *Hindenburg* engines sang a soft hum that brought deep sleep to the stowaways who slept past dinner and past the alarm that vibrated on Theo's wrist.

Had it not been for the fact that Murphy's ear flopped across Theo's nose and cut off his airflow, the teens might have slept until the next morning.

"Ugh, Murph, get—" Theo gave a gentle shove and moved the sleeping robot from his face. He pulled his wrist in front of his eyes and touched the screen to illuminate the face of the watch.

"Gracie!" Theo tossed the blanket so quickly that Murphy was tossed awake too. "Gracie! Get up! It's past midnight!"

"*Pfui!* Why didn't you wake me?"

"Oh, I ran to the hold and got my backpack so you'd miss the fun. Zikes, Gracie! I was asleep too!" Theo paced the floor while his hands moved from running through his tousled hair to rubbing across his face and back to his hair again.

"Okay, okay. Calm down. It's not like we're landing in five minutes." She turned onto her stomach and slid her legs off the bed until she was able to stand on the bottom bunk and step down to the floor. "We have time. Besides, this may be better. Everyone's asleep, right?" She sat on the floor where she could pull on her boots and lace them.

Theo's arms fell to his sides. He nodded as he bent down to pull his shoes to the side of the bed. Gracie stood and walked to Theo's side and placed a hand on his shoulder for reassurance. He looked up and knew Li'l Grey was right.

Gracie looked into Theo's eyes for a few more seconds until she was convinced that he was with her mentally. She gave him one last shoulder shake then moved to the cabin door. With the stealth learned as a street urchin sneaking in and out of locked shops, she cracked open the door and peered into the hallway. "Coast is clear. Let's move," she whispered.

"Wait! I'm not going to let Murphy out of my sight until I plant him in the hands of the boys. Murphy! Roll, boy." Murphy cocked his head but obeyed his master and rolled into a shiny ball. Theo tucked Murphy into his hoodie, not caring that his left side looked to have grown a lump.

The duo slipped quietly into the hallway and crept down the long corridor. The dimly lit hall provided enough shadow for them to sneak undetected all the way to the end, where locked doors displayed a sign stating, CREW ONLY ACCESS. Gracie's nimble fingers worked the lock like a master thief, and with a quick turn of the wrist, the mechanical latch lifted and the door opened.

"That was a little too easy for you," Theo chided as the door popped open.

"Shhh," Gracie hissed as she pointed to the closest cabin door in the hallway. A light from the room popped on and lit the space between the bottom of the door and the threshold, casting an eerie glow into the hallway. The two teens watched as the L-shaped handle slowly turned downward. The door cracked open a bit, allowing light from the room to pour into the dark hallway. A passenger suffering from insomnia innocently stepped into the hall. Before his eyes could focus in the darkness, Theo turned and tackled Gracie, knocking them both through the crew-only door and into the restricted area of the *Hindenburg*. They hit the metal catwalk with a thud of bodies falling and a grunt of Gracie having the wind knocked out of her lungs from the fall. Theo quickly turned and, with a soft kick with his foot, shut the door. The only new sound was a soft click as the latch settled into the striker plate and again held the door closed.

"That seemed a little too easy for you," Gracie mocked, pushing the boy off her and quietly standing up.

Theo threw an index finger across his lips to signal silence and forced his eyes to see down the catwalk into the first cargo area.

Gracie shrugged off Theo's warning and turned toward a light and sounds of a faint commotion of men playing cards where the catwalk ended in an open room. "Great. Now how do we get around that?"

Theo didn't answer right away as he scanned the farthest edges of the lighted cargo hold for a possible way around the gambling crewmen. He looked up, left, right, then down, and without another word, he grabbed the railing of the catwalk and leaped over the side. Gracie swallowed her gasp as she watched the boy from the future leap over the side of the catwalk. She leaned over the side to see him staring up at her, motioning for her to follow his lead. She cocked her head sideways in a "why not?" fashion and bound over the catwalk safety rail and landed without a sound on the balls of her feet.

"Again, too easy." He laughed quietly at his partner's cat-burglar-esque abilities. "This way," he motioned, pointing to an area ahead that was packed with passengers' extra cargo. Without a sound, they snaked their way through the maze of boxes, crates, and suitcases. The noise of the rowdy men above them grew louder the more they gulped down the homemade brew. Theo was glad for the commotion above. The noise of the inebriated men and their card game made it easier to sneak along the passage underneath the crew. There was little chance of any accidental missteps being heard as the teens crept aft on the airship.

Their trek through the cargo hold eventually led them to another wall. A single door provided the only means of entering the next cargo area. Gracie scanned the door lock for a few minutes and shook her head in disgust. "I don't think I can open it," she mumbled in defeated tone.

"Seriously, we've made it all this way just to give up? Don't you wanna at least try?" Theo wasn't sure what their next move should be if Li'l Grey couldn't pick the lock. "Maybe I should unroll Murphy. Maybe he can open this door with no problem."

"If you hadn't forgotten your stupid backpack, we wouldn't need to open this door."

"Sure, get mad at me now that you can't get us through," Theo retaliated as the frustration of the situation was starting to discourage both of them. "What happened to 'We were both exhausted' and 'Don't feel badly'?" Theo could feel his face heating up in an embarrassed anger when he threw Gracie's words back at her.

"Whatever!"

Theo wanted to scream but was pretty sure the drunken crew members would hear him despite the noise they were making. He let out a sigh of frustration and swung a fist at the door handle. The momentum of his fist swing tilted him in toward the door where the handle took the brunt of his explosion. As his hand made contact, the L-shaped handle gave way, spilling him to the ground. "Ow."

"Well, whaddaya know," Gracie chirped mockingly as she stepped over her friend sprawled out on the metal floor. She pushed on the door and laughed as it opened. "You just gonna lie there?"

"Whatever," Theo mumbled as he pushed himself up from the floor.

The card game overhead was turning violent. The noise and commotion above them crescendoed. Theo was thankful for the chaos that covered the noise of his fall and prevented their exposure.

He stepped through the door and almost jumped out of his skin when it snapped shut behind him. Theo spun around, ready to swing his clenched fist at his attacker, but he lowered it when he saw Gracie's smiling face. "Easy, Tiger. You don't want to take it there," she joked, watching as he lowered his hands and tried to relax. Theo knew his nerves were on end. He also knew control was a must. For one thing, there was nowhere to escape from a balloon in the sky. For another, he was tired of being outplayed by a girl.

Annoyed at Gracie, Theo started navigating his way through the supply area. This second area had stacks of crates filled with food and drinks, along with boxes of dried food and extra rations in case of an emergency on the airship. The weather was forecast as clear for most of the trip, but Erich had told them of a possible delay in landing the dirigible due to a strong headwind.

They made their way through the second cargo hold without incident and began to feel confident that they would be able to retrieve the missing book and backpack. They slipped through another unlocked door and entered the cargo area where they had been stowed when the voyage began. A high stacked crate covered with a large drop cloth and netting blocked Theo's view. He pressed his body against the cargo as he moved along the side, hoping for a better view of the room. Once he crept to the edge of the tall crate, he dipped down to a crouched stance and peered around the corner of the freight.

Before he got his entire head around the corner, he jerked himself back and swore silently under his breath. Cautiously, he took one more look to double-check what he thought he had seen. Was that really who he thought it was? Men in military dress were standing out in the open, looking through the crates, including the one used to sneak them onto the airship. A stoop-shouldered man in a long black coat moved restlessly around the perimeter.

"Wha . . ."

Theo shook his head violently, stopping Gracie from even whispering her question to him. He motioned with his head for her to look around the corner. She leaned around him enough to peer around the corner and came back with eyes wide open and the same shocked look on her face.

Gracie looked up at Theo and mouthed the words, "What now?"

Theo shook his head in disgust and shrugged his shoulders in defeat. They leaned back on the cargo and carefully scanned the cargo hold around them. Gracie tapped Theo lightly on the shoulder and then pointed up.

Theo followed her finger pointing upward and studied the catwalk above them. The interior triangular framework of the airship could easily be scaled, but he was worried the men in the center of the room would hear them. He pointed to his ear and made a climbing motion, which drew a very strange look from Gracie.

Before Theo could come up with another plan, Gracie slipped around behind the triangular support beam and started quickly and silently scaling upward. Her hands and feet worked in unison as she zipped up the beam and sat waiting for Theo and watching the men and black-clad beast having their conference. Unable to hear what they were saying, she lay flat on the crossbeam.

Theo knew his height would help him scale the distance to the next level of beams, but he also knew he didn't have the catlike dexterity of Gracie. Knowing he could use leg muscles toned from years of drift boarding, Theo smoothly and silently pulled his legs into a squat position. He had watched Gracie keep her body close to the beams to prevent detection by wandering eyes below. In a fluid motion, Theo pushed up with his legs and reached above his head with extended arms. He grasped the beam and started his climb, catching his hoodie on the beam. He was so focused on the climb that he paid no attention to the tug at his side until he felt the weight of a ball kick against his side as Murphy jumped from inside the hoodie.

"No! Murphy!" Theo swung one arm after the unrolled sphere, but Murphy was in a full-speed run down the beam, headed in the opposite direction.

Neither Theo nor Gracie moved anything but eyes as they watched Murphy run undetected to the end of the room, where he slowed and inched down a vent that led to the main floor of the cargo hold. As if he knew the mission, Murphy sniffed the floor, moving silently in and out of boxes until his nose snuggled against the strap of Theo's backpack that lay against the open crate where he had hidden a day earlier.

Theo silently prayed that Murphy would not be noticed and jerked his arms tighter around the beam as a tick sound came from the far side of the room. The men standing around the crates looked in the direction of the sound, away from Murphy, and the stoop-shouldered creature in a black coat wandered toward the sound.

Theo looked up at Gracie, who was perched with a crooked grin on her face and her hair hanging down around her face. Theo knit his eyebrows until he saw Gracie point to a series of bolts on the beam where one was missing the nut that held it on the beam. His eyes drifted back to Gracie, who was dangling the elastic band that usually held her hair. She grinned again and pointed at Murphy. All that Theo saw was the tip of a tail as Murphy disappeared into the backpack.

Theo grinned back as he shook his head and let his thoughts give credit where it was due. *Leave it to my girl to find a way to make a slingshot distraction.* Theo couldn't help but admire Gracie for her way of keeping him and Murphy safe. With Murphy safely hiding in his familiar backpack, Theo pulled and crawled up the beam, stopping close to Gracie, who curled up until she sat with her legs under her. For a moment, she was content to lean against Theo's shoulder and place her hand on the knee squatting beside her. She had a freshness about her. Theo wasn't sure if it was a scent or just a softness that radiated from her heart, but he knew that whatever happened, he would never forget and always love this girl. Perhaps she knew.

"Theo?" Gracie leaned away from Theo and looked at movement below.

"Theo?"

"Yeah?" Theo willed more time with Gracie.

"Theo, I think those people are huddling up for a meeting or something." She gestured to the group below them. The momentary distraction Gracie had created only delayed the purpose for the small group assembled in the cargo hold. A stoop-shouldered man in a long black duster restlessly moved around the outskirt of the assembly that stood directly below the beam where two silent teenagers sat frightened of detection, determined to finish their mission.

Catwalk

"**G**ENTLEMEN, STOP BICKERINK! Must I remind you of all I must report to vonce ve land in die United States? Die *Society* vill not take any excuses if you fail yet again to find tat boy and *das Buch*!" Though she stood with her back to the teens, the woman's stern voice filled the room. She had no worry for being in a restricted zone.

"My apologies, *Frau*—"

"*Enough* apologies, Colonel Erdmann! You tree vere specifically placed on tis dirigible for two tasks." Point by point, two slender fingers were lifted into the air. "First, to find *das Buch*, and sekunt, to prevent die Communist *Red Peace* from vhatever ist planned. Der führer does not allow *anyting* to embarrass das Reich!" the gray-haired woman reprimanded the high-ranking Nazi officers with absolutely no regard for their position and prestige.

Theo and Gracie looked at each other in disbelief that a woman was tearing into German officers like a teacher correcting bad schoolchildren. Without talking, two minds asked the same question. *Who is this woman?* They both returned their stares to the group below in an effort to focus. Never did they suspect the cruel words they heard next.

"Ve gleaned little usable information from tat man . . ." The woman cocked her head toward a tall man standing beside her dressed in an American raccoon coat and tan fedora. "Gustav, vat vas his name again?" To this point, he had remained silent. Shadows and distance prevented any clear view of his face.

"Möeller." The man hesitated and tipped his head back as if looking at the catwalk lacing the air to find written the victim's name.

"Ah ya, Jahile Möeller. He vas vone of de last *Beschützer* for de *Watch* tat ve know of." Gustav Wilhelm Kaercher's matter-of-fact reply expressed zero emotion for having tortured another human.

"Tis ist a huge loss for . . ."

Theo turned his head to the side, having a hard time letting the words sink in and their meaning register in his brain. Though he had learned much of the Deutsch language during his time in Germany, he could not fully understand. "Gracie, what did he mean by *bes*—"

"Protector," Gracie exhaled the word before Theo could repeat what she did not want to hear.

"Loss? Gracie, what are they saying?" Theo let his whispers trail into silence. Then as the shock of the words started to dig into his soul, his eyes widened in horror and he choked back a scream. A soft gagging noise came from beside him. He turned his head to see Gracie biting down on her hand, her eyes filling with tears and her face reddening with venomous rage for those who stood below her. With increasing determination, Gracie unclenched her jaw from her fist. She quietly straightened her legs to stand on the beam, ready to pounce on the enemy below.

Theo reached over and put his hand on hers. She stopped her movement and crouched down to look at him with a tear-stained face. "You can't do this now." He leaned his mouth close to the side of her face and whispered barely enough for her to hear. "He wouldn't want you to do this. He sacrificed himself for you."

Gracie didn't respond with words. Her rage seized her body and mind. The only thing she understood was the man she loved as a second father had been taken from her just like her papa had been. She pointed her finger at the man who had spoken. She just kept pointing at him, her arm shaking uncontrollably.

Theo watched Gracie as she struggled internally with emotions that threatened to explode out of her like a ton of dynamite. He relaxed as she sank back down to lie on the beam, keeping herself hidden from sight. Convinced that she would not stand and leap off the ledge onto the Nazi officers and *Society* informants, he turned his attention to the meeting below. They hadn't stopped talking. Theo feared they may have missed hearing useful information.

"Ve vill dismiss until after breakfast! You stay here and guard tis evidence of die Amerikaner on board." Again, the slender finger of the woman pointed and moved from the dark-cloaked jaeger to the backpack lying near a crate. "From here on, no vone gets in or out of here vitout our permission. Ve must capture tat younk man and also look for members of *Red Peace*. De Communists vould have no problem destroyink tis airship!" Without a word of dismissal, the woman spun on her heels and moved toward the exit. As if ordered by a silent command, the tall man and the German military officers followed until the door closed behind them with a sharp click.

Suspended fifteen feet directly above a nightmarish monster, Theo wasn't sure how to help Gracie. Seeing her body shake from her silent weeping caused his insides to burn. He understood her sadness of loss. He wanted to comfort his friend.

Theo also struggled against tears at the news of Herr Möeller's death. His thoughts swirled in memory of the man who had nursed him back to life after the vicious beating he received at the hands of the *Hitlerjugend*. He understood the pain of losing a man who stepped in to be a father when no other parent was there to comfort, to listen, and to hold him through the good as well as through the evil. Theo's mind started to wander. He thought about the conversations he had had with Jahile Möeller. That man had been patient and understanding. He was incredible. Somehow, he had managed to save them from jaegers and SS officers.

Thoughts that crossed Theo's mind convicted him, and he knew Gracie was feeling the same: they were responsible for Herr Möeller's death. What drove him to sneak away from Herr Möeller's home that night to find Brack and the leather book? Why did Gracie follow him? If only they had stayed in that night, Herr Möeller wouldn't have come to their rescue and fought the jaegers. Herr Möeller wouldn't have been forced to threaten the enemy by exposing the triquetra branded onto his arm. He would still be alive, maybe even be with them right now. Their guardian would have helped get them safely to the United States. Instead, he was gone—gone from their lives, gone from this world.

Theo choked on his tears and turned away from Gracie to focus below him. He watched the jaeger pace around and around. After watching the repetitive hobbles, Theo noticed the pacing was actually a pattern. The creature was systematically walking through various sections of crates to view the entire cargo area from different angles. Nothing or no one on the floor of the cargo hold would be able to get past this monster. Theo knew he needed to avoid the jaeger's path to get to the floor of the cargo hold long enough to retrieve the backpack.

From his perch on the beam, Theo could clearly see the canvas backpack beside the crate. He watched and he understood—the sole purpose of the beast's presence was to guard the backpack. So how could two unarmed kids descend fifteen feet, lift the pack, and get out of the cargo hold without alerting the jaeger? This was not just a man or a creature. It was an indestructible killing machine securing the room for one of the most lethal and ruthless militant groups ever formed in the history of man.

Theo closed his eyes to focus and create a plan. He released the beam with the hand he had used to stabilize himself. His movement drew the red tear-stained eyes of Gracie down on him. He remembered seeing that same look, that same expression, once before. Gracie's eyes held the same pain his father's eyes held the day of the accident that took his mother's life. It was a look of pain welling up from inside, a look of irreversible loss.

Gracie pulled her eyes from Theo to the crate that had been used to smuggle them on board. She watched as the beast below finished another round of security check in the cargo bay. She shook her head in disgust, believing that very creature could be responsible for ending Herr Möeller's life. The red of her eyes slowly began to match a crimson in her cheeks as sadness returned to rage. She vowed to herself that she would avenge her guardian's death.

"*No!*" Theo mouthed the word and shook his head, seeing the change in her face.

"They killed him!" she spoke the words almost inaudibly, but they resounded in Theo's ears with a crash. He opened his mouth to reply when a movement below caught their attention. They gasped as the backpack lying in the middle of the floor began to squirm and move around like it was possessed.

"Murphy!" Gracie gasped.

Theo punched her in the arm to get her attention then held an index finger to his pursed lips to quiet her.

The two teens weren't the only ones to notice the movement of the backpack. In a flash, the jaeger appeared in the middle of the room where he kicked the bag and sent it flying into a large stack of wooden boxes. The noise from the impact made Gracie and Theo both shudder as the backpack gave very little protection to Murphy's robotic body. The pack smashed through the thin plywood box and wedged between the splintered wood.

Theo and Gracie watched in horror as the creature started walking toward the stack of boxes. Uncontrollable swelling and stinging in Gracie's eyes came with tears that challenged her ability to focus. The abuse of Murphy was a final blow, and she couldn't be strong anymore. The painful losses of parents and surrogate father had mounted in her heart. Now the lovable robot dog that had already saved her life lay lodged in a pack waiting to be destroyed by the soulless shape of evil.

Tears borne in her heart streamed down Gracie's cheeks as muffled sobs tried to escape. She leaned forward to wipe her face on her T-shirt. Too late she sucked in a breath to pull back uncontrollable tears that fell fifteen feet to the floor below them. Gracie impulsively reached out to catch the drops of falling emotion. The quickness of her motion tipped her weight too far from the beam, causing her to tumble from her perch. Seeing her movement in his peripheral sight, Theo instinctively reached out and grasped her arm just below her shoulder. The upper half of her body dangled in space as the iron grip of Theo's fingers held her body in limbo. Only her feet and knees remained across the beam. Theo grimaced. He clamped his teeth as he held her with one hand while the other white knuckled hand grasped the iron beam. He fought a battle of mind and strength as the pull against his hold of the beam weakened the grip of his fingers. He tried leaning back to use his body weight as a counter level against Gracie, but he couldn't pull himself back far enough.

He grunted against the sweat of exertion that threatened its toll on his muscles. Fighting gravity, Theo and Grace watched the tears that seemed to be falling in slow motion finally splash down on the floor of the cargo bay directly in the path of the jaeger.

The black leather-clad beast stopped halfway through its stride. The toe of the creature's knee-high combat boot stopped less than half an inch away from the nearly imperceptible wet spot on the floor. He took a moment to examine the insignificant spot that a normal person's vision would have missed then lifted his foot for another step. A second tear splashed down on the creature's shoulder stopping him midstride. Turning his head, black eyes buried in a deformed face peered at the tiny drop on his shoulder. With a black-gloved hand, he swiped across the spot and lifted the finger to his bulbous nose to sniff the tear. The arms of the beast dropped to his sides as he tilted back his head and bellowed. The roar combined with a heightened stench threatened nightmares for years to come, if not immediate death.

The jaeger squatted then sprang off the floor of the *Hindenburg* with the velocity of a cannonball. The long arms of the beast swiped at the vulnerable girl dangerously dangling from the crossbeam. The black-gloved hand sliced through Gracie's hair and closed a split second too late. The angry beast landed on the ground with nothing to show for its effort. Again, it uttered an angry snarl and squatted to set another try.

Gracie screamed as the stench and the waft of wind passed in an attempt to latch onto her face. "Pull me up!"

"I am trying!" Theo moaned, red-faced, as every muscle in his upper torso strained to keep both of them from plummeting to the floor. "Hang on!"

Theo used every ounce of energy he could muster to squeeze his hands tighter. He inched his fingers farther around the beam to give more surface for his sweaty palm to grip. He knew his leg muscles were strong. With stubborn tenacity, he started to rise from a squatted position. He knew his quads would support both his weight and Gracie's. He braced his feet and pushed back with his legs to throw all his weight backward. The quick change of direction jerked Gracie upward enough that she could get a grip on the beam. With Gracie's weight suddenly off his muscles, Theo took a few quick, awkward steps before he tumbled backward, landing against the next beam.

Gracie pulled herself up to brace and catch her breath. Theo had caught himself on a beam parallel to Gracie's. They looked at each other with a "that was close" look then down just in time to see the jaeger's second attempt to reach them. This time, its leap awarded success as one hand locked onto the beam where Gracie sat. The man-creature began to pull itself up with one arm.

Gracie stood and sprinted across the skinny catwalk with the poise of a gymnast on a balance beam. She sprang into the air and came down with a thud on the monster's grip hand. She kicked her boots downward to land with all her weight on its fingers. Theo watch as the unfazed beast lifted itself with one arm and reached for Gracie's foot with the other.

Theo didn't hesitate. With all the speed and balance he could muster, he sprinted dangerously fast over the narrow beam. One misplaced step and he would fall to the hard, unforgiving floor beneath.

Gracie jumped away from the attacking arm and tried to dislodge its hand once more. Again, the beast didn't move and yanked itself up again and made another swinging grab for her foot. Theo came crashing down on its hand with more force and weight than Gracie could generate. Even with his huffing breaths, Theo heard and felt cracking bones under his shoes. Using his momentum of movement, he made a powerful kick to the jaeger's head between eye and ear, forcing the creature's body back, causing him to fall to the floor and lie in a motionless heap.

"No way that thing's dead," Theo offered as they both stared down at the crumpled leather mass on the floor beneath them.

"Great, now what?" Gracie panted heavily between breaths.

"I honestly have no idea. We're in a ton of trouble. I wish Herr—" He stopped and glanced up at Gracie and dropped his head in sadness. His head spun with dizzying emotions that flooded back into his mind.

"This isn't the time!" Gracie's voice shook as she tried to be strong in the face of peril. "We have to get away from this thing and find Erich or Joseph."

Theo glanced away. She was right. He sniffed back tears to examine the situation below them. "Where did it go?" Theo's voice came out as a whispered scream.

"Look!" Gracie pointed down at the shattered crate.

Theo jerked his head around just as the cabin boy named Werner Franz streaked out from behind stacks of dried foods. He kicked the broken slats of the crate until he could pull out the backpack. The young boy looked up at them. Werner had been in every room, level, and niche of the airship and had crossed those beams a hundred times. He knew more about the ship than even the designing architect. "*Folge mir!*" he shouted with a wave of his arm and disappeared into the stacks.

"What?" Theo turned his whole body, trying to watch the young cabin boy.

"Follow him!" Gracie slipped around Theo, who was clinging to a vertical beam. She ran then leaped like a cat across an open space, landing lightly on another beam moving her farther back into the depths of the dirigible.

"Seriously," Theo moaned then moved around the beam and jumped to the next. He had a hard time keeping up with Gracie as the months of living on the streets had honed her skills. Theo watched in amazement as she went from beam to beam with little effort or worry, jumping over large open spaces that would have ended their journey if either of them fell. Twice, he stopped to judge distance before he jumped with all his might over the stacks and piles below. As they maneuvered along the catwalk, he saw they neared a wall. He sped up his pace, fearing what was behind and below him and not wanting to lose the cabin boy or the curly-haired girl. His fear of the unknown superseded his fear of falling, quickening his movement from beam to beam, closing the gap between himself and the other two.

Theo didn't raise his eyes from the beams until only one beam lay between him and the wall. Then hope yanked from his soul when he raised his eyes but saw no one ahead of him. He looked down and saw a cart of bed linens with a noticeable indentation. He traced the shape on the linen pile with his eyes then shook his head. He turned a full circle in an attempt to catch a glimpse of Gracie. Tilting his head and squinting as if to measure, he looked back down at the pile of linens.

"You've gotta be kidding me." He recognized what could be a Gracie-sized impression. Once again, he shook his head at the agility of his companion. With a quick breath and quick step, before he could change his mind, he stepped off the beam and prayed there would be enough cushion to ease the force of his landing.

With a soft thud, he landed in the cushion of bed linens. The cloth absorbed his blow but cradled around him, submerging him in a coffin of tangled white linens. He twisted and turned, trying to free himself from the soft fabric, but escape did not seem possible. Theo could feel his heart pounding. Panic set in. The feeling of being closed in the tunnel crept under his skin. Being submerged in darkness threatened to smother him. In a reaction, he thrashed with both arms and was trying to scream when one hand covered his mouth and another cradled his head behind his neck. He struggled against the soft hands that muffled his scream. More hands grabbed his arms just below his shoulders and tugged, pulling him from his capture.

The hands that covered his mouth and wrapped around his head released their firm grip. Theo stopped wrestling and was able to see Gracie kneeling beside him in the linen cart, one hand on his mouth and a finger on her lips telling him to be quiet. She nodded in the direction where they had been on the beams. Theo did his best to turn and look, but his legs were still tangled in the linens. He looked down at his bound legs and watched the young boy move quickly to untangle Theo's limbs from the mess. Theo noticed his pack was slung across the boy's back. Finally freed, Theo turned and saw why Gracie had covered his mouth.

The jaeger that had fallen off the support beam was walking through the crates and stacks of cargo. All three youths had no doubt the beast was looking for them. The man-creature stalked through openness and shadows. It stopped every few steps to take a deep breath like it was trying to locate them through smell. Theo and Gracie locked eyes for a moment. Theo's breathing had calmed. He nodded, and she took her hand away from his mouth. She opened her palm and offered Theo her hand.

Theo winced as the cart holding the linens creaked loudly just as Gracie stood and was pulling to help Theo climb out. They froze and held their breaths to see if the beast had heard the noise. Convinced they had not been detected, Gracie pulled as Theo used his muscular legs to push his way out of the cart. He eased to the floor and stood, still holding on to Gracie's arms.

Gracie, Theo, and Werner hid in the shadows, silently watching the black-clad jaeger turn back toward the area where he had—for a few brief moments—been nothing but a heap on the floor. They watched in horror, wondering what it would take to permanently stop him. They looked at each other then back to where the jaeger disappeared around some crates.

"Tis vay," Werner whispered and turned toward the rear of the ship. The duo followed their guide, having to stop and hide in the shadows to elude a crew member making his rounds. The cabin boy Werner was hyper aware and seemed to have unprecedented knowledge of every nook and cranny on the dirigible.

"Werner, where are you taking us?" Gracie was grateful for his help, but her life on the streets had made her wary of trusting.

"I show you sometink," he said with broken English.

"What?"

Werner didn't answer Theo. He just put a finger over his lips then pointed above them to the support beams that ran the entire length of the airship.

Theo and Gracie gasped and looked straight into the soulless eyes of the jaeger they thought they had escaped. Theo instinctively threw his arm in front of Gracie to protect her. Gracie ducked her face, then straightened, and pushed his arm away.

Theo looked at Gracie, slightly embarrassed by his reaction and slightly hurt by hers. *Focus!* he mentally chided and braced himself to spring into action. The beast crawled above them, stopping to sniff the air every few steps. Theo realized this jaeger—maybe every jaeger—was blind. *The Watch* could use this information! He elbowed Gracie a little harder than he intended, this discovery giving him a burst of adrenaline.

"Ow! What?" she mouthed the words and scowled as she rubbed her arm.

Theo pointed to his eyes then up to the creature that was crawling away from them. He mouthed the words "Can't see. Only smell" as he pointed to his nose.

"Oh!" Gracie formed the unspoken word, but the jaeger immediately stopped and turned around so quickly the trio almost screamed. It scurried across the support beams so fast that Theo started to rethink his previous statement about it not being able to see. It stopped directly above the three youths and took in a deep breath through its grotesquely misshapen nose and snarled viciously as it caught a whiff. As it took another long deep breath through its nose, saliva spewed from its mouth and fell on the tip of Gracie's shoe.

Theo feared Gracie's reaction. He watched as the look of fear on her face faded. He turned from Gracie to lock his eyes on the jaeger. He knew full well that they had very little room for error and could not get caught off guard again by its stealth.

Werner hadn't moved or uttered a word but suddenly snapped out of his shock and tapped Gracie on the shoulder. The movement caught Theo's eye, and he understood the boy's motion to follow. Gracie turned from Werner to Theo, who shrugged his shoulders.

Gracie turned back to the cabin boy just in time to see him slip through a crack between the large stacks of cargo they had been using for cover. She quietly followed through the opening and helped pull Theo's big frame through the entirely too small hole. She almost laughed as Theo sucked in as much of his mass as he could and still winced as he scraped his body on the rough cargo containers. He gave her a pathetic look and rubbed his sore, bruised chest.

Engine Car

THE DUO FOLLOWED Werner as he weaved his way through the cargo holds and the back regions of the ship. He seemed anxious to show them something he did not want to talk about in the halls. Eventually, the cabin boy came to an abrupt stop and pointed at one of the most amazing things Theo had ever seen. At the end of a very long gangway loomed a section of hydrogen-filled gasbags, which gave the airship the ability to float.

Theo stared with his mouth hanging open. He remembered a history lesson when Mr. Medi explained the construction of the gasbags. A kid in class had interrupted Medi's lecture about the *Hindenburg* by making a wisecrack about how the school could probably float in the air since there seemed to be a lot of "gasbags" in the office. Theo grinned remembering how Mr. Medi was not happy about the play on words and how he decided to respond with a lecture of how the bags on airships had been made from cow intestines but the *Hindenburg* used a new technique of cotton infused with gelatin. *Funny*, Theo thought, *how a mouthy teen actually caused a lecture that now made a lot of sense. Now I'm standing here looking at 1937 modern technology.*

The back of the dirigible offered less light. Gracie squinted to understand what she saw. From where she was standing, the walkway appeared to pierce into the inside of the hydrogen-filled cotton bags, puffed bags that filled the entire diameter of the airship.

"They're gone," Werner whispered in a sad and shocked voice then turned sharply to stare back the way they came. "Someone's comink." Theo and Gracie listened closely to the mumbles of the perplexed boy. Without another word, Werner took off in a sprint toward the gasbags then crawled over the guardrail of the gangway. He disappeared in the darkness of the ship's underbelly.

"Wait! Werner! Don't leave us!" Gracie watched in disbelief. Their navigator and guide was leaving in a hurry. They were lost in a maze of the ship without Werner's lead.

"Where's he going?" Theo snapped his head around.

"What do we do now?"

Theo opened his mouth to answer Gracie but was stopped by the slam of a door behind them.

"*Was macht ihr zwei hier? Ihr dürft hier nicht sein!*"

Theo looked from the very angry, very surprised engineer then to Gracie for a translation, but he knew they were in trouble for being so far back in the dirigible. "He's not happy, is he?"

"Not at all. He wants to know what we're doing here. He's telling us to leave. I don't think we have a choice, Theo."

"Great, we can avoid the SS, the *Red Peace, the Society*, even their psycho assassin jaegers, but this guy catches us and blows our cover." Theo's expression and tone were harsh with disgust.

The engineer cautiously moved toward the two teens. His shock of seeing civilians in this part of the ship hadn't quite worn off. He had woken from sleep just minutes earlier for his shift at the portside aft propeller. The engineer was still groggy and not thinking clearly. "*Dreht euch langsam um und fangt an zu laufen!*"

Gracie leaned close to Theo and whispered, "He wants us to turn around and start walking."

"Whatever." Theo turned and started heading down the gangway toward the gasbag ahead of them. Gracie frowned but followed her companion down the walkway, her eyes searching for the cabin boy and anywhere they could escape.

"*Was macht ihr zwei hier? Was habt ihr vor?*" the engineer spoke with anger.

"He asked what we're doing back here," Gracie translated for Theo before he had a chance to ask.

"Tell him we came back here looking for Ulla, to feed and to walk her."

"Good one, Theo. I'll make a street rat outta you yet." Gracie grinned then, without hesitation, translated Theo's idea to the engineer. "*Wir sind hier Ulla zu finden, um sie zu füttern und mit ihr spazieren zu gehen.*"

"*Lustigen, kleiner Mann war gerade vor ein paar Stunden hier. Er darf nicht hier sein,*" he grumbled.

"He's not pleased with that excuse. He must've already had a run in with Joseph."

"*Nehmt die Leider!*" he ordered and pointed to a gap in the railing where a ladder disappeared into the darkness below.

"Take the ladder, Theo."

Theo peered over the edge down into the darkness and noticed a little farther down the catwalk a small travel trunk pushed up against the exterior of the hydrogen gasbags. *That's strange. Why would luggage have been left there?* The trunk spiked Theo's curiosity.

"Theo?"

"Uh, yeah, the ladder, where does it go?" He looked back over the rail, trying to remember the location and planning later to ask Erich about the out-of-place trunk.

"I have no idea. Just do it! We don't need him any madder than he already is!"

"Fine," Theo grumbled reluctantly. He turned and started down the ladder but stopped about halfway down when he heard a loud thud. Gracie screamed, echoing throughout the vastness of the hold. "What's wrong?"

"Climb faster, Theo! It found us!"

"What found—ugh!" A stench wafted down. Theo realized they had to move quickly down the ladder, but he didn't know how much farther to the bottom. With swift thinking and action, he covered his hands with his sleeves and gripped the outside of the metal ladder, then he hugged the outside of the ladder with his feet so he could slide to where the ladder ended. The exhilaration ended quickly as he came down hard on the next platform. "That was awesome!" Theo blurted out, despite the burning in his palms and the seriousness of the current threat.

For the moment, Theo had forgotten Fritz's warning that a constant threat of danger could make a person a little braver or a little more numb. Theo teetered on a dangerous line between courage and overconfidence. "Hurry, Gracie!"

"Do you honestly think I'm taking my time?"

"Well, no, but—"

"Shut up and run!" With a thud, Gracie dropped beside him on the platform.

"Run where?"

Gracie glanced each direction of the catwalk then looked up, listening for the jaeger's heavy steps on the rungs of the ladder. She tugged Theo's hand and started running toward the rear of the ship. They heard a clang of the creature's footstep echo in the metal corridor.

"Where are we going?"

"Away from that thing!" Gracie sprinted down the dimly lit walkway. One slip or misstep threatened capture. Her heartbeat pounded as she commanded her thoughts. *Keep a steady, fast pace! Keep upright! Look for escape!* The outline of a door and a heavy wheel lock almost tumbled her to a stop. "Quick! Help me open this door!"

She could hear Theo's panting breaths as he fumbled in the shadows until his hands firmly gripped the lock wheel. He muscled a quick turn, but it didn't budge. He took a step back from the door, inhaled a deep breath, and squeezed his hold on the wheel. Again, he took a commanding step forward and heaved on the wheel. Nothing.

"What's wrong?"

"It won't budge. Do we even know where this goes?" The idea of a dead end behind the door, or even something worse, frightened Theo as much as facing the odious beast.

"How should I know?" Gracie's eyes searched the darkness behind them for any signs of the blind beast. She knew all too well that just because she couldn't see or hear the jaeger didn't mean it wasn't closing in on them as they struggled with the door. "We really need to hurry!"

"I know. I can do this." The concern and worry in Gracie's voice made him more determined. Theo readjusted his grip on the thick wheel lock. He sucked in a deep breath then leaned into the door, driving with his legs to put all his might behind the effort.

The wheel refused to give way. Theo began to weaken from his explosion of effort and adrenaline. A wisp of defeat nearly swept through his mind. Suddenly, the wheel creaked and slightly turned.

"I . . . think . . . I . . . got . . . it," he grunted through clenched teeth as he forced the wheel.

"It's close. I can smell it."

"I'm trying, Gracie, I promise."

"I know."

Theo moved to the left side of the handle and grabbed it like a baseball bat. He fell to his knees, using his body weight to force the metal wheel to turn. "Umph." Theo's downward pull was fueled by a determination to survive and by an even stronger desire to save Gracie. "Umph." He held his breath as he pulled downward until a dull grating sound hinted the turn of the wheel. He grasped the top of the wheel and pulled again and again and again until the turning stopped with a click. With a hard tug, he opened the heavy door. Biting his lower lip, he put his head through the doorway. Exasperation flared as he stared at another short, slightly better-lit gangway that ended at yet another door with a spinning wheel lock.

"You've got to be kidding me!"

"What is it?"

"It's another keel gangway with another locked door!" Theo grumbled and stepped over the ledge of the oval-shaped threshold and into the next passageway. From behind him, Gracie stepped past Theo and started down the gangway toward the next door. He leaned against the heavy door to close it behind them and spun the wheel to the right until a dull click locked it once again.

Theo turned to follow Gracie when something slammed into the door. He spun around where lifeless eyes stared back at him. The beast's breath steamed the double-paned glass as it sniffed the air for signs of its prey. Theo caught himself on the railing in frightful reaction to seeing the demented face. He regained his balance and jogged down the walkway.

He gripped Gracie's shoulders and leaned to her ear. "It's at the door."

Gracie didn't question Theo's warning. For a moment, she looked back at the door. A gasp escaped her lungs as she caught a glimpse of the creature before it disappeared from the small window. She reached back and rubbed her neck to fight the chills that crept under her delicate skin.

She shook the shiver and tried to refocus by grabbing the lock wheel. Theo watched the dainty girl. "Here, let me help you." He reached around her shoulders and grabbed the wheel on either side just above her hands. "On three. One, two, three!"

The teens both pulled the wheel, answered by a solid clunk of unlocking the mechanism. Gracie ducked underneath Theo's arms, allowing the room he needed to yank the door open. He leaned back hard, braced with his legs.

The oval door gave to the pull, admitting a wind that blew into the triangular passageway, dropping the temperature dramatically. Gracie and Theo looked at each other then peered out the door.

"Whoa." As far as Theo could see was sky around him and ocean below him.

"I usually find your descriptions a bit lacking, but I think you nailed this one." Gracie couldn't hide a wide smile as she tried to take in all the blue of sky and ocean that was spread out in front of her.

The only disruption to the early-morning hazy dark-blue sky was a ladder that led to an enclosed compartment hanging from the lower side of the dirigible.

"What do we do now?" Theo looked at the ladder that led to the rear propeller engine room. "Why couldn't we choose a room that's built inside the ship? I feel sorry for the guys who have to climb out on this ladder every day just to get to the engine room."

"If it makes you feel any better, there are three more external engine cars attached to the outside of this big balloon. We only need to get into one of them." Gracie gave him a pat on the shoulder. "Come on, if you can balance on a driftboard, surely you can balance on a ladder to another room."

"Uh, yeah, but my driftboard doesn't hover five hundred feet above the ocean, and I can't kill myself by falling off!" Theo looked around the compartment where they were standing. "I just wish there were some other way."

"We can't go back that way." Gracie pointed back to the door behind them.

Theo pointed to the attached engine car. "If we get trapped in that thing, that could be the end!" Theo's concern was thick in his words.

"What choice do we have? Maybe, if someone else is in there, that thing won't come after us. We'll probably be safer getting caught by the crew than *the Society* and its thugs."

"Good point. Okay, I'll go first. Be careful." Theo wiped his sweaty palms on his jeans before he turned and gave Gracie a hug. "Hold the door." He squatted and backed to the doorway, placing both feet on the ladder bridge suspended between ship and engine car. He knew not to look up again at the face of the brave street urchin before he started stepping backward until he could grip the suspension cable with both hands. About halfway across the suspended ladder bridge, he stopped to look down. He could see white caps of the waves splashing into one another below him. He looked up and noticed a darkness permeating the thick, heavy clouds forming on the horizon.

"Looks like a storm." His words carried to Gracie as she backed closer to him.

"That's not the only storm on the horizon!" Both teens looked up at the outside of the airship. The door lock started to turn. "Theo, hurry!" Gracie shouted to be heard over the air currents. She feared being attacked on the bridge.

Theo quickly continued his descent until his foot rested on the side of the engine car. He dropped the lower half of one leg through the rungs and straddled the ladder bridge. "Here goes nothing." He lifted the heavy door, exposing the turbine inside churning loudly. With a glance back at Gracie to ensure she was still moving, he pulled both legs under his body and jumped down a short ladder inside the compartment. A quick look around suggested no one else was in the small outboard engine car. He stepped up the short ladder and braced himself against the open doorway with one arm and reached out to grab Gracie by the waist. Gracie reached back with one hand as her feet crossed the threshold. Turning, she put her hands on Theo's shoulders for extra support as he gently lowered her into the room. Physically standing inside a secure structure after crossing the chasm of air crashed in the hearts and minds of the teens who stood in a silent but tight embrace. Theo released a sigh, letting his hand slide from her shoulder down to her tiny hand. He stepped away to pull shut and latch the door.

"I think the man that was yelling at us was next on duty," Theo guessed aloud. "We may have just doomed ourselves."

"Maybe we can find something to hold this door shut. If Werner finds Erich, he'll search for us after he realizes we are missing. We just need to wait."

"Erich won't have time to worry about us. He and Joseph were pretty busy finding out what *Red Peace* is planning."

"You're probably right," Gracie conceded. "But we're safe for now."

Theo shrugged then searched for something to jam the door. He turned sideways to slip past the enormous engine that turned the propeller. He wiped sweat from his forehead. Air inside the small room was heavy with heat thrown off by the engine.

"Jackpot!" Theo yelled, rifling through a toolbox at the front of the compartment. Recklessly, he tossed tools to the floor as he frantically searched for something big enough to secure the door. His thoughts continually flashed back to scenes of the jaeger's strength, reminding him that a door jam would only buy them a little time. His mind warned him with memory of the jaeger's grip when it grabbed Theo's leg in the Kaiserdom tunnel. The beast could have easily shattered his bones with its hand. Theo shivered and tried to shake off the memory that seemed so distant but had happened only a couple of weeks ago. He willed his mind to forget and focus as he wrapped his hand around a very thick and heavy monkey wrench. "Got it!"

Again, he slipped carefully past the motor and gave Gracie a slight smile to reassure her that everything would work out. He wished he could convince himself. Climbing the small ladder up to the door, he slid the huge wrench through a latch on the door and jammed it into place. The creature would have to work pretty hard to snap that cast-iron wrench in half to open the door. Theo smiled as he put the final touches on his self-made security door.

"Do you think that will stop it?" Gracie's voice sounded insecure. Her time on the streets of Germany had given her too many chances to outwit the enemy, and too many times she had failed.

"Nope, but it's sure gonna have to work a lot harder if it wants to get in here." Theo winked at Gracie.

Gracie flashed her smile at Theo then went to work searching the tiny car. She opened a few small built-in drawers but found nothing of use. She ran her hands along the rough, sturdy fabric walls. Slowly her fingers moved along the seams as if sending messages to her brain. With her arms extended out to her side, she mentally measured a panel that seemed about a meter square. On the wall beside her hand, she noticed a metal ring inside a narrow strip of metal. As she studied the flat metal ring, she calculated that this was an outside wall of the engine car. Acting from her curiosity, she pulled the metal ring. The entire panel slid down, creating a small hole to the outside.

"Check this out!" Gracie shouted above the gusting wind and loud engine roar. She stepped up on a ledge at the base of the wall and peered out the newly created window. The invigorating wind blew through her hair. Just as she had not feared small spaces, she had no fear for the open air so far above the sea. She pulled her head back inside the room, continuing to study the wall. She didn't see any actual handles or footholds, but she noticed vents and ledges they could use if they needed to climb out the window to escape. She shook her head. *No, not if we need to escape, but when we need to escape.*

"Did you find an egress?" Theo smirked.

"Nope, no small birds out here." Gracie laughed at her own joke.

"Ha, ha." Theo laughed sarcastically. "Anyway, what did you find?"

Gracie slid the panel back up to its closed position where the lock clicked back into the metal strip. She stepped down from the ledge. "If we go out there, we better have no other choice."

"Great." Theo exhaled heavily, smoothing his windblown hair and holding the back of his head in frustration. He went back to the toolbox and grabbed a small wrench that he slipped through a back belt loop. "Here take this." He flipped a large flathead screwdriver to Gracie.

"Thanks." She handled the tool to get accustomed to its weight and balance. "This might come in—"

Gracie stopped midsentence and looked at the door. Someone, or something, was banging on the door, making it move. She glanced at Theo and was pretty sure he wasn't breathing. The fear of what was trying to come through that hatch was taking hold of both of them.

The steamy compartment seemed hotter as the noise at the door became louder. Theo faced the door. His eyes zoned in on the wrench wedged in the latch, as he was convinced that the door would not open without tearing through the iron wrench. As he watched, hope changed to fear that the pounding on the door would create enough movement to cause the wrench to fall.

Gracie and Theo stood nearly touching in closeness but ready to spring in defense. The relentless pounding suddenly stopped. The only sound they could hear was the humming of the engine and the wind as it battered the outside of the car. Neither said a word as they listened for the slightest sound and watched the door for the smallest signs of movement.

Gracie scanned the sides of the engine car for any indentations from the jaeger crawling around outside. The creature would have strength to combat the wind turbulence and be able to make its way on top of the compartment. Her gaze went from the roof of the engine car to the side panels. She adjusted her grip on the screwdriver in her right hand. She turned to face yet back away from the outer wall as she realized that it might even have the grip strength to crawl along the side to the small hatch in the wall.

"Where did it go?"

A black-gloved hand wrapped with tattered and bloody bandages exploded through the thinner metal plate of the small hatch. Gracie screamed and tumbled into Theo as she lost her balance.

Theo's wrench clanged heavily onto the floor. He caught her under her arms and pulled her against him He dived forward, grabbed the wrench, and rolled toward the danger. He used his forward momentum and all his strength to swing the wrench down onto the flailing arm of the jaeger.

The wrench swung through the arm, and Theo felt the bone crushing under the blow. The creature's arm hung awkwardly from the elbow down. It dangled at an unnatural angle with a large piece of bone sticking through the skin.

"Oh sick." Theo gaped at the grotesque sight. His hands started to shake and sweat profusely. The wrench slid from his grip. He bent with his hands on his knees and vomited on the engine room floor. "Seriously," he mumbled as he wiped his sleeve across his face.

He looked away from the mess on the floor and almost fell backward from the shock of the arm missing from where it had hung inside the window. "What! Where'd it go?"

"I don't know! It was there—then gone!"

"Watch the sides of this engine car for indents. That monster's weight will be too heavy and push the metal down, giving away its location," Gracie ordered Theo with hope in her heart that her guess would prove true. There was no other way to track the jaeger. Even his odious smell wouldn't permeate the fabric covering of the airship.

Theo readjusted his grip and moved his eyes around the small compartment where they were trapped. The engine hummed smoothly but radiated waves of heat. He grabbed a rag and wiped the wrench to help keep a firm grip on his weapon. He ran his forearm across the top of his brow in a feeble attempt to soak up the sweat trickling down his face.

The air was thick and heavy. Gracie noticed the base of Theo's heaving throat and put a hand up to her own throat. They were both pulling air with deep breaths, trying to get oxygen into their lungs. "I can't take this! It's getting too hot in here." Gracie hated being the first to complain. Her dark curly hair was almost as damp as the hair of the brown-haired boy on the other side of the compartment.

"No kidding. Do you think something's wrong with the engine? It shouldn't be this hot in here, should it?"

"How am I supposed to know? I have no idea how an engine should work. All I know is, if it doesn't cool off in here soon, I'll take my chances outside with that monster," Gracie threatened.

She slid to the floor but kept a tight grip on the screwdriver she held in front of her. A strange hissing sound exploded, and steam poured from the engine, intensifying the heat. Both looked at each other then at the mechanical apparatus in the middle of the room.

"What the heck was that?" Theo yelled over the teapot-sounding hiss screaming into the confined car.

A louder click sounded. Automatic airflow doors began to slide open. Gracie sprang up and bumped into Theo, who had also turned to look at the doors opening at the front of the engine car. Loudly rushing air drowned out any chance of hearing each other. Gracie pointed to the wrench lodged in the escape hatch. Theo nodded and, in a few sprinted steps, reached the door they had entered. In anger, he struggled to dislodge the wrench and open the door for a way out.

"Augh! The heat expanded the metal! I can't get the door unjammed! It's no use!" He jumped down the ladder leading up to the door and stared up at the wrench, trying to figure a way to escape the heat and danger.

A scream reached his ears over the loud rush of wind and the humming of engine. He turned just as Gracie thrust her screwdriver into the face of the jaeger as its head bolted through the clam-shaped doors opening to cool the engine. The sight of the blood squirting and the animalistic screams made Theo choke back the urge to vomit again. He winced as he caught sight of the handle sticking out of the beast's eye socket.

Gracie wiped the slimy blood on her hands against her blood-splattered clothes. She turned and ran to Theo. "Hurry! That beast won't stop until we're dead!"

Over Gracie's shoulder, Theo watched in horror as the jaeger thrashed in pain, trying to climb inside the airflow door with one arm as the other one flapped uselessly in the wind. Theo spun and jumped up to grab the end of the wrench wedged in the door's latch. "Augh! Come on! Move!" He knew the wrench held them between the beast and safety. Both hands gripped the handle as he willed his body weight to jar it loose. His hands slipped. "No!" Theo yelled and kicked against the steps leading up to the door. His body swung away from the wall of the engine car. His swinging weight threatened the grip of his sweaty hands.

Gracie screamed from below, "Theo! Use your legs!"

Again Theo reached for the steps with his legs, but this time, he caught a rung and stood with both feet. "Fine! I can't pull you down, I'll . . . Ugh!" Sweat poured down his face and stung his eyes. Adrenaline and determination shot through him as he strained against the heavy metal wrench. He bent his knees slightly then gave one last explosive push off the steps.

Gracie wasn't sure which hit the floor first, Theo or the wrench. She bent down to help Theo back to his feet, but he sprang up just as she took his hand. The thick air caught in her nostrils with a smothering stench. She jerked upright and looked over her shoulder.

"Run!" Theo screamed and coughed from the stifling smell.

Gracie ran up the steps to the hatch, punched the latch with her hand, and gulped a breath of fresh air as the door popped open to a cloudy sky and the silver exterior of the airship's main body.

"It's coming! Move!" Theo screamed from beneath her.

She crawled out through the top hatch. Though the suspended ladder to the dirigible swung and shook, her only fear was the screaming, wounded animal that stood inside the engine car. She gripped the cable that ran along the ladder bridge and half crawled, half climbed back to the safety of the dirigible. Still kneeling on the ladder bridge, she reached for the handle in the side of the airship just as the door flew open from the inside. She let out a cry as a hand grabbed her by the shoulder.

"Let me help you, *mademoiselle*." Joseph extended his other hand.

Gracie reached up and took the outstretched hand that effortlessly pulled her inside the ship to the triangular walkway. Her body began to shake uncontrollably at the sight of Joseph and the floppy-eared dog sticking out of the backpack worn by the young cabin boy, Werner.

"Get up, dear, you must get up!" Joseph's voice was soft but commanding as he again lifted her from the floor. He was not an imposing man, but he was incredibly strong for his petite size, with a body of muscle that had been forged over countless hours of gymnastics and calisthenics. Once he had her standing, Joseph turned back to the door of the airship, where he reached out for Theo's arm.

Gracie gave Murphy a quick pat on the head as she slipped past Werner to make way for Theo as Joseph pulled him inside.

"Let's go!" Theo yelled in a panic as the jaeger's good arm emerged from the hatch of the engine car.

"No. Not yet." Werner looked at Joseph like he was waiting for a sign.

The jaeger pulled itself out of the engine room and started across the ladder bridge. The handle of the screwdriver extended from the eye socket, and its mangled arm hung uselessly. It tipped back its head and howled in a scream of terror, pain, and anger.

Joseph stood stooped over, unflinching. Werner moved to the other side of the open door.

"What are you waiting for?" Gracie knew this was not a game.

Joseph did not turn away from watching the creature move up the ladder bridge. "Wait for it, Werner." His voice was calm and strong.

"Wait?"

"For what?" Theo and Gracie yelled at the same time.

"This." Joseph laughed loudly as he nodded at Werner. They squatted and reached outside the door to pull two large pins from the ladder. The jaeger's disfigured face held a look of horror. It lunged and scrambled to get a good grip with its only usable hand. The ladder dropped away from the side of the *Hindenburg* and pitched toward the ocean below.

The wounded beast wasn't quick enough to save itself. The swinging ladder mercilessly slammed into the side of the engine car.

The strike against the car shook the jaeger's one-handed grasp and sent it plummeting to the freezing waters churning below.

Theo grabbed Gracie and pulled her into his chest to block the bloodcurdling scream that faded as the creature fell to its death.

Joseph watched the beast fall and disappear into the dark-blue waters. He stared at the spot where the ocean water swallowed until he was convinced the monster was destroyed. He slammed the door shut to the outside world and to one less demon.

Theo and Gracie collapsed on the floor. Exhaustion and terror grabbed them and sapped their bodies of any remaining strength or will to move. They sat on the cold metal walkway and looked at each other. The teens knew they had outwitted a brush with death that neither could have done alone. Theo covered Gracie's hand with his.

Joseph secured the airship from inside and paced around the triangular walkway to check for anything out of place. Once satisfied, he made his way back to the teens resting on the floor. He reached out and offered his hand to Theo.

"Jahile would be proud of you, boy. Not sure I know anyone besides him who has escaped a jaeger." Joseph's voice was cheerful, but he noticed a look of sadness on the teenager's face.

Theo winced at the words—a reminder of a friend who cared beyond reason, now gone from this world. He looked at Joseph then around to Gracie, who was holding back a flood of tears. "Werner, help her back to the cabin."

"Absolutely!"

Theo waited until Gracie and Werner had gone from the walkway then recalled to Joseph the details of their early morning adventure, which included overhearing the *Society* members talking about Jahile.

Dog Spy

IF A MEMBER of the crew had been guarding the back catwalks, he might have heard strange whispers coming from the crates in the cargo hold just aft of the crew sleeping quarters. Early morning shifts were about to change for the breakfast hour. Most people were in their small rooms preparing for a day of drifting over the Atlantic Ocean in their four-day journey to Lakehurst, New Jersey. Hidden in the makeshift dog crate where Joseph's show dog, Ulla, was housed for the journey, three souls had escaped an angry Captain Pruss and also had welcomed a secret place to talk. The tall dog sat in a regal pose beside her master, who continually pet her from head down to tail, smoothing the soft German shepherd fur.

"So what's the plan, Joseph?" Theo couldn't hide the anxiety in his voice.

Gracie nodded in agreement. She was starting to feel claustrophobic on the airship and wanted to be on solid ground before Theo figured it out. Her thoughts continued to wander. *Why is the land called New Jersey? Where is the Old Jersey? I have a new appreciation for Theo wandering around Germany. I need to control my fear of being in a country I don't know.* She secretly prayed, *Oh, let Fräulein Amelia be at the landing field. She sounds so nice. Oh, please let me get out of this crate before my mind convinces me I have no more air to breathe!* Gracie shook her head to get control of her thoughts and her breathing.

"We need to wait until Erich gets here. We have a lot to discuss and—"

An adjoining crate scratched along the floor of the cargo hold as it was moved to reveal the group's hiding place. Erich stood with a concerned look on his face, which was overpowered by the fact that his hat was falling halfway down the side of his face. He could feel everyone staring at him, at his hat. He quickly removed the cap and pulled the crates closed behind him. "I swear I'm getting a smaller cover before we set off back to Europe," he complained under his breath, causing a small outbreak of laughter from the rest of his group.

"Welcome, Erich, I was just saying that we needed to wait for you and your hat to get here before we could start." Joseph flashed a large smile, provoking more laughter from the two teens sitting on empty peach crates.

"Ha, ha." Erich laughed mockingly then threw his hat harmlessly at the nimble gymnast, who ducked and caught the extra large cap on his own head. He took an extremely deep, overexaggerated bow to the soft applause from Gracie and Theo and flipped the hat back to its owner.

"Now, Erich, if you're done fooling around, can we start this meeting?" Joseph quipped sarcastically while pointing to another crate to be used for his seat. His tone of voice gave his dog, Ulla, a cue to lie down at his feet. He turned his attention to the American youth and the beautiful girl who had been challenged to wait patiently. "What were you two thinking going that far back on the ship? Do you have any idea how much trouble you two could have been in had you been captured or, worse, killed by that jaeger instead of you killing it?"

"Wait a minute!" Erich looked first at Theo then at Gracie. "First, there was a jaeger on board, and second, you guys killed it?" Erich was dumbfounded at the thought of one of those beasts being on the closed flight. He had never seen one himself, but their legend knew no limits in the ranks of *the Watch*. He shook his head and shivered, unable to imagine where the dead beast might be.

Theo leaned toward the young rigger, anxious to recount their adventure now that a day had passed. "It was amazing, Erich. That thing was coming after us in the engine room—"

"In the engine car? I heard a report that one had been damaged. Uh, so you two knew about the engineer attack? I assumed, since

Werner was the one who found him, that the engineer was confused when he said he was attacked by a beast of a man. I actually covered for Werner by convincing Chief Knorr that the engineer took a hard-enough knock on the head that he wasn't thinking straight!" Erich stopped talking long enough to narrow his eyes and give each teen a questioning look. "Joseph's right. How did you two end up all the way back there?"

"Well, Werner took us—"

"Werner! What were you two doing with Werner all the way back there? Don't you realize how much trouble you could be in had they caught you? I can't believe—"

"Erich, seriously, dude, let me finish!" Theo blurted out, wanting to tell their story.

"Sorry, continue, but if you had been—" Erich interrupted a fourth time, scolding the teens, but the look on their faces let him know they wanted to finish their story.

Theo relayed the events of the prior evening in as much detail as he could remember, with Gracie eagerly interjecting a few parts here and there that he had forgotten or wanted to forget. When the teens had exhausted their memories, Erich and Joseph looked at each other in disbelief. The idea that two young kids could destroy one of those walking nightmares and survive was unimaginable.

"Amazing." Erich looked from Joseph back to the teen. "And, Theo, thanks for sharing the part where you lost your lunch." Erich tipped his head and gave a sideways grin. "But you two left out a very important part of the story. What you were doing that far back in the first place?"

"We went to find Murphy. Got chased by a jaeger. Werner showed up out of nowhere to rescue us," Theo offered an explanation with some true details and quite a few left out.

"Right, and once we thought we were safe, Werner wanted to show us something. We didn't mean to get into trouble." Li'l Grey had a way of making dangerous decisions sound innocent.

"That's right! He started rambling on about 'they weren't there' or something. Next thing we know, he disappeared. We were going to come back up front, so we headed down a ladder to the level where we could get back to the room." Recounting their trek, Theo's memory recalled a flash of a small trunk where the catwalk passed one of the gasbags used to keep the airship aloft. "Hey! Wait a minute, I did see a box that seemed out of place near one of those giant gasbags." Theo's forehead furrowed as he remembered seeing the luggage in an odd location.

Joseph listened quietly to the kids' adventure but stood up at the mention of the trunk. Mental cogs began to spin as missing puzzle pieces began to set in place, making a clearer picture laid out before him. "That must be part of whatever the members of the *Red Peace* are up to! Erich, it would be good of you to go back there and take a quick look around. When do you have to report for landing?"

"Well, I came back to tell you that we received a message from Lakehurst Airfield that the weather forecast is not ideal for landing. They think if the bad weather does hit the coast, we'll need to push back our approach time and shift our direction. That's good and bad for us, I think. Gives us more hours to search for an out-of-place trunk but gives *Red Peace* more time to set up and the Nazis more time to hunt for these two." He waved a pointing finger between the two teens.

"More time could work against us. That does complicate matters a bit," Joseph agreed, rubbing his temples with his fingers, a remedy that he found helped him think and relax before his shows. "While you guys were on your little adventure, I was schmoozing with as many other passengers as I could. I think I've narrowed down our search a little more, but I need a few more mealtimes to pin down the *Red Peace* culprits who aren't worried about this airship having a safe landing. Problem is, I can't be everywhere to eavesdrop on every conversation."

Gracie almost fell off her crate with excitement. "Oh! Oh, I've . . . Uh, we've got a way to solve that problem. Theo has a girlfriend on board and promised his new sweetie that her two brothers could play with the toy metal ball that he has with him." Gracie spoke quickly and purposely avoided looking at Theo when she mentioned his girlfriend.

"Metal ball?" Joseph raised his eyebrows to elicit more explanation.

Theo jumped at the pause in the conversation to explain and to defend himself. "First of all," he didn't cover the anger in his voice and looked directly at Gracie, who had a huge smirk across her face, "I don't have a girlfriend or a sweetie. She's just some girl I ran into by accident. Second, Murphy has a few special talents."

The beagle that had been sleeping soundly during the entire conversation sprang to life and landed in Theo's lap before anyone had time to blink.

Both Joseph and his dog, Ulla, sat up straight and tilted their heads at the animated dog panting on Theo's lap.

"Besides being very agile," Theo laughed as he ran his hand lovingly down his beagle's back, "he can also morph when he needs to."

"Morph?" Erich was confused by the word he had never heard in either the German or English language.

Theo paused, trying to think of a good way to explain. "I'll just show you." He looked down at the dog stretched across his lap. "Murph. Hey, Murphy." He gave a quick double scratch from ear to ear and had to say the name twice to get the dog's attention. Murphy hopped into a sitting position on Theo's lap and stared intently at his master, waiting for a command. "Sphere time, Murphy!"

Erich and Joseph waited on the edge of their seats but exhaled slowly as nothing happened. Instead, Murphy looked at his master and cocked his head as if he questioned the order.

"Listens almost as well as my Ulla." Joseph chuckled.

Theo glanced up at eager eyes then back down at Murphy. "It's okay, boy. Go ahead."

Murphy sat back on his hind legs and put his front paws on Theo's shoulders and licked his face. Then he pulled back a bit to look Theo in the eyes then licked him again. "I love you too, Murphy. C'mon. Roll, Murphy!" With one more loving tongue swipe, Murphy sprang using his hind legs and rolled into a solid ball of silver that landed gently in Theo's lap.

"What in the . . . ?" Joseph shied back.

The German shepherd gave a soft whine and jumped to her feet. She stretched her snout toward Theo's lap and whined and nudged the silver ball. Uninterested in the shiny ball, she returned to lie down at Joseph's feet.

"Whoa, that was incredible. What kind of dog is she?" Erich reached toward the silver ball.

Before Theo could correct the "she" mistake, the ball spun off Theo's lap, and in a flash, Murphy growled angrily where he stood beside Erich's legs.

"Murphy! Mind your manners!" Gracie scolded the beagle that seemed to enjoy making the young airship rigger nervous. "He didn't mean anything by it, for heaven's sake."

The robotic dog gave one last growl at the man fearing he would be bitten then trotted to Gracie. He rubbed against her leg and looked at her with big brown beagle eyes. "Murphy is a very special *boy* dog." Gracie stressed the word *boy* as she reached down to pat the begging dog.

"My apologies, Murphy. I didn't mean to offend you!" Erich offered an apology, hoping the unusual dog would understand him.

The group chuckled as Murphy jogged over to a very nervous Erich and rubbed against his leg. "Good boy," Erich said stiffly as he carefully held the back of his hand down to the dog.

"That, my friends, is the meaning of *morph*!" Theo was pleased to have an upper hand for once.

Joseph kept his eyes on Murphy but returned to the business at hand. "Well, amazing trick, but how does that help us?"

Theo and Gracie looked at each other, questioning who would explain more of the dog's ability. Theo nodded at her with a smile.

Gracie took the lead to explain their plan. "Murphy can actually hear conversations and send them to Theo's watch." She pointed to Theo's bare wrist. "We can hear what people are saying around Murphy. So we were thinking that Theo could share Murphy, I mean, the toy ball with Walter and Werner, two little boys who had their toy taken away. We think they'll be anxious to play with the ball and will carry it with them. If we can ask Irene, their sister, to give Murphy to the boys before breakfast, we can eavesdrop on most conversations in the dining quarters!"

Joseph listened to the teens' plan and started to formulate more of his plan. "That will be a tremendous help! I think we need to use your dog's talented services. He's truly an amazing creature! I do have one question, however." Joseph looked at the two teens. "How is it that you two can heroically defend yourselves from the jaeger and traipse across half of Germany unharmed despite the best effort of Viktor Brack and *the Watch* but you can't seem to follow simple instruction?"

The two teenagers looked bewildered, not sure what instruction Joseph meant.

"The jaeger wasn't our fault."

"We—"

"You wouldn't have had to worry about that dangerous beast if you had stayed in your room like I instructed you when we first boarded this silly contraption. You've put yourselves in danger and have taken unneeded risk. Besides, how do you know that these kids—the Doehner boys—how do you know their parents aren't the members of *Red Peace*? Surely, you know by now that we are looking for the people from the Communist society, and they may be looking for you!" Joseph nearly spit the words with anger as he finished his rebuke.

"Oh, trust me, sweet Irene would never rat on her new boyfriend. Even if she were Hitler's daughter." Gracie intentionally threw in an unneeded jab!

Theo glared at Gracie with a "what the heck" look then tried to explain his version of the story. He was finding it very difficult not to scream at Gracie. *What's her problem? I really don't understand girls at all!*

Erich and Joseph grinned at each other, knowing exactly what was going on between the two teenagers. Seeing the bewilderment on Theo's face made the situation funnier to the two, who were a little better versed in the ways of the opposite sex. Joseph broke the ice forming in the air between the teens. "Let's give the toy ball a try. What can it hurt?"

Erich yawned loudly. "Well, if that's the plan and we have nothing else to discuss, I'm going to bed. I need to sleep before my shift starts. But I am curious, so I'll run back to see if that box still happens to be next to the gasbag. See everyone this evening." Erich pushed his hat back into position and pushed open the large crate to slip out.

Joseph stood up and stretched his taut muscles. He wasn't a person who liked being cooped up in an airship for so many days. He needed to train, to flip, to make people laugh. Right now, these two youngsters didn't appear to want a laugh from a thirty-two-year-old acrobat. He slapped his leg. "Kennel, Ulla!"

Obediently, the German shepherd returned to the mat at the back of her kennel and lay down as her master left her crate.

Joseph smiled at the two teens and made his way to the exit. "Give Murphy to the boys then get in your room and stay there. Do you understand?"

"Yes," Gracie and Theo answered in unison.

Silence sat heavily between the teens during the awkward wait time while Joseph made his way back to the passenger zones. Gracie was the first to stand in a stoop to leave Ulla's crate, but she struggled with the weight of the large cargo crate that each man had pushed aside and reset as they left before her. Theo had to stoop over even more as he stepped behind her and nudged her gently out of his way. He pushed on the crate and cringed with its loud scraping noise. So far, they had been undetected, and he didn't want to press their luck. He reset the crate just enough for them to reset Ulla's crate door and to slip into the hallway.

Gracie and Theo stayed alert though no sound or looks passed between them as they walked back to their room at the end of B deck. Halls were empty, allowing them to pass only one passenger and a working crewman. Gracie mentally dealt with her anger toward Theo and Irene's new friendship. Theo couldn't convince himself whether or not he even wanted to think about his pretty friend's strange behavior ever since they had met another girl on the dirigible. For a moment, they stood outside the door of their cabin until they were forced to look at each other and decide who would take the spherical Murphy to Irene's brothers.

"I don't even know what room Irene's brothers are staying in. Besides, I suppose you want to go see *Irene* to give her Murphy." Gracie's terse words punched out Irene's name.

"What's your deal?" Theo exploded on the unexpecting Gracie. "Seriously, what did I do? It's not my fault if she has a crush on me. I've done nothing to provoke her or you!"

Murphy looked up at his master and at his friend. Even as a robot, he couldn't understand why they increased their voices. He turned and faced down the hallway as a door creaked open, revealing the source of all the trouble.

Theo followed Murphy's gaze until his eyes rested on Irene. He started to give an order, but by the time he looked down, the brown-and-white beagle was gone and a silver ball of metal was resting at his feet. *Good boy, Murphy*, Theo thought, impressed by the dog's almost-humanlike intuition.

"Oh, look. It's—"

"Enough," Theo cut off Gracie's latest jab before she could finish. "I'm sick of it. This is going to help us, so get over it." Theo bent over and picked up Murphy. As he stood up again, Theo noticed Gracie was slipping quickly into their room and wiping something from her eye.

"Whatever," he mumbled under his breath as he walked toward Irene's room.

The young German girl closed the door behind her and started down the tiny hallway toward the handsome young American boy with the deep-blue eyes and shaggy hair. She had to concentrate to hide the smile of excitement of getting another chance to talk to the mysterious boy.

They met awkwardly in the hallway. Theo smiled, not knowing what to say. He took a step back as Irene took a step closer to him, which, in his estimation, made things much more embarrassing. The teens stood not really knowing what to say, so the silence built to a crescendo forcing Theo to react by just holding the ball in front of him.

Thoughts tumbled in Theo's head and prevented him from speaking. *Things are never this awkward around Gracie. We can talk about anything. I can't even talk to girls from my own time and country or even to Irene standing here! What am I supposed to say? It's so easy to talk to Gracie. I don't have to think about what to say. I guess almost dying a few times with someone will make talking much easier.* Unintentionally, a grin crept into Theo's countenance, and he chuckled aloud.

"What's so funny?" Irene tipped her head in a coy but pretty fashion.

"Oh, uh, nothing. Just thinking about something Gracie said earlier," he lied.

"Oh." Irene's smile disappeared in jealousy at the mention of that pretty girl with beautiful curly hair. "What did she say that was so funny?" Irene feigned interest in the girl who seemed very important to Theo. Irene knew she should at least pretend to care as she took another step toward him.

"It was, uh, well . . . It, uh, it . . . It wasn't anything." Theo stumbled over his lie. *Why does she keep getting closer to me? Man, I think I'm sweating.* Theo moved the silver sphere from hand to hand as he wiped his hands on his jeans' pockets.

"She seems wonderful. So pretty! Don't you think?" Irene probed.

"*What?*" He didn't have to pretend being confused.

"Oh, come on now. Gracie is beautiful. I know she's not really your sister. How do you two know each other?"

Theo broke out in a sweat as a fear like nothing he had felt before started creeping up his spine. *All these questions. What's she saying? What does she want? Am I supposed to disagree with her? Should I tell her I think she and Gracie are both pretty? Girls!* He held the sphere in one hand as he raised an arm to wipe off the beads of sweat forming on his brow. *Zikes, I don't know what's worse—being interrogated by a girl or being chased by a jaeger! I didn't know how lucky I was never to have a girlfriend before!*

"Is she your half sister?" Irene persisted, trying to find out a few more details. "Maybe a cousin?"

"She's . . . she's, uh, my friend is all," Theo answered over a lump that threatened his airway. "We're traveling back to America together to meet her Aunt Amelia for a vacation in Florida or something. I really don't pay attention to all the details."

"Are you two close?" Irene took another step toward the obviously nervous boy. She giggled as he slammed into the wall trying to take a step back. "Have you known her for very long?"

Theo lifted the sphere up to his chest, putting it like a makeshift shield between him and the German girl. "Yeah. Long time. It seems like we've known each other a very long time."

"Oh." Irene's small mouth pulled up into a cute pout as she could not hide her disappointment from the boy's response.

Theo sensed the unintended disappointment and felt he could move his way out of this mess. "We just get along so well that it seems like we've been best friends forever."

"Oh." Irene lowered her head and took a half step backward.

Theo immediately felt badly that he had hurt her feelings, and once again, he was unsure what to do. He didn't want to be mean to the nice girl, who was pretty in a simple way. He just wanted to pass his spy dog to her brothers. He took a step toward her, impulsively putting one hand on her shoulder as he lifted the sphere with the other hand.

"Oh, here's that toy ball I promised for your little brothers." He hoped his offer would break the silence and serve as an apology for hurting her feelings. "I thought they would like to play with it after breakfast."

"Yes, they would like that very much." Irene's innocent expression made Theo wonder why he had cowered against the wall.

Theo handed her the silver ball. She pulled it into her arms, cradling it with care. "I'll make sure they're careful with it. Wouldn't want to have to buy you a new one." Her eyes danced up at him.

"Not sure that's possible," Theo answered with a laugh, putting a smile on the girl's face and brightening her countenance. "It's pretty indestructible, but I'm positive that it's one of a kind!"

"Thank you. They will enjoy this. They've been quite bored since the captain took away their toy panzer tank. But I would rather them be bored than have them set this ship ablaze with a silly spark. Wouldn't that be awful?"

Theo shuddered at the thought. "It really would be terrible."

Irene turned to go. Theo let down his guard a bit too soon, though, as she turned back and tiptoed in her tiny satin slippers to plant a soft kiss on his cheek.

"Oh" was all he could say as he reached for his cheek and his fingers brushed Irene's hair. Out of the corner of his eye, he noticed the movement of his room door just as it quietly clicked shut. *Great. I'll never hear the end of this one.* His thoughts were of Gracie as he raised his eyes to look at Irene.

"Will I see you at breakfast?" Irene's voice held a lilt from the success of her stolen kiss.

"Oh, probably not, I . . . I mean, Gracie has a special diet she has to eat. She has a very sensitive stomach. If she eats the wrong thing, she'll be in the restroom the rest of the trip." He giggled. *I hope she heard that too!*

"Oh my, that sounds awful. Well, if you get bored, we'll be on the observation deck until lunch. My father and mother just love meeting all the people."

"Okay, sounds great." Theo scarcely quit talking before he turned and headed for his cabin door. He gripped the handle and leaned aggressively against a bit of pressure to quickly open the door and catch the would-be spy off guard. He smiled even though he heard a light thud.

He closed the door behind him and watched as Gracie rolled to her side on the floor and rubbed her backside. "You did that on purpose," she accused him angrily with a hand up asking for assistance.

"Yep." Theo said no more as he ignored the outstretched hand and crawled onto his bunk and started searching through his pack, looking for the watch to connect with Murphy.

Eavesdropping

"**I GET IT FIRST!**" ten-year-old Walter shouted when his older sister offered the Doehner brothers a new toy. The wonderful silver ball looked heavy but was light as a feather when he ripped it from her hands, almost causing himself to tumble with unneeded momentum.

"That's not fair, Walter!" whined the youngest of the siblings. "Why do you get to play first?"

"It's simple really. If you were older, you'd understand." Walter knew he didn't have a valid reason why he should get the ball first. All he knew was that he hadn't had anything fun to do since that mean captain took away his toy panzer tank.

"That's what you always say!" Werner crossed his arms over his chest, trying to hold back tears of disappointment. He, too, had been terribly bored since the novelty of flying on the airship had worn off. He was really tired of listening to old people talk about war and other boring stuff. "I should get it because I'm the youngest!"

"No way! You'd probably lose it out a window." The older brother spun the ball around in his hands, amazed by the smooth metal. He couldn't find a seam or mark from the ball's construction. Walter remembered a small village outside Mexico City where he watched a man blowing glass to make ornaments. The man created at least a dozen multicolored spheres. Werner had made it a game to find where the apprentice separated each ball of glass from the long blowpipe.

Irene watched her brother spin the ball around and around in his hands. "Walter, what on earth are you looking for?"

"There's no seam! What's this thing made of?" With curiosity, Walter balled his hand into a fist and hit the silver sphere, expecting to hear the echo of a hollow object. Instead he heard a low thud. "I think this ball is solid metal. I've got to show this to Father!"

"Absolutely not!" Irene shouted and tore the ball out of her brother's hands. "I'll take this ball back if you do! Do you understand?"

"Why can't I show Father? He'll be confused and like it too, just like me."

Irene turned to her brother, who was listening through his sniffles. "You're always confused, Walter! Here, Werner, go to the observation deck and have some fun. I have to give this back to its owner tonight."

"Fine!"

"Oh! Thanks, Irene, thanks so much! I needed a toy." Werner sniffed and knew his older sister would always protect him. He shot a quick glance at Walter and stuck out his tongue.

"What was that for?" Irene was surprised to feel his short, little arms reach around her waist.

"Thank you for being my sister."

Irene returned the hug and gave him a kiss on the top of his blond head. "Go have some fun, silly boy." She smiled and wagged a finger at Walter. "You go have fun too, and be nice to him, you hear me?"

"Fine," he mumbled and jetted for the door.

"I couldn't hear you." Irene playfully blocked his escape route.

Walter looked up at his sister and smiled a devious smile of an older brother ready to pounce on his younger prey once the pseudoparent was out of the way. "Yes, dear sister."

Irene stared at her brother's blue eyes, checking the mischievous glint in them. "I'll be up shortly. Be nice." She stepped out of the doorway and reached for a quick hug, which was rejected fiercely as her brother ran past.

Once free of his sister's watchful eye, Walter caught a glance of Werner turning the corner to the stairs leading up to the upper deck. He sprinted after his younger sibling, determined to play with the ball too.

Werner stopped when he heard the pounding of running steps. He sneaked a backward glance to see his older brother heading straight for him. Dashing up the stairs with the ball tucked tightly under one arm, he giggled and pushed himself up the last short flight of stairs, his brother hot on his trail.

Walter hit the landing at the top of the second flight of stairs just a step or two behind his younger brother and reached out to grab his sleeve just as Werner turned the corner and ran into a black leather coat and fell to the deck. The ball came loose from his grip and rolled back toward the stairs. Werner cringed as he watched Walter scoop up the ball. The black leather gloves reached out and grabbed Walter by the shoulder, causing him to turn with a sheepish grin.

"Hello, Walter." Lieutenant Hinkelbein's voice stopped the older Doehner boy. He turned and offered his other hand to the younger boy who hadn't moved since crashing into him. The lieutenant helped the boy to his feet then pushed both of them to stand side by side in front of him. Removing his hat, he knelt down on one knee to be eye to eye with the children.

As lieutenant in the German Luftwaffe, Claus Hinkelbein's military assignment was flight duty as an observer on the *Hindenburg* for the 1937 season of flights. Although his purpose was to learn long-range navigation and weather forecasting for flight, he and fellow military officers Colonel Fritz Erdmann and Major Hans-Hugo Witt had filled part of their flight time getting to know other passengers. Thus, it was often that Lieutenant Hinkelbein shared a meal in the dining hall, having good discussion with Hermann Doehner and getting to know the rest of the Doehner family who were on the flight. At age twenty-six, Lieutenant Hinkelbein enjoyed listening to the animated storytelling of the boys, Walter and Werner, while allowing his uniform to keep the professional distance from the children and their antics.

"So what's the rush, boys?" The lieutenant folded his hands in front of his buttoned uniform, content to wait for an answer. He noticed a silver ball cradled behind Walter's back. "What do we have here, boys?" He nodded to the poorly hidden toy.

"Sorry... uh, sorry, sir," Werner stuttered with fear. He knew Father would be furious if he found out that he had crashed into the lieutenant while messing around. "I didn't mean to run into you, sir. See, I was just trying to get up here to play with our toy." Werner grabbed the ball from behind Walter's back.

"Hey!" Walter grabbed for the ball but was stopped as the officer snatched the ball away from Werner's hands. Walter dropped his eyes to the floor, anticipating an eventual scolding ending with another toy taken away.

"Where did you get this fun toy?" the Nazi officer asked as he tossed the ball into the air.

"My sister!" Werner offered with excitement.

"Interesting," the officer mumbled as he stood up holding the ball in his black leather gloves. He spun it around in his hands. Something was familiar about it. "Should we be running, boys?" The officer never took his eyes off the sphere as he wondered what made the ball seem important.

"No, SIR!" both boys shouted in unison.

The officer smiled at the boys' enthusiasm and began to walk away with the silver sphere.

"Sir?"

Lieutenant Hinkelbein stopped and looked over his shoulder at the two boys still standing at attention. "Yes, Werner?"

"Can I have my ball, sir?"

Walter held his breath to hide his fear from showing on his face. He knew better than to ask for the ball back from a Nazi officer. He stood up a little straighter, waiting to be scolded by the lieutenant for his little brother's breach of propriety.

Lieutenant Hinkelbein looked at the two boys, letting a long silence fall between them, then down at the silver ball in his hands. He turned to walk away, and without looking back, he smiled and tossed the toy over his shoulder. "No more running, boys. Do you understand?"

"Yes, sir!" Their reply was heard in unison.

"Thank you, sir," Werner added. His older brother might have caught the toy, but that was better than not having a toy at all.

The boys walked carefully to the lounge area, where they made a game of sitting a few feet apart and taking turns tossing and rolling the ball to each other. Every few throws, the ball would veer off its intended course and roll underneath a few of the adults sitting in the room talking, knitting, or reading. The boys had a good laugh as the silver ball seemed to have a mind of its own.

Werner gave the ball a hard roll toward his brother, but it stopped halfway between the two of them. "Wow! Amazing!" He jumped up from his cross-legged position and reached for the silver ball, but it zipped to the port side of the ship, almost like it was trying to get away from him. "Hey!" he shouted in surprise then laughed as he chased the ball under the legs of two people having a hushed conversation.

The adults didn't notice the ball or the small boy standing very near where they sat. Werner slowed and tried to tiptoe up to the crazy ball. Trying to not be noticed, he squatted, and just as his fingers were about to touch the cool metal exterior, the ball rolled under the legs of the young woman in conversation. Werner was at a loss as to his next move. He looked at the ball, at the lady, then back to Walter, who was waiting for his turn with the ball. The young boy wasn't sure what to do, but he was sure he shouldn't interrupt the adults.

Werner walked back to the corner where Walter's patience was wearing thin. He stole a quick glance back and was almost positive that his crazy ball had rolled between the old man and the young woman at the lounge table.

"That silly boy has proven to be less than helpful," the senior passenger complained, removing his thin wire-framed glasses and rubbing the bridge of his nose in frustration. He jostled in the comfortable, cushioned chair as if something unseen agitated him. Imperceptibly, the silver sphere near his feet rolled in slight movement to prevent being kicked by the man's shoes as he nervously flexed his legs.

"Maybe we should remind him that if he doesn't help us secure a safe place for the device, his sweet Keila and her daughter will not be heard from again." Not wanting her poignant comments to be overheard, the sophisticated-looking woman crossed her legs, leaning closer to her companion.

The man slid his glasses back up the ridge of his nose and scanned the lounge for any sign of someone trying to eavesdrop on their conversation. He took notice of two children arguing in the corner. Another passenger in the lounge was a journalist who eagerly shared his profession with other passengers on the flight. Never was he seen without a small notepad and pencil in his hands and a congenial smile on his face. A story of flight on the *Hindenburg* was more than his passage to a higher position as a journalist. It was a story born from his passion for people and the lives they lived.

The old man knew the eager journalist couldn't overhear their conversation as he was in heavy conversation with a photographer from Bonn who was flying as a publicity photographer for the dirigible company and for personal family ties in America. The old man smirked as he watched the people in the lounge interested, or at least feigning interest, in the lives of complete strangers.

"Lewy, Lewy, my dear, what has you so—"

"Sorry, Gissy. You know how much I like to people-watch." He laughed and patted her wrist as he continued to watch Nelson Morris, the meat-packing tycoon, and his friend and fellow Chicagoan Burtis Dolan chatting and trying to brighten the serious countenance of Miss Mather, an heiress from Rome who was never fond of traveling overseas by zeppelin but less so by ship. A year earlier, the media had made a spectacle of Nelson Morris. Everyone knew of his turbulent divorce that made headlines in the new era following the 1920s and his recent marriage to a French comedian, Blanche Bilboa, who shared his love for philanthropic causes.

"They all have their own stories, then they blend into each other's. It's fascinating, don't you think, darling?" He listened to his wife as he continued to watch the group that had assembled in this same lounge. He turned and offered a blank stare to Nazi lieutenant Hinkelbein, who stole glances at them when he thought they weren't looking.

"If you keep taunting that SS, he'll be over here questioning us without reason." Gisella's words became a terse whisper. "Is that what you want? Unneeded Nazi attention? Those animals don't think. They just react. We can't take the chance of him acting irrationally and detaining us for something he only suspicions."

"You're right, as usual, my love." Lewy smiled warmly at Gisella. He knew they had much to accomplish in their loyalty to *Red Peace*. It would not be prudent to risk their plans being derailed by the very Reich they were trying to embarrass.

"I understand that you want to throw that monster out the window and watch him splash down in the cold Atlantic Ocean below, but we must operate carefully and intelligently. The cause is counting on us to blacken the eye of this foul regime," she whispered, laying her soft, caring hands over those of her older husband.

"So right, Gissy. So absolutely right," Lewy spoke softly, lifting her hands to his lips and kissing them gently.

"We need to move forward with the plan. If Keila is unable to help us by forcing her ties through Erich Spehl, then we must do whatever is necessary to ignite this monstrous symbol of the Nazi regime and Hitler's growing power." The soft visage of the beautiful woman exposed lines of worry as she spoke through clenched teeth. Anger that had been hidden under the guise of a tourist began to boil inside her body as she thought about the man and his military.

A cynical smile broke across the husband's weathered face. "That's what I love most about you, my Gissy." He laughed at the confused look his young wife gave him. "Your passion keeps me young."

"Well, what *is* our plan moving forward? We were close until that, that *thing* interrupted us." Gisella shuddered at the memory of the strange, odious man-creature that had appeared out of nowhere while they were trying to set the trunk on the catwalk.

"I say we put the device back where we had it at the aft of the ship near the portside engine. It was just bad luck that those kids showed up when they did. I think I can attach it to the underside of the catwalk this time and keep it out of sight of the crew and any meddling outsiders," Lewy spoke in a matter-of-fact calm without looking at his wife until he finished.

The younger extremist stood up, still holding her husband's hands. She pulled his hands toward her, prompting him to stand. "Come along, Lewy. Let's go back to the room and get things prepared. This weather delay should give us time to—how shall I say?—perhaps map out the rest of our plan." She leaned over and kissed her husband's forehead.

Before Lewy and Gisella walked even a few meters from where they had sat, Walter swooped in and snagged the silver ball that had eluded his younger brother. He held the ball tightly in his hands, determined not to let it get away from him again. Walter walked back to the corner.

"I've got it. Let's play." Walter grinned and knelt down on the soft carpet before he rolled the ball to his younger brother. He kept a watchful eye on the ball as it rolled across the red carpet, ready to move quickly if the crazy ball went off course again.

The boys played what seemed like only a short time to them, but hours and miles flew by until Matilde Doehner called for them to clean up for dinner service. "Let's go, boys." Matilde Doehner had not been able to relax or hide her anxiety about this flight from anyone, especially her two boys.

"Coming, Mother!" The boys sprang up to follow her back to their rooms on the lower, less crowded B deck. This time, Walter took the responsibility to hold the ball firmly under his arm, with Werner tagging along behind him. The boys made it through the first crowded deck, but as they stepped onto the landing of the lowest deck, the ball began to shake and spin.

The ball popped out from underneath Walter's firm grip, bounced off the wall, then zipped through the surprised Werner's legs. The two young boys looked at each other then back at their toy as it rolled rapidly down the hallway. The ball shot to the far end of the hallway toward two Luftwaffe officers, so caught up in a private conversation that they took no notice. Both boys held their breath while the ball veered and slowed, certain to roll across the feet of the two Nazi officers. Instead, the rolling ball slowed on the lush carpet until it rolled to a stop in a doorway nearest the two men.

Walter shook his head in disbelief as he took one last look at the silver ball. He grabbed his little brother's hand and walked him quickly and quietly to their room to get changed for dinner.

"Who was on duty to watch the cargo hold?" one of the two men in military dress questioned a subordinate officer with a mixture of suspicious alarm and angst.

A young SS officer nervously rubbed the back of his hands as a way to avoid eye contact with his superior. "I haven't seen him. It was a jaeger. I started missing his blasted smell two nights ago. Since then, I've discreetly searched through the cargo hold where we held our meeting to discuss this escapade. No luck there. I've even searched cargo holds farther back."

A heavy sigh of disgust rolled from the higher-ranking officer's nostrils. "I've never known one to go missing or disobey a direct order like this before." He turned and scanned the halls as he spoke more to himself than to the other servant of the Reich.

The soldier nodded in agreement and put his gloved hand to his chin, trying to think of what could have detained or stopped the fiercest and most devoted beast he'd ever known. "I'll go after dinner and check the cargo holds again. I'll set the other two on that rigger, Erich, and get some answers as soon as I can."

"Excellent. If he's working for who we think he is, then he should be able to answer a few important questions. Keep up appearances during dinner, then slip out as soon as you think no one will be suspicious." The higher-ranking officer of the Third Reich looked the other in the eye to put power behind his command.

"Sir. Heil Hitler." A raised arm saluted before the lower SS headed down the hallway. He stopped briefly at the first door. He looked down, not sure what he thought he would find. He could have sworn he'd seen a silver flash streaking down the hallway, but he only saw a child's toy ball tucked against a door. The toe of his boot made a dull thud as he tapped the ball and watched it roll to the door on the other side of the hall then dismissed it as nothing. Quietly, with impeccable posture, the SS officer methodically stepped down the long hallway and headed for the dining room.

May 6, Early Morning

*K*RISTALLNACHT, A NIGHT of terror that historically would not happen until the next year, flashed through unsettled dreams as Theo tossed in his bed. The tinkling of shattered glass connected times of annihilation coursing through his mind. Thoughts tried to formulate within the nightmare. *No, I'm not seeing Kristallnacht. Sounds—glass or screams? What glass is shattering?* Visions appeared of crystal goblets sliding across dining room tables, tipped and tossed across a room leaning at a forty-five-degree angle. *What am I seeing? I feel like I'm living through the Titanic, but this is not 1912. This is 1937. May 1937. Where am I? Why am I feeling threatened? Why do I feel I'm headed for a destination of doom?* Theo tossed back and forth, trying to quell visions intertwined in a nightmare of darkness and noise. Surely, if dreams could recall smell, he would have sensed the smell of fire burning—burning furniture, burning dirigible, burning humans.

Mr. Medi! Theo sprang upright in his bed. *No, no, it can't be. Medi, come on, get into my mind. What was the lesson? What was the lesson? Was it something about the Hindenburg? When? What year? 1940? No, that's getting into wartime. It was sometime around Hitler, I think. Zikes, I can't remember any better now than when I flunked the timeline on Medi's test. I think, augh! I don't know what to think. Why is my mind so unsettled? Hindenburg crash, ugh, the date was 19 . . . 1936? No, I would have heard about it. It was, um, 19 . . . 1937. Yeah, I think that's right. Which flight? What year is it now?*

"Gracie! Gracie! Wake up! Please, wake up!" Theo stood on his lower bunk shaking the girl who slept above him and sweating as if a fever had overtaken him.

"What?" Gracie rolled to look from the hand that shook her to the face beside her shoulder. "Theo? Theo, what happened? Are you sick? Is Murphy okay?"

"No, no, Gracie, get up. What year is this?"

"Seriously? You woke me up to ask me the year?"

"Gracie, this is important. Is the year 1937?"

Gracie shook her head in exasperation. "Yes, it's 1937 and has been for the past four months. If you want to fill out your calendar, today will be the May 6. If you want the time, it's the middle of the night. Now, can I go back to sleep for a couple more hours?"

Theo's heart beat faster. "You have to get ready. I'm so stupid not to remember. We have to do something, tell someone! I need to get word to Irene."

"Slow down." Gracie threw back the blanket and lowered her legs over the side of the bunk. Theo didn't move from where he stood on the lower bunk, causing him to stand even with Gracie's shoulders. "Did something happen? I didn't hear anything. C'mere, Murphy." Gracie dangled her hand down in the direction of the blue light collar where the dog sat still in the darkness of the room. "What time is it? Theo, are you even awake?"

"Gracie, we're doomed! We're gonna die! This flight doesn't have a happy ending!" Theo's voice was strong and deliberate. Gracie leaned away from Theo.

In the darkness, Theo could not see the wary look in Gracie's eye, but her silence gave him time to realize his forearms were holding most of his weight perched on Gracie's bed. He lowered himself down to the floor and mentally chastised himself before speaking again.

"Sorry. Yes, I'm awake. I had a nightmare, but it was more than that—it was truth. Noise in my dreams seemed real even though I've never lived through such horrible times. Mr. Medi—my history teacher—taught me about events in history that were living nightmares. Really. I think my brain scrambled history, but the nightmare helped me remember. I remember a lesson about May 6." Theo sank to the floor beside his bunk and pulled his legs up to his chest and laid his forehead against his knees. "Oh, please, God, tell me what to do." Theo's words no longer spoke to Gracie.

Gracie slid down from her top bunk and sat on the floor beside him. She stared at the profile of his tipped head and gently put her hand on his shin. "You wanna tell me what this is about? Today is May 6. It's still early—probably between three and four—four-thirty at the latest. Maybe you're confused because we were supposed to land at six this morning. Remember, the late start put us a little behind, but we'll still land today." Gracie paused and looked at Theo, who hadn't lifted his head or responded in any way.

"Maybe you're subconsciously worried about any problems Brack or the SS will cause when we land." She softly rubbed his shin with one hand while placing her other hand on the back of his neck. Murphy wedged his way between the two of them and mostly draped across Gracie's lap. "Hey, you're tough. You've been through a lot, but I know there's nothing now that Brack will do that can keep you away from your dad. You'll be fine. I just know it."

Words that Gracie hoped would soothe Theo's troubled thoughts only caused him to shake his head as he raised to look her in the eye. "No. Gracie, we can't rewrite history. The *Hindenburg*, this airship—it will crash—tonight—when we try to land." Theo leaned away from Gracie just long enough to wrap his arm behind her and pull her to him. "I'm sorry, Gracie. I should've remembered history. I never should've allowed you to be on this flight. I'm sorry. I'm so, so sorry." Theo pulled her head against his face and neck. Gracie accepted his comfort while her own thoughts spun as a storm in her mind.

"Theo? What do we do now?" Gracie tried to mask any shock in her voice with resolve to move forward.

"I don't know." Theo squeezed his eyes shut in an attempt to think rationally and see a plan of action. His dad always made lists—a trait that sometimes annoyed Theo but that also seemed to give direction. Mentally, he tried to list steps for alerting the people who could control the landing. He gave a sigh of resolution—alerting the people would change history.

"I have to let people know."

"But how? Who will believe you? You'll be treated as a troublemaker. Remember, we have to avoid the crew, especially the captain. We're stowaways, remember?" Gracie spoke with reason, but in her mind, she knew that if Theo was right about the disaster, they would need to alert people—at all costs.

"I don't know how to convince people, but I've got to try. I'm not afraid of being in trouble. This is too big, Gracie."

"Okay." Gracie turned her face to Theo. Even in the darkness, a glimmer of determination shone out of the eyes of Li'l Grey. "I'll help. Where do we start?"

Theo gave Gracie a strong hug of thanks and stood up. He hadn't realized his legs were beginning to cramp from sitting on the floor. "Whew. Maybe if I can get my blood circulating again, I'll be able to think straight."

Murphy raised his head to look at Theo then snuggled against Gracie as if to protest and convince her to stay and hold him longer. Gracie gave Murphy a quick double rub on his head, making his ears flop. "Okay, Murph. Up we go." Murphy tumbled to the floor as Gracie stood beside Theo.

"Should we wait until morning?" Gracie's question was more of a suggestion as she shone a light on a nearby clock that read 4:43 AM.

Theo grinned and nodded in the darkness. "Okay. You win. I'll wait until six." As he spoke, Theo rolled back down onto his bed. Gracie climbed back to the top bunk, while Murphy lay down with a disgruntled sigh to voice unhappiness with his bed on the floor. Theo looked over at the blue flashing collar. "Okay, boy, come on." Before Theo could pat the blanket twice, Murphy was on the bed and turning in three circles to make his nest.

The early morning brought restless sleep to the two youths who knew so much and could do so little.

Although Theo little expected it, he dozed in and out of sleep for the next hour. By six o'clock, he was down the hall with a fresh set of clothes and a visit to the washroom. His movement about the cabin woke Gracie. She lay staring at the ceiling, trying to recall the discussion of the night and sort out reality. Reluctantly, she slid from her bunk, gathered her clothes, and headed for the ladies' washroom.

Two youths in two separate locations moved through daily routine while questions, ideas, hopes, discouragements, courageous intents, and insecurities literally tumbled from one thought to another weaving a challenge to be surmounted. By 6:30 AM, each had returned to the cabin where plans were made behind the locked door.

Gracie and Murphy sat on the lower bunk. Theo pulled a chair up to the bunk and propped his feet on the mattress. For all looks of being relaxed, the hearts of Theo and Gracie kept fast beats that threatened to expose their anxiety.

"Okay. First, we don't move from this room without having all we own with us at all times."

Gracie tilted her head and raised her eyebrows. "Give the lecture to yourself. I'm not the one who left the backpack and book in the cargo hold."

"Whatever. I'm just making a clear plan that we can both follow." Theo inhaled and paused before continuing. "We should stay together as much as possible. If we separate during the day, we need to let the other know where we're going. By evening, we need to be together at all times. I'll keep Murphy with me."

"You don't always pay the attention he needs. What if he runs off, or what if Walter and Werner want to play with him?" Gracie matter-of-factly tried to list all possible scenarios.

"I said he stays with me." Theo's voice was firm. He saw Gracie's shoulders drop, and he realized how sharp he sounded. "Sorry. I'm just a little tense. You're right, I need to have a reason to tell the boys that I'm keeping Murphy." He reached across to the bed to pet the snout that was tipped back and snoring. "And you, Murphy! You must mind me today! You'll get plenty of sleep time because I plan to keep you in the backpack most of the day." Murphy's front paws ran a quick race in his sleep, making the teens laugh at his reaction.

Theo sat back and continued, "Next, we need to decide who needs to know and how to tell them."

"I've been thinking about this," Gracie interrupted. "Of course, we need to tell Erich and Joseph. If we leave it to them to tell the captain and crew, we'll never be detected."

"True. So how will they convince the captain that the *Hindenburg* is about to crash?"

"How would two teenagers convince the captain that the *Hindenburg* is about to crash?"

"*Touché.*" Theo crossed his arms and sat back in his chair.

Gracie had noticed that when Theo wrinkled his brow, he had hit an unplanned mental roadblock. She knew this was a time she could express her thoughts without seeming to be pushy. "Maybe Erich can convince Captain Pruss that the headwinds will not allow the airship to safely land at the Lakehurst, New Jersey airfield. Maybe landing will be safer in another location."

Theo shook his head. "You don't understand the willpower of a captain. He not only has his orders, but people in those positions don't listen to amateurs make suggestions just because of a little wind."

"Well, what if Erich tells the captain that he overheard a newspaper reporter on the flight who has discovered the danger of using hydrogen instead of the less flammable helium? He can convince the captain that the reporter will leak the news and create war between Germany and the United States if the airship lands at the time and place originally planned."

"I don't know. Maybe Erich has an idea. But I do know that we need to tell Erich first." Theo paused and kept his eyes on his arms resting across his chest. "I need to tell Irene."

Gracie's head snapped up. "What? Why does she need to know? What can she do except scream, get scared, and cause problems?" Gracie's voice rose to a volume too loud for the little cabin.

"Calm down. I just think she needs to know. She's our friend and a passenger who can help since she has a family on board," Theo snapped back at Gracie without making eye contact.

"Oh well, let's just go down the passenger list and tell everyone. Everyone on this ship has a right to know and panic!"

"Gracie, you're blowing this out of proportion."

"Oh, am I? We're here on a secret mission. I've been with you since last year and have been by your side to help keep you alive. I even believe you and all of your stories of coming back from the future and of things you know that will happen in history. I've believed you beyond reason. Now all of a sudden, a pretty little face is the most important thing to you on this airship. Go ahead! Tell sweet little Irene. I don't care. Go ahead! Help her when we crash. I don't need your help!"

Gracie stood and enumerated points on her fingers until her shouting was cut short by the slamming of the cabin door. Theo leaned his head in his hands and closed his eyes.

Endings

THE LIFE OF a cabin boy on a dirigible appealed to Theo and Gracie as Werner Franz spent every spare minute of the four-day flight exploring and nosing around with them. He not only helped them find ways in and around the *Hindenburg,* but he shared laughs and friendship with his new friends. Theo wondered how much of Werner's broken English was actually unfamiliarity with the language and how much was just a way to say things and misuse words to cause Theo and Gracie to burst out laughing. The three teens had become good friends. In truth, Werner had tried in earnest to get Gracie's attention in a special way. He always felt a bit clumsy around girls, but Gracie was different. It wasn't that she didn't seem feminine, but she did seem comfortable climbing and running and exploring like the boys back home. It was her touch of ruggedness that not only made Werner feel at ease around her but also made him look forward to their time together. Yet Werner never tried to be more than a friend since he had seen the special way Theo looked at Gracie, though Gracie herself didn't seem to notice.

Werner had a little free time before the airship would be approaching its final destination. "Theo! Hey, Theo!" Werner waved and called out to his American friend from behind him in the hallway.

Theo recognized Werner's voice, but the German words were unfamiliar. He turned and waved to Werner. He waited for Werner to catch up, but he didn't want to risk letting Murphy out of the backpack. "Sorry. I'm still learning German. Do you mind speaking English?"

"*Tut mir Leid* . . . uh, I mean sorry, *Mein Freund*. I asked if you want to encore more of the ship."

Theo grinned in response. "Uh, I think you mean *explore* the ship."

Werner's blond hair bounced with his laughter and bobbing head.

"I guess we can. What time is it?"

"If you mean do I need to be workink, we're not yet over America, so I have time before we land."

Theo's smile faded as he looked at his friend. He couldn't shake from his mind the impending tragedy that hung in his mind. He mentally promised himself that although he could not rewrite history, he would stay alert and save his friends from danger.

"You okay, Theo?" Werner's voice shook the older teen back into the moment.

"Yeah. Uh, yeah, actually, I think it would be great to hang out with you. Maybe I can even help you when we get ready to land."

"So let's find Gracie and see if she wants to *explore* with us." Werner spoke carefully to pronounce his English words correctly.

The next hour was filled with the three friends helping themselves to snacks in the kitchen until they were found and run out by the head cook, spying on a trio of young businessmen who spoke loudly over one another, and begging Joseph to take them back to the cargo hold so Murphy and Ulla could be in pictures with them as they posed for Joseph's movie camera. For the time, Gracie gave no show of being upset with Theo. However, a discerning eye could have seen a flinch or a sudden move if, in their activities, Theo reached out to touch her arm or to hold a door open for her.

By midafternoon, Werner was paged over the speaker to go to the *Laufgang*, the walkway, between the lower staircases to be assigned his landing duties. Theo glanced over at Gracie, who suddenly had a look of concern as she returned his glance. "Werner, uh, maybe Gracie and I could go with you, huh?"

"*Nein*. My work is fun, but in the eyes of Chief Knorr, work should be hard enough to make me drip water. He doesn't seem to like me, so I don't think he'd like three of us. I might see you as I'm doing my work, and I promise to look for you on the ground before you leave." Werner's vow to his friends was sincere and sealed with a huge grin and wink toward Gracie. He spun and headed to the nearest *Treppenaufgang* where Theo and Gracie could hear the clamor of his stomps on the staircase.

A sudden lump in Theo's throat almost made water amass behind his eyes. Gracie's gaze was still on the now-vacant hall. In a whisper, Gracie spoke the hearts of both teens. "He's such a very good friend."

This time, Theo was not pushed away when he wrapped an arm around Gracie's shoulder. He pulled her close. Willingly, Gracie laid her face against his chest, allowing him to wrap both arms around her and place his chin against her forehead.

Two teens stood silently in a dimly lit hallway, and Theo never questioned what sounded like a muffled cry against his chest.

"Theo, what do we do now?" Gracie's voice cracked as she broke the silence.

"I really don't know."

Whether by accident or intent, Gracie wrapped her arms around Theo and locked her hands onto the canvas backpack that hung across his back. She could feel the movement of a ball inside the pack, and she patted her rolled-up friend. Stepping back, Gracie dropped her hands against her sides. "I'd better make sure my own case is packed even though it's not a nice one to hang on my back and hold my best friend."

Without moving his eyes from hers, Theo reached out and cupped her face in his hands and drew her up to his face. For too long he had wanted to tell her how he had grown fond of her. He had resisted the urge to grow close for fear of losing her and leaving another black hole in his heart filled only with a memory. Now, on the cusp of change, he realized he had no choice but to bare his soul to her, to give in to wanting to love her, to tell her how he felt. In the darkened hall, two teens stood with delicate hearts and tough exteriors that were willing to admit that even those out of time and out of place needed someone to love.

"Oh, excuse me!" Irene's voice shook the silence and the possibilities of the moment. Theo dropped his hands.

"Irene!"

A small sound came from Gracie's throat. Theo didn't look at Gracie to see if the sound was a cry or a growl.

"Hey, um, Irene, I've . . . I mean, we . . . You know, Gracie and I, we've been looking for you . . . to, um, tell you, uh, we think that . . ." Theo couldn't gather his thoughts and really didn't know what to tell Irene that she would believe anyway.

Gracie spoke up, not loudly and not soft, just matter-of-fact. "The *Hindenburg* is scheduled to land at four fifteen. Everyone should be ready to get off as soon as possible."

"I know we will soon be on American soil. Father is so very excited and has told the boys to gather their toys. They were so sad not to have your toy ball today. I very much thank you for the toy you let them use, Theo. They, and I, are grateful to you for your kindness."

"Yeah, well, we're concerned with more than toys, but you probably don't understand adult matters." Gracie's expression gave no hint of any feeling, but her words were terse with no softness in tone.

"Gracie!" Theo reacted, embarrassed that the young girl would think him to be part of Gracie's rudeness. Gracie turned to stare Theo in the eye, and he knew he had to cover. "Uh, Gracie, you're right that we needed to remind Irene that it's time to pack up. I understand the winds are still strong, so perhaps we should brace ourselves by the promenade windows so we won't fall if the airship tips a bit while landing." He felt obligated to warn both girls about the landing, and he knew he could not tell the truth. Theo felt his pulse quicken and his mind spun until he feared he would be sick. "Actually, I think I'd better go find a place to sit for a bit. I'm not feeling so well right now." Theo turned sideways to pass the two girls and leave them behind him in the hall.

Irene's innocent eyes showed compassion for Theo and a desire to distance herself from Gracie's glare. "I'd better check on the boys." She could not have scurried quicker from the hallway.

Gracie's stare did not follow Irene. She didn't even glance in the direction Theo left. Instead, her stare was broken by a squint that closed her eyes tightly as her leg raised to plant her foot on the wall with a side kick of anger before she ran down the hall and found refuge in the bunk cabin.

By four o'clock, the voice of Captain Pruss came over the speaker with a static introduction and a buzz that caught everyone's attention. "Passengers. This is Captain Pruss. First, let me thank you for a most pleasant flight. I do apologize for the fact that we did not make our six AM landing. Some people—" He cleared his throat. "Uh-hum, some instances had to be dealt with and caused our delay." He paused briefly to cover his anger for the late takeoff from Germany and continued in a lighter tone. "We have had a challenging flight through cloudy skies, but I am happy to announce, we are over the land of America."

Although Captain Pruss paused, cheers from crew and from passengers could be heard in lounges, in halls, and even over the depressed button of the intercom. The captain waited for the brief celebration to settle before he continued. "Second, I find I must apologize again. The weather is unstable with high winds. Ground communication recommends we spend more time in the air to use fuel and lighten the load for landing." In a quick addition, Captain Pruss added, "There is no danger, and we'll circle in a large flight pattern to allow you a splendid view of the nation's capital as we pass over. For now, visit the viewing windows of the promenade, pour a cocktail, and enjoy the additional sightseeing. We will return to Lakehurst Airfield for a newly scheduled evening landing." The speaker squealed off.

Joseph fidgeted—not in the usual sense of his inability to remain still for very many minutes at a time, but in the sense of a worried state of mind. He nearly passed Theo before he recognized the young man sitting by the observation window. "Ah, my young friend, are you watching for the landing already? I have many more pictures to record with my new movie camera, and I can't seem to settle to sit."

"Do women ever confuse you, Joseph?"

Though Theo's question was in earnest, Joseph couldn't help but release a belly laugh as he put a friendly hand on the young man's shoulder. "Theo, my boy, I am married with three children, one of whom is a girl. Even with a wife and a daughter, I am no wiser about women!" Joseph bellowed in laughter that he welcomed. He had needed a chance to settle his own anxieties about landing and reuniting with his family. "I'm bringing Ulla home as a gift to my children. I know they'll be excited. I can already hear my wife's first comment! 'Now, Joseph! Who will clean up after this animal?' But I know she'll be just as excited as the kids about the new pet. It's just in a woman's makeup to confuse the liver out of a man."

Theo's smile proved that Joseph's humor was just the medicine he needed for his unsettled soul.

"Well, keep an eye out for land somewhere in the middle of that pea soup outside the window, Theo. I'm headed aft to check on Ulla. I can't give the kids a skinny dog, you know." Joseph turned the camera to Theo's smile then tipped his hat as his legs appeared to twist and stretch and move three steps before his body caught up with the acrobatic legs.

Theo pulled his canvas backpack around to his lap where he lifted the flap and stuck his hand past the zipper to give his own dog a pat of care. "Well, Murph, whaddaya say we go find Erich and see what he's up to? Surely, the crew's activity in preparing to land tonight will be more interesting than looking out a window at dingy clouds. I'm sure that wandering among the crew will be safer than thinking about girls."

Murphy's nose poked up through the open zipper. The flashing blue lights on the collar had slowed without a need to translate Joseph's mix of English and German and Irene's mix of Spanish and English. Flipping the cover over the half-opened zipper, Theo flung the strap across his shoulder, tucking the canvas bag under his arm. Theo grinned, realizing his best friend was both physically and emotionally close to his heart.

Grounding

SUPPER HAD SCARCELY ended, and plates had been removed from the dining room tables. Goblets still stood half filled with water and dinner wine while travelers finished their drinks and conversations. Although passengers were aware that the unkind weather had plagued their flight with clouds and periodic turbulence, smiles and laughter were the fare of the evening as the landing in New Jersey was promised to be soon.

The table designated for cabin workers included chairs to keep Theo and Gracie out of view of any who sat and digested more politics than food and conversation. Their beginnings as stowaways had handily been covered by keeping them in quarters reserved for youth who worked to clean and maintain guest cabins. Likewise, their dining table was reserved behind a screen in the back of the dining hall so the workers would not be associated with the higher-class passengers.

"Landing soon, eh, boys?" Joseph stuck his face around the doorframe of the small dining room designated for the workers. Only a very alert watcher would have seen the momentary eye contact between the upbeat acrobat and a *Hitlerjugend* dressed in cabin boy's clothing sitting beside Theo at the dining table.

Nothing looked unnatural. Nothing looked suspicious. Yet Joseph felt an unrest of spirit. He noticed Gracie did not join Erich, Werner, and Theo at the table. She had pleaded no appetite and chose to rest on her bunk under the guise of wanting to be ready for her new experience in America.

"We'll be landing soon, boys. Werner, mind your duties." Erich dismissed himself to the back of the airship.

"Theo, I'm back on duty to clean up the officers' mess hall. Perhaps you can come talk with me in there. The view from the windows in the officers' quarter is really quite good." The two boys sauntered into the kitchen, where Werner began his dishwashing duties while comparing notes with Theo about the East Coast of America. Finally, by 7 PM, the horn sounded to signal the crew to prepare for landing.

Erich poked his head through the kitchen door. "Theo, Chief Knorr has told the deckhands to prepare the landing lines. We are approaching the airfield. If what you have told me is truth, you must be prepared." Erich left as quickly as he had come.

Theo's heart skipped a beat then picked up a rapid pace of anxiety as he stood and lifted his backpack from beside his chair and strapped it to his back. For the first time since riding his driftboard through the streets of his hometown, Theo clicked the waist strap that secured the pack on his back.

"Werner, it's best that you stay close to—" Theo's words were cut short as a loud pop seemed to pull down on the back of the *Hindenburg*. Theo moved the curtains aside that led into the dining room in time to see crystal goblets sliding down tilted tables. "Get to a window, Werner!" Theo yelled over his shoulder as he ran to the hallway leading to his cabin.

Indeed, Werner did plan to get to a window for a good view of the landing, but just as he opened a cabinet door, the ship's tilt unloaded the cabinets. Dishes fell around Werner and crashed to the floor. He ran to the doorway and looked to the aft where a ball of fire belched out of the gas pods lining the ship. Werner turned to run to the front of the ship, but the angle of the hall along the keel caused him to slip and fall. Facedown, Werner began sliding down into the inferno that threatened to spew up the hall. Frantically, he grabbed for a guide rope lining the narrow hall. He could hear his voice panting and grunting as he sucked in air and tried to climb the rope and move to the higher end. The heat of the fire threatened him, and his hands gripping the rough rope cried out in weakness that they could not pull his body strength. His legs almost lay against the tilted floor. "Help me!" Werner choked out a scream, but the popping and roar of the fire was deafening. He forced his head to hug the rope that prevented him from falling into the fire but also kept him from moving upward.

Suddenly, a lilt from the burning dirigible upended an unbalanced ballast of water. The water crashed like a waterfall over Werner. He gasped and spit the water that poured over him but challenged him to fight back. Looking around, Werner saw the hatch for loading supplies. Drenched and determined, Werner steadied himself with the rope and crawled to the hatch. Gripping the wall with one hand and the door latch with the other, Werner pulled down on the metal handle. Nothing seemed to give. "No! Ugh, ugh." Out of anger and out of a will to survive, Werner kicked and kicked and kicked the door. "Augh!" Relentless kicking sent pangs up his legs until there was a snap and the door fell from its hanger. Werner sprang forward and put a hand on each side of the hatch, looking out into the air that also sucked the fire from within.

"Jump!" Werner could hear a man below him. The ground did not look welcoming at the distance, but the fire flaring around him promised death. Werner jumped.

The *Hindenburg* tilted, and voices called out commands and confusion. "Gracie!" Theo's voice joined the shouts as he ran to their cabin. Just as he reached for the doorknob, the door opened and Gracie lunged out of the cabin in fear of knowing the unknown. "Run, Gracie! We need to be near a window!" Theo reached for her as she willingly gripped his hand and ran with him. A sudden jerk that shook the entire ship tumbled the two to the floor. "Get up! Get up!" Theo lifted Gracie and ran until she could get her legs underneath her and her stride in full motion.

Windows of the promenade on the upper deck were filled with expectant faces since Captain Pruss had announced their soon arrival to the Lakehurst Airfield. The airship tipped forty-five degrees, throwing passengers into panic sliding down the carpeted floor, stopping only by hitting the back walls of the dining room.

Mrs. Doehner remained at the tipped dining table, sending the boys to the floor with toppled chairs. In matronly instinct, she wanted to gather her family to her arms and find a place of safety. "Irene! Werner! Walter! Come, children!"

"Over here!" a voice commanded passengers who were reaching out to stop their fall. Joseph Stahl stood at the front of the dining room. Seeing a red flash, Joseph thought perhaps lightning had reflected off the open glass windowpane. But the booming sound that accompanied the flash was not a thunder from the skies but one that literally shook him to the bone. He turned his camera from filming the landing to filming the melee inside the airship. People were running and screaming. One man was momentarily pinned against the lounge wall when the lightweight Blüthner grand piano slid down the plush carpet. At the sight of Theo and Gracie climbing up the tilted floor, the camera continued to roll even as Joseph dropped his arm to his side. "So this is it?" Joseph looked at Theo.

"Get out! We have to get out!" Theo's grip on Gracie's arm and his crying yells were born out of the nightmare coming to life.

"But my Ulla . . ."

"Get out!!" The youth became a strong-voiced man of command and knowledge. Theo forcefully lifted Gracie to the ledge of the window. "It's not far. Jump!" Gracie didn't look back but kept her eyes down at the ground below her where a Navy sailor broke her fall.

Joseph lifted himself to the window ledge and knew the twenty-foot fall was nothing his gymnastic agility couldn't handle. He sprang into the crowd of ground crew running to catch people jumping from the giant canvas firebrand falling from the sky.

Theo had hung one leg out the window when he saw Matilde Doehner running, screaming commands, and pushing Walter and Werner up the tilted floor. Irene was behind Matilde. Theo pulled his leg back inside the window. "Walter, Werner, here!" With both arms, Theo grabbed for the boys and lifted them to the window ledge. "Jump! Don't be afraid! Jump!" He turned to help Mrs. Doehner, who was already escaping from the ledge of the next window. He turned for Irene.

"Irene!" Theo could feel the heat and smell a pungent burning that singed the inside of his nostrils. The young girl was nowhere in sight. "Irene!" Theo's smoke-filled eyes saw only bodies without identity running toward where he stood at the front. "Irene!" Passengers and crewmen who had made it to the front of the airship pushed against Theo. The movement of the mass was as if a liquid bubbled and oozed in a continuous flow. Theo didn't remember jumping but obeyed the Navy man who lifted him from the ground and yelled for him to clear the ship.

Dazed and in shock, Irene didn't want to leave without her father. "Mother, where's Father? Father! Father!" Irene pushed against people screaming and running to the front of the ship. "Father!" Her soft cries were not heard above the rushing crowd. Irene fell over a toppled chair. Rubbing her shin and slowly looking around, Irene uprighted the parlor chair and stood grasping the back of the chair. "Father?" Her voice, no longer frantic, had a frailty that matched her shaking legs as she sat in the chair.

"*Fräulein*, you must get out!" Irene gave an empty stare to the crewman pulling on her arm. "*Fräulein*, get out!"

"But Father—" Irene gave in to the tug on her arm and stood.

"Get out, *Fräulein*!" The crewman turned and ran to a window that had just emptied.

Brushed and pushed with the crowd, Irene followed the surge to the window ledge. Just as a crewman turned to lift her to the ledge, her hair and dress were caught by the fire that started with a spark on the red carpet. The crewman helped her crawl and fall through the window before he jumped after her. Below, a ground crew of sailors eased the burning girl to the ground and smothered the fire that fell with her. The man who lifted her to the windows looked through blurry eyes to try to find details in the burned face of the child. He gave in to the voice that beckoned him away to treat his burned hands and stand clear of the airship fully consumed in fire.

Staggering through the masses, Gracie looked out across the destruction with eyes set in a face bruised from her fall and smudged from ashes of dirigible canvas floating across the tarmac. Heavy breaths hit against her vocal cords and threatened to scratch them, but she could not hear her own breathing that was drowned out by the pulse of surging blood that hit against her eardrums. Sounds.

Everywhere were sounds, yet nowhere were words. The cacophony around her was a tempest of voices, sirens, and wails that pierced downward through her heart and lodged with pain in her stomach. She blinked to clear her vision, but the dark cloud of smoke billowing from the skeleton of a burned dirigible prevented any clarity of sight.

"Theo." Li'l Grey's words were scarcely audible as she mixed the words she wanted to scream with the thoughts that wove through the confusion in her mind. *I must get away from the fire. I am lost. I am a fighter. I can't, I won't give up. Fight, Li'l Grey, fight!* she commanded her thoughts as she crawled on hands and knees across the rough terrain.

"Theo."

"Ma'am, are you all right?" Gracie looked up at the voice connected to the hand that touched her shoulder but could not respond before it finished. "She'll be okay. She's not burned."

She ran away. "Theo? Find him. Find—" Gracie coughed as her words tangled in the smoke and in the tears that were gushing unhindered. She tilted her head, trying to distinguish unearthly, high-pitched wails. Through the dark fog, she could see two small figures standing with arms locked around each other. "Boys?" Enveloped in confusion and trauma, she crawled toward the screaming figures. What lay beside them that made them wail so?

As she neared the figures, people in sailor uniforms and people with red crosses stitched on their shoulders massed around the object on the ground. "Boys?" Gracie tried to lift her voice to call out, but nothing could be heard over their screams. She paused to listen, commanding her ears to distinguish between the screams of sirens and the screams of souls in pain. She had either no strength or no desire to stand—she didn't know and didn't care which. So she continued to crawl on hands and knees, forcing her way between soldiers and medical staff around the object on the ground.

"Let me see. Let me in." She crawled through the mass until her face hung inches above the object. *Is this a face? Is this a body? Is this someone? Why can't anyone answer me?* Her eyes tried to focus. She choked as she inhaled the smell from burned remains. Gracie realized her tears were pouring down onto the charred cinders that threatened to strangle her. She crawled under the people working. She wanted to understand what made the two young boys scream. She crawled along the charred form until she saw something she recognized. No longer crawling, she rose on her knees and began to shake. She heard her hoarse voice scream as a soldier gently pulled her away while she clutched a delicate red satin slipper that had fallen beside the burned and lifeless body of Irene.

Gracie lay curled up on the tarmac a hundred yards from the smoldering wire cage of catwalks that once was known as the *Hindenburg*. A soft hand brushed the hair from her face, but she had no desire to talk or open her eyes.

"Medic, take this young girl to the temporary infirmary. She doesn't appear to be physically injured, but her heart is breaking and she's in shock. Don't try to take this satin shoe from her. It must be from someone she loved." The nurse stood and walked to the next victim lying on the tarmac.

Adrenaline moved Theo as his eyes searched the grounds filled with Navy men and medics tending to victims of the crash. Cries of people drew his attention as he jogged away from the burning airship. In a matter of seconds, the hydrogen-filled canvas radiated a red heat before it disintegrated into air. The winds that had tormented the landing now carried away ashes of proof that a white balloon filled with passengers had ever graced the sky over New Jersey. Theo welcomed the unrelenting wind that blew his hair and held at bay the heat of an inferno behind him.

"Gracie! Joseph! Erich! Werner! Gracie! Joseph! Erich!" Panting the repetition of names, Theo succumbed to the strength of emotion that burst from his heart. "Please answer me! Gracie!"

"Sir, keep moving away from the airship! Sir, you're turning back toward the flames! Sir!" The voice shouting at Theo seemed deaf to the ears of a young man frantically searching for people he had grown to love. A hand grabbed Theo's arm and grabbed again as the young man spun from his grasp and continued plodding across the airstrip. "Sir, you must stop." Strong but gentle arms of a Navy man wrapped around Theo's chest and backpack to stop him but held tightly as the disoriented young man collapsed to the ground.

"I have to find them. Please, let me go. I have to find them." Theo wept through his words, his adrenaline soaked up by fear.

"Tell us your name, young man." A man with a clipboard had rushed to the side of the Navy man who gently lowered Theo to the ground.

"Theo. Theo Marshall."

"What are the names of your friends and family?"

"Gracie, Joseph, Erich. Can you tell me where they are?" Tears had made runnels through the ashes staining Theo's face, but he looked into faces equally stained.

"Nurse!" The man with the clipboard stood up and motioned for a lady with a cross on her sleeve. "Get this young man over to the hangar. We'll continue searching for passengers."

The woman with the red cross knelt down to lift Theo's arm over her shoulder. Theo started up and pulled away.

"No, I have to find Gracie." Theo's pull was too strong against the slight grip the nurse had on his arm, and again he started to stumble across the tarmac. About a hundred yards from the nose of what had been the dirigible, Theo recognized the small stature of a man limping toward the hangar.

"Joseph! Joseph! Wait! Joseph!"

The limping man looked up in Theo's direction. "Theo, is that you? Oh, you're a sight for sore eyes! Come give this broken acrobat a hand, will you?"

New energy surged through Theo's body at the sight of his friend, and he ran to put his shoulder under Joseph's arm.

"What happened, man?" Theo's height towered above the small-framed gymnast, so he stooped to help Joseph walk.

"Can you believe it? I can balance on skyscrapers and do tricks and never fall, but a twenty-foot jump from a burning airship and I twist my ankle. Theo, do you see Ulla? Surely, someone got her loose. Do you see her, boy? Did she make it out of the ship?" Joseph's voice digressed from strong to pleading with the reality that his dog had been trapped in the burning vessel. "Tell me she's out, Theo. She's a sweet pup. I got her for my kids, Theo. Tell me she's alive, Theo."

Theo felt the weight of his own dog tucked in the backpack and understood the sadness of his friend. He didn't speak or nod his head or even look in the face of the man who made millions of people laugh but limped away with no way to soothe his own heartache.

"Can you walk with me over to that hangar, Joseph? It looks like everyone is being carried over there. We'll look for Gracie and Erich, okay, Joseph?" The two men bonded by ties of political right and by ties of friendship headed for the hangar that had become a makeshift hospital.

"Names? Hey, names?" Another man carrying a clipboard walked toward Theo and Joseph as they approached the doorway of the hangar.

"Sorry. I'm Theo Marshall, and he's Joseph . . . Uh, Joseph, I don't even know your last name."

"Späh."

"No kidding? Are you the acrobat Späh?" For a brief moment, it seemed the clipboard man would forget his duties and fall into casual conversation.

Theo stopped walking. *Where have I heard that name before? Späh . . . Späh . . .* He remembered hearing the name being spit through a German tongue translated by Murphy. *Späh . . .* Theo could hear again the sound of the name, the sound of—yes! The sound of Viktor Brack's voice as he and Murphy lay under the floor of the wooden building in the concentration camp where he landed with the time jump. *What was said about Späh? Think, Theo.* For the first time in months, Theo willed his mind to recall the concentration camp where he met and left his new Jewish friend, Yari. *Oh, I know. It was something about Späh and the government. Whatever it was, if it was against Viktor Brack, then Joseph really is my friend—I don't care what he did.* Theo's thoughts were disrupted by the clipboard man tapping him on the shoulder.

"Come on in, sirs." The clipboard man pointed to the left of a row of bodies being treated for burns and injuries from falling. "Go over there. A medic can check out your leg, Mr. Späh."

"Thank you." Joseph nodded at the clipboard man. "Boy, walk me the long way around down these rows. I want to look at these people and see if I can find Erich. I wish the light were better. I'd even film them as evidence against the Reich . . ." Joseph's words trailed into silence as he began looking intently from person to person to recognize a face of a friend.

Although he was thirsty and wanting to rest, Theo agreed to pull the hobbling gymnast down each aisle, weaving in and out of medics and Navy men tending to the injured. He wanted to search too for Erich and Werner and Irene, especially for Gracie. Staggering as a two-headed inebriate, the young and the younger walked slowly, scanning faces and bodies. The lightning was fighting the evening sky consuming the area where a disaster had ended airship travel forever. Lights came on in the hangar, but even the strength of their beams struggled to show the features of the many bodies scattered across the floor.

"There! That's his hat! I'd recognize that oversize cover anywhere!" Joseph picked up speed by hopping on one leg and nearly dragging Theo along with him. "Erich! You old son of a gun! What are you doing lying in here?"

The face of the young rigger turned toward his friend's voice. "Joseph? I should have known—"

"Excuse me, mister. Do you know this man? Can you tell us his name?" A pretty lady with a cross on her shoulder tipped her face in front of Joseph's to get his attention.

"This man? Yeah! I know this man—best rigger on the ship! Write it down and get it right. This man will be thanked someday for his work to save the people of Germany! This is Erich Spehl. That's S-P-E-H-L." Joseph stood balanced on one leg with his arms proudly crossed against his chest. "Yes, Germany will be proud of him someday."

The eyes of the man on the makeshift infirmary bed looked directly at Joseph. Raising a burned finger, Erich tried to motion to Joseph to come near. "Joseph," the soft voice beckoned.

Joseph turned to Theo. "Move over so I can get next to my friend." Still using one leg, the small frame lowered to his knees with his face beside the badly burned rigger. "I'm here, buddy. Talk to me, Erich. Tell me what to do. I'll stand against any Reich for the both of us. Talk to me."

In a whisper that came out of burned lips that had curled into a grin, Erich breathed, "Tell my girl, Joseph, tell my girl, '*Ich lebe.*'"

"You bet I will, my friend." Joseph balanced back up to a standing position next to Theo. "You hear that? I gotta get to a telegraph to send a message back to Erich's girl. He lives! Did you hear that! Get me to a telegraph, Theo. He lives!" Looking back down to his friend, Joseph promised as Theo slipped the arm of the small-framed man over his shoulder. "I'll send word, Erich. Get better. I'll return. I'll send word." Then he leaned away from the bed, allowing Theo to help him hobble to the end of the infirmary.

As they stepped away, Theo didn't hear Erich's last breath, but he was certain he heard a sob from the bowed head that hung close to his heart.

At the end of the row, Theo lowered Joseph to a place on the floor where people with less critical injuries were being treated by young medics. "Joseph, I'll be back. Wait for me here. I have to find Gracie," Theo spoke as if reassuring a child. The gymnast with the bowed head gave a visible nod and then laid his head across his arm that rested on his uninjured leg.

Theo continued up and down the rows. Toward the end of the fifth row, a woman's voice caught his attention.

"Amelia, perhaps the girl in the corner is one you're looking for." The woman stood pointing to a small bundle against the wall of the hangar.

"Amelia?" Theo turned to see a pretty young woman walking up the aisle between rows of victims. He turned again to look at the bundle leaning against the wall. "Gracie? Gracie?" Theo ran and knelt beside a girl with her face buried in the sleeve of her jacket. "Gracie?"

No other voice could have made Gracie's heart skip a beat as it did at that moment. She rolled to look into the face of her friend. Embraced in each other's arms, the two welcomed the chance to cry for friends found and to cry for friends lost.

Neither was aware that a woman stopped to talk to Joseph, to give him a hug, and to nod her head as they both watched the teens against the wall. She sat while Joseph's ankle was taped and crutches were supplied, then together, they walked to the teens.

"Theo, Gracie, you've been through a lot, my friends. I'll take it from here. I'll be doing stunts off the tops of these crutches in no time."

Theo gently brushed Gracie's curls to the side of her face, revealing a small smile for Joseph. The teens helped each other up from the floor of the hangar and turned to the two adults.

Joseph looked at the youths. "Now, let me introduce you to Amelia Earhart. She'll take good care of you and help you with whatever connections you need to make here in America. She has a passion for flight and, naturally, has friends in high places. So if she can't get you what you need, she knows the people who can!" With a twist on the toes of one foot, Joseph turned to face the lady known as Amelia. "Miss Earhart, I now leave with you two inspiring young people who are on a mission to right the wrongs of the world and find adventure in the journey. Please meet Theo and Gracie." Standing on one leg, Joseph used a crutch to point to the teens.

All with slight smiles and nods, the three shook hands and said their hellos.

"Thank you, Joseph. I've always appreciated your ability to find mavericks. Theo, Gracie, our friend Jahile sent kind words ahead of you. I think you'll find we have similar likes and dislikes in people. We'll talk later. For now, let me encourage you. The more one does and sees and feels, the more one is able to do, and the more genuine may be one's appreciation of fundamental things like home and love and understanding companionship."

"I couldn't agree more, Miss Earhart. So I'm off to appreciate my own fundamental things of home, love, and companionship with my wife and three children. Theo, Gracie, the pleasure has been mine." With his last words, Joseph bowed with an arm across his waist. It wasn't until after the bow that Theo noticed Joseph held in his hand the hat of a rigger, which he twirled up to place on his head in a lopsided, slipped-down-over-one-eye sort of fashion. Then he turned and used his crutches to walk away without looking back.

Amelia Earhart smiled at Theo and Gracie. "I understand you have a small friend in your backpack who will be anxious to meet me. Today, you will rest. Tomorrow, you will meet my dear friend, Eleanor."

I'm halfway home. Theo looked around the triage area of the New Jersey airfield. He felt a wiggle against his back from movement where a nose poked out of the canvas flap of his backpack.

Someday. Someday, Murphy, we'll go all the way home. Theo shook his head to bury the thoughts in his memory while he pulled an arm out of the strap holding the canvas bag and slung it around to his chest. Without prompt or command, Murphy wiggled out of the pack and into the arms of his master where he could press his snout under Gracie's hand that reached out for him.

In the shadows, a man in a raccoon coat awkwardly wiped ashes from his fedora before he pressed his bandaged hands together to drop a picture of a young Jahile, a woman, and a smiling girl onto the hangar floor to grind it with the heel of his scuffed shoe.

ABOUT THE AUTHOR

Jimmy Adams teaches high school history and coaches teens. He enjoys woodworking and outdoor activities, including running and swimming. He and his wife, Chelsea, have two dogs, Lincoln and Penny, and one cat, Bella.

Brenda Heller has retired from thirty-four years of teaching high school and college. She fills her days with volunteer work. Her hobbies include camping, trail riding, and hiking with her husband, David. They have two daughters and five grandchildren.

Though both authors keep busy schedules, they desire to encourage others to know the impact history has made on life today; thus, their passion for writing historical fiction has given birth to the TimeWorm series.

CPSIA information can be obtained
at www.ICGtesting.com
Printed in the USA
FSHW011321080120
65809FS